Tannion

(Book One in the Tannion Series)

Wayne Elsner

Excerpt from Tannion Stepping Out Copyright ©2014 Wayne Elsner. All rights reserved.

ISBN-13: 978-1500635305
ISBN-10: 1500635308
Library of Congress Control Number: 2014913360
CreateSpace Independent Publishing Platform
North Charleston, South Carolina

Cover Design by SelfPubBookCovers.com/Shardel

Visit the author's website – www.wayneelsner.com

Printed in the United States of America

To my wife Carrole, our sons Mark and Kent and our daughter Laura.

1

Jim Tannion had no idea that this day would be any different than any other day. It began innocently enough and pretty much the same way every workday had started for the past few years. Getting up at six thirty for work had become a habit.

As he walked out of his apartment, he thought about how much he loved living downtown. He enjoyed having the freedom to walk to work or to his favorite bar and the restaurants that were close by. He wasn't that interested in going to work though. He knew there would be lots of paperwork to do, but he was thankful that he didn't have to sell anything. Somebody had to do the paperwork to ensure everything was kept straight. His economics degree got him the job, but he wasn't sure what good it had done him since.

The money was decent enough, but it could have been a lot better. The work was adequate and he liked the people he worked with, but he yearned for more excitement in his life. He knew he had fallen into a rut and had never found the time to put a resume together to look for a better job. He didn't like the feeling of complacency, but not enough to do anything about it.

The morning hours passed quickly and at least he could enjoy his noon break. His lunch usually tasted better when sitting in the park watching for girls. Lunch hour always went faster than any other hour in the day so, too quickly, it was time for him to make his way back to the office. Today he left a little earlier than usual as he had decided to stretch his legs with a walk along the river bank.

After he had walked for a few minutes he noticed there were fewer people along the way. Glancing at his watch, he decided he had better hurry back. He looked up and only then noticed that the sky had gotten very dark. A major cloud was passing over, but blue sky could be seen on both sides. It didn't seem to be a big storm, but Tannion knew that he could still get very wet. It was probably a good time to get back to work.

Before he stepped off the sidewalk he had to first wait for the light. The light turned green and the little man indicated that he could walk. He took another quick look up at the sky and thought it would be best to hurry a little.

He never heard anything, felt anything, or saw anything until he woke up lying on the ground with people all around him and sirens getting closer. Thoughts were flitting about half-formed in his head. The sirens led him to considering the Doppler Effect and wondering what the siren would sound like when it went past him, but it didn't. The siren stopped quite near him.

He couldn't talk or move, but he could hear everything being said.

A man in a light blue suit said, "It happened so fast. I didn't see it, but I heard it." Tannion noticed little things like the small stain on the guy's tie and the stubble on his chin.

The woman he was talking to nodded and replied, "I heard it too, but I wasn't looking in his direction. Until someone screamed, I had no idea he had been hit." Tannion hoped that it wasn't his scream she had heard.

It wasn't until he was in the back of the ambulance that Tannion was able to get a few words out. When he asked what truck had hit him, he was told that he had been hit by lightning and was lucky to be alive. He thought he'd been hit by a car or maybe one of the crazy bike couriers that zoom in and out of traffic and up on the sidewalk whenever they have to.

By the time the ambulance reached the hospital, he was feeling fine. He couldn't tell that he had been hit by anything, except that he had a good-sized headache and his suit jacket was rumpled. He also seemed to be missing his right shoe. Looking for burn marks or any other sign of the incident, he was a bit disappointed that there was nothing obvious. Luckily one of the paramedics had picked up his shoe and it was sitting on the gurney beside him.

They kept him in the hospital for a few hours. It appeared that all he had was a headache, but the doctors hadn't seen too many lightning strike victims and had decided to run more tests than usual. They probably kept some poor guy out in the waiting room for hours while they fussed over Tannion's tests. Finally, when they couldn't find anything wrong with him other than a slight concussion from when his head hit the sidewalk, they sent him home.

He had missed an afternoon of work. Luckily he had been able to phone the office after sitting in a hospital bed for a few hours. He had caught the receptionist on her way out, explaining what had happened.

"Sorry Jim. Everyone's already gone for the day," she informed him. He knew he would have some explaining to do in the morning.

Tannion was told by the doctor to take it easy and that he would have to find his own way home. He caught a taxi, and by the time he got home all he wanted was to go to bed. He thought that a few hours sleep would probably do him a world of good. They had given him a remedy in the form of a couple of painkillers, but he hated to take drugs of any sort. He knew he would have to handle it himself and sleep was usually the best cure.

When the alarm sounded the next morning he woke up feeling unusually refreshed. Unlike most nights, he didn't recall waking up once, not even to go to the bathroom. He occasionally had to go in the night, but he chalked it up to being a little dehydrated after yesterday's strange events.

He went to work as if nothing had happened. He had to tell the story a few times, but overall it was just another day at the office. In the back of his mind he had this feeling that something had happened that was greater than he knew, something that he couldn't explain. It wasn't until much later that he found out what it meant.

2

"Did you hear about the guy who got hit by lightning, Mike?" Bill Pansloski asked. Pansloski had stuck his head around the door to his partner's office in the building the FBI was using in Wichita. Mike Rallin waved him into the only other chair in the room.

Mike Rallin had spent a couple of years in the navy. When he got out, he applied to the FBI and was put on the street. That was twenty-two years ago, and since that time the Bureau had changed considerably. He had been a witness to it all.

Bill Pansloski had been with the bureau a little longer than Rallin, but saw himself as second on a team of two. Pansloski enjoyed being someone's partner and had been Rallin's partner for more than ten years. He felt he knew what Rallin was going to say before he said it.

"No. What happened?" Rallin asked.

"You saw that unexpected storm that passed through here early yesterday afternoon, didn't you?" Pansloski queried.

"I saw it. We only got a bit of rain, but I heard the thunder."

"If you were walking downtown you might have seen it as well as heard it. This guy was walking along and then he was on the ground. I just talked to one of the locals," Pansloski said.

"Did it kill him?"

"No. It sounds as if he got off without a scratch."

"Lucky guy," Rallin said.

"No kidding, but it happens once in a while," Pansloski muttered, not sounding completely convinced.

"More often it kills whoever it hits. Damn lucky. What are you working on?"

"I'm looking into that missing person who might have crossed over the border. It's been quiet. Not much going on," said Pansloski with a shrug.

Rallin could relate. Crime was down overall, and even fewer of the crimes required the FBI to step in. They were a small unit, still there was barely enough work to go around. Rallin looked at the file he was working on. The DEA had contacted the boss and asked for some help looking at what they saw as organized crime moving into the downtown area and getting into the drug business.

"Have you seen this file from the DEA yet?" Rallin asked Pansloski.

Pansloski hadn't, and he took the file and spent a couple minutes looking through it. "It doesn't look like much, Mike."

"I agree. This isn't a big town, and I'd think if anything big was to move in we'd have heard about it before now."

"There's always a bunch of drugs moving downtown. Other than a couple gangs we know about, it's been calm, almost peaceful."

"I agree Bill, but I need to go through the motions. The boss will expect at least that much."

Pansloski took a last look at the file and threw it back on Rallin's desk. "I think I'm better off with my missing person."

Rallin laughed as Pansloski slid out the door. He thought he might just be right. Both cases looked like losers, but there was nothing else coming at them. He would have to make do with what he had. He just wished he had more.

Rallin realized he hadn't even asked Pansloski if he knew the name of the guy who had been hit by lightning. "Not important," he thought as he looked back at the file on his desk.

3

It was two weeks after the lightning episode when Tannion noticed something different. Lying in bed thinking about going to sleep, he felt something touching his hand. He couldn't see anything, but he could have sworn that something had touched him. He wrote if off to imagination and rolled over to go to sleep.

He was busy knocking off some of the paperwork in his office a few weeks later when he felt the same sensation, and this time it didn't go away. He looked at his hand and could tell there was something there, but it was too small to see.

He found a magnifying glass in his desk. He still had no idea what he was looking for or looking at. When the feeling went away again, he suspected that it would be back and decided he would be ready when it did.

The next day just after starting work, the feeling was back. It was still somewhere between a touch and a brush, but he was sure that something was touching the skin on his hand. This time he had a magnifying glass, hand lotion, and a nail file. After a minute of searching, Tannion realized again that he didn't have a clue what he was looking for. Then he spotted it. Just slightly below the knuckle on his left index finger a small spot appeared under the magnifying glass. It was somewhat raised and a lighter color than the rest of his skin. The feeling was definitely coming from this tiny bump. He worried and wondered about it for the rest of the day.

That night Tannion found a Q & A page online where someone had written about a bump similar in description to what he had found. The answer appeared obvious and simple. It was the start of a wart.

He had seen warts before, but he didn't remember ever noticing them in the early stages. The little ones must go unnoticed until they got to a certain size. Tannion was puzzled as to why he had spotted this tiny guy at this stage in its life.

Looking very intently at the tiny bump, he tried to determine why he could feel it. He then went to get the crap you put on warts to get rid of them. He didn't have any in the medicine cabinet, and it was too late to go to the drugstore to buy some. He decided to leave the poor little guy alone for another day.

The next afternoon Tannion's hand had a completely different sensation. At first he thought that the wart remover was burning, but then he recalled that he hadn't applied any. The feeling had changed slightly to a sensation of movement. Tannion stared intently at the bump, and that was when it happened. There was a momentary loss of vision. The hand was there and he could see it clearly, but it was as if he had another pair of eyes and he could see more than he had ever seen before.

In front of him he could see what looked like a little blob of moving strings, and he knew immediately that they were wart viruses. He didn't know how he knew. The thought just popped into his head. He had seen a website about warts and assumed that it must have had a picture of what the virus looked like under a strong microscope.

When he saw the viruses he thought that he would rather not have them in him. The thought had barely registered when he saw an increase in blood flow from tiny blood vessels near the surface of the skin. The blood very quickly enveloped the viruses and just as quickly destroyed them. Within a few seconds he knew that the last wart virus was dead. His skin and blood flow went back to normal.

Needless to say, Tannion didn't get much sleep that night. The next day at work he couldn't concentrate, and finally he told the boss that he was sick and went home. When he got home he sat down on the recliner for a nap. As he relaxed he could hear and feel his heart beat. Heart palpitations weren't uncommon for him, but this time he decided to pay very close attention. He had always fancied that if he concentrated he could slow his heartbeat down. As he relaxed and listened to each heartbeat, he felt a natural slowing of the rhythm of his heart.

Tannion looked up at the clock on the wall and started counting. He calculated the number of beats per minute. His first count was seventy two beats per minute. He thought that was a little above normal. Concentrating and relaxing his breathing over the next few minutes, the number of beats reduced to sixty, then to forty-eight, and on down to thirty-six. He doubted it had ever been that slow before.

Maybe he was doing something to affect it, but he couldn't think what. He was only relaxing and thinking about slowing his heart down. He kept counting and his heart rate continued to drop. At twenty-four beats per minute Tannion got a little freaked out, but he kept counting. His heart rate jumped to over seventy. There's nothing like a shot of adrenalin to punch things up a little.

Tannion sat for a long time, thinking about what was happening. Thinking about what he had done with his heart. Wondering if there was anything else he could do. He thought about a bruise on his arm and considered what would heal it best.

At the thought of healing, the area around the bruise grew warm, the blood flow increased, and started to clear away the old blood. The internal bleeding had stopped several days before and it was mostly just discoloration with a little sensitivity. Within a few minutes the bruise cooled off and was gone. There was no color left and no sensitivity.

He spent most of the night trying to figure out how this could have happened. The only thing he could come up with was that it had to somehow be associated with the concussion he got when the lightning struck. Somehow it must have awakened an ability to control some of his body functions. Or perhaps it was the lightning strike itself that sparked something in his brain.

He knew that there were a lot of body functions that people subconsciously control every day. How does the heart keep beating? Lungs draw in air without anyone having to order it done. Why do people have control over their bladder and bowels even when they sleep? He knew that the autonomic nervous system took care of these things without thought. Perhaps during his accident something triggered his ability to control this system in his body. What else could be done? What might be possible? Had only thinking about healing the bruise been enough?

Having control over his heart and blood flow didn't seem that far-fetched. People have been able to control their breathing and heart rate through meditation for centuries. He had never heard of anyone being able to control blood flow with their mind, but why not?

Tannion started to think of what else he might be able to do. The problem was that he was relatively healthy and didn't have anything to cure without causing something first. He had healed one very small bruise, so it made sense that he should be able to heal bigger bruises. He thought of hitting himself on the thumb with a hammer, but then he thought about what would happen if he couldn't heal it. He didn't want anything that would slow him down or hurt like hell. Finally he decided to just drop the hammer on the back of his left hand. How bad could it be?

The hammer hit him in the middle of his left hand and it hurt like hell for a few seconds, and that was it. It didn't appear to bruise or hurt enough to need fixing. He didn't think he had done anything to stop his hand from hurting or bruising. Obviously, it hadn't been enough to actually do any damage.

Finally he decided to cut himself and see if he could heal it. But where? He didn't want to have it bleed too much, or leave an ugly scar if he couldn't heal the wound. He thought maybe a small cut on the palm of his hand like the ones used to make blood oaths might work.

He made a half-inch cut in the center of his palm. First the cut hurt, but the pain soon stopped. He had thought it would be nice for the pain to go away, and then it did. He assumed that he had blocked off the pain receptors. Pain is only the body sending a warning to the brain that something is in trouble. As long as he knew what was in trouble, and knew that it could be fixed, there was no need for the pain signal. Why not shut it off? He wondered what he would have to do to heal the cut. He didn't have to wonder for long. A minute later the wound felt as if it wasn't there. Tannion washed off the dry blood to find nothing underneath. No cut. No scar. Nothing.

4

It was relatively rare for Tannion to go out for lunch, but when the guys from work asked he usually went along. The two-block walk was quick, and they had a nice meal at the corner restaurant. As they were walking back a voice cut through their conversation.

"Spare some change for something to eat?"

Living downtown, he probably got more of that sort of thing than the rest of the guys from work did. Everyone ignored the guy and walked on. No one looked to be in the mood to drop a few coins into the homeless man's hat, and he quickly recognized he was getting nothing from them. Resorting to his departing gift, the man called loudly, "Have a good day, God loves you," to their backs. Tannion walked on without saying a word as he always had, but the thoughts going off in his head occupied him and he ceased listening to the others' conversation.

Tannion never went out of his way to look for a confrontation, which is why he ignored the bums on the street, but he always had the same feeling. He would often think when a guy asks for change that he should stop and tell him that he wouldn't give a penny to someone so they can go and buy a bottle of cheap wine and get drunk. He was sure that the chances of that person using it for food were one in a million.

Even though he had put a lot of thought into this tirade, he had never used it. He had, however, come up with a list of the four types of people living on the street. There are the helpless, the hopeless, the useless, and the lazy. The first two may get a little of Tannion's sympathy if they at least tried. These are people who need help because they are unable to help themselves.

The last two categories got no sympathy and definitely no help from Tannion. These are the guys who want to be on the street. Either too lazy to get a real job, or too useless to hold down a job. Drug addicts and alcoholics would fall into these groups. He always saw the bums on the street asking for handouts to be in the last two categories.

That afternoon he was in a good mood. He had a date. His date was with an old friend he had seen off and on since high school. Female, yes, but not the type of relationship that he expected would get intense. Just someone nice to go out with, talk to, and who maybe would even hold hands. He hadn't been on too many dates lately, but he had known Jane for a long time.

Tannion met Jane at her apartment at seven with the idea of going to a seven thirty movie. When they got to the theater none of the movies looked that interesting to either of them, so they decided to go for a walk in the park instead. Tannion liked the idea of talking and catching up with any gossip as they hadn't seen each other for a few weeks.

Of course, Jane knew about the lightning strike, but Tannion had no apparent ill effects from it, so his health was not a topic that came up in conversation. He also had no intention of telling her about the way he was seeing his body. He wasn't too sure that he believed it yet, and he sure as hell didn't think anyone else would. They would think he wasn't in his right mind if he started telling tales of physically assaulting himself to see if he could heal it with his mind.

After cutting his hand the first time, he had tried at least a dozen more times and each had the same result. Each test got more extreme than the last, and each one healed as quickly. He knew there were things that were best kept secret.

As they walked across the street and into the park, Jane took hold of Tannion's hand. Walking hand in hand into the park, Tannion had a sensation that was becoming fairly familiar. There was a touch and a hint of understanding all at the same time. He couldn't tell what it was, but he knew where it was coming from. It was Jane. He didn't know exactly how he knew, but he knew the feeling was coming through the connection of their hands. There was something in Jane begging him to take a look.

Jane was a good friend, but he didn't think he could just ask her to take her clothes off in the park so he could see where this sensation was coming from. Even if she did, he had no clue what he was looking for and would have only been distracted. He tried hard to see what it might be, which resulted in his not being very conversational. Luckily, Jane was going through some issues at work and his silence made Tannion look like a very good listener.

Tannion could feel whatever it was Jane had. As he concentrated, he could feel that it was coming from her hand and arm, but it had started somewhere else. Mentally working his way inside her body, he finally figured out the problem. Jane had a virus. It was not a very serious virus, but it was prevalent through her bloodstream and would probably make her mildly sick that night. He had been listening to her for twenty minutes.

Tannion wondered if he could ask Jane's body to fight the little buggers just as his body had fought the warts. Once again the thought process appeared to be the catalyst. Jane quit talking and looked at Tannion queasily. He watched as a bit of a flush came over her.

"Oh my," she murmured.

"What is it?" He asked nervously.

"I just… felt a bit… a bit warm!" she said slightly embarrassed, "I have no idea what… I mean, I'm far too young for hot flashes," she joked, trying to hide her discomfort.

"Do you think you may be coming down with something?"

"There is a flu going around work that has a few people down. It's probably one of those twenty-four hour bugs that make you violently ill for a day and then goes away as quickly as it came."

He continued to hold onto her hand, but he couldn't feel a thing. He thought that the bugs must be gone. It's amazing what the body can do if it has a mind to… or in this case, if a friend has a mind to.

"It's passed," Jane noted. "Must have been the twenty second flu!"

The rest of the evening went pretty fast. Jane had talked herself out and, having had the listener she needed, she was feeling better. They decided to take in the late show. When the movie was over Tannion walked her home. He even got a good night kiss at the door. He wondered if he might be able to work this friendship into a relationship yet. Jane was certainly not hard to look at, and she was easy to talk to.

He decided he would just have to see what the future had in store.

The future was on Tannion's mind when he went to bed. He was lying there thinking about what was going on and what had happened with Jane. Then he thought that maybe he should get some rest. The next thing he knew it was morning. Jane was still on his mind, but he knew that his thinking about sleep was all it took for his body to put itself to sleep. Now he wasn't so sure who was controlling what.

It felt strange enough being able to look at his own insides with some sort of internal eye, but it was another thing altogether to look into someone else's body. It took him a little while to get over the idea of looking in and seeing things he had not seen before.

Now the question was how far could this go, and how could he take it there? It had taken almost half an hour of holding hands on a warm summer evening before he had even noticed that something was wrong with Jane. It might have been the moisture on her skin that was important, or maybe it was more important to know what to look for, or where to look. When he had thought about healing the flu bug it seemed to happen quickly, but could he have found it faster?

The next few days at work he tried to shake hands with people and touch others in what appeared to be a normal way. Nothing. He couldn't believe that everyone he touched was in perfect health. Each contact lasted only a few seconds and he suspected that this brief contact just wasn't enough.

There had to be a way to test his theory. He needed to find people who would allow him to touch them for extended periods. Holding hands with Jane had worked. If he could get someone to hold hands with him again, he might find out if what happened was a fluke or not.

Tannion decided that what he needed was to find sick people. There had to be people with illnesses that they knew about. People who were in a position where he could hold their hand to comfort them, or at least lay a hand on their arm or shoulder and leave it there for a few minutes to allow a proper read.

He thought that the perfect place was obviously a hospital. A hospital would have lots of sick people. He could probably go and visit someone who would let him hold their hand, but he was not likely to know what was wrong with them. It may be better if he could be looking for something in particular.

The solution finally came to him. He needed to visit a cancer clinic. There would be people who were very sick, close to death even, who could use comforting. Their health problem would be obvious, and it would be the most serious thing they had. Now he just had to find one.

5

Tannion found out there were a couple cancer clinics nearby, but he felt it would be wise to go out of town. He was sure he shouldn't let anyone know about his secret, at least not until he completely understood it. If he went to a different city, he should be able to do it anonymously.

Topeka was a little more than a three hour drive from Tannion's home. He decided to make it a day trip so he wouldn't have to stay overnight and leave any paper trail. He even went so far as to pay cash for gas. No one was going to be able to trace him.

He had looked up the address of one of the clinics. After driving around for a while he found it and pulled into the parking lot. It was then he realized that he hadn't thought about a cover story. He had found the place with the idea of seeing someone, but hadn't put a lot of thought into what he was going to say when he got there. All he knew was that he needed to get into a cancer clinic and talk to a patient he didn't know.

A few minutes of thought and he had a game plan. He wanted to keep it simple and try not to raise any suspicions at all. Tannion walked into the front entrance and up to the counter. He saw that it was almost eleven thirty.

"Good morning, when would I be able to see Mr. Smith?" Tannion asked.

The nurse behind the desk looked up at Tannion with slightly sad eyes and said, "Visiting hours start at one, but there is no Mr. Smith here."

He thought for sure this place would be big enough to have a Smith. Now what? So much for his brilliant plan.

"No problem. I'll call my aunt and see where he is. I thought she said this was the place."

Tannion hoped it was a reasonable explanation. Now he didn't have a clue what to do. As he walked out of the door a couple of people in white jackets, who he took to be doctors or clinic staff, were coming in and he took a chance.

"Can you tell me if a Mr. Adams or Abraham is in the clinic today?"

One of the fellows looked at him and his answer caught Tannion by surprise. He thought they would say they weren't allowed to talk about the patients or simply say no, but the man stopped and said, "No, but Mrs. Adams is here. Were you looking for her husband?"

"No. That's fine, thanks," Tannion said and kept on walking.

Tannion almost went home, but upped his nerve and continued. He waited until exactly one o'clock and walked up to the front desk and thanked God that a different nurse was on duty. He asked for Mrs. Adams's room. The nurse was busy filling out some papers. Without looking up, she asked if he was family. Tannion told her that he was just a friend. It seemed to be good enough for her because she waved him down the wing to her right.

"Room 103," she said, raising her hand to point the direction, her face never lifting from the papers on her desk.

Mrs. Adams was in the third room just down the hall. The clinic wasn't nearly as large as he had originally thought, and it was really only a central lobby with wings to the left and to the right. Mrs. Adams was awake when he walked into the room, but she looked to be heavily sedated. She managed to look at him and said a weak "Hello."

"Hello," Tannion responded nervously. "I... I was here to visit my uncle, but he's asleep. Would you like to talk?"

She smiled gratefully and nodded. He took her hand as he sat down and knew she would be quite comfortable with him holding it for a while. She was on pain medication and it showed on her face.

He held her hand as she drifted in and out of sleep. All the time he was searching. Not knowing how to search, but having an idea of what he was looking for. After a couple of minutes Tannion felt the sensation that was becoming more and more familiar. He could tell that she had something wrong, but at first he could not tell what. The fact that he was in a cancer clinic was his obvious clue, but a person could have cancer of just about anything, so he was still searching.

It finally happened almost like a veil being lifted. If he was looking for cancer, he found it. There appeared to be a fairly large tumor wrapped around some of her internal organs and many of the cells in the organs were not right either. It must have been the type that was inoperable, and he guessed that she didn't have long to live.

Now that he had found it, Tannion had to ask himself what he should do. Mrs. Adams was probably in her late fifties and looked as if she had been a very lively and vibrant woman before the cancer. She was very thin, but he got the impression that before the cancer she had never been fat. This did not look like a woman who should die.

First thoughts are much like first impressions, they stick. He knew that he had done something, but he had no clue what. The body can do amazing things given the chance, or maybe just given the instructions. By now he was convinced it was possible that whatever he wanted to happen could happen. It was just a matter of setting out a recipe and the rules.

Tannion said good bye to Mrs. Adams, not really knowing if he had helped her or not, and walked next door. The occupant in the next room was sleeping and didn't look very good. He was very thin and looked very old. Tannion quickly made the decision to move on. He walked into four rooms and made the same decision in each. In the last room he checked he was surprised at what he saw. It looked to be a little kid. She could not have been older than ten or twelve.

Tannion stood at the doorway for a few seconds. The fact that a young kid had cancer is hard, but why would she be in this clinic? Don't they have kid's hospitals for this kind of thing? As he moved closer he realized that it likely didn't matter where she was. It didn't look like she had too long to live. She was heavily medicated, probably because of the pain, and could barely keep her eyes open.

"Hi, what's your name?" he asked softly.

"Sarah," was the quick, but drawn reply. She was obviously tired, but it didn't look like she was expecting a visitor so he sat down. Tannion wondered where her parents were and why she was left alone at the beginning of visiting hours. He put his hand on her arm and between touching her arm and holding her hand, he was able to make contact with the cancer.

It was deep in her lymph nodes, and based on her color and strength it didn't look like she had that many more sleeps. The thought process went to work and although he couldn't be sure he had done anything, just like with Mrs. Adams, a little color rose in Sarah's cheeks making him think that something might have happened. He looked at his watch and thought maybe ten minutes had passed. That was less than half the time it had taken with Jane, but if he was to use this thing he would still need to find a situation where he could touch someone for longer than is usually socially acceptable. Either that, or figure out a way to speed the contact up.

He left Sarah's room and started back down the hall looking in the doors on the other side of the corridor. Each room was filled with the smells and sounds of death. Each room had someone who looked like they already had one foot in the grave. Finally he walked out the front door and got into his car to head home. Tannion had come to the clinic to test his new-found skill, but was leaving with a scar he didn't have before.

Tannion had never really been around death much. One of his grandparents and a couple of aunts and uncles had died, but he had seen them only after the fact, never a few days before. The experience in the cancer clinic touched him deeply. The pain, misery, fear — and worse, the acceptance of their impending doom were etched in his soul.

Monday turned into Tuesday and it was Thursday before anything happened. In one of the back pages of the newspaper there was the mention of two people being cured at a cancer clinic in nearby Topeka. The article noted a mystery visitor, but had no explanation for the miracle. Tannion was happy to see that they didn't have much.

His happiness didn't last any longer than the next day. Tannion heard it first on the car radio as he drove out for groceries, then he turned on the television in time for the six o'clock news, and it was the lead story. The radio and TV news had picked up on the newspaper report.

The reporter announced, "A couple of patients in the Grant's Care Cancer Clinic had a miraculous cure of what was considered to be incurable cancer. Names were not released, but officials said that both patients reported having a strange male visitor last Sunday afternoon. A dark-haired male in his thirties was seen visiting the clinic, and the nurse on duty remembered him."

The news report then flashed to the nurse Tannion had seen at the clinic. "He was about six feet tall, maybe two hundred pounds. Looked like he was in pretty good shape, but I don't recall much about his face," she said.

Tannion watched the telecast with his heart in his throat the whole time. "Christ, if they are able to draw a composite picture or figure out it was me, then what?" he said to himself. Tannion was sure that the nurse hadn't looked up enough to see much of his face or to even know how tall or heavy he was, but she must have looked at his back as he walked down the hall. Then the TV flashed the composite Tannion had been dreading.

Luckily, the composite didn't look like anybody Tannion would recognize. The features were ordinary and generic. He bet the nurse was embarrassed that she didn't get a good look and had a composite drawn from what she thought he would look like based on the back of his head. Tannion knew she never looked up and he had gone out the front door without her even knowing he was there.

The TV broadcast ended without mention of any further action. After all, two people had been cured, not killed. Had he done something wrong, or had he done something right? If someone walked up to him on the street and said, "Hey you're the guy who cured the cancer patients," what would he do? Would he say that they had the wrong guy? Would he take pride in the fact, or would he run like hell?

6

"Hey, Mike. Did you see the paper this morning?"

"What are you talking about, Bill, the obits? I didn't see your name," Rallin joked.

"No, you dumb shit, the section on the cancer clinic. Two patients are miraculously cured and there is talk of a mystery stranger."

"I read that too. I have an aunt in a cancer clinic, so it caught my eye."

"Do you think it's worth taking a look at?" Pansloski asked

"You mean as a case file?"

"Sure, why not? It's been so quiet lately. It might be worth looking at. It might be interesting."

"Not likely, Bill. Even the local cops won't be looking at it."

"More reason for us to look."

"Maybe. I've been with the FBI for a long time, and I've seen cases built around a lot less than that. We would need to tie it to something though."

"It was a hospital, right?" Pansloski asked

"It said a cancer clinic, so much the same I would think. Why?"

"Under federal law we have jurisdiction over anything relating to health care fraud. All you need to do is make it sound as if you are taking a look at it to see if there might be fraud. Maybe they were never sick at all, which would be insurance fraud. That's a federal offence as well."

"Might work, Bill. If you're interested in helping with it, I'll talk to the boss and see what happens. I can admit to being a little intrigued by the case, and a little bored. It is Friday."

"Sure, why not."

The request went more or less the way Rallin expected. Talking to the division head got them the go ahead to start a file. Not quite an X-file, but 'cancer mystery, possible fraud' would do. Crime was not so rampant that different or off-beat cases couldn't be opened. A file like this in New York or LA would never see the light of day. Mind you, it may be opened, but may never be worked on even in Wichita.

"I don't know if this is the type of case I want, but I've got it. That damn Pansloski came up with the idea and now I'm stuck with it," thought Rallin.

A couple of phone calls to the local police and their file on what was now an FBI case was faxed over to Rallin's office. The locals had collected a little data, but they must have had the same thoughts Rallin was having. Where was the crime? Rallin gave them the line of investigating for possible health care fraud in order to justify taking over the case. They were more than happy to pass the case to the FBI. Other than a few notes on the patients and a composite drawing, it was pretty bare.

The file indicated that two cancer patients appeared to have had miracle cures. The first patient was a fifty-eight year old Caucasian female. Mrs. Margaret Adams had been diagnosed with a large non-operable malignant tumor wrapped around several internal organs and blood vessels. She had been given only a few weeks to live.

The second patient was a nine-year old Caucasian female. Name: Sarah Jansen. Sarah had a rare form of leukemia that attacked the lymph nodes and she was given only a couple of weeks to live.

Both patients had been visited by a Caucasian male the day before they started feeling better. They both indicated a warming sensation throughout their body and an increase in energy the next day. Both patients started feeling better and tests found that Mrs. Adams's tumor was gone and that there was no sign of Sarah's leukemia. Both were considered to be healthy and were sent home to recover their strength.

There were no opinions in the files, only facts. There were no thoughts on a connection between the stranger and both patients' sudden improvement. If there was a connection, what did this man do? How did the two patients suddenly find themselves healthy again? Answers to these questions had to be very important to anyone with cancer or anyone working on a cancer cure.

Rallin knew he would have to talk to the people involved. The file at least had names and addresses. They had also developed a pretty good sketch, but that was all they had. The patients had been on heavy sedation and didn't remember much. The nurse had not seen much either. But between the three witnesses, they did get the composite.

Rallin picked up the file and took a last look. His aunt was dying of cancer and he had seen her a couple of times. He found the place very depressing. Going to another clinic would only make him think of her.

He decided to take a last look at the composite before the file was put away and probably forgotten. Maybe nothing would come of all this. After all, was it really a crime?

7

Tannion spent the next few weeks living in constant fear. Images of a hand reaching out and settling on his shoulder with some guy in a dark suit saying to come with him haunted his waking moments. He had trouble concentrating at work. Each night he would sit inside his apartment, afraid to go out in case someone recognized him from the composite.

Luckily the picture was not a very good likeness. The two patients were pretty sick when Tannion was there, so he should have expected that they didn't get a good look at him. The nurse had been busy and had barely looked up when she had directed him to Mrs. Adams' room. Still there was always the chance that one of his friends or co-workers would think the picture looked like him. Either they didn't see the resemblance, or they hadn't seen the picture. At least, not yet. He knew he needed to be careful.

One thing that did come out of sitting at home in front of the TV was a chance to practice. Sleeping had become a wonderful thing. He would be asleep in seconds and would sleep like a baby with gentle dreams, waking refreshed. He still didn't know why or what any of the medical terms were, but his body seemed to know what to do. His body was able to release a chemical cocktail equivalent to a great sleeping pill and the next thing Tannion knew it was morning. This restful sleep never left the groggy hangover that pills would often produce. Instead he would be energetic and ready to tackle his day.

He focused his energies on ways to get his eyes inside his body. He looked at his heart by thinking of his heart beat. He checked his lungs by coughing and thinking of his breathing. His liver was tough, but he got there. Bladder and kidneys were easy, if a bit uncomfortable.

Tannion needed to practice. It became an obsession. If not for the fear of being found out, he might have done almost anything. After thoroughly researching every vascular system and every square inch of skin on his body, the urge to research on someone else was overpowering. Yet he couldn't think of a safe way to play this new form of doctor. The news had let go of the 'miracle cancer cure story,' but the constant fear kept him cautious. Finally Tannion was struck by a brilliant idea. He could go home.

Tannion knew that he could meet his mom, give her a hug, and leave his arm around her for as long as it took. He knew that his mother had a few problems. She had high blood pressure, high cholesterol, and a sore back. Those were the ones she would complain about every once and a while, but there were probably more. Tannion could search and experiment on her to his heart's content, and she would be thrilled to have him there. She was constantly complaining that he didn't visit often enough.

When Tannion got to his mom's house, she met him at the door and, as always, was very glad to see him. Just as he knew he could, he hugged her and walked into the house with his arm around her making sufficient contact. Tannion knew he could have waited until much later to take a look, but he couldn't resist. As he held on to her, he began to probe and look for the signs.

The first thing that came through was a weakness in an arterial wall that could have led to an aneurysm. This was obviously very serious and popped up very quickly. Tannion was surprised that it was there in only a few seconds. He knew that it was something she wasn't aware of, so he could fix it without her knowing. Then there was the start of an ulcer and a partially blocked artery. Then there were the items he knew about, and finally a bruise on her leg.

His first instinct was to fix everything, but he had already almost been caught because of the cancer clinic incident. Even though this was his mother, he decided to take it slow. First fix the ones she didn't know about and that could kill her. The potential aneurysm was easy as her body sent additional cells to the area and strengthened the wall. The ulcer was caused by small bacteria, which he killed. He didn't bother repairing the damage, deciding to let it heal on its own. The cholesterol was simple as well. He broke down a large quantity of arterial plaque, allowing the body to eliminate it naturally. With the blockage broken up, the high blood pressure would go away in no time.

This scanning and repair only took a few minutes while they talked about what he was up to lately. She never showed any sign of even subconscious awareness. Tannion stayed the night, which pleased her to no end. Driving home the next day, Tannion was feeling good about what he had been able to do, and pleased with the knowledge that he was improving. He was getting the feeling that he could fix everything and anything that was wrong, and do it in a matter of minutes. With his mother, each illness had taken less than a minute. By the time he left, his quickest time was under thirty seconds. Tannion began to think that his skills had improved to the point that a simple handshake just may be enough time to command a body to repair itself.

For the next couple of weeks Tannion shook hands with anyone he met, always trying to look inside. He found that he was unable to see into anyone with only a quick hand-shake, but with each new attempt he had the feeling he was getting closer.

There were a few times at work when he was able to extend the contact for longer. With that extra few seconds, he would have the time needed and would cure whatever ailed them, so long as he knew he could get away with it. He was able to get to a couple of guys by wrist wrestling with them. Several of the married ladies in the office didn't seem put off by his resting his hand on their forearm as he told a short story. He found that he would do anything to extend contact long enough.

In a matter of weeks, he had his time down to a few seconds. It still was slower than he knew it had to be. He was beginning to think that the time would always be at those few seconds when he had a breakthrough.

Tannion went at it in a slightly different way. Instead of looking inside randomly to see what was wrong, he started with a preconceived idea of what was wrong. He went looking for cancer each time, and almost immediately the problems appeared. If people had cancer it announced itself instantly, but if they didn't then any problem they had would be there just as fast.

He was beginning to think that he could heal the world.

8

Tannion and a friend from work went out for a drink after work and they stayed for several hours. When they finally made it a night, they said their goodbyes and split up to head home. Tannion had a few blocks to walk. As always, the bums were out. He had already told a couple of younger guys that he didn't have any change when he came upon the last guy sitting on the sidewalk with a hat in front of him. For one reason or another, the guy wanted to talk.

"Spare a quarter for a cup of coffee."

"No, I don't have any," was Tannion's practiced reply.

But the man didn't just let it go. "Can't you spare a little for a hungry homeless guy?" As Tannion was repeating that he didn't have any change, a thought hit him. This guy was probably in his late forties or early fifties. It could be hard to tell with these guys on the street as they lived a hard life. He looked and smelled like a hard drinker. Alcoholism is considered a disease, and Tannion wondered if he could see it in this man and perhaps cure it.

Reaching into his pocket, he brought out a dollar and went to hand it to the bum with his left hand. As the bum reached out for the bill with his right hand, Tannion grabbed it and shook it with his right.

The bum was surprised, but he caught himself and shook Tannion's hand while thanking him. He wasn't the only one surprised. As Tannion looked inside, he discovered extensive damage that would probably kill the guy in a matter of months, if not weeks.

Tannion shook his head, and an involuntary thought must have triggered something. The bum took his dollar and settled back into his spot. Before Tannion had taken a couple of steps there was a small sound like a sigh. When he looked back he could see that the man had drooped over, apparently quite dead. He kept on walking, but he knew what he had done. He hadn't meant to do it. Or had he?

Tannion checked the paper for the next few days, but there was no mention of a homeless bum dying on the street. It just wasn't newsworthy. There didn't appear to be any reaction at all. The coroner must have seen it as natural causes. Even if they did an autopsy, they would have come to the same conclusion. Tannion knew he hadn't done anything that wasn't going to happen anyway, but he also knew that he made it happen sooner. Life and death. Were they his to give, to take, or was it what fate had in mind?

He had reached a new point in this gift, or curse, whichever he wanted to call it. He could heal himself, he could heal others, and now he could kill. The bum was pretty bad off and it didn't take much, but that wouldn't have made any difference. Tannion knew that he could have killed him in so many ways it was scary. He could have triggered any number of arteries to leak and cause slow internal bleeding that would kill in a few hours. He could trigger a heart attack, like he had with the bum, on anyone. He could have attacked any one of his internal organs. The list was long, and Tannion knew it. The real question was why hadn't he cured the man?

Time eases anything. In a few days Tannion had more or less forgotten the dead bum on the corner and went about life much as before. He was also starting to get past the feeling that he had to keep looking over his shoulder. He continued to experiment with as many people as he could. Shaking all hands that were offered and looking deep inside. He cured a friend's prostate problem before he knew it was a problem. His uncle had high blood pressure that Tannion eased over time to make it look like his eating habits had caused the change. A little healing here and there eased his conscience. The longer he went with no one noticing the more confident he became.

It had been about four months since the lightning strike and Tannion was feeling like he was getting pretty good at his gift. As he was walking home from a local pub one night, he took a shortcut through a darkened alley. He saw a guy coming at him. This guy looked a little scruffy and although the area was usually safe, all Tannion could think was that the bums were out.

"Not another bum looking for a handout," he muttered dejectedly. Tannion didn't want to deal with the bum, but he had no choice. There was no other route. When Tannion got within a couple of feet, he made sure not to make eye contact. It obviously didn't help.

"Hey, mister," came the original opening. "Can you spare a quarter?"

"No, I don't have any change," Tannion said without slowing down, trying to get enough distance so the guy would drop the conversation. He didn't get that lucky.

"Come on, you must have something you can spare for me," the bum said taking a step in Tannion's direction to make sure the couple of steps Tannion had taken didn't allow the required distance to occur.

This was not a normal response, and by this time Tannion had stopped and turned around. It was then that he saw the knife. It wasn't a big knife, but it looked sharp.

"Don't fuck with me asshole, give me your wallet," the guy said.

There was no chance of anyone hearing them as they were very much alone. The bum had made sure that they were in an area where he wouldn't be seen trying to mug someone.

Tannion quickly looked at his options. He could probably outrun this guy and the best the guy could do was to throw the knife at his back. They were standing only a couple of feet apart and Tannion thought that the guy might be able to get a thrust in before he got started. Tannion also knew that he could pull out his wallet and give the bum what he wanted, but that was the last thing Tannion wanted to do.

"I don't think so, you useless shit," Tannion snarled. It took the guy a little by surprise.

"I'll stick this in your gut if you don't do as I tell you," the bum hissed. Tannion heard a small hesitation and it wasn't hard to tell that all of a sudden maybe the bum thought that he had bitten off more than he could chew. Instead of a businessman who would give up a few bucks rather than take a chance, maybe this was not going to be so easy.

"That little pig sticker? You're only going to get yourself hurt with that thing," Tannion bluffed.

The bum took a step forward and tried to slash Tannion with the knife in his right hand. Tannion had never been in a fight in his life, certainly not one with a guy with a knife. He stepped back and the knife only caught the sleeve of his shirt. Tannion stepped in to hit him, but underestimated the guy's speed and missed. This gave the bum an easy shot at him. The knife went in under Tannion's left arm, grazing along his ribs. The pain shot through him and almost took him to his knees.

Tannion was prepared for this possibility though. Immediately he stopped the pain and the bleeding. That was his edge. The bum had expected Tannion to either fall down in pain or cry out that he gave up. Instead Tannion grabbed him by his arms. He saw the weakness, and it was all over. The bum shuddered and went limp. The weak spot was in an artery to the brain. The massive brain hemorrhage was quick. They were still alone, so Tannion took the body over to the side of a building and dumped it.

As Tannion made his getaway, he quickly finished healing his wounds and went home to cleanup. He had to throw his shirt away, as it was cut and bloody. After washing up he looked in the mirror and saw that everything was healed, just like the cuts he had made on his hand. No scar. No nothing. It looked as if nothing had happened at all.

Tannion's thoughts were all over the place that night and he didn't get any sleep. He knew that he had a power that could be used in many ways. He could obviously cure almost any disease or ailment. Hell, maybe every disease. He could use it for good and for evil. He could kill in an instant and not be overly concerned about his own health. The only problem was he had to get close. He had to touch them.

If he had to get close, he knew he would have to see about protecting himself. Body armor or a bullet-proof vest seemed to be the best bet, but he didn't want to wear anything that was noticeable. He knew that he could heal himself very quickly without pain, but there was always the chance that a bullet or a knife could hit that vital area that would kill him before he could think.

After a little thought the idea came to him. He needed to find a way to use his own body to protect itself. The first thing he had to do was gain strength. Tannion usually worked out a few days a week. Now he found that he was able to lift weights and gain strength, making it look as if it was the workouts that were doing all the good. He made sure that some of it never showed. He didn't want to get much bigger, merely increase his strength several times over.

By changing the muscle structure, reinforcing the tendons and connections to the bone, increasing bone and muscle density, and adjusting the nerve fibers to fire faster, Tannion found he was getting stronger and faster. At just over six two, his normal weight was just over two hundred. Tannion didn't look that much bigger, but every time he got on the scales he could see the difference.

Tannion figured that the only way he could be killed instantly would be a shot to the head or the heart. Anything else gave him a chance. He increased the bone density in his skull and enhanced his neck muscles to compensate for a heavier head. He then thickened his ribs, closing the gaps between them to protect his heart. He knew that a big enough bullet in the wrong spot might still kill him, but didn't see how he could do much more. As it was, he had to make sure that he never got in front of an x-ray machine. Those kinds of questions were the last thing he wanted.

Everything was going as well as he thought it could. His body was improving and he was gaining strength and agility, but he still had to work on his mind. He always thought that he was well adjusted, but it bothered him a little that he felt no compassion for having killed. Another loser dead on the street. An unmarked grave with no tears at the grave site.

9

Bill Pansloski showed Rallin the file late that afternoon. A homeless person dead on the street is not a complete rarity, but those sorts of things tended to happen more in the winter than in the fall. Still it happened. The difference is they usually don't die of natural causes with a knife in their hand and blood on the knife that didn't belong to them.

"Bill, what type was the blood on the knife, and what was the blood type of the bum?"

"That's homeless person Mike, not bum. The knife was AB positive and the bum was O."

"Thanks, but a bum is still a bum. The coroner's report says the guy died of a brain hemorrhage. Now I ask you, is it possible for a guy in a knife fight, who by the looks of the blood on the knife appeared to be winning, to suddenly fall over dead?"

"Guess so. The sudden exertion could have caused an artery to give."

"Yeah and the other guy gets lucky. We need to find that guy. You check with the hospitals. I'm going to the scene to take a look around."

"Sure. Knife wounds are automatically logged with the locals and it should only take a little while, but it's possible that whoever was knifed may not have gone to a hospital."

"It's possible, but by the size of the knife in the picture and the extent of the blood on it, it looks like the other guy got stuck good and would probably need a little help."

"I'll give you a call as soon as I get any info," were Pansloski's last words as he left the room.

In all his time with the FBI, Rallin had never broken a big case or been in the limelight. Hard working and stable, he had never gotten the lucky break or the lucky case. As a result, he had stayed right where he was. He was a detective in the FBI, but not in the largest bureau nor in the biggest city. Not a whole lot happened out here. Now his next case was a dead bum. Not much to get excited about. He wasn't even sure why this case had made it to the FBI. Couldn't the local guys handle a dead bum?

The back alley where the deceased was found was a few minutes away. As he swung into the alley it was easy to note that the fight could have been hidden from view. The alley had enough of a curve and there was a large garbage container and assorted boxes that could have made it very secluded. Not much light either. No witnesses had come forward and none had been uncovered in the sweep the local guys had done when the body was found.

The marks were still visible on the ground where the body was found. Circles around small blood drops indicated that the other guy probably went out the other end of the alley. The police tape was still up waiting for Rallin to complete the investigation.

The coroner had put the time of death sometime between midnight and two a.m. The report noted that all the shops on that end of the street would have been closed. When the shop owners were asked the next morning, they said they had already gone home and hadn't seen anything out of the ordinary before they left. If someone had walked out of the alley, he may have been seen, but not really noticed. If they were limping badly or holding themselves as if they were badly hurt, someone would remember seeing them. Problem was there may not have been anyone there to see anything.

"Well not much to see here," Rallin said to himself. He looked at his watch and the digital timer indicated it to be well past five in the afternoon. "Might as well go home," he decided. Rallin called in to the locals to have the scene released and headed for home.

Pulling up in front of his modest three-bedroom house always made Rallin feel good. He would have liked to live in a better neighborhood and in a bigger house, but this was home. Inside he knew his wife would be waiting. A beer would be in the fridge, but only because he bought them himself. Arlene didn't like him to drink, but a beer after work was allowed if he bought it.

Arlene would always ask him how his day was and often they would talk about his cases. He knew the big guys at the bureau wouldn't like that sort of thing, but he found Arlene's insight to be very good. Her questions often helped him think the case through.

After telling her most of the details of the dead bum, they were both at a loss.

"It looks like the only way you will solve this one is when the guy shows up for stitches at some clinic. Other than that, you've got a guy dead from natural causes and no case," Arlene said.

"Yeah, you're probably right, if no one saw a thing and the other guy doesn't appear, we have nothing. If someone is out to rob or kill the street people, there won't be the public outcry that rapists or serial killers get, but we don't even know if the guy who was stabbed was the victim or the perp."

"How is this an FBI case?" Arlene wondered aloud.

Rallin shrugged. "The only reason this has become a federal case is the possibility of someone preying on the homeless. Maybe the brass is concerned with someone cleaning the homeless off the street. This is the second dead guy on the streets in a few weeks, and both were from natural causes."

Arlene could usually cut right through all the bullshit and get to the point very quickly. She didn't disappoint Rallin.

"Next case," was all she needed to say.

10

Tannion found once again that time could heal almost anything. The physical wounds took only minutes to heal. The emotional and psychological wounds would take longer. In this case, he hadn't forgotten the beggar. He had simply set him aside for another time and moved on.

He couldn't get excited about his work at the office. The feeling of power every time he touched someone became what he lived for. That and working out. Tannion started working out more often and the muscles continued to pile on.

Tannion would get a euphoric feeling after a workout that he had never felt before, and he liked it. He felt as if he could do anything, but at the same time he felt alone. He hadn't told anyone about his "gift," as he had begun to consider it. Despite knowing lots of people and having several friends, he started to look inward more and more and started spending more time by himself.

"I am probably the only one in the world who can do the things that I can do. I am as close to a superman as the world is ever likely to see, and yet, I don't dare tell even my family or closest friends."

Tannion tested himself in little things. He played mental memory games. Buried himself in books and found his reading speed to be much faster. He would go for a run, and when he was alone he would pick it up until he was really moving. By making changes in the nerve and muscle fibers he thought he could be the strongest and fastest person on earth.

With all the time he spent working, working out, and honing his skills, the rest of the year passed easily. Christmas was a couple of weeks away and he hadn't even thought of gifts. He needed something for Jane. He usually bought something small for a few of his friends, and would get something nice for his mother. Christmas Day was always a day at his mom's house with friends and family. He was looking forward to it as he always did.

He went shopping at the downtown mall near his apartment. He walked up and down the strip trying to think of what to buy with the hope that something would jump out and say 'pick me!' It didn't happen. Discouraged after hours of shopping, he trudged to the parking lot. He had driven, just in case he had a good haul.

As he was putting the key in the car door, he heard tires squeal and a loud thump followed by a crash. Over his shoulder he saw a couple of people running towards a car that was obviously in trouble. The driver had come around the corner in the parking lot a little too fast and hadn't seen the teenager on a bike coming at him. The bike had gone under the car and the rider had gone up on to the hood.

As the car swerved and braked, it had thrown the kid off and hit another parked car and bounced to the left. The kid had fallen in front of the car and ended up pinned under the front tire. He was screaming in pain as Tannion got to the scene. It was only a few cars away so he was one of the first to get there. It was obvious that the car had to be moved off the kid's leg, but it would be a while before the fire trucks could get there.

Without thinking Tannion grabbed the front end of the car and lifted. The first few inches were taken up by the springs, but a few more and someone grabbed the kid and pulled him out. Tannion dropped the car down and took a look. There wasn't any blood, but the boy's leg looked like it was probably broken. It could have been a lot worse. He thought about touching the kid, but there were too many witnesses already.

The cops questioned Tannion and people thumped him on the back. Before he could escape, a news crew came in and did an on-the-spot interview. Tannion claimed that the adrenaline must have been pumping, which gave him extra strength, but he knew better. He could have lifted a lot more weight than the car had to offer, and although he had started lifting without thinking it through, he had enough sense to make it look difficult.

Tannion found the sense of power to be almost overwhelming. Was there anything he couldn't do? Was there anyone on earth who had ever been stronger, faster, or better? The euphoria felt great and the only question left was what next? His secret was becoming too good to keep to himself, but short of putting on tights and a mask, Tannion had no idea how to do the things he wanted to do.

Tannion's favorite comic book hero was never Superman, Batman, or Spiderman. It was a character called the Flash. The Flash would use his great speed to fight crime. Tannion thought it would be fun to have a tight suit and mask and go around saving people, but that was for comic books and not real life. There must be something that could be as fulfilling.

Tannion had grown up in a good home, had a good education, and throughout it all he was always the good guy. As Tannion sat there thinking about his life, and how he had to keep his secret to himself, he knew he had to do something. The frustration of not doing anything was going to get to be too much, and eventually he would explode.

The question was what. The movies and comics always made it look so easy with bad guys everywhere, but in real life Tannion didn't know one guy who he could call a bad guy. No one he knew had ever been in jail or had stolen a car. Still, Tannion knew he had to do something. Curing colds and high blood pressure was never going to be enough.

If he was going to do something with his gift, it was going to be for the good. It had to be for the good. There might not be any rich megalomaniacs out there vying for world domination, but there were murderers and rapists, thieves, and crooks just waiting for him to stop them. Now he had to go out and find them.

11

"Did you read this morning's paper, Mike?" Pansloski asked

Rallin looked up at his partner and picked up the paper. "Yeah, what part you talking about?"

"The city section on the third page," Pansloski said as he leaned over Rallin's desk.

"Where?" Rallin asked, and after Pansloski pointed to the right page he added, "You mean the article about the strong guy picking the car off some kid?"

"Yeah, that's the piece. Quite something, huh?"

"So what does this have to do with anything?"

"Think you could have lifted that much in your time."

"Piss off Pansloski! This is my time, and no, I would never have budged that car. He had to have lifted close to a thousand pounds just to get that corner off the kid," said Rallin. The grin across his face belied any harsh words that may have come out, and it was clear to his partner that was the point. "That's a big car not a dinky toy." he added.

The banter between the two cops was as good natured as always, but as usual there was an undertow of reality. Good friends they were, but they were also good cops. Rallin took a few minutes to read the story of a kid being rescued, and before he could voice the thought, Pansloski did.

"Wouldn't mind getting a look at this guy, but doesn't look like they took any pictures."

"The press always takes pictures," said Rallin. "They may not print them, but they were bound to have had a camera there. They never throw any of that stuff out. Let's have a go at seeing what this guy looks like." Pansloski had tweaked Rallin's curiosity.

One quick call to Rallin's contact at the local paper assured them both that a few pictures had been taken. As they had suspected, the pictures were not in the junk bin. Having a contact at the local paper was always a good idea for any cop, and Rallin had one of the best.

The call had confirmed their suspicions. "Sure, come on down and take a look, we've got them, but they'll never make the paper. We just never got a real good shot of the guy. He seemed always able to be at an angle or looking down so none of the pictures are of the quality we wanted to print, but they're good enough to get a good look at the guy," Pete offered.

"Pete always comes through for us," Rallin muttered, hanging up the phone. Rallin and Pansloski headed for the car, eager to see what a strong man looked like.

"We didn't have any luck with the dead bum case, maybe this strong guy could be interesting," Rallin said as they arrived at the newspaper. Both Rallin and Pansloski knew they were there only to satisfy their curiosity. It wasn't a case at all. This one would never be a case.

Pansloski had never heard anything from the locals about anyone showing up at a hospital with a knife wound, and both Rallin and Pansloski had buried the dead bum case. There had been one guy at Central, but he had been stuck on the other side of town. He had the wrong blood type too.

Pete was easy to find and he took them back to his little cubbyhole that served as his office. Rallin had been there a number of times over the years, and it always looked the same. Books were piled up high enough to kill small animals or children, if or when they fell. At the same time, they were always clean and in a neat row.

"You're right, never a good angle, Pete. Who was the cameraman?" asked Pansloski as he peered down at the pictures.

"It was one of our best guys, but it didn't matter. Almost like the guy didn't want the publicity."

The pictures were good, or at least they were very clear and bright, but the guy never gave them what they wanted. They could see him well enough to be able to spot the guy on the street if they saw him again. Sure didn't look like a big enough guy to have picked up that car, and Rallin said as much.

Pansloski answered, "He looks trim and fit and fairly big. Probably works out, but I was kind of expecting a real big guy like a biker or a linebacker."

Rallin looked closely at the picture. There was something about the man that looked familiar, but he couldn't put his finger on it. "Does he look familiar to you?" Rallin asked Pansloski. The more he looked at the picture, the more Rallin thought he had seen this guy before.

"No, can't say that he does, Mike. Might not hurt to run his picture against the mug file and see what comes out or fits the description. Although I'm not sure what you might be looking for. Looks like a nice kid who happened to be in the right spot at the right time and able to do what needed to be done."

There was nothing left to do at that point. They thanked Pete for being helpful. Both Rallin and Pansloski knew the worth of having a good relationship with the press.

Back at the office they both had some paperwork to do on other files they were chasing. Nothing interesting and nothing that would close a case or catch a bad guy, but files needed updating. The strong guy story still had Rallin bugged.

That night after supper, Rallin sat with a cup of coffee talking to Arlene. "The guy was big, but not that big." Rallin said.

"Well they say that people can pump a lot of adrenaline in times of emergency and do things they wouldn't normally be able to do," said Arlene.

"Yeah I know, but there was something else. He seemed to look like someone I've met before or something."

"What was he like?"

"Well he was pretty tall. Probably just over six feet and over two hundred pounds. Dark hair. I'd say right around thirty more or less. Good looking young guy."

"I've heard you use a description like that a number of times over the years." Arlene chuckled. "He probably fits the description of lots of guys you have either arrested or talked to in the years we've been here."

"That's it Arlene. Fits the description. Pansloski said those words too. They always talk about someone fitting the description when they draw a composite picture of someone. I think this guy looks a little bit like one of the composites I've seen this year."

Rallin kept copies of many of his files at his house. After a quick search he came up with a few composite sketches. He looked at a couple of them until he came to one that made him stop.

"Look at this one, Arlene. I think that big guy might look a little like the composite they drew of the guy who visited the cancer clinic last summer. This guy could be him."

"I don't know, Mike. There might be a little resemblance, but not much."

"Still worth checking," said Rallin. "He does fit the description the locals got."

When Rallin got back to the office early the next morning, the first thing he did was show the composite to Pansloski.

"What do you think, Bill? Could the big guy be the same guy as this composite from the cancer clinic?"

Neither Rallin nor Pansloski had kept a copy of the picture that Pete had shown them the day before, but he thought Pansloski could remember what he looked like.

"Not much chance of that, Mike, but it's still an open file and it's on your desk, so you might as well follow it up. He might look a little like the strong guy, but then again so could hundreds of people."

"Yeah, you're probably right. Arlene tends to agree too, but I think I'll take the time to talk to this guy."

"Go for it. The case is still open," Pansloski said again as he went back to his own desk and his own apparently endless supply of paperwork.

Rallin took another look at the composite picture. The guy in Pete's photo may be a little close, but it definitely wasn't anywhere near a match. Height, weight, and build were close, but he never knew about composite sketches. Would be a hell of a fluke if it was, but he had a few minutes to kill early in the day, and the address Pete had given him was close by. What the hell, why not?

The drive took Rallin to a three-story walk up that dominated that part of the inner core. Not quite downtown, but definitely inner city. The buzzer down in the lobby was a two-way speaker and Rallin was pretty sure he was on camera somewhere. Rallin had been told that the guy's name was Jim Tannion and that he worked as a sales accountant with Clarke and Moore downtown. It was still early and Rallin thought that Tannion might still be at home.

The buzzer rang upstairs and after a couple of seconds Rallin heard a click. "Yes," came the vaguely disjointed voice that those machines always seem to make.

Rallin answered immediately, "FBI, Mr. Tannion, I would like to have a few minutes of your time."

There were a few strained seconds of silence, and finally the disembodied voice came over the little box. "What for?"

"I just want to talk to you about the kid you picked the car off of last week." Rallin had come with a game plan to discuss the accident as a cover, when all he really wanted to do was ask him about the cancer clinic. The accident would probably get him in the door, but the clinic was his real question.

"Okay, come on up," Tannion finally said.

The apartment was one of the newer three-story walk ups built on the fringe of the downtown core. Of course this meant no elevator, but the stairs were well marked. It only took a minute to climb the four sets of stairs to the third floor.

A knock on the door brought instant results, as Tannion was obviously waiting for him. Rallin had his FBI credentials out before he got to the door. Tannion took a quick look and backed away, inviting Rallin in. His apartment struck Rallin as being clean and neat, but there was an obvious male presence without a hint of fluff that might indicate a female.

Tannion led Rallin into the living room. Rallin noted a nice sectional in gray leather and Tannion invited Rallin to sit down. A large TV set was in the corner and Rallin guessed that it must be at least fifty-five inches. Another no female mark.

"So what can I do for you, Mister Rallin?"

Tannion was obviously alert, as he had read Rallin's name off his ID in the couple seconds that Rallin had given him to look at his credentials. The interview notes from the paper indicated that he was college-educated and in his late twenties.

"That's Agent Rallin, Mr. Tannion. I saw the picture of you after you picked that car off that kid the other day, and I thought I may have recognized you. I have a few questions. How long have you lived at this current location?"

"I have been here for over a year, but what does this have to do with the accident?"

Rallin knew that if he continued asking questions, Tannion might get very defensive even if he was not guilty of anything. He cut to the chase. Rallin had had a few of these types of conversations in his years with the force. He found if you came right out and asked the tough questions without beating around the bush, the answers may surprise even the guy giving them.

"It's got nothing to do with the accident, but I would like to know where you were on July seventeenth of this year?" With any luck, even if the answer was not what he was looking for, Rallin thought that Tannion's reaction or his body language would tell him something.

Tannion took a breath and let it out slowly, pointedly thinking. Not much help for Rallin. No obvious reaction and the body language didn't help. It only looked as if he was trying to remember a day a while back.

"What day of the week was that?" Tannion asked.

"A Sunday."

"Well, on Sunday I usually sleep in and then watch some sports on TV. Maybe I'll go for a walk around the park or for a work out, but I have no idea what I might have been doing on that particular Sunday. That was a few months ago. They all run together after a while. Why do you ask?"

"Just a case I'm working on. You fit the description of an individual we want to talk to. You're sure you were in town that day? Did anyone see you, or did you do anything that would have left a record of you being in town that day?" Rallin asked knowing that this was his last chance. If the answer was non-committal, and if Rallin didn't have any evidence putting Tannion at the cancer clinic or even out of the city that day, he was screwed.

"No, I don't remember anything that I did on that particular day, sorry."

"Okay, thanks for your time. I'll find my own way out."

Tannion showed the FBI agent to the door anyway. Later in the car Rallin tried to go over everything that was said from the time Tannion answered the buzzer. Nothing stuck out. All he had now was a composite picture that didn't look much like Tannion. He could get a copy of the one from the newspaper, but it didn't show the best likeness of Tannion. The best he could do was show it to the cured cancer patients and see what happened.

Rallin stopped at the newspaper office and picked up the best picture of Tannion they had. First thing to do was to look up those cured cancer cases, then show them the picture of the strong guy and see if they recognized him. It was a long shot, but worth a try. Things were still slow at the office. At least, for the moment.

Rallin looked through the file. There wasn't much in it, as neither he nor Pansloski had spent a lot of time on the case. "Maybe I should have gone a little further when I first opened the file," thought Rallin.

The drive was uneventful and Rallin pulled into town just before eleven. He had the addresses for both Margaret Adams and the Jansen's place, but decided to go to the cancer clinic first. When Rallin called he was told that the nurse who was on duty that Sunday morning in July would be on duty at noon.

The cancer clinic reminded Rallin of the clinic where his aunt was. She was not doing very well, and he suspected that was why this case interested him so much.

His aunt was in her early sixties and didn't deserve to be in a cancer clinic living out the last few weeks of her life. She was young and had been a very active person. His aunt and uncle used to do a lot of traveling together. Up until she was diagnosed with lung cancer, she had loved life. If there was a cure around for cancer, he sure would love to have it happen to his aunt.

Rallin had something to eat just down the street from the clinic and then found himself at the front desk at noon. He walked up to the desk and saw the nurse on duty. She looked Rallin up and down, as if measuring him for a suit, and then asked what she could do for him. Rallin had the impression that she knew he was a cop, based on the way she looked at him. He showed her his credentials.

"I'd like to ask you a few questions about the afternoon of July seventeenth. The police report indicates that a man entered the clinic and talked to a couple of your patients. They were Sarah Jansen and Margaret Adams. Both of them appeared to be near death and then they were suddenly cured. Please tell me what you remember."

"That was a few months ago and as I remember telling the police at the time, I never did get a good look at the guy. We don't expect to get people in here that aren't friends or relatives, so the visiting policy is very relaxed. I remember a man wanting to see Mrs. Adams and I told him what room she was in. I was busy and don't remember looking up at him."

"Did you help build this composite picture?" Rallin asked as he showed her the composite made at the time.

"Yes. I saw him from the back and helped a little with the shape of his head, but I never saw his face."

Rallin pulled out the picture of Tannion he had picked up at the newspaper. "Have you ever seen this man?"

She looked intently at the picture, but shook her head. "I don't think so. This could be the guy, but so could almost anyone. I'm sorry. I'm not much help."

"Do you know if there was anyone else on duty that day who might have seen the guy?" Rallin asked. The original police report hadn't helped. No one interviewed could remember seeing anyone out of place that day. He knew he was grasping at straws.

"Sure, Doctor Valdez was here, but I'm sure he already told the police that he didn't see anyone visiting any of his patients that day. Visiting hours for most people start at one and Doctor Valdez is often here in the morning and through part of the visiting period. He's with one of his patients right now."

Rallin asked her to page Dr. Valdez and took a seat in the small waiting room. Dr. Valdez took about ten minutes to come down the hall and Rallin rose to greet him. He was a man in his late forties with a Latino look that fit the name.

Rallin introduced himself and showed him his credentials. Without wasting any time on pleasantries, Rallin started with his questions. "Were you at the clinic on the afternoon of Sunday July seventeenth?"

"I'm usually in for a least a few minutes almost every Sunday. The police already asked me if I had seen anyone that day, and I don't remember seeing anyone at the clinic except my patients and a few of their family members visiting. No one out of the ordinary."

Rallin took the picture of Tannion out of the envelope. "Have you ever seen this man?"

Valdez took a careful look. "This guy does look familiar. As I told the police before, I don't remember seeing anyone unusual on that day during visiting hours, but I am pretty sure that I have seen this man somewhere before," Valdez said.

"Where do you think you might have seen him?" Rallin asked.

"It might have been here, but it could have been anywhere. He certainly looks familiar, but I can't tell you where from."

"Have you been out of town recently?"

"No, not for a while," replied Valdez. "I haven't been out of town this year, and except for a two-week vacation in Jamaica, I haven't been out of town for a couple of years. I'm much too busy here at the clinic and at my practice to do a lot of traveling. If I saw him, it would have been in town."

"Then you would have seen him recently?"

"I think so. It would have been here and probably in the last year or so. The face is familiar, but not from my past."

Rallin thanked the doctor and gave him his card, asking him to call him if he happened to remember where he had seen Tannion before. Already Tannion was starting to look good to him. If the doctor had seen him, it meant that Tannion had been in Topeka recently. That was something at least. It was time to talk to the healthy patients. With a little more luck, who knows?

The first stop was to talk to Sarah Jansen. Her parents met Rallin at the door, and although they were a little reluctant, they let him show her the picture.

"Have you ever seen this man before?" Rallin asked kindly.

She took a good look. "Mmmm... I don't think so."

"You don't think that you saw this man, perhaps at the clinic?"

The girl shook her head in confusion. "I don't really remember much from there. I didn't feel good when I was awake. I was so sleepy." She shrugged helplessly and then smiled sweetly.

Sarah was full of smiles and energy. She was very polite, but by the way she was bouncing in her chair, Rallin could see that she was eager to get up and run. Probably something that she hadn't been able to get enough of since getting well. Her little miracle had not been wasted on someone who didn't care.

The little of Sarah's personality that Rallin saw in the few minutes he had with her made him think that she could be much older than he knew her to be. Lying in a bed in a hospital where everyone was dying would mature anyone, and Sarah was no exception. There was no doubt in Rallin's mind that the kid shouldn't have been in that kind of place, but as she had, it had made an impression on her.

After the interview, Rallin thanked Sarah and her parents and walked back to the car. The next stop was at the home of Margaret and Philip Adams. Margaret Adams met him at the door and he immediately had the same feeling he had when he left the Jansen's. Here was a woman full of life, not wasting a minute of it.

"Come right in, Agent Rallin. Please sit down," she said as she backed into a nice living room. Rallin sat down on an oversized couch of soft brown leather. Mrs. Adams and her husband lived in a small, but very neat, house near the out-skirts of town. The walls were covered with small shelves and each of these was in turn covered with little pottery pieces and knick-knacks.

"Thank you, Mrs. Adams," Rallin said, but was very quickly interrupted.

"Please, call me Margaret."

"Okay, Margaret. Thank you. You're looking very well."

"Thank you, I'm feeling great. I still have difficulty believing what has happened."

"I take it that you are in good health?"

"Oh, yes!" she gushed. "The doctors tell me there isn't a trace of cancer anywhere in my system. I haven't just gone into remission, but have been granted a complete recovery. I can only thank God for this gift of life that he has granted."

Rallin knew if Margaret Adams wasn't religious before she came down with cancer, a miracle cure would probably swing her in that direction. His own religion wouldn't suffer from a miracle now and then either.

Rallin pulled out the picture of Tannion and showed it to her, asking whether she had ever seen him before.

"I don't think so," was her cautious answer. "He looks a bit familiar. Why do you think I may know this man?"

"I'm wondering if this might be the man who visited you at the clinic a day or so before you started your recovery."

"Oh, I see. I do remember a man coming into my room and talking to me. He was such a nice young man, but I can't get a mental picture of him. This picture could be him, but it could have been almost anyone. What I do remember was that he seemed to be a little thin and should be eating better."

Tannion was anything but thin. If that was her recollection, Rallin thought he might be off base with Tannion. Rallin thanked Mrs. Adams and showed himself to the door. The drive home gave him a few hours to think. He didn't have much to add to the case file except that Dr. Valdez thought Tannion looked familiar. If he knew Tannion, it would not be from anywhere outside of Topeka. That could prove important down the road.

Even with the added data, if Tannion was the man at the clinic it would probably be impossible to prove unless he confessed. And then what would he be confessing to? Visiting sick people is not a crime, but something in the back of Rallin's mind said there was more to this than meets the eye.

Unfortunately, right now it looked like a dead end. The file would be put back in storage and probably it would only gather dust. There were always other files to work on.

12

Tannion was still shaking hours after the FBI agent had left. He had almost shit when the buzzer went off and a voice said it was the FBI. FBI, for Christ sake! His first thought was the dead bum. Then it was the cancer clinic. What else would bring the feds to his house? And then the questions the agent asked!

Tannion thought he had acted normal. He knew now that it had been a good idea not to leave a paper trail when he went to the cancer clinic. The big question was whether they had a positive ID or was the agent just grasping at straws.

"I don't think the composite looked enough like me to even get this close. Must have been only that I fit the general description," was Tannion's hope. "I didn't do anything wrong! Why would they care if they did catch me? Lifting that car might have been a big mistake if the FBI got involved as a result," he muttered to himself.

Tannion had taken some time after the agent had left to get his thinking in order, let alone get his heart rate down. What if they did ID him and come back? Should he do something like move to another state or what? Finally Tannion decided that if they had anything more concrete, they would already have dragged him downtown or whatever they did.

Tannion thought he was probably safe as long as he stayed out of the spotlight for a while. He certainly had no plans to go public, or to push himself out into the limelight. But he hadn't planned on lifting a car off a kid either. If he was going to do anything with his talent, it needed to be as silent and obscure as he could make it, and he could not do anything for awhile, lest he catch their attention again.

The days before Christmas went by quickly and uneventfully. Tannion did manage to get his shopping done and then spent Christmas day with his mom. He hung around close to home or his mom's house for a few weeks after Christmas and was very cautious in using his gift. Nothing was going to look suspicious if he could help it.

As Tannion was walking back to his apartment late at night, he passed an obviously drunk man on the sidewalk and was surprised that he didn't get asked for money. "Must be so drunk that he doesn't even see me," he thought.

A few steps later and he looked back to see what this guy was doing. Muttering to himself, the man's volume increased drastically. Not quite shouting, but close. The bum reached into the pocket of his heavy coat and brought out a whiskey bottle with only a couple swallows left in it, quickly knocking it back.

"Well that will really shut him up," Tannion thought, but he wasn't prepared for what happened next. With a very awkward, but surprisingly hard throw, the drunk launched the bottle in the direction of the building next to him where it easily went through the large plate glass window of a department store.

Tannion moved without even knowing he had. The next thing he knew he had grabbed the drunk by the collar and sat him down next to the curb. "Just sit there and you won't get hurt. We're going to wait for the cops." Tannion wasn't sure he was ready to be seen by the police, but felt he had no choice.

With the alarms that were going off, Tannion knew it wouldn't be long. There must have been a car in the area, as it only took what seemed like a few seconds before a cop car pulled up alongside where they sat. Two cops got out and started to pull their guns. When they realized that Tannion was holding onto the drunk, they holstered their guns and went over to get his story.

Tannion filled out the police report in the precinct house. The drunk, Peter French, was taken to the drunk tank. Tannion was informed that there would be an arraignment the next day and he was asked to testify.

"Christ, that's quick," Tannion muttered, but thought that would be good.

The next day at about two in the afternoon a much more sober French stood in front of a judge and pleaded guilty to mischief. Tannion was asked to testify so that the judge could get a feel for appropriate sentencing. All the time Tannion was talking, French glared at him, and as Tannion sat down he mouthed the words, "You're dead." Or at least that was what it looked like. After Tannion's testimony, the judge sentenced French to a week in jail. He was also required to pay for the window and attend a treatment program for his drinking problem.

Tannion didn't think much of it, but a little more than a week later he was approached as he was walking home after a night out with the boys. There were four men sitting on the steps of one of the buildings he passed. They began to follow him. Tannion was immediately aware of them, but not too worried. Finally when they got to the spot they had obviously chosen, they made their move.

Two of the men ran into the street around a parked car and were in front of Tannion. Two men remained behind. Tannion took a quick look and knew they were trying to push him into an unlit alley. "If that's the game they want to play, it meets my needs," Tannion thought and took a few backward steps into the mouth of the alley.

The four men thought that they had him now. For the first time, one of them spoke directly to Tannion. "You thought you'd get away with putting me in jail, didn't you, asshole? Me and the boys are going to fuck you up good and you'll think twice about sticking your nose where it don't belong. That is, if we let you live."

Tannion hadn't recognized the guy until he spoke, and then he knew why this was going down. The drunk was back and obviously trying to make good on the words he had mouthed in court. He had received only one week in jail and had probably got out a day or two early. Obviously French held a grudge and, unbelievably, he had friends. His friends didn't look too warlike. But four to one odds probably left them feeling invincible.

As they walked forward, Tannion took a couple more steps into the alley where the light was even poorer. He was sure that with the light coming in from the street behind the four guys, he was probably at a slight advantage. Then he saw French take a baseball bat out from under his coat. One of the other guys did the same.

"You don't want to do this," Tannion said as he took another step back into the alley.

"Like shit we don't. Okay guys let him have it," French said to his three buddies, who quickly closed in trying to form a circle around Tannion. The first one to move in was the other guy with the baseball bat. As he swung, he made the mistake of swinging for Tannion's head. Tannion ducked under the bat and planted his right fist in the guy's gut. He then grabbed him with his left hand, and with a quick twist took the bat out of his hands.

Tannion brought the bat up just in time to block the swing that French had aimed at his head, and the bats made a loud crack as they hit. The bat in French's hand flew into the air. Tannion's bat kept its momentum and French's head took the worst of it. French's last two friends came in swinging. Tannion ducked and moved to his left. With a quick right the first went down and the second soon followed. Tannion stood over the first guy who was still lying doubled up on the ground. He reached down and touched him on the back of the neck. There was a small sound and then silence.

Tannion left all four of them lying right where they landed. The only thing that he took was the bat. He looked to make sure there were no witnesses. As they had been pushed back into the dark alley, there was no one around. Tannion knew his fingerprints would be on the bat in his hand, but nowhere else. The bat would make a nice souvenir. No witnesses should mean no problems.

13

The fight in the alley started Tannion thinking. Much of this thinking was around the comic book heroes he had read about when he was a kid. Tannion had the skills, or at least serious potential, for fighting crime. The comic book hero life of a crime fighter had a certain appeal. Perhaps it was a bit childish, but the problem that slowed Tannion down was not the immaturity. He had no idea how to go about it. He didn't want to be in the public eye, which in the comic book world meant a disguise. Yet a disguise always seemed to do exactly the opposite and create someone the media would either love or love to exploit. That would probably put him right in the public eye, which is what he wanted to avoid.

Thinking, dreaming, and contemplating it were getting him nowhere. He finally decided to just take the plunge and go out and try to be a crime-fighting hero. He picked a street that was constantly in the papers for arrests relating to drugs. He put on an old coat, jeans, and a baseball cap, thinking it would be enough of a disguise for dark streets without being a bizarre costume that would draw unwanted attention. If things got rough enough, Tannion knew he didn't have to leave any witnesses.

Tannion left the house at eight thirty on Friday night. He walked several blocks in the wrong direction and bought a bus ticket. Getting on the bus, he made sure that the bus driver didn't get a good look at him. The bus had a few people on it and Tannion kept his head down, not looking anyone in the eye. He wasn't worried about anyone remembering him or recognizing him, but when the feds come to his door, as they already had, he couldn't help feeling a little paranoid.

Tannion got off the bus a couple of blocks from his determined stop. He didn't want to be associated with a closer stop, just in case. As he walked a few blocks from the bus stop in the general direction of city hall, the scenery started to change. It was getting darker, which added a sur-real look to all the shadows. The houses changed from nicely kept three story walk-ups, to more run-down brick apartment buildings, and finally to old office buildings that looked to be condemned, but still had lights on in some of the windows.

The street Tannion was looking for was only a couple of blocks away, and already he was being approached to buy drugs. This is what he was hoping for and had been expecting. He had his game face on and a game plan in mind.

The plan was to let the dealers come up to him. It always happened in the movies. At first he would pretend that he was interested. When he saw the stuff, he would proceed to destroy it. Either by letting the powder go into the wind, or throwing it on the ground and stepping on it, depending on what they were trying to sell him. Tannion was expecting everything from pills, crack cocaine, marijuana to heroin, but with his middle-class All-American upbringing, he wasn't sure what anything would look like. If he had to rely on what he had seen on TV, it could be interesting.

When he finally got to the place he had more or less picked out, there was a guy there. The guy approached Tannion and was immediately his best friend.

"Hey buddy, how you doing'?" he asked.

This guy was black, early twenties, and was dressed in the baggy jeans and shirts the crowd that age wears. He was not a bad looking guy and didn't appear to have the glaze Tannion was expecting from a heavy user. Tannion made the assumption that he was a seller, but not a steady user. This could make a difference in the future if he needed to take a look inside.

"Good. What you got?"

"You name it and I've got it," the man offered.

"Show me the stuff so I can make up my mind."

"No way man. Don't work that way. Show me your cash, name your poison and I'll hand it over," he said.

Tannion hadn't brought any money, or for that matter any ID, so that wasn't going to happen. He had left his keys to his apartment in a safe hiding place so his pockets were empty. If needed, he could strip to his underwear and go home and still be okay. Tannion was prepared for almost anything, but it didn't look like this was going to happen the way he thought it was.

"Forget it, man," Tannion said and went looking for the next guy.

"Fuck you," the guy muttered and walked away in the opposite direction.

Tannion had gone a little less than a block when a couple of guys stepped out of an alley and made their way towards him. They were both black and looked a little older and a lot scruffier than the last guy he had talked to. The first was probably a little taller than Tannion and skinny with a shaved head sticking out from under a baseball cap. The second guy was a little shorter and stockier, and obviously the leader.

They came right up to Tannion, who stopped to wait for them. Tannion thought if this was going to be some kind of a shakedown, it would be better to take it into the alley on his right. Tannion moved a little into the alley, away from the light. The road had streetlights on every block, but two of them weren't working. The spot they selected was one of the darker areas. The move towards the alley must have looked like Tannion was trying to evade them, and they made a bolder move in his direction.

"Hey, you," the shorter punk said. "We saw you talking to Jaymar. What did he sell you?"

"Nothing, man." Tannion didn't get the drug dealer's name, but figured it must be Jaymar. The two of them obviously knew Jaymar and knew him for what he did best.

Tannion could see where this was going. As he hadn't bought anything off Jaymar, he had nothing to show them, but Tannion knew that wouldn't be good enough. They would want to see something, but there was nothing he could show them.

"Bullshit. That's not how it works here. Just give us what you bought and you won't be hurt," the larger of the two men said.

A little tingle went up Tannion's spine. Either it was a touch of fear, or this was what he had been waiting for. He knew they didn't have a chance, but he wasn't sure exactly how to do it. If he used muscle and beat them senseless, leaving them out in the cold, then it would look like murder. If he made it look natural, he would have to hang on to each of them and then drag them farther into the back alley. All possibilities had their inherent risks, but Tannion had decided that whenever possible he would use natural causes, or what would look like natural causes.

Tannion took a couple more steps towards the alley. They both took it as if he was going to run.

"Don't let him get past you," the shorter fellow told his friend, and he yelled at Tannion to stop.

The tall guy had pulled a knife and had taken a few running steps in order to cut Tannion off. He stopped short before colliding, but Tannion was close enough to grab him by the wrist before he could move. Tannion squeezed hard and the knife fell from his hand. The guy fell almost at the same time. Tannion had taken a look and found a heart weakened slightly from drug use and simply stopped it.

The dead guy's friend was on Tannion almost as the first guy hit the ground. His friend was dead without making a sound. As the shorter guy went for Tannion, he had an eye on the ground to look at his friend. That was the end of his time on earth. Tannion caught the short guy's right wrist, which contained a deadly-looking switchblade, and wrapped his right hand around the man's throat.

Killing them the same way might look strange, but having two dead friends in an alley was going to look strange enough that it really wouldn't matter how they died. The short guy went as quickly as the first. Tannion grabbed him by the scruff of the neck so he wouldn't hit the ground.

Reaching down, he grabbed the tall guy by the shirt collar with his other hand, quickly dragged them both into the alley, and dumped them into a nearby dumpster. He then used a tissue to pick up the knives. Wiping them down, he tossed them into the dumpster as well.

Tannion hesitated a moment, then slammed the lid closed. If he was lucky, the bodies would not be found before they made it to the landfill. Part of him felt bad about the possibility that these men might have family and mothers who may never know what happened to them. He forced the thoughts aside. They would probably be found eventually. This was simply to give him time to get away.

As he strolled casually out of the alley, Tannion was feeling pretty heady. He had rid the streets of a couple of small-time thugs. Debating going farther, he thought better of it and decided that it would be best to go home and lay low for a few days. Go to work, keep his regular routine, and see if anything showed up in the papers. He needed to keep a low profile. It had been a good night's work, but the season on these guys had just opened.

14

"Hey, Pansloski, who've you got under the sheet?" Rallin queried, strolling into the morgue.

Pansloski had called Rallin at home before he left for the office and told him that he should come down to the morgue. He didn't tell Rallin why, but he didn't act like it was a big secret or anything. Just a quick "come and see this!" and then the line went dead.

The morgue was never Rallin's favorite place to visit. Suspecting Pansloski knew it, he wondered if, on occasion, Pansloski would set up a meet at the morgue when somewhere else would have worked just as well. Rallin wondered whether this was one of those times.

"Yeah, Mike, come take a look. Recognize this guy?" Pansloski asked as he pulled the sheet off the guy's face.

"Sure, that's Jerome Alexander. We've had a warrant on him for more than a year," Rallin answered. "Where did you find him?"

"The local guys picked him and a buddy out of a dumpster a couple of days ago. When they finally figured out that he had a federal warrant, they gave us a call. The desk took the call and I found it when I got in early this morning. The coroner passed me the autopsy reports and things..." Pansloski scratched his head, "just don't add up."

"What do you mean?"

"Well, the locals found both him and his friend in a dumpster down in an alley off thirty-third. Looks like a dump and run, but when the doc tears them apart, he finds some smack and other barbiturates in their systems. That's not what killed them though. What killed them was a massive coronary. Jerome has an aortic something or other and the other had something very similar where an artery burst."

"You mean they both had heart attacks at the same time and both died in a dumpster?" Rallin asked incredulously.

Pansloski gave a knowing look. "Doc says he has never seen it happen quite like this in anyone, let alone two guys found together in the same dumpster. He thinks maybe the drugs had something to do with it and has written it up as drug-induced natural causes or something like that. It just doesn't ring clear," Pansloski said. "You know, this kind of reminds me of the bum a while back. The one who died of what the doctors said were natural causes after knifing someone."

"Did one of these guys knife someone too?"

"No, but each of them was known to carry a knife. A couple of blades were found in the dumpster beside the bodies."

"You mean the knives were not in their pockets."

"It says here that two knives were found in the dumpster. They had the dead guy's prints all over them. Definitely not in their pockets. And there's more," Pansloski gestured for Rallin to take another look at the corpse under the sheet as he kept talking. "The report notes that Alexander had slight bruising around his right wrist. His friend, by the way his name was Winston Sweet, has a similar bruise on his wrist and some bruising around his neck."

Rallin lifted the sheet off Alexander and took a closer look. He always found it very disturbing when he saw what the coroner did with an autopsy. To him it was pretty much tearing the guy apart and then it looked like he forgot how to put him back together again based on the rough stitch job on the guy's chest. Rallin had seen several over the years and it always got to him a little.

After looking at the bruising on the wrist and noting nothing on his other arm, Rallin asked the attendant to show them Sweet. Sweet was a couple of drawers down and looked a lot like Alexander from the coroner's point of view. The bruises were similar on his wrist, with some additional marks on his neck.

Rallin scratched his chin. "If these were from fighting, where are the other marks?" There were no marks on the knuckles or anywhere else. "If this was a fight, it sure was over quick. These guys didn't even get one punch in."

"It's possible that the marks were made when the bodies were dumped in the dumpster," Pansloski said. "It should say something about it in the report." He skimmed quickly through it. "The report says the locals checked for prints, but there was nothing on the dead guys that they could make out."

A further look at the coroner's report indicated that the bruising was done when the heart was still pumping blood. "It had to be before they were dead, but it was possible they were alive when they were dumped and then bled out internally in the dumpster," Pansloski theorized.

"Well it looks like someone, or something, did us a favor," Rallin muttered, not sounding particularly grateful.

Pansloski replied, "With the coroner's report saying natural causes, it doesn't look like a case here... but it just doesn't make sense. I think we need to keep our eyes open and ask a few questions. The DEA is still looking around too, in case it was bad drugs."

"Did the locals do a good job of looking for any witnesses who might have seen who dumped these guys in the dumpster?"

"I think so. I haven't read the full report. As it wasn't a federal issue until they found out that Alexander had a federal warrant, they dealt with it on their own terms."

"Okay. Let's let them deal with it and all we need to do is to take a warrant off the books and close a file," Rallin said, choosing the easy way.

"You never did catch a break on that dead bum case, did you?" asked Pansloski, although he already knew the answer. No one ever did show up in any hospital with a knife wound that would match what they were expecting. The case didn't have anywhere to go.

"Nope. I shook down the usual group, but I got what I was expecting from that bunch. A lot of nothing."

"That's what I thought," Pansloski said.

"The only thing that this case has in common with the bum is that somehow things just don't add up." Rallin insisted. "First a bum dies of natural causes. All he has on him is a knife that apparently belongs to him, with blood on it that's not his. Who did he stick and why couldn't we find the guy?"

Pansloski went on to finish what Rallin was thinking. "Yeah, and then these two dead guys show up in a dumpster, having died of a similar natural cause. They both have minor bruises, but nothing indicative of a real fight... and they had knives with them."

"And, who dumped them into the dumpster?" Rallin hated asking the question.

"Right. That's the part that has me confused. If they had gotten hold of some bad stuff and died as a result, you could see that. The bruises could have occurred before they died either by fighting with each other, or maybe with whoever sold them the drugs, but how did they get into the dumpster?" Pansloski was getting Rallin into this case, and he could sense it.

"And why were their knives not in their pockets? They didn't have any prints on them but the dead guys. So they either brought them into the dumpster themselves, or the killer was careful," Rallin said.

Police work may be paperwork and chasing clues, but sometimes the best way to an answer is to talk about it and ponder the possibilities. "What if they got into a fight with the drug dealer and they got the bruises from him. Then they died after downing the drugs, and it was the dealer who threw them in the dumpster?" Rallin asked.

"Nah, I don't think so. The stuff would never react that fast. And if they got into a fight, they should have other marks on them. The marks make it look like someone very strong grabbed hold of his wrist and made him drop the knife."

"But there were two of them," Rallin said. "How could one guy grab one of them and not have the other guy all over him?"

"Maybe they were two different cases. Some guy dumped them in the same dumpster after two different attacks," Pansloski proposed.

"No, I don't think so. The report says that these two were known to hang together all the time. I doubt they were killed in two different locations and then dumped together. More likely they were killed at the same time which may mean that there was more than one killer." Rallin mulled it over for a bit then shook his head. "How did they make it look like natural causes?"

"Christ if I know," Pansloski said.

15

Tannion couldn't wait to go on the hunt again. Nothing came out of the first hunt but a couple of dead guys and almost no notice. The papers said a couple of small-time hoods, one of them having a federal arrest warrant on him, were found dead in the downtown area. The article indicated drug-related and possible gang-related activities, but there was absolutely nothing on what really killed those guys. There was no follow up. It looked like no one really cared.

People were probably glad to be rid of some low-life scum and didn't get upset about how they died. Still, caution must rule. Tannion knew that the next one would have to be different natural causes, or maybe even look like an accident. Too many unwanted people go dropping dead of heart attacks, and even the police couldn't keep ignoring it. This time he was going to have to plan better.

Tannion's biggest defense would have to be a disguise. He needed to buy a few things, but he decided it was time for a road trip. Making sure not to leave a paper trail, he got in the car and drove to the next town. He bought a baseball cap and sunglasses. The big finds were a blond wig and some cheap mustache stuff that he found at a novelty store.

If he was trying to fool someone who knew him, he wouldn't stand a chance, but as long as he could get away without being recognized in a dark alley, he had what he wanted. Tannion made sure to buy the stuff in a couple of different places and, of course, he paid in cash.

Tannion headed out on Monday night, wanting to break the weekend routine. He drove to a spot that was a nice long walk back to the general area of his last encounter. His choice was still going to be the local drug punks. Tannion thought it would be better to hit the chain higher up, but he had no idea where that would be. Maybe in time he would learn more and move higher up the ranks of bad guys, but today his mark was the first guy who came along and offered him something.

Tannion had his disguise on. It didn't take long for some-one to approach him, just like the first time. A guy approached Tannion from a doorway. "Looking for a good time?"

"Let me see the stuff," Tannion muttered, checking his mustache carefully.

If it went the same way as the first time, and this guy wouldn't show Tannion the stuff, he had decided to take it from the guy and provoke what would come.

"Sure, take a look," the man offered as he opened a bag he pulled from a pocket. He had a light jacket on with big pockets in front. They appeared to be filled with lots of small baggies of whatever he was trying to sell. Tannion found it hard to believe that the cops would have trouble finding these guys, but figured there was probably a lot he didn't know.

The baggie the man showed to Tannion was full of pills. There were a few different colors, but they were all mixed together as if it didn't matter. Tannion took a quick step for-ward and pulled the bag from his hand.

"Hey," the man hollered. "Don't fuck with me! Give those back." He was moving forward at the same time and grabbing for the bag. Tannion knew this guy looked a little on the small side, but in his business he would know how to handle himself. Tannion wasn't that surprised when he started to pull a gun out of the other pocket.

Tannion didn't let it get out of hand. Quickly stepping forward, he hit the man as hard as he could on the chin, launching him up and back several feet. The movement was quick. The man hadn't been able to get the gun completely out of his pocket. When the man hit the ground, the gun fell out of his pocket and skittered across the ground.

Tannion ran over to him, but the guy was already gone. At first Tannion wasn't sure if he was just out cold, so he bent down and took the man's pulse. There wasn't any. He checked the man's breathing and found that missing as well. Tannion knew he was dead.

One punch and that was all it took. Tannion emptied the guy's pockets of all the junk he carried and ground it into the dirt. He wanted to send a message. The message being that a drug dealer just died. Whoever killed him didn't want the shit he was dealing.

Tannion took one last look around, put the guy's gun into his own pocket, and walked away. He took a round-about route back to his car. Taking off the wig on one street, he stuck it into his pocket. He tore the fake moustache off on the next street. By the time he got back to his car he looked considerably different. His jacket was reversible with a different color on each side. If anyone saw him hit the guy and walk out of the alley, they would be describing a very different person.

Tannion drove the car home and went upstairs to store all the paraphernalia away, including the gun. He knew keeping the gun was a risk, but the wig and makeup stuff was enough to make people suspicious if they were ever found.

Tannion spent the night going over what happened, so he didn't get any sleep. "So much for planning to have it look like an accident," he thought. "No, let's hit the guy so hard he's dead before he hits the ground."

Tannion could only wonder what the paper would say on this one. He also worried about what the cops would think. He had hit the man so hard that they would probably think the guy had been hit with an iron bar. He would be okay with them thinking that. Definitely it wasn't natural causes this time.

16

The next couple of days went by without incident. The paper mentioned a murder in the core, but didn't release any names or pictures. It said one man was dead and that it could be another drug or gang-related incident, but it didn't release a cause of death.

Murders weren't very common in town, so the fact it was a murder and not natural causes resulted in this one getting a little more press. The idea that the town even had drugs or gangs was something that most of the population didn't want to admit. As a result, the papers and the cops usually didn't make a big deal out of it.

Tannion had no idea where this could go, but the feeling of power when another crook was off the street was very enticing. He knew it had only just started. During the next few weeks he chose the day very carefully. Tannion wanted his attacks to look as if they were random, completely unconnected events. Sometimes he killed with brute force, sometimes not. Some would die on the spot, some would take a few minutes, and others would take a few days to die. The only thing they all had in common was they were trash and they all died.

Most of the people Tannion hit dealt drugs, but there were a few exceptions. A big guy was dealing, but he was also throwing his weight around, roughing up a few people, when Tannion met him. Tannion shook his hand as if congratulating him. Later that night the guy's kidneys failed, then his other internal organs shut down. He died in agony in his own bed. He didn't even know enough to call an ambulance and died without calling anyone. Tannion was improving every day.

A little white guy pulled a gun on Tannion in a back alley in what looked like a simple robbery. Tannion looked him in the eye and then took the gun away before the guy knew Tannion had moved. When Tannion grabbed him by the arm, his heart gave out. The heart was still the quickest and cleanest, and now he had another gun for his collection.

Some of Tannion's work showed up in the paper. The cops usually still called it drug or gang-related, as that was the easiest way to write off a few punks who they were glad to be rid of. He never heard much after that. The police couldn't have been putting a lot of effort into the chase, and why should they? Tannion was solving cases that hadn't even happened yet. And he was having fun.

He was having fun, but he was still being very careful. If he thought there was any chance of getting caught, he simply didn't do the deed. Or he would make it a slow and obviously natural death that happened hours later. In those cases, if the people he touched knew what was wrong, they could have gone to a hospital. They didn't expect a thing, and by the time it hit, it was too late.

There wasn't one that Tannion regretted. Well, there was one guy who looked him in the eye with that bewildered 'what have you done to me' look that made Tannion think for a second. He still didn't regret what he had done. He only regretted having to do what he was doing. These guys were all scum of the earth. Drug dealers and petty thieves. Sure, they all had mothers that may have loved them, but they had forfeited all that and got only what they deserved. A quick and, if they were lucky, a painless death was their way out of a useless existence.

17

The local cops hadn't put a great deal of effort into a number of the deaths they had been tasked with. It wasn't just because they thought it was good riddance to bad rubbish, but also because the feds had taken over. The feds didn't use the press until they had to, so there was very little known about the deaths outside police headquarters.

"Pansloski, what's the count up to with that last guy in the four hundred block?"

There were now twenty-two known deaths in a few blocks' radius. Twenty-two coffins, but not nearly as many mourners. Mostly drug dealers, users, and punks, but citizens just the same. Sixteen of them appeared to have died from natural causes. Six had been beaten to death.

"Twenty-two, Mike," Pansloski answered. "The last one died almost the same way as Alexander did a few weeks ago. Coroner says a heart failure, but his report indicates similarities between this and at least eight other deaths. Talk about too many for a coincidence!"

"That theory you had is starting to sound possible, but still I don't know," Rallin said.

"It's possible, I guess, but I find it hard to believe that someone is out there pushing some kind of poison. First, you'd think that one of them would think it was not a good idea to take the shit, what with all the dead guys around. Then, what about the coroner's report? Most of the stiffs had some kind of junk in their veins, but there's nothing consistent."

"Then it must be something that can be added to whatever the guy has already in his system," Rallin insisted.

"It would have to be something that doesn't show up on the tox screen. And what about the dead guys that weren't natural?"

"Whoever is doing this must be a pretty big guy. If the mark doesn't take the drugs, he beats the shit out of him," Rallin said.

"And the stuff can work fast or slow. Some of these guys drop dead on the street, others show up after they take it home and die in bed."

"Whoever this is, if it's only one person, they want these guys dead. That means it isn't your ordinary drug dealer. They would need their customers alive. Your idea of a vigilante killer has to make sense."

"Yeah, I think that has to be it, but what is the weak link? How do we catch this guy and what if it's a gang thing and there's more than one? You'd think that a group would be more likely to make a mistake," Pansloski said.

"If the shit is bad, and kills that quickly, then why can't the coroner find any trace of it in their system? What the hell is killing these guys? It just doesn't add up. Christ, it seems like every case that I get this year just doesn't add up."

To make matters on these cases even worse, there were absolutely no leads. Although the victims all had something in common, none of them had a lot in common. They didn't work for one guy, or run in the same gangs. Some pushed dope, but not all of them. The dealers all ran for different people. Nothing fit. Except that there weren't too many people sad to see any of them gone.

It would have been nice to have even one lead to go on. At least someone to talk to, but there was nothing. They did the usual, searched for physical evidence, talked to potential witnesses, and interviewed known associates. All proved worthless and nothing or nobody was coming forward. A bunch of dead-ends, all with a dead guy at the end.

The brass was tired of not getting anywhere, but they also understood why. The newspapers had cooperated and many of the deaths didn't get reported. At least that stopped talk of a serial killer. Rumors like that could panic the general population. The local cops were out in force, talking to anyone on the streets, telling them to watch themselves and to stop anything that looked drug-related.

They had also increased patrols in the areas. It hadn't helped the last guy. He was dead in a back alley. Not even dumped into a dumpster this time. The killer, or killers, must be getting more daring. Yet in his gut, Rallin knew it had to be one guy, but what guy was big enough to take all these others down?

Even the stakeouts didn't show anything. There was the usual activity that was to be expected, but even that was much reduced over the past weeks. Fewer people were on the streets, fewer people were dealing, and fewer were using. What more could the city ask for? The locals knew it, and although they never wavered, Rallin knew their hearts weren't into it. The streets had never been so clean.

18

Tannion quit his job. He thought it would be harder than it was. He walked in and dropped his letter of resignation on the boss's desk giving two weeks' notice. Tannion was more than happy to be paid the severance and have security walk him out of the building.

If it was a job he really loved, that would have been worse, but this job was only for the money. Tannion had slowly grown apart from most of the people at work over the past few months. He had been a little preoccupied. Most of his friends thought he was nuts to quit. When Tannion told them that he was going to move to New York, they really got on his case.

Jane almost cried, making Tannion think that maybe there could have been something there. He had more or less ignored her for the past few months, and had never gone past second base. The biggest issue for most of his friends was that he was going off to New York without any idea of what kind of job he would get.

Tannion lied to his mom. He told her that he had a job waiting for him. Fact is, it wasn't really a lie, just that the job Tannion had in New York tended not to pay very well. The last three times he had gone out he couldn't get anyone to come near him. The streets were barren. When he did see someone, they usually went the other way. There were a number of times he thought the only guys on the streets were cops. Tannion knew his job was more or less done and it was time to move on.

The local papers were all eagerly reporting the lack of crime in the city, even if they didn't talk about the deaths. Some of the guys Tannion had run into were indirectly a big part of the break-and-enter scene in town. Without them the town was safer. With fewer drugs on the street, a large group of users and thieves had packed their bags and moved on. It was the users who were the small-time hoods breaking into homes and stealing anything they could get their hands on to pay for their next fix. It was Tannion's turn to move. If he wanted more of the same where else to move but to New York?

New York was bigger than life in Tannion's head. He had never been there, but with all the TV shows and movies it seemed as if he knew it long before he spent his first moment there. Tannion had saved every penny he could for the past few months and having sold his car, he had a few thousand dollars in the bank and a bit of a plan.

Tannion wanted to find a place that would allow him to stay relatively close to the action. He thought Harlem might be good, but being very white, he thought he would stand out too much, even if the number of potential clients might be high. He really had no idea. The movies always painted Central Park as a really bad area, so that was probably his best starting point.

If he could find a place to live only a short bus ride away, or within walking distance of any part of Central Park, then he should be able to find plenty of clients looking for his business. He would also have to find a job that left him free on evenings and weekends. Tannion knew he could live for a few months without a job, but that was about all.

Tannion bought a bus ticket to New York, and it was leaving on Thursday. He had said most of his good-byes already, so he had Wednesday night free. He wanted to go around to all of his old haunts and say goodbye to anyone he knew, but more to say goodbye to the life he had led. He had already got rid of his stash of guns, a baseball bat, his wig, and mustache. He was leaving nothing of his old life behind.

Wandering the streets Wednesday evening, Tannion realized that he had never really been anywhere. His life had been a quiet existence in a quiet town where people still looked after each other and life was good. It was only in the last few years that modern society had caught up to this place. With it came some of the modern problems. Tannion had caused many of these new problems to disappear, and now the town was coming back to where it had almost forgotten it used to be.

The movie theater in the mall was playing a few first-run shows, but he had either already seen them or didn't want to. He met a couple of people he knew, and they went for a beer. Tannion shook their hands and cured a couple of minor ailments that they probably didn't know they had.

That was the way the evening went, moving from one old hangout to another. Occasionally running into someone he knew, he would shake hands. Seeing their problems and healing what had to be healed, but not really connecting with any of them. By the time Tannion was home and in bed, he knew with incredible clarity that he was doing the right thing. He had to move on, and New York offered only excitement and wonder. Tannion was feeling like a young kid on his first date.

19

The bus pulled into the station in the New York Port Authority Bus Terminal. Tannion thought it had to be the biggest bus station in the world. It sure made his little station back home look tiny by comparison. Thousands of people filled the halls and stores from one side to another. He wondered how many buses had pulled in and were emptying out into these corridors. How many bus loads of people were getting ready to board?

Tannion once thought, "If I touched everyone for just a few seconds, I could cure the world of all its ailments and everyone would live healthy and happy lives." What a dumb thought. If he could touch someone new every minute, he would be dead before he had cured half of New York let alone the world. The sheer volume of people in one bus station was enough to make him re-evaluate what life was all about.

Tannion thought he was prepared, but when he stepped outside the terminal he was still very surprised by the number of yellow cabs. The cabs were lined up three deep as far as he could see. This made finding one very easy, but when he got in he drew a blank.

"Where to?" the driver asked.

Tannion's brain raced for a minute before he could answer, and the cabby broke in before he could gather himself.

"I said where to?"

"Uh right. Central Park. Can you take me to Central Park? I want to find a place to live near the park."

"Sure, buddy. Central Park is only a few blocks away. Where do you want to live? Maybe that will help," he asked.

"I don't know. Didn't give it much thought. This is my first trip to New York. I just thought I could find an apartment near Central Park and then go look for a job."

"Yeah, right buddy. Like you're the first to think New York is a dream place to come to make your fortune. You'll be lucky to live a week if you end up in the wrong part of town. Other parts will cost you a fortune. My advice is to go home, but I'm sure you'll ignore that. Am I right?"

The cab driver was an average-size guy. By the accent, and his look, Tannion assumed he was of Italian descent. Obviously he had lived in New York for all, or at least most of his life. A New York cab driver has got to have seen it all.

"Yeah, I know. Pretty dumb, but I got tired of home and had to come. How about landing me someplace near the park that won't get me killed and won't cost me a fortune?"

"Okay, your best bet is off Manhattan. The way the subway system works here, the park is only a ride away. You're much better off in Queens. I'll show you the Queens Midtown tunnel and we should find a place that will have a vacancy by driving around for a few minutes... if you can afford the fare."

"I need a place, and as long as it doesn't cost me a month's rent for the cab ride, let's go."

It took a few minutes to get off Manhattan and to the tunnel. Very quickly they were in Queens.

"I know this area because I grew up here. Lived here all my life," the cabby said. "I think I know a place that has a furnished room to rent for not too much, if it's still available. I'll drop you off and introduce you to the land-lady. She's an old friend of mine."

"Just what I need," Tannion thought. "Find a cabby who's going to set me up with some old Italian relative and I'll feel I have no choice but to rent some hole of a room and then find it takes three bus rides and a subway to get to Central park and back."

Tannion didn't want to be a long way from where he was going to do what he wanted to call his work. At the same time, he would need to get an apartment and a job. He might as well take a look.

The cabby drove down a street that had a number of older brick walk-ups that all looked much the same. Tannion knew he wouldn't want to get drunk and forget his address in this area. He could wander around for days trying his key in different locks. When the cab finally pulled up in front of one of them, the cabby jumped out and obviously expected Tannion to do the same. They walked up the few stairs and rang the doorbell. It was a few seconds before the door opened.

The woman who looked out was in her forties, but still had a look that could turn men's heads. She obviously knew the cabby because they exchanged pleasantries. Tannion introduced himself. The cabby went back to the cab and took out Tannion's bags as if to say, 'here you are and here you'll stay.' Tannion shook his hand and cured a couple of minor ailments that would have bothered him in a couple of years. He was quite surprised at how healthy the cabbie was. An obvious smoker, but relatively clean lungs.

"I think you'll like the apartment here. It has one bed-room and a separate bath with a small kitchen. Do you cook?" Mrs. Patelli asked.

"Thanks, Mrs. Patelli. I'm sure you're right. I do some cooking, but I do eat out a lot." Tannion responded as she showed him up to the apartment.

The apartment was much as she said, and although it wasn't big, it was clean and tidy. More or less what Tannion would have been looking for, if he had been given a chance.

"How long does it take to get to Manhattan from here?" Tannion asked.

"Oh we're real close. The bus takes thirty to forty minutes. A cab is less than half an hour. Are you thinking of working downtown?"

"Yes. I thought I would go tomorrow and look for a job right away. I might even look into working evenings." Tannion thought it couldn't hurt to get that out in the open so she could expect to see him at all hours of the day and night.

"Sure, the paper is always full of jobs, and a lot of them are in the city. A good-looking strong guy like you shouldn't have any problem."

When she finally left, Tannion got a better look at the apartment. The fact that he took it and didn't object to the nine hundred and fifty bucks a month didn't seem to faze her. Tannion couldn't tell if she was giving him a good deal or was hosing him. He decided that he should never play poker with that woman.

Tannion did manage to shake her hand on the deal and found a couple of interesting items that he left alone. He saw that one kidney was only working at half speed. He could have fixed it and the small hernia he found. Other than that, she was fairly fit for her age. Tannion decided to wait to cure her ailments. He couldn't be too sure what ailments she knew about and then he might heal something no one could explain later.

The apartment was only a few hundred square feet, but it had a separate bedroom with a kitchen/living room combo and a bath off to the side. The furnishings were old, but looked to be in good shape. Tannion hadn't brought much as he had decided to travel light. He'd have the rest sent after he got settled. His mom wanted an address, and this was one way she was sure to get one.

After a few minutes of unpacking, Tannion realized he was hungry and decided to either go find a food store or a restaurant, whichever he found first. He didn't know what kind of neighborhood he was in, but at the same time it didn't matter. He knew nothing could hurt him, with the possible exception of being found out.

A walk of a couple blocks brought Tannion back to the main street he had seen on the way in. There, he found almost everything he knew he would need. There were more than a few restaurants, a couple grocery stores, and at least one market.

Tannion ate a quick meal from a Chinese restaurant and went back to his room for the night. He surprised himself and walked directly back to the room. He didn't miss a step. He even enjoyed the walk on a surprisingly warm night. Spring had almost sprung.

He would have to buy a TV, as the room didn't have one. For the one night he had a book to read and he could dream about the next few days. This was all happening easily and quickly. Something had to give. Finding this place had almost been too easy. He was sure that when he got a long string of luck, some of it was bound to be bad.

20

It didn't take nearly as long as Tannion anticipated to fall in love with New York. It happened on the second day. Tannion took the bus downtown and wandered around Times Square and up and down the streets of Manhattan. Although he was very impressed by the size and beauty, it wasn't obvious where it got its reputation. He had to keep telling himself that it didn't look the same after dark.

Tannion applied for a couple of jobs he saw signs for and thought he would get a paper and see if there was anything he might like. He had doctored his resume a little to eliminate his degree and make it look like he was suited for more of a laborer job. His last job had bored him to tears. It didn't matter what he did as long as the job didn't drive him nuts, but paid him enough to live. His real work was yet to start, and it was bound to get his adrenaline going.

Tannion decided to take it easy the first night and wander around a bit just to take a look. He thought he had an idea how much action he would be able to get into. It was going to take a while to scope out the area enough to know where to go, but he also thought there had to be lots of places that would be good. If nothing else, he could always wander around Harlem or Central Park late at night.

Tannion noted a few spots that were likely and witnessed a couple of drug deals going down as he wandered, but he left everything alone. No need to get in a rush. The first thing to do was to get a real paying job.

Over the next few days Tannion was offered a couple of jobs. Offers of minimum wage just weren't enough. When the third place offered him a job in a warehouse not far from the docks, and the wage was decent, he took it. They took one look at Tannion and his resume and they tested his strength. Tannion had no problem lifting the hundred pound sacks and they hired him on the spot. The few bucks an hour to start was going to be enough to get him through and more.

Tannion started the next day and it didn't take long. He was the new guy and the others soon let him know it. He was given all the shit jobs and all the heavy lifting. Tannion didn't care as long as they paid him. Much of his duties were carrying whatever had to be lifted manually and loaded into what ever needed to be filled. The perfect job.

First, it was sacks of potatoes from a truck onto pallets to go into the warehouse. Then there were large boxes of something from one pallet onto a truck. Tannion thought all this could have been done by machines, but a lot of it was done by strong backs and usually weak minds.

"Hey, kid." They immediately started to call him kid even though he was older than at least two of the guys there. "Take that package down the line and give it to Fred."

Tannion was sure that the last thing Fred wanted was the package they gave him. It must have weighed over a hundred pounds, but he lifted it up and took it to Fred. He knew he would have to stand up for himself eventually and was very prepared for it, but it was going to be at the right time.

"Hey, Fred. Here's that package you wanted."

"Package. What fucking package?" Tannion got the answer he had expected almost word for word.

"Take that goddamn piece of shit back to where you got it and don't bring me any shit again unless you want it shoved up your ass."

Tannion could have made this incident the one where he stood up for himself. Instead, he took the package back to where he got it and went back to work. He was still in training, but it didn't take a rocket scientist to have the routine figured out in the first fifteen minutes. Tannion knew the work would become routine, but if he didn't have to think about the work, it gave him time to think about lots of other things.

It was on the Tuesday of Tannion's second week on the job when it finally happened. Just after nine in the morning, he was unloading a pallet off a skid when Jake came up behind him. Jake was the shift foreman and one big son of a bitch.

"Hey, kid, take this package down to Fred."

"I don't think so, Jake. He didn't like the last package I took him," Tannion said.

"I don't give a shit if he loved it or not. When I tell you to take Fred a package, you take Fred the goddamn package. You got it, kid? Now get your ass out of here."

Tannion knew the time was now. If he took Fred the package it would be Fred on his case and not Jake. Fred was smaller than Jake and probably not as prone to violence, but then violence was the least of Tannion's worries, and Fred was the boss. Tannion knew it was time to push.

"No, Jake. If Fred wants the package so bad, he can come and get it, or you can take it to him yourself."

Tannion had purposely said this with his back to Jake to see what he would do, and it didn't take but a second. Jake grabbed Tannion by his left shoulder and swung him around. Tannion was fully expecting a fist in the face, but Jake wasn't ready for that yet and was still talking.

"Kid, when I tell you to do something then you fucking well do it, and do it now." Jake was almost yelling by now.

Tannion thought it would only take one more push, and he was right. "Get out of my face, Jake," he yelled back.

"You son of a bitch!" Jake yelled as he launched a right hand. Jake had to be just under six feet, but well over two hundred pounds. He was probably a good street fighter, but the punch was telegraphed and to Tannion it might as well have been in slow motion. Tannion made just enough of a move to make it look like he luckily made Jake miss, and then he stepped back.

Jake was thrown off balance for a second, but for a big guy he moved pretty quickly. This time he wasn't going to give Tannion a chance to get out of the way. He charged right at Tannion. He probably thought that Tannion would move back and that his momentum would carry them into the wall.

Instead Tannion took a quick step forward and swung both hands and caught Jake on both sides of the head with his open hands, slapping him hard. Jake was going to have a good headache when he woke up. He moved his hands back to his head in an automatic reaction and started to slump. Tannion grabbed him and quickly threw him onto his shoulder, then into a nearby dumpster.

"Okay, who's next?" Tannion yelled. He had a good shot of adrenaline and was having fun. He hoped like hell there would be follow up. He wasn't disappointed. Three guys jumped forward and came towards him. It looked as if they had done this before.

The first guy slid by Tannion with a punch which Tannion ducked. In the next few seconds there were punches, kicks, grunts, and groans. Tannion made sure not to hurt anyone badly, but he also made sure that no one even touched him. If these guys thought this was going to be easy, Tannion was going to show them that not only was it not easy, it wasn't even possible. After a few seconds, all three of them limped away nursing bruises and bangs. No one else was coming forward.

"Hey, kid," Tannion heard from behind him. Jake was crawling out of the dumpster. To Tannion's surprise, he had a big smile on his face.

"Been a long time since a new guy got the best of me. Christ, that hurt, and I got to see most of what you did to the other guys. Where the hell did you learn that?"

"I told you I did a lot of this sort of thing back home, but you didn't listen," Tannion told him. He had mentioned that his last job had been with a rough bunch, but he had never mentioned fighting at all. It's always interesting to see what you can get away with.

"Yeah, well, we're listening now. Okay, no more kid. You earned your stripes. Now get back to work."

And just like that Tannion was in. He was now an accepted member of the apparently loosely knit group of warehousers. All he had to do was get to the point of not taking any more shit and then taking it to the physical stage. He didn't have to win and that was pointed out only a couple of days later when the next new guy finally told Jake to take a hike. The new guy put up a game fight, but Jake was too big and too fast. Jake didn't take it easy on him, but Tannion could tell that Jake was only interested in a good fight and not on hurting or killing the guy. After they picked the new guy up off the ground and handed him a rag to wipe some of the blood off, he was one of the group too. The only way someone didn't get in was by not fighting. Those guys didn't last very long before they were run off.

Tannion spent the next few weeks with work and getting to know the town. Tannion found New York to be much like any other city. It was big, but all he had to do was break it down into smaller chunks.

The Manhattan area with Central Park, then north into Harlem and the Bronx was what Tannion considered to be his area. He would work at the warehouse all day and then go out to eat in some restaurant near Central Park. Then he would wander around looking for the right area, getting to know what the people were like and what he should expect. He wasn't in a hurry to get started and he was being cautious. He was finding it a little hard to get a feel for where the right place was, or for where the right people were, but this had to be the right, or maybe rather the wrong, part of town.

21

After almost two months in New York, Tannion was finally ready to go out with a purpose. He had found a number of likely places in Harlem, the Bronx, and an area of Central Park that wasn't particularly safe after dark. Maybe he was finally on his way.

Tannion put on an old shirt and went to one of the spots he had picked out. After walking around for several minutes, he noted that nothing was happening. He was considering going home, and started moving back toward the subway.

"Hey, you," someone called from behind him. Tannion turned around to see three black youths walking towards him. They looked to be in their late teens and were trying to look and act tough. These were not the kind of guys he was looking for. Tannion thought that with a little guidance these kids could turn out okay. They could also end up dead in a back alley or spending time behind bars just as easily. They didn't look to be part of a gang with any obvious signs, so his first reaction was that he should just teach them a lesson.

"What can I do for you?"

"You can get the hell out of here is what you can do," said the apparent leader.

The guy to his right piped in, "Yeah, white boy. You're not welcome here."

Tannion was expecting a little rougher language. The lack of it solidified his first impression that this was not something they did on a regular basis, but were only trying to look tough in each other's eyes. Tannion decided to talk to them until they couldn't take it any longer and either buggered off or decided to get physical. He knew if it came to the latter that he was going to have to go easy to not hurt them.

"Hey, guys, I seem to have wandered off the beaten track. Can you tell me where I am and how to get to Beaton?"

"Beaton. What you mean, Beaton? There's no place called Beaton around here. Now if I was you, I'd get my ass out of here before someone decides to take exception to the likes of you around here and lay a beaten on you." This all coming from the one Tannion assumed to be the leader.

"You guys go to school around here?"

The smaller one started to say that they did, but the leader shut him up with a curt remark. "None of your goddamn business."

"Just asking," Tannion said as he tried to keep the conversation going. "Can you tell me what you do for fun around here?"

"The only fun you're going to get is a knife in the ribs and a good ass kicking."

Tannion had decided that they would probably let him go if he told them that he was leaving, but that wouldn't teach them anything. He pressed.

"I don't think three little pipsqueaks like you would be able to scare my mother. Why don't you run off and play, or send me your big brothers." Tannion thought that might be enough and he proved to be very right.

One of them took immediate exception. As they were close enough, the kid took a swing with a curse on his lips. Tannion was ready for anything and stepped back. As the kid's fist passed within a few inches of Tannion's face, he reached in and slapped him hard enough to knock him to his knees.

The leader and the little guy were stunned by what they had just seen, but weren't ready to back down yet. They both came at Tannion. Within seconds they were on the ground with very sore heads, and Tannion hadn't even closed his hand.

"Okay, boys. I could kill all three of you in less than ten seconds if I wanted to, but you look like the kind of guys who might make something of yourself. You need to keep in mind that there is always someone faster, bigger, and tougher than you out there. As long as you go looking for a fight, you'll find one or it will find you."

Tannion turned his back on them and walked away. As he went around the corner he had a second to look back at them and to think about what he had just said. He realized how corny and stupid it must have sounded.

"I probably made three not-so-tough kids into three guys wanting revenge, rather than sending them packing back to their mothers," he thought. He decided that if he ever had a similar feeling about anyone else that he would tell them to bugger off and walk away.

Tannion hoped those three had big brothers and that he would run into them soon. Real soon.

22

Finally the big day arrived. Tannion went to work as usual. He ate a light meal after work and went for a walk, the same as he had been doing for the past few weeks. If anyone saw him they would know that he was on his routine schedule and think nothing of it.

It was a cool late spring night so the fact that Tannion had a jacket on was not unusual. If they had looked in his pockets and seen the extra long ski hat with blonde hair sticking out from under it and the glasses that he had never worn before, they might have thought something was up, but no one needed to see inside those pockets, and no one asked.

Tannion walked to the end of the street and caught the bus into town as usual. When he reached one of the first stops he got out and took a different bus into Harlem by a different route. He had done this only once before, but had no trouble finding his way. Tannion was heading to a spot he had picked out as being a local drug corner where he had seen a number of drug deals go down over the past couple of weeks. He was looking for one particular dealer who he had seen rough up a couple of guys when he thought they were alone.

Tannion waited for over an hour just out of sight before the guy finally arrived. He came out of a side door, and if

Tannion hadn't been paying close attention, it may have looked like the man had appeared out of nowhere. He wasn't a big man, but he carried himself with an obvious swagger, as if he knew he was important and he wanted anyone seeing him to think so. He also wanted to look a little dangerous. To Tannion he looked like a little guy and an easy mark.

Tannion had already determined how it was going to happen. It was going to look like natural causes, and it would take a few hours for it to happen. As Tannion approached, the man hesitated, obviously not expecting a blond white guy in the neighborhood. As Tannion got closer he put up his hand.

"That's close enough, what the fuck do you want?" he said in what Tannion was getting used to as one of the New York accents.

"Heard you might have some interesting stuff," Tannion said while he kept getting closer.

"What kind of stuff you thinking about? You a cop?"

"Shit, no, I'm not a cop. Do I look like a cop?"

"Yeah, you do. What do you want?"

"Let me see what you got," Tannion said, while at the same time bringing out a roll of cash obviously large enough to buy some of whatever the guy had. Tannion thought it would be better to carry some cash with him, but letting anyone take a look under the top couple of bills would not have been a good idea. Tannion put the roll back in his pocket. It was only for show. Things had changed since leaving home. Tannion carried cash and he even had his ID on him.

"Okay, okay, take a look," he said obviously deciding that Tannion wasn't a cop. He pulled a bag out of his jacket pocket and showed Tannion the contents.

Tannion's research on street drugs was still limited, and he had no idea what the guy had. Tannion looked the assortment over. "I'll take a few of the red ones."

The dealer picked out a few and tucked the bag back in his pocket. "Good choice, man. That'll be forty bucks."

Tannion reached into his pocket and handed him the money. As the guy handed over the pills, Tannion reached over and shook his right hand. The guy had a cloth glove on, but there was enough touch through the cloth to make contact. Tannion started a small leak in his right aorta, knowing that it would take a while before he bled out. Tannion made it so the damage would continue to increase a few cells at a time until there was nothing anyone could do, even if the guy was lying on an operating table.

Tannion walked away knowing that there would be one less drug dealer on the street. He felt pretty good about it as he knew what this guy was like. He had decided that he didn't want to make any mistakes and kill someone who didn't deserve it. The drugs went into a garbage can down the road. It was full enough that they would never be spotted. Tannion didn't mind paying the forty bucks to know that this guy was done.

Tannion didn't bother to get a paper the next day. No way would a Harlem thug dying of heart failure cause a stir. At least not enough to make the Times. Over the next couple of weeks Tannion tracked and disposed of four more dealers. He thought if word got out that a number of dealers were dying of heart failure, users might think the shit they were selling on the streets, and obviously taking themselves, was bad.

Tannion didn't have any grandiose idea that he would be saving some young kid from a life of hell as an addict, but if he was going to go after someone who deserved it, drug dealers were a good start. He would rather have gone after rapists and murderers, but they didn't usually conduct that sort of business on the street corner where he could find them.

Tannion did get lucky in Central Park, though. He was walking through the park on a Saturday night after midnight when a couple of hoods approached him. He knew before they got close that they would tangle. One had a knife out that Tannion could see long before they got close, which assured him that at least that one was not too bright. Tannion could have easily run in the other direction when he first saw the knife.

One of the things that Tannion had been working on was his eyesight. It was already very good, but he knew it could be better. With a few adjustments here and there his daytime sight was more than twice as good as it was before. Then he started on his night vision. It wasn't perfect, but it was good enough to see things at night that the other guys thought the darkness hid. In this case it was the knife.

As the two got closer, the guy slid the knife into the pocket of his worn out old jacket and kept walking towards Tannion. When they got close enough to make them feel comfortable, the first guy pulled out the knife and put up his hand. "Hand over your wallet," he ordered.

Tannion had a mental flash of highwaymen in merry old England a few hundred years ago stopping people on the road. He thought better of saying anything and simply attacked. It was probably the last thing they expected, and was certainly the last thing they saw. In only a couple of seconds Tannion broke both their necks. The first took a hand to the side of the head so hard that it snapped his neck. Tannion then moved behind the second guy and gave his head a twist. The second guy didn't even have enough time to think of yelling before Tannion was behind him.

Drug dealers were one thing, but Tannion had no qualms about taking out armed robbers. The only difference was that it didn't look like natural causes. These guys had obviously been killed by someone.

At least when the cops took a look at the two dead guys, they wouldn't make any connection to the dead drug dealers that had been showing up in the past weeks. That had to be a good thing. They might even think they had been killed by more than one person.

Tannion knew that the cops were not his enemy, but they could get in the way. He knew if they got close, he'd have to leave New York. He would just have to make sure they didn't get close.

Tannion quickly left the area and made his way home. He knew he had to sit still for a while and stay out of the area. He went for walks every night to make sure the neighbors didn't see a change, but he moved to a different area and kept to himself. With all the shit that goes on in New York, it was going to take a while before he put a dent in it and made the streets safe. It would probably take years, but he was prepared. If nothing else, he was having fun. Cleaning the streets was just a bonus.

23

Jeff Martin was a typical long-serving New York detective. He knew his way around, had his eyes and ears who worked for him, and did a pretty good job on the paperwork.

As he pored over some of the seemingly endless paperwork, the phone rang. The voice on the other end was an old friend from the coroner's office telling him that there was something he should come down and see. It seemed to Martin as if too much of his work started at the morgue.

Phil Canbow knew when Martin would come in. Martin had done this so many times that his immediate arrival could be timed within seconds.

"What do you have, Phil?"

"Hi, Jeff. Good to see you. Come over here and take a look."

Canbow handed Martin a sheet of paper, and it was obvious that Martin had seen many like it before.

"So, what am I looking at this time?"

"That's the coroner's report on a guy they found in the street a few days ago. The blood screen is noted at the bottom. You notice that it's clean. No drugs of any sort in the guy's system," Canbow said.

"So what? Most people will give you that result."

"You'd be surprised, Jeff. Most people have some over the counter drugs, caffeine, nicotine or some shit in their blood, but this guy was squeaky clean."

"Okay, you found some stiff with good blood, so what?"

"The thing about this guy is that he's a known drug dealer who was found dead on a street in Harlem. And that's not all. At least four known drug dealers have been found dead in the past few weeks. All died of natural causes, but if you look at the other reports on my desk you'll find that the others were all using something. The natural cause in each case was much the same. A leaking aorta causing pulmonary collapse. Of course, we all thought it was some bad shit on the street. Then this guy comes along."

"And this guy is clean, but died of the same thing?"

"That's right. What are the chances of another drug dealer dropping dead of the same thing that has killed three of his compatriots, and yet we know it was not drug-induced?"

"So what is the theory today?"

"We don't know. The sort of leakage around the heart is very rare and yet here we have four of them. All we know is that this is very strange and we have put word out to watch all the morgues for more of this sort of thing. We may be dealing with an unknown virus or bacteria, but nothing shows up in any of the cultures we've run. If it was virulent and killed this way, we would probably have an epidemic on our hands. That's why I called you. This is starting to look more like a homicide, rather than a medical problem."

"Homicide? How can you jump to that conclusion?"

"Well, if there is one thing I've learned over the years it's that when things just don't want to add up, there must be some outside influence. In this case, these dead guys are all the type who some people would like to see dead or at least off the streets. Therefore, homicide is plausible. Or it may be that we're just running out of ideas. If it's in your area, at least you need to be aware."

"That does sound suspicious," Martin agreed.

"Also, there are drugs out there that can cause a heart attack that are virtually untraceable. If this is the case, then he wouldn't have taken it willingly. Therefore, it's murder in my books. I plan on doing a little more work on the blood tests. Run a full panel and look for more exotic substances."

"Thanks, Phil. I can't see you being right on this one, but stranger things have been known to happen. If it is, I've been warned. Let me know if you come up with anything at all. For now, I can't see me doing anything."

With that Jeff Martin left the office and headed back to his car. Phil Canbow looked after him as he went through the door into the hallway and thought, "I hope like hell I am wrong, but if I'm not, at least one of the good guys knows about it." There wasn't much else he could do but watch Martin leave.

24

Bill Worthing was a big man. At well over six feet and close to three hundred pounds, Worthing didn't take shit from anyone. For the most part, he would and could do what he wanted when he wanted. The bar was his usual drinking hole, and he had his usual table. As he worked his way across the room, he could see that his table was occupied. This, of course, was a common occurrence, but it wouldn't last for more than a few seconds. It was always the same when some poor unsuspecting fool had chosen the wrong table at the wrong time.

"Okay, asshole, move," Worthing said as he assumed a menacing posture resting his knuckles on the table.

The man at the table looked up at him over his beer and didn't say a word, only lowered his eyes and looked back down at his drink.

"Hey asshole! I said move. This is my table," Worthing was almost yelling already. The knuckles on the table had gone white as he placed more weight on them. A few more pounds and the table might have caved under the pressure.

The guy at the table slowly got up and Worthing could see that he was almost as tall as he was, but he knew he had almost a hundred pounds on the guy. There was no need to worry. The guy was probably done already. What he didn't expect was what came out of the guy's mouth.

"How about you and I stepping outside and seeing if we like each other," the man muttered.

Worthing couldn't be happier. If there was anything he liked almost as much as sex and drinking, it was a good fight. This guy looked big enough and in good enough shape that it might almost be a good fight. A short fight, but this guy might even get a lick or two in.

They left the bar by the back door into the alley. Almost the entire bar followed them and they took their positions along the walls of the surrounding buildings. They knew what to do. They knew what was coming. They had seen Worthing in action more than a few times in this alley. They had seen Worthing come in and knew that the new guy was at his table. The fight was a bit unexpected, but was always good entertainment.

They didn't have long to wait. Worthing moved forward like a big bear expecting to grab the stranger and squeeze him. Then he would hold the guy in one hand and lay a licking on his face with the other. Several of the people standing along the walls had seen this happen a few times before.

The stranger didn't move as Worthing came close. Worthing grabbed him around the ribs and started his squeeze. The stranger seemed to shrug and Worthing was on the ground. There had been a good number of yells, but with that one motion the crowd was silent. Worthing got up and the stranger still hadn't moved. As he got closer, Worthing moved with more caution.

Worthing had thought this was going to be easy when he put his arms around the other guy, and then he was on the ground. He had no idea how he got there. What had gone wrong? He moved forward looking more for an opening, thinking about what the other guy had done. As he moved forward the other guy still didn't move. 'What is with this guy?' was the first thought in Worthing's head. Worthing was more of a bull-type fighter. Moves were straight ahead and with power. He never expected to have any trouble with anyone unless they ran. This guy was different.

Worthing reached out with one big paw trying to grab the stranger by the hair, but the stranger ducked and slapped Worthing across the face. It looked harmless enough, but Worthing was on the ground again.

Worthing never saw the move or the slap, but he did feel it. It shook his head like a child's rattle. His teeth felt loose and his sight wavered with flashing lights going off. What happened next was not something he could have prepared for.

With an audible gasp the crowd of onlookers saw what Worthing could not or would not believe. The stranger was on Worthing almost as soon as he hit the ground. He grabbed Worthing's shirt with his right hand. With his left hand he grabbed the pants at Worthing's crotch. Without any apparent difficulty, he raised Worthing over his head and threw him the couple of feet it took to hit the brick wall of the nearby building.

Worthing hit the wall at least six feet off the ground, and as he fell, the stranger hit him three times. Twice into the face and the last one into the stomach with enough force that it almost stopped his fall. Worthing hit the ground like a sack of potatoes with a thud and a groan, but that was all. Worthing was out cold.

The stranger hadn't even worked up a sweat. He dusted his sleeves off and walked back inside. The crowd watched him leave, and after a few seconds they finally realized it was over. Almost as one, they walked over to the prone body of Big Bill Worthing and someone checked to see if he was alive. Finding a pulse, they called for an ambulance. No one thought to follow the stranger. He had walked back into the bar, paid his tab with a generous tip, and walked out the front door without comment. The few people left inside the bar who had seen him go into the alley with Worthing had a look of wonder on their faces when only the stranger came back in, but no one said a word.

After the ambulance and cops arrived there was a lot of talk and confusion. Some of the people said the guy was bigger than Worthing. Some said he was a little guy who knew Kung Fu. Others said they didn't get a good look. In the end the cops wrote it up as a back alley brawl with no charges filed and no report to write. They liked it better that way anyway. After all, the only guy hurt was Worthing, and he would live.

25

Jeff Martin hadn't got a good night's sleep the night before, and for the most part he looked like shit. His hair was thinning and more than a few gray hairs were present that were not there last year. It looked like he had combed his hair in the morning, but that was all. He wasn't worried about what he looked like.

This morning he was reading a number of reports that had been dropped on his desk the night before. More of the same was all Martin could think. The last item, however, caught his eye. A drug dealer was found dead in Harlem and the autopsy report indicated natural causes. "If this turns out to be the same type of natural cause," he thought, "bullshit it was natural."

One phone call placed to the right source filled him in on the missing information in the autopsy report on his desk. Sure enough, it was some fancy heart-sounding infarction or something. The number was growing and was now up to nine. No one was getting upset as the causes appeared natural, and these guys were scum. They were not the type of people anyone really cared about.

That didn't matter to Martin. This was a mystery. A puzzle. Martin enjoyed solving puzzles, and this one looked like the type of puzzle that most people didn't even see as a puzzle. The intrigue was too much for him to resist. Martin didn't really care that much for solving the case, only in solving the puzzle. The next phone call was big.

"Jeff, haven't heard from you in a long time. How are you doing?"

Martin had placed a call to an old friend and colleague who had quit the force and moved on. Fred Hines used to be a New York Cop, but after only a few years he saw the bright lights put up by the feds and moved over to the FBI. Taking a New York cop usually meant retraining him to lose all the bad habits, but they saw the potential in Hines and gave him a chance. They hadn't been mistaken, and Hines had turned into a top-rate agent.

"Hi, Fred. Yeah I know it's been too long and it seems the only time I call is when I need something from you."

"Sure, Jeff. What's going on?"

Martin took a few minutes to tell Hines the story. He told him that the cause of death looked irregular only because of the numbers. Hines wasn't as sure as Martin that a puzzle existed. But eventually the volume of coincidences was too much, even for him.

"Nine dead and all known drug dealers. The FBI has a task force on dealers in New York. I'm sure they're aware of this, but it hasn't got big enough to hit the general radar."

"What I need is any data that isn't already in the files. I don't even know what that might be, but if you can talk to the task force, maybe they have something," said Martin.

"Those guys can be very tight-lipped, but I have a couple of contacts. I can at least check. Boy, this sounds like one for the X-Files. I'll see what I can do."

Martin thanked his buddy and hung up the phone. "Christ," he thought, "the FBI have a task force on drug dealers in New York, and now we have dead drug dealers. Coincidence maybe, but there is no way in hell these guys are going to tell me anything."

Martin hoped Hines would be able to get something out of them, and with luck it could be something he could work with. If the FBI had a task force, maybe they were behind the deaths. Wouldn't that just be the answer? Rogue FBI agents inducing something that was untraceable into the veins of dealers and then dumping them back on the streets to die. Even Martin couldn't believe that one.

Martin knew that he was out of leads at this point, and he had other cases to work on. Real cases to work on. If Hines didn't come up with anything, then the case would only sit. There was some first-hand data in the files, but with the deaths being natural the cops hadn't pursued any action. Only thing to do now was wait. There really was no case as the deaths were all written up as natural. Nothing for the cops to do.

26

Things were going as well as could be expected. Every few nights Tannion would go out and try to find where the action was. About one out of every three times he would get lucky. He had already run out of the guys he had spotted and tracked earlier. Now he had to rely on chance. Chances were pretty good if he hung out in the right spots. Most of the time this meant bars of some sort in the rougher parts of town. On occasion he could get lucky and find a tough guy.

The next step wasn't obvious, and he almost missed it. His job since moving to New York had been physical. After a while he found it easy to forget that he had other skills. If nothing else, hauling large bags and boxes around all day had made him even stronger. He hadn't got back into the routine of a workout schedule, but with this job he didn't have to. Unfortunately, it wasn't a job to stretch anyone's mental capacity.

As Tannion passed one of the buildings in Manhattan, something, caught his eye. One of the local hospitals had placed an ad in a paper, and someone had posted it in the window. They had probably posted the page because of the article on prostitutes, but the ad was on the same page.

The ad was for an accountant with a few years experience and with good computing skills. Tannion knew his job experience back home was not exactly what they had in mind, but he had the degree they wanted, and they had what he wanted, access to a hospital. The job was in a nearby hospital. It would be filled with all kinds of ruffians that he could get close to and make the kind of decision that he liked to make. The possibilities seemed too good to pass on.

As soon as Tannion got home he dusted off his resume. He made some changes and added his degree and work history back in. If all went well, this could be the way in. Maybe the bad guys could come to him for a change. If he could get the job.

The next morning Tannion dropped his resume off on his way to work and then set in to wait. It didn't take too long before he got a call from the hospital for an interview. He had made the short list based on his education and experience, but after the interview he didn't think there was much hope. This was prophetic as he received a call the next day telling him that the job had been given to another. He didn't have the type of experience they were looking for.

If he really needed the job it would have been different, but he was making enough money to live where he was. It wasn't the job, but the opportunity that he found exciting. He would have had relatively free access to a hospital that could have had who knows who in it. Guys coming in with knife wounds they got in a gang fight. Cops with bullet holes in them. Who knows? He could have patched the ones who deserved it and eliminated the ones who needed elimination, but in such a way it would look like they succumbed to either their wounds or to a secondary infection. All he had to do was be there and touch them.

Of course all he had to do was get a job at a hospital and the opportunities were there. He began looking very seriously at a career change, and after a few days he found the spot that could do it. A hospital in Queens was looking for a janitor. A few adjustments to his resume and he was off to the races.

The job wasn't automatic, but Tannion's physical strength was what got him the job. They showed him the janitor's room and there was a large pail of detergent on the floor which should have been on the shelf. Tannion bent over and picked it up with one hand and placed it on the shelf. The reason it was on the floor was because the last guy couldn't lift it. He almost got the job on the spot, but they showed some composure and hired him the next day. Tannion was in.

The first day at the job gave him the right impression of what the job was going to be. He spent the day mopping floors and taking out the garbage. Tannion didn't know a place could have that much garbage or that many hallways. It was only a good size hospital, but to someone new, it seemed enormous. Tannion, however, got the chance he wanted.

Tannion was in the hall outside the emergency room when he heard the noise of someone coming in. It must have been serious as they didn't wait for any triage or to ask the patient whether he was insured. They brought him in on a gurney and the nurses were there before the doors were closed. Tannion found out later that he had been stuck in the ribs and was not in very good shape.

He had been admitted immediately and the doctor must have looked at him right away. Tannion kept on mopping in the general area and tried to look busy and inconspicuous. He mopped the hallway and then went to empty all the garbage, and then went back to mopping. All the while watching to see where they took the man.

The man was left in the emergency room, and after the doctor had left, Tannion had his chance. He moved into the area, still mopping the floor, and got a look. The guy was white, in his late twenties to early thirties, and he was lying in the bed out cold. He had a few monitors around him making beeping sounds and an IV drip was in the back of his left hand.

He must have been in better shape than the doctors or nurses originally expected, since they had left him alone. Tannion walked over to him and touched his arm. The sensation was there in a flash and he could see the damage. Tannion knew immediately that he could heal this guy as easily as kill him. The knife had entered just below the ribs and had cut upwards, just missing the heart and one of the major vessels around the heart. A small decision on Tannion's part could make it look like the blood vessel had been nicked. The blood flow would start slow and then increase until the guy bled out inside.

Tannion could just have easily taken the worst of the wound and healed it on the spot, even ensuring that secondary infection wouldn't get him. The problem was he had no idea which was the right decision. Was this guy the one who should have died in a knife fight? Was he an innocent bystander or the victim of a robbery in some liquor store? Without knowing which, Tannion could do nothing.

Tannion was going to have to feel his way around for a while before he could make those types of decisions. It was going to take time to set up a plan and to put it into action. The job was going to take second fiddle, but he still had to do enough to keep the job. Of course that wasn't hard. All he had to do was work hard for a few hours. With his speed, he could get all his work done and then only make it look like he was working the rest of the time.

A few weeks in and he got a bit of a break. At first it didn't look like it was a break. It might have been his end. Tannion had walked into a patient's room to clean the floor and went over to the man and touched him, just as a nurse walked into the room.

"What do you think you're doing?" she demanded.

Tannion didn't have a good answer. After a bit of a stammer, he told her he had heard the patient moan and had gone in to see if there was a problem that he should tell someone about. She obviously thought that it was the truth, as she immediately told Tannion she was sorry for being harsh and walked him out of the room with a smile.

Tannion had made a friend. Dorothy Perkins was probably a few years over fifty and was what might be called matronly, but she knew her stuff. Whenever he got a chance Tannion would take some time and talk to her. She had been a nurse for thirty years, with the last twenty at this hospital. She knew everything there was to know.

Tannion told Dorothy that he might want to become a nurse or a doctor someday. As if that was likely at his age. He would ask her all kinds of questions with that in mind. He was then able to ask her questions such as, what was wrong with the patient in 405 or 309.

When the right one came along, Tannion was ready. Dorothy told him about the guy who had just come in from emergency with a gunshot wound. The wound was serious, but he was going to live. Dorothy told Tannion that he had killed a cop and had taken a bullet in the action. When Tannion managed to make it to his room with the cover of taking out the garbage, he took a look and saw a guy in his late thirties or early forties with long greasy hair and tattoos. Tannion quickly touched his arm and left the room.

It was a couple of days later that Dorothy told him that the guy with the tattoos had succumbed to his wounds despite the best efforts of the doctors. Tannion's first strike appeared to be a good one. The guy had shot one cop and held out for over an hour before the shot that took him down. He had been rushed to the hospital, where the doctors had worked on him. There was talk around the hospital, and it was always of the sort that said it was a good thing that the guy had died. Saved the taxpayers a lot of money was the usual response.

No one was sad that he didn't make it. No one was going to his funeral, but he was supposed to live.

27

Tannion was really starting to like his life. Work at the hospital was easy if a little boring, but there were so many people around to talk to and to watch. People are very transient in a hospital. Except for the workers, there are patients, patient's friends, and relatives. Most stay only a few minutes, some may stay for up to a few days.

Tannion tried to stay away from some units, but his job was to mop every floor in the building. Eventually he got to every place. The worst was the sick kids ward. He felt he should cure them all, but he knew it would have been his downfall.

The best was the emergency department. He never knew what would come in. There would be everything from knife wounds to heart attacks, burn victims to bad coughs. Every day was different with different people.

The emergency department was used as a training ground for young doctors and nurses, but it was also where all the doctors who didn't have a department specialty had to move through.

This meant new staff on a regular basis. Of course there were the emergency specialists too, but they had their job to do and stayed out of his way. Every few days there would be someone who was pretty banged up. With some minor research, Tannion could find out about them. If they were a likely candidate, he could follow them to the room they were to die in.

All of them died peacefully and with little pain. Tannion made sure that death came in the night when the doctors were as far away as possible, in case the patient knew what was happening. Most just went in their sleep. He made sure that what killed them looked like what brought them into the hospital.

Tannion did make a couple of mistakes. They looked like good candidates, but when he got the real answer they didn't always fit the profile. One guy, based on the way he looked, made Tannion pretty sure he was on track, but he turned out to be an undercover cop.

Tannion decided very quickly that this was probably going to happen every once in a while, as the system wasn't perfect, but as long as he could keep them to a minimum they were acceptable losses. He needed to remember to always do the research and take nothing on face value.

Tannion's relationship with Dorothy was going very well. She was easily his best friend at work. He found that the hospital was more like a family and it could have been easy to get close to people. Too easy. He had to make an effort to keep most people at arm's length. If someone got too close he never knew what he might say by mistake.

It used to be that his worst fear was being placed on a table and dissected. That was replaced with whatever the justice system thought of his mercy killings. He definitely thought of them as a form of mercy killings or better yet, a service to society. The justice system would see them as vigilantism at best. At worst, murder.

The laws had been written a long time ago and, in Tannion's opinion, the justice system was run by bleeding heart liberals who thought the law was all there was. As a result you had murderers and rapists walking the streets. Gang bangers and drug dealers harassing people where Tannion walked. Many of these criminals were well known, but were on the streets due to a technicality. Lack of a search warrant to gather evidence didn't slow Tannion down.

The hospital easily became a second home and maybe in his case, because of the room he lived in, it was more like his first home. Tannion spent most of his waking hours in or around the hospital. Luckily it was also a fairly large hospital and although like a second home with his family everywhere, there were still a very large number of the staff who didn't have a clue who he was. He came and went more or less as he pleased. If anyone asked him a question, he always had the right answer.

28

Eight weeks. It had been eight weeks and there hadn't been one dead drug dealer. Harlem had been losing one or more a week for several weeks, and now nothing. Sure it could be all the bad stuff had gone up someone's nose or maybe whoever was planting the stuff finally got the guy they were after or whatever. All Detective Jeff Martin knew was it didn't smell right. Why so many, and now none. It didn't add up.

Cases like this didn't come up very often. First it wasn't even a case. As far as everyone else was concerned, dead drug dealers are a good thing, but ones who died of natural causes were even better. No need to waste any public money chasing whoever killed them. In this case Martin had no authorization, no permission, no nothing, but he couldn't get them off his mind.

"But I do have cases," thought Martin. The file on his desk was flipped open and the name jumped out at him. Reginald Baxter Wilton. Now who would call their kid Reginald? Baxter was probably a family name, but to stick the kid with Reginald. Another kid growing up to hate his parents.

Didn't matter much now. Reggie was dead. He had been shot twice at relatively close range by a twenty two caliber handgun. The autopsy report indicated cause of death to be internal bleeding. The medical report indicated that the bullets had penetrated the upper chest and abdomen and were lodged deep in the back. Both bullets were removed at Queens General Hospital and that the operation had been a success. The patient was supposed to live, but during the night an artery that must have been nicked by a bullet, and which must have been missed in the surgery, kept on leaking. Eventually it burst open, and he bled out internally.

His killer or killers had gotten away, and that was the case. Reggie was an undercover cop. The picture in the file made Martin think that Reggie was probably good at what he did. The mustache and hair looked the part, but the kicker was the tattoos. Reggie could go into deep cover and no one would think him to be anything but a biker or hard case. Deep cover was Reggie's specialty.

There were a few leads in the case, but not much. Martin had already been to the crime scene and talked to anyone he could in the vicinity. He had also read the reports from all the beat cops who had canvassed the area. The coroner's report included information from the hospital that was not the usual type of data you see in a coroner's report. The attending physician at Queens General hospital had worked on Reggie and had reported him to be in satisfactory condition. The coroner's report said that Doctor Fred Anton was sure he hadn't missed any nicks or leaks that eventually killed the patient, and he was shocked that he had died during the night.

"This man should not have died," read the report.

Martin decided not to see Doctor Anton immediately as there were always better things to be doing. In this case the coroner's report indicated the bullets to be from a twenty-two caliber handgun, and ballistics had matched the bullets to a handgun recovered in a robbery in Queens that same day. The gun had been dropped as the scum got away on foot, but they had a pretty good lead on who he was.

So the doctor could wait. Now it was time to find the guy behind the gun. The lead had them in the north end of the Bronx, and when Martin got there the area was covered with squad cars and a standoff was underway. The area precinct had sent Lieutenant Roland Chambers to head the operations. It took a few minutes to find him in the melee. Martin told him his part in the operation. As he was outside his jurisdictional area, Martin was only able to watch, but he made damn sure Chambers knew why he wanted this guy, and that he wanted him alive.

Chambers knew about Reggie's death and was sympathetic as all cops are when one of them is hurt or killed. He would do what he could, but you never know what may happen in these situations. Standoffs like this were often very volatile. Accidents could happen, but he would do his best to keep the guy alive.

As often is the case with this type of situation, the temperature got real hot for a while and then slowly cooled off until the guy came out with his hands over his head. The local guys almost tore his head off getting his hands behind his back and cuffed. He was in the squad car heading to the seventh precinct, where Martin knew he could find him.

Because of the possibility that this guy was a cop killer, Martin got a shot at him early. After talking to him for a few minutes he knew he wasn't going to give him anything, but he felt the guy was guilty. There were witnesses who would be able to pin Reggie's killing onto this guy, as well as evidence which included ballistics. The forensics looked good enough to convict. All that was left was to work on the paperwork and send the case to the courts.

Martin still hadn't talked to the doctor about Reggie's death and thought it was as good a time as any. Then he could put something into the case file. The local guys had the gunman in custody and a couple of their guys were talking to him. It would all be in the report on his desk in the morning.

Queens General was built in the post war years when all they seemed to have to build with was red brick and mortar. The outside looked institutional, and the smell inside said definitely institutional. That distinct smell of antiseptic can bring back distant memories. "I had my tonsils out in a hospital that smelled just like this many years ago," thought Martin as he headed down the corridor in the direction that the information desk pointed.

Martin had called earlier and knew that Dr. Anton was in. Dr. Anton was the head of ER and Martin had needed to book an appointment to see him. "You can never tell what emergency would put me second in the queue," thought Martin as he approached the door. Anton's office, if you could call it an office, was next to the ER and it was easy to find.

Martin knocked and heard a muffled voice that might have said come in, but may have been bugger off for all he could tell. Martin wasn't in the mood for bugger off, so he took it as come in and walked in.

"Detective Martin of NYPD I presume," Dr. Anton said.

"That's right," Martin replied. Dr. Anton stood and reached across his small desk to shake hands with Martin.

"Yes, come on in. To what do I owe the pleasure?" Anton pointed to a chair beside the desk for Martin to sit in.

"Well, Dr. Anton, a colleague of mine died here last week. I read your report and thought I should ask you a couple of questions. A police officer by the name of Reginald Wilkins was brought in here with a couple of bullets in him, do you remember the case."

"I sure do. When he came in he was badly shot up and had lost a lot of blood, but he was wide awake. He had a lot of guts this friend of yours. He talked to me as we were taking him down to the OR. He asked me what his chances were, and I told him I couldn't tell yet, but that he was in good hands. He looked like a real hard case and I thought the worst of him as he lay on the gurney. I thought this guy had probably held up a liquor store or something, but when he talked to me it was obvious that he was well educated, and the hair and tattoos didn't fit the voice."

"What else did he say to you?" Martin asked, hoping to take some notes that the original team had missed as Anton dredged up memories that he may have thought unimportant at the time.

"Not much. We put him under right away, and after I scrubbed up I went in. He had a bullet lodged in his back between the…" He stopped for a second and then went on. "Sorry, no reason to get technical. He had a couple of small caliber bullets in his chest that I had to get out. One had hit him high in the chest and was mostly a flesh wound, and the other had cut into his intestines, but had missed all his vital organs. I repaired everything as peritonitis is not a fun way to die. I cleaned out the area and went back in to see if I had missed anything, and I hadn't. There was no way this guy should have died. When I came in the next morning I was extremely shocked and disappointed that he had died in the night. I made sure that I was present for the autopsy. They found that he had bled out internally from a tear in a major blood vessel. I know that tear wasn't there when I closed."

"What do you mean?"

"There was no possible way that the bullet could have cut or even nicked that artery. The bullet entry and path had to be at least an inch from that area. Our team would have noticed any other fragments and there were none found in the autopsy. It almost looked like a natural aneurysm."

"What are the chances of that," Martin asked.

"A man is shot and almost bleeds to death, survives a complicated surgery and then, as he sits in the recovery room, an aneurysm lets go that we didn't know about or see when we were in there. I don't think it's probable, and in this case, looking at the physical condition of the patient, not very likely. Not likely at all."

Martin thanked the doctor and found his way back to his car. He didn't have anything new for the case file, but there was something wrong here just like there was something wrong with the number of dead drug dealers. Natural causes were written on all the death certificates, and now this included a dead cop, but none of the deaths seemed to make any sense.

On the bright side, Reggie's killer was behind bars, and unless the court system failed again, he would be staying behind them for a long time. At the same time, the possibility of his death being by natural causes didn't help. If his killer's lawyer uses that data in his defense, you never know.

Martin was having trouble putting the pieces together. Nothing fit. All the dead people died of natural causes. He decided to talk to Dr. Anton again to see if he could make some sense of it. They met again the next day.

During his appointment, Martin told Dr. Anton everything he knew about the death of the dealers and then Reggie. Dr. Anton wasn't sure how he could help, but Martin saw him as someone in the business, and Dr. Anton agreed to be available to discuss the case. It had touched a chord in Dr. Anton, and it may have been more than just Reggie's death that got him on side.

Doctor Anton asked Martin if there were any other deaths that could be considered mysterious. Martin decided to look back over the obituaries and see what might appear. He spent several hours over the next few days going over old files to see if anything popped up. He wasn't sure what he was looking for, but thought he would know it if it appeared. Maybe he needed more help.

29

Martin was going over the New York papers looking at all the obits, but nothing struck him as abnormal. The work was slow, and he had real cases he needed to work on. There had to be a faster way of looking through the obits than him looking at fiche in the library. Then he had his first good idea in a long time. Martin had a source he hadn't used in years.

A friend of Martin's worked in records at the FBI, but they had lost track of each other. They used to be an item a number of years earlier, but when they split they had remained friends. Then she moved to California, and they lost each other.

She had been with the FBI in Sacramento, so that was his first call. When he asked for Sarah Haskill, the operator asked him who was calling and passed him through. First time lucky. Sarah had been with the FBI when they first met, and now she had been at Sacramento for more than ten years.

When Sarah came on the line it was as if the last ten years had not existed. They were both really excited to talk to each other, and after they had spent several minutes catching up, Martin had almost forgotten what he had called for.

"Sarah, it's been nice to talk to you again, but I do have a problem that I was hoping you could help me with."

"Jeff Martin. I thought this was just a social call," Sarah said, but you could hear the smile in her voice.

"Well it should have been. It's been far too long, and I blame myself for not calling years ago."

"Don't beat yourself up, Jeff, I could have called too." The smile was gone and was replaced by a somber tone.

"Yeah I know, but the time seems to be flying by so fast that I barely have time to wake up and then the day is done. What I was hoping on this one is that you could do some fancy footwork for me to look up a few things in old newspapers."

"Sure, anything to help a fellow cop, what are you looking for?"

"I have a case. Well it isn't actually a case, but it has me bugged. A number of drug dealers have died in New York over the past few months of what looks like natural causes, and then an undercover cop gets shot, but even when the operation looks to be successful, he dies. The death certificate says complications from surgery following a gunshot wound, but when I talked to the doctor who operated on him, he told me there was no way he missed anything that would have killed this guy. I think there's something going on and I'm trying to find out if there have been any other mysterious deaths anywhere over the past five years. I searched the New York papers by hand and didn't find anything, but it took far too long and now I want to check outside New York."

"Jeff, hold on," Sarah said.

Martin hadn't realized how fast he had been talking and slowed down to complete the thought. "Sorry Sarah. I get into it sometimes. This one has done it. I would like to look over the papers of all the major cities in the US to see if there has been anything similar over the past five years. I thought maybe you have access to a database that might have the type of data I'm talking about."

They talked for a few more minutes, and then she informed him that the FBI had a database that included all U.S. deaths with date, time, and cause of death. She asked questions that would narrow the search and they decided to check over the past five years only for men who died of a heart condition, but were under the age of fifty.

Sarah told him it might take a few days to get authority to run the report and then only minutes of CPU time to get the results, which she would email to him.

Three days later Martin had an email at home that was a little more than what he had expected. Apparently in the past five years there were over fifteen hundred deaths from heart failure that matched the criteria. He was going to have to revise the input parameters to reduce the number.

Martin called Sarah back, and she was expecting him. "I knew you wouldn't like the number, have you come up with revised search criteria?"

"Does your database have occupation?"

"I think so. Assuming it does, what are you looking for?"

"I want to match the characteristics of what we have in New York. The dead guys are all drug dealers with the exception of the undercover cop. So if we can eliminate any-one who appears to have a real job, maybe we can get lucky."

Sarah said it wouldn't take as long because she already had clearance to help him, so he should have an answer the next day. He was only a little surprised to find an email on his home computer when he got off work that night. This time the number was more like something he could handle.

The list was easy to read and contained just under a hundred names. The list was alphabetical and was sorted by location. There was one dead in Akron, Ohio. Another one in Atlanta, Georgia and a couple in Boston, but nothing looked out of the ordinary until he got to Wichita, Kansas. Wichita had nine deceased with none of them having a full time job. One had a comment indicating that he was living on the street, a couple had prior convictions for drug dealing, and the rest were young with arrests for theft or assault on their records.

Martin felt that he had hit the jackpot. This had to be it. The similarities were too strong. He had hoped for more drug dealers, but most people don't put drug dealer down as an occupation on the city census. The number was three times as large as any of the other cities, and Wichita isn't that big of a city. When compared to some of the other cities with much greater population, this put the per-capita deaths extremely high in Wichita.

Martin felt elated for several minutes, but finally came back to earth. So what if there were similar deaths in Wichita. The question was how to change from big deal to something that may spring the clue loose that would give the answer he sought. He wasn't sure where to go from there, but he had to tell Sarah what her report had come up with.

When Sarah answered the phone she was way ahead of him. Not only had she seen the large group in Kansas, but she had looked up the directory and found the name of the FBI bureau chief in Wichita.

The call to Wichita was fruitful with the bureau chief giving Martin the name of the two agents on the cases. The problem was the cases were cold. Nothing had happened for several months and the leads had dried up, so there was precious little to go on.

"Well, maybe I have a new one here in New York," Martin said to himself.

Bill Pansloski and Mike Rallin. That's the names the bureau chief had left, along with their phone numbers. The chief sounded more than happy to have his guys talk to a New York detective if it meant getting a lead on a number of old cases. Including the nine that had shown up on the list, he told Martin of an additional thirteen deaths, some of which did not include natural causes.

"Now to contact the agents and see what we can shake up," Martin thought. A couple of phone calls later and Martin had Bill Pansloski on the line.

"Agent Pansloski, This is Jeff Martin of the NYPD. Can I take a few minutes of your time?"

"Sure, no problem, is it Detective Martin?"

"That's right, but I'd rather be known as Jeff."

"Sure, call me Bill. What's on your mind?"

Martin filled Pansloski in on the number of dead drug dealers and how he had been informed of him having similar cases of his own. Pansloski told him that he and his partner Mike Rallin had more or less forgotten about those cases and had moved on, but there was something in the cases that had stuck with them as they just didn't add up. When Martin told him that it was the same problem he was having, Pansloski understood.

They made arrangements for Martin to come out to Wichita and pay the FBI a visit. The only problem was he had no reason to be going to Kansas on official New York police business. Because he had quite a lot of vacation time coming, he decided to take a week off. Next stop Kansas.

30

Tannion almost made a big mistake. There had been a gang fight and a number of young Asians were admitted with knife wounds of all sorts. Big machetes can do a lot of damage, and it looked like these guys let each other have it.

Tannion saw the first of them come into the ER. It looked like there had to be a lot more than three badly hurt. There was a lot of blood. Altogether there were nine patched up guys in nine beds in the ER by the end of the night and two had been sent to surgery for more serious patching. The staff didn't know which gang these guys belonged to or if there were some from each gang, so they took them into separate rooms for the night. They didn't want to take the chance of putting rival gang members in the same room and having them finish the job during the night. There were cops all over emergency.

Tannion waited and watched from afar as all this took place. With the nurses and doctors running all over the place and routine patients coming in and out, it was easy not too be noticed. When he had a chance he went into one of the rooms. There was a kid about sixteen lying in a bed with a bandage around his head and another that looked to be holding his shoulder on.

He checked a couple more rooms and decided they were only kids and left to see how the two were doing in surgery. Both were in recovery by that time, so it took a few hours of waiting around, mopping floors to see them moved into single rooms.

Tannion made it into the first guy's room, this one looked a little older and was obviously in rough shape. He had taken a good slash to the chest that was bandaged, but based on the tube sticking out with bloody fluid coming out of it, the knife must have gone in deep.

Tannion went over and touched him and made sure that the bleeding never stopped. He then stepped into the next room and saw what must have been the worst case of a knife fight he could imagine. This guy must have lost a lot of blood, and he must have had his guts nicked or worse. He was bandaged almost head to toe, and what wasn't bandaged appeared to have tattoos. This guy looked to be in his early twenties, and based on the age of the other two he could have been the leader.

Tannion walked over to him and placed his hand on his arm and stopped. He almost started the internal bleeding that would kill him and realized that he had never killed two on the same night. He didn't want to have Queens General look like a place to die so he had been careful to kill only those who looked like they could die. If he killed both of these guys the attention may come down on the hospital. The problem was, this looked like the guy who should die and the other should live, but it was already too late. This guy got to live.

Tannion was being very careful. Only one a week or so could die, and only those who were obvious. The last thing he needed was an investigation at the hospital. People died in hospitals every day, but too many would cause suspicion. He was always able to augment his need in Central Park or in Harlem, where one or two murders could happen any night.

The hospital had proven to be as good as Tannion had expected, but he had found that he couldn't move nearly as quickly as he would have liked. He thought it might be time to move on. If he wanted to increase the total he may have to start taking risks, but it wouldn't be tonight.

Even though the hospital had been good, it was always a waiting game and he felt as if he was never hitting the right guys. The big guys never got hurt and never crossed Tannion's path, and working at the hospital didn't drag him into any circles that would include anyone bigger.

Tannion really wanted the top guys. These were leaders who got kids into drug running or using. The pimps might be easy to find, but who ran the entire operation? Tannion was just not into the scene enough to know much at all and it was frustrating. He needed to get in deeper. It wasn't happening where he was.

31

The first meeting took place in Mike Rallin's office on the third floor of the FBI building in Wichita. Detective Jeff Martin was not that surprised to see that it was rather nondescript with only the typical FBI plaque out front that said you were entering a place that only a few wanted to enter.

Rallin struck Martin immediately as a solid guy with his head on his shoulders. He filled him in on what was going on in New York, and Rallin completed the picture that Bill Pansloski had started on what had happened a few months earlier in Wichita.

"You mean you don't even have enough to open a file in New York?"

Martin told him how there were a few dead guys, but nothing that immediately pointed to anything but natural causes and nothing that the NYPD thought important enough to put a detective on.

"And you're here in a completely unofficial capacity, that right?" Rallin said as he walked over to the chair behind the desk and sat down.

"And to make things worse, I'm officially on vacation."

That was enough for both Pansloski and Rallin to have a couple of laughs at Martin's expense, but they also knew that it was not really a laughing matter,

"I got the information on Wichita and thought that there may be something going on that can help me figure out what's happening in New York before the situation there becomes worse," Martin said. He sat down in the chair across from Rallin, and Pansloski continued to stand over by the door almost as if he was getting ready to leave.

"If there's a connection, then we need to find it. If what happened in Wichita has simply moved to New York then there are a lot of people in grave danger. To make matters worse, there are a lot of people who see the dead guys for what they are and are glad to see them gone. This only results in fewer outcries to catch someone and pin something on them."

"That's already happening," Martin said.

"The crime rate went down considerably during the few months this was going on and hasn't come up noticeably since. We've always known that a large portion of the petty crimes were caused by drug users needing to get their hands on cash to feed their habits. With a few of the users and many of the dealers dead and gone, and a fear that whatever or whoever was killing them may still be around, we saw a large volume of the criminal element leave town. We don't know where they went, but we know they aren't here," Pansloski said.

"I think the problem is New York is so many times larger than in your area, and the number of dead guys so minimal, this couldn't even make a dent. Too many people have been dying the same way and to me that means murder and not disease or bad drugs."

"If we have more than a coincidence then there must be something or someone in common. All we have to do is find the common denominator and we have the answer," Rallin said.

"Agreed," Martin said nodding his head.

"At this point I think we have to rule out everything but the people factor. If this is not someone, then it isn't something we can even look for." Pansloski said. "That means we need to see if someone used to live in Wichita or visit Wichita on a regular basis and now has moved to New York. Unless anybody has any other suggestion that's the only thing I can come up with."

"As good as any I have," Martin said.

Rallin made a quick phone call and told them he had someone looking for any data that indicated that someone had moved from Wichita after the last death they had on file. This would mean a search of vehicle registration, business licenses, dog licenses, or anything that would indicate that someone had moved. "We don't have big brother watching as close as some people think we do," Pansloski said. "However, the credit card industry will be our best bet."

Martin met Pansloski and Rallin the next morning just after eight. As before, they met in Rallin's office and Martin was beginning to wonder if Pansloski had an office. Rallin made a quick call to see if anything had shown up on the data request he had made from records and was told there was a list, but more data was being run.

After Pansloski had left to go pick up the list, Rallin and Martin had a chance to chat, but after only a few lines of small talk, Rallin couldn't help but get right into the case.

"Bill and I have been following this case for close to a year now and we don't appear to be any closer than we were when we started. We at first thought it was a bad batch of cocaine or something that was killing these guys, and then a few dealers were killed by someone obviously very strong."

"I'm sure there were some in New York killed that way too, but they get lost in the shuffle," Martin said.

"When the list of dead dealers and punks started to get a little longer we realized that the natural causes and the beating deaths had to be connected. There was just too much in common with the victims in each case, but no one was able to figure out how someone could be responsible for the natural cause deaths, then it all ended, we ran out of leads, and it all came to a halt."

"We have one case that didn't fit at all," Martin said. He then filled him in on the one guy who was squeaky clean and how drug use just didn't make any sense any more.

Rallin got Martin thinking that there may be other deaths that were not included in the list he had. If there were dead guys who had been beaten to death who he had not been counting, then the number of dead could be a lot higher. In New York there were enough of these types of deaths that it may be impossible to make a connection to the possible drug induced cases.

It was a few minutes before Pansloski came back with papers in his hands. When they took a look at the list, it contained more than five hundred names. There were bound to be a few who simply disappeared without leaving a trace who they would never pick up on, but there were more than enough to start with.

"Jeanie in records is still running the list, and as there were a few areas that hadn't come through yet the number will be higher," Pansloski told them.

"Now we need to cross reference the list with where they went to see how many went to New York," Rallin said.

It took a few minutes to cross off the names that never were seen in New York. There were a couple of people who had gone to New York, but then had moved on prior to the date Martin was using for the start in the city. When they were finished they had a list of seventeen people.

"Well seventeen is a number that we can deal with," Martin told them. "Now I guess the next move is up to me. I'll find these seventeen people in New York and see what they have been up to for the past few weeks. I'll also look for any other suspicious deaths, especially drug dealers or users during the same time period. If the physical is connected to the natural causes, we should be looking for a pretty big guy."

"You can probably reduce the list very quickly if you knock off the single women, and there appears to be three on the list," Pansloski added.

"They might have big boyfriends who may have been doing the deed, and if the woman is the bread winner, the guy may not show up on the scan," Martin said as he was picking up his jacket and getting ready to leave. "Leave them on the list, but I'll leave them to last."

Martin had taken a full week's vacation and this was only Tuesday, he was going to have to find something to do for a few days. "Nothing's going to happen in this case that a few days of R and R will hurt," Martin told himself. "As long as when I get back to New York I can talk the captain into letting me have this as a case." Martin had asked Rallin to call Martin's precinct and ask them to set up a case assisting the FBI, with Martin as the detective in charge. He hoped that would do the trick without causing too much trouble for him.

Martin was still going to catch shit from above for doing an end around on this one, but he was willing to pay that price.

32

Tannion was walking down one of the streets not too far from his place when he was approached by one of the hookers who worked that part of town. It didn't have to be the raunchiest part of town to attract the hookers, and this was a pretty nice area of businesses that was usually frequented by hard working New Yorkers, but the hookers were there.

When the lights went off and the shops closed, the street life came alive. For the most part the hookers weren't trouble. Sometimes the Johns were trouble and usually the pimps were the hard cases, but the girls were hard working.

It's not like Tannion hadn't been approached before. Some of the areas he had been wandering around in New York brought him into contact with this element all the time. The fact that he hadn't been laid for a long time might have been on his mind, but he still couldn't go to that level.

Not that he was worried about catching anything, but he still couldn't go there. What it did, however, was make Tannion think about another element of the night life. The hookers did a service that probably keeps some crazies from doing something a lot more drastic.

Some of the Johns were the type of guys Tannion could feel good about getting rid of, but only some of them, and he didn't think he could easily tell the good ones from the bad. This then left the pimps. Everything he saw or heard regarding these guys told him that the world would be a better place without them.

He knew he couldn't put any trust in the hookers, but without them he probably would have trouble finding the pimps. The only way was to sit and watch and hopefully the pimp would visit and Tannion would be able to recognize him when he came. Then he would follow the guy to someplace where he could shake his hand or wring his neck, which ever worked the best.

Tannion found a good spot to watch the strip. There were four girls working and he could see them all. They appeared to be working in pairs with two on each corner. Tannion had been there for over an hour, and in that time each of the girls had been approached by at least one John, and two of them had gone off to conduct business.

After three hours Tannion gave up on this idea altogether as he had seen the girls come and go, but had no idea if he had even seen a pimp. He knew there was a lot that he didn't know about this side of life, and unless he was willing to dig deeper into it and become part of it, he wasn't going to learn what he needed to know.

As he walked home he was surprised to see a large group of people on the street a few blocks from his place. As he got closer he could see they were coming out of the church on the corner. Christmas was coming and Tannion assumed they were attending a late night mass or something.

He was in some kind of mood. It must have been from watching the hookers being picked up and dropped off and then being pissed off that he couldn't catch a pimp that way.

He was walking through the crowd not really caring if they moved or not and he bumped into several people before he passed through.

Several people told Tannion to watch it, but he never said a word and kept on walking. Tannion wasn't sure what might have happened if one of them would have given him a bad time. It may not have been pretty.

So here was a bunch of probably quite good people coming out of a church, and the only thoughts Tannion had were 'stay out of my way.' As they saw him bust through, they were probably thinking the same of him. Thank God he didn't have an urge to touch any of them.

So it didn't look like pimps were his game. The hospital was working for him, but it was too slow. He could find a few of the types he was looking for by wandering along Central Park or going to the obvious drug haunts, but this was a city of big crime. Murder, rape, and assault were all around him, but Tannion wasn't in the middle of any of it. He had been in the city for months and still he hadn't found his way into the inner circle. He didn't even know where to look.

Maybe he only needed more time, or was it possible that New York wasn't the hot bed of crime that he thought it would be. He was no longer sure.

33

Jeff Martin was back to work on Monday morning. When he sat down at his desk there was a very visible note sitting where he was sure not to miss it telling him to see the captain.

"Now the shit begins," Martin said to himself.

Martin walked the few yards down the hall and knocked on the captain's door, without waiting for an answer, he pushed the door open and walked in. The captain's office always looked the same. There were a few piles of folders on one side of his desk, a picture of his wife and kids, and not a computer to be seen.

"Morning, Sam," Martin said. "What's on your mind?"

"Morning, Jeff. I think you know the answer to that question. You also know I hate it when I get a call from the Feds, and especially when I have no idea that it's coming. What the goddamn hell have you been doing? You go away for a week's vacation and just before you get back I get a call from the FBI to inform me that I must support you on a case that doesn't even exist." Sam's voice got louder and louder throughout his tirade.

"Are you done, Sam?"

"I'm done, and now you better fill me in or your hide will find itself with a few more weeks off."

Martin filled his captain in on what was going on in New York and how it appeared to be connected to Wichita. He failed to go into any detail as to how the connection was made. Sometimes there were contacts that were best kept anonymous. When he was finished with his story his captain could only agree that something had to be done, and with some reluctance he told Martin to hand all other cases back and to go full time on this one.

"Next time, Jeff, come and see me. I can be reasonable once in a while you know," the captain said as Martin left his office.

"Yeah right, chief," Martin thought as he walked out. "About the same time hell freezes over will be the time he goes against the book. He won't take any risks now that he's this close to retirement."

Martin walked back to his desk with a bit of a smug smile on his face. He knew for once that he was going to be on a case he actually wanted to be on and not just one that appeared on his desk or when the phone rang.

"Now to the list," Martin thought as he picked up the list of names the FBI had provided. This list was the quick list produced through motor vehicle searches, a more definitive list would be arriving later based on credit card and bank purchases.

The list had seventeen names on it and all he had to do was start at the top and work his way to the bottom. He knew he could cross them off the list only if they could provide an iron-clad alibi for more than one of the victims. It was going to take some foot work, but the last known addresses and phone numbers were on the list so he might as well start calling.

By the end of the day Martin had contacted eight of the people on the list. Six weren't home, and three were no longer at the number he had. He made appointments to meet three of them the next day and he felt he had done a good day's work by the time he went home.

"Well that was three up and three down," thought Martin the next morning as the first three turned out to be way off the mark. The first was a gay Latino man who was not only much too small to have hurt anyone with his hands, but had already been living in New York for a couple of months when the last dozen or more hits were made in Wichita.

"Not sure why he was even on the list," thought Martin. "Must have taken a while to get his vehicle registration changed."

The next two were pretty much the same. The rest of the day was made up of contacting as many of the no-shows as possible, including finding new numbers for the three that no longer had the number the FBI came up with. The last of that three had moved from New York over a month earlier so he crossed him off the list.

It was just after three when the fax came in from Wichita. The FBI had come up with the list from the credit card and bank angle. He hoped this would be a more detailed list, and when Martin took a look he wasn't surprised to see the same seventeen names plus eleven more.

Eleven more names was still not a bad number. It might take a while to chase everyone down. It was only a small chance that he would find anything anyway. As Martin reached for the phone to begin the search for the day it surprised him by ringing first.

34

Bill Pansloski had just faxed the list off to New York and made a copy for Mike Rallin. Rallin scanned down the list without any real purpose, but when he got a list of names handed to him, it was human nature to look at the names to see if he knew anyone on it. He was almost to the bottom of the list when a name registered.

"Shit, Bill. Look at this," he exclaimed as he held his copy of the list in front of his partner. "Look who's near the bottom of the list. Do you recognize that name?"

"No. Can't say that I do," Bill said. "Jim Tannion. No, doesn't ring a bell."

"This is the guy who saved that kid's leg a few months back by lifting a car off him. Remember. I went out and talked to him because he looked a little like the composite of the guy in the cancer clinic case."

"Sure, I remember now. Your aunt was in a cancer clinic at the time so I remember your interest. How's your aunt doing by the way? I haven't heard you say anything about her for a long time."

"Yeah, that was why I was interested and she's doing okay, but it is only a matter of time. That's the way cancer is. You fight it and I guess every once in a while you win, but more often you lose."

"So what about this Tannion?"

"This guy was able to lift a big car off that kid, he was in Wichita, and then moved to New York. That's got to be enough to move him to the head of the class. Hold on. I'm going to give Martin a call and fill him in."

"Martin," said the voice on the other end.

"Good morning, Jeff, this is Mike Rallin in Wichita. How's everything in New York this morning?"

"Son of a bitch. He's been up for less time than I have with the time difference. He shouldn't sound so damn good in the morning," Martin thought, but he said, "Morning, Mike. Things are pretty good here. I just received the new list. Thanks."

"You're welcome, Jeff, but you may like something else I have too. One of the names on that second list is Jim Tannion. He used to live in Wichita and moved to New York, but what I remember him from was when he saved a kid's leg by lifting a car off him. I talked to him after the incident and this guy is young, fit, and obviously very strong. He might be a good place to start. I'll fax you his picture."

Martin didn't know if it meant anything, but if Rallin thought it was somewhere to start he might as well. After thanking the FBI agent and hanging up the phone, Martin took a look at the list to see whether Tannion's name was on it. Being alphabetical the name was very near the end, but it was there.

The list provided some information on each of the people on it, including last known address, phone number, and employer if known. Tannion's address and phone number were there and noted his current employer as Queens General Hospital where he appeared to be in custodial services. "I assume a janitor," thought Martin.

On the other end of the telephone line, Rallin put down the phone and turned to Pansloski. "Martin said he might as well put Tannion at the top of his list. Nothing has turned out to be promising so far, but he's eliminated a few from the list."

Rallin had a little time to think before he went to his next call. He had a visit down to the morgue in store for him and he thought he could put it off for a while as he put his feet up on the desk.

If Tannion was the guy it might make sense as he certainly had the strength to put guys away based on his ability to lift that car, but this guy had worked in an office as an accountant when he was in Wichita. Not the type of guy you expect to be out killing dealers.

Then how did that account for the dead dealers who weren't killed by force. Some of these guys had marks on them, but for the most part they had died peacefully. Some of them apparently even died in their sleep.

The list said that Tannion had switched professions and was now in custodial services. From an accountant to a janitor. Rallin wondered if that had any meaning.

There wasn't much for evidence in this case even if Tannion looked promising. He hoped that Martin could figure it out. "Well I guess it's down to the morgue for this cop," Rallin said to himself as he lifted off the chair, put on his jacket, and headed out the door.

"That is a case that sure could use a break," Rallin said as he closed the door behind him. But Rallin knew that breaks in most cases didn't just happen, they took hard work. He hoped Jeff Martin was doing the work that might just break this case.

There was still a nagging thought in the back of his mind. Whoever had bumped off a few dealers and users had dropped the crime rate down, and the city cops were happy to see these guys gone. So why should anyone care to catch the guy responsible? Maybe New York was getting the same benefits, but it was probably too big of a city for the benefits to show up in the statistics yet. They may never show up. Maybe this is one case that should be dropped, but Martin seemed to have his teeth in it. "I guess I wouldn't," Rallin thought.

35

"Hi, Dorothy," Tannion said as Dorothy walked into the lunch room and sat down beside him. Dorothy had bought the special no matter how many times Tannion had told her not to.

"That stuff will kill you. You need to look after yourself better than that you know," Tannion said.

"Right, buster," she countered. "What have you eaten today? I hardly ever see you eat any more. You've been holding out on the lunch room staff these days, Jim."

Dorothy had become a good friend of Tannion's. Maybe his only friend. Being a nurse in the hospital with several years of seniority, she had opened a lot of doors for him that his position as the mop and glow boy would not have opened.

There were quite a few marks that he had found mostly because she had mentioned them. She was always more than glad to talk about her patients to someone she knew and trusted and someone who she thought had the patient's welfare in mind as much as she did. She didn't know, however, what type of welfare Tannion had in mind for some of them.

Dorothy had aged even in the short time that Tannion had known her. She had to be quickly approaching fifty-five if she wasn't there already. With the number of years she had put in at the hospital, a pension had to be possible. Problem was she would probably rather die at work than leave for any reason. In the few months he had known her, it looked like she was getting closer to that moment.

Tannion had never taken an internal look at Dorothy. He realized he had no idea if she had anything wrong with her or if she was as healthy as a horse. Tannion reached over and took her by the hand, trying to make it look as if he was helping. The picture came up as quickly as he knew it would, and he wished he had been wrong. This was one sick nurse.

Dorothy had a number of ailments and they all came at him at once. Dorothy had cancer, emphysema, gall stones, and gout to name a few. Nothing that Tannion couldn't fix, but they might be things that she knew all about.

Tannion left the major problems, but fixed a couple of annoying symptoms and started the process to have the gallstones turn to powder and be absorbed. The other problems would have to wait.

"Dorothy, I need to talk to you," Tannion told her. "I don't think I can continue with this job. It's been getting to me lately and I thought instead of just quitting I should talk to you first." It was probably time to move on, but the question he wanted to ask Dorothy was where to. She told him that he had to do what made him happy. Working at the hospital was no longer making him happy.

Tannion dropped off his letter of resignation the next day and was told that they were sorry to see him go. Tannion found himself unemployed. It had been a while since he had been unemployed, but he had been saving money since he had gotten to New York and had almost fifty thousand dollars in the bank.

Tannion had brought most of that money with him after he sold his car and moved to New York. He had enough to last for quite a while and he was in no hurry to get another job that would not allow him to do what he had to do.

Tannion thought he had made some serious mistakes over the past eighteen months since the lightning strike. The most serious was that he had allowed too many people to die of the same ailment and he was worried that it might be seen as too much of a coincidence. How many heart attacks or heart failures could a population have, and with most of them not that old.

He needed something that appeared to be natural. It had to be something similar to a plague like virus that couldn't be traced or cured. Doctors might think it was air born, passed by fleas, rats, or as a sexually transmitted disease.

Tannion locked himself in his room for the better part of two weeks coming out only to get something to eat and occasionally a walk in the park. He looked at every angle of his body and read whatever he could find on disease. He used his own body as the guinea pig and did things to it that would have killed anyone else if they didn't have the ability to stop it and then reverse it. He was happy only after he had what looked to be a very virulent strain of some bug.

Tannion thought he had what he needed, but now he needed to test it on someone other than himself. He needed to see if his virus would kill when he wanted it to kill, and it had to look natural. Anything else was unacceptable.

36

Jeff Martin walked out of the precinct house early. It was Tuesday morning and the spring in his step said that he had someplace to go and that he was eager to be on his way. A few days working with the list of people sent to him by the FBI had left him with only Jim Tannion as a possibility and today was the day to take a look at this guy.

Rallin had told him that Tannion was a good place to start, and Martin had told Rallin he would check him out. Martin decided, however, that it would have been premature to go in that direction and continued to work down the list in alphabetical order. When he got to Tannion there were only a couple of names to go, so he had skipped over him until today.

A call to his home phone number had not been answered and Tannion didn't have an answering machine. "Who the hell doesn't have an answering machine these days," thought Martin as he had looked down the list. The list said he worked at Queens General Hospital, so that was where Martin was off to early this morning.

Martin met with the head of security at the hospital and was told that Tannion had quit a couple of weeks before and hadn't indicated why or where he was heading. That meant going to the guy's home. The head of security, Phil Anderson, was interested in why Martin was looking for Tannion, and Martin proceeded to tell him the majority of the case feeling an instant camaraderie with him.

After spilling his guts for the few minutes it took, the head of security looked at Martin and started filling him in on the types of people who had died in the hospital during the period that Tannion had worked there. A few minutes looking at some data and he had a list of people who had died after being brought in with gunshot wounds or knife wounds. Martin was very impressed with the database that the hospital security kept.

"So all those guys were gang members or suspected gang members or drug dealers, and they all died here?"

"Not all. There was one undercover cop with them and a few that we didn't have any idea what their past was," said Anderson.

"Shit, that's right. I forgot all about Reggie. He was a case of mine, but after we caught the guy who shot him I closed the file and that was the end of it."

"Maybe for you," replied Anderson, "but he became a statistic on our files and one that I would rather not have. When the doctors get their shit hot because someone dies that they think shouldn't have, they start looking for answers. Sometimes those answers look like there may be an outside influence and then they're on my case."

"I know Dr. Anton thought Reggie should have lived," Martin said.

"Dr. Anton didn't like how he died and he was sure that someone must have interfered somehow, but there was nothing that I could find," Anderson said. "Now with you looking for Tannion and with the types of dead guys on your list, maybe there was something there after all. I didn't know Tannion very well, but I talked to him a few times and he always seemed to be a very nice guy. As far as I could tell he didn't have a great many friends at the hospital, but he did spend a lot of his time with one of the head nurses. Her name is Dorothy Perkins, but I think she's not on shift today," he said after consulting a paper Martin had to assume was the shift roster.

Martin said goodbye to Anderson with a promise to keep in touch if he found anything and headed downtown to Tannion's address. After talking to his landlady, a Mrs. Patelli, he found that after spending a few days in his room without going out much, Tannion hadn't been seen for a couple of days.

"Shit. Now the hunt begins."

Martin headed back to the office to get someone started on running credit cards to see whether Tannion used his in the past few days and if so when and where. He still didn't know whether this guy was the one, or for that matter if he had anything to do with anything, but circumstantial evidence wanted to point in his direction. If it was willing to point, he was willing to look, and when he caught up with Tannion, he'd be in for a few interesting questions. Martin also knew he would have to talk to Dorothy Perkins.

37

Tannion left the apartment and caught the first bus that stopped at the bus stop close to his place. He didn't really care where it took him as long as it took him away from where he was. The apartment was a great place to stay or sleep, but over the past few days he had spent far too many hours cooped up inside.

It had taken that kind of a sacrifice to perfect the next step. Now it was time to rid the world of the pests he saw on a daily basis. He also knew it was time to be more cautious and at the same time, more open. It was time to put his agenda into action.

Tannion got off the bus in an area of the city that was completely foreign to him. The one thing he could tell was that this wasn't the upscale part of town. This was definitely near the edge of trouble. He walked into the closest bar, and it didn't take long. As he walked up to the bar, a long legged, but rough looking girl sat down next to him.

Tannion looked at her closely. She had hooker written all over her. "Buy a lady a drink?" she asked with a voice that obviously belonged to a long-term smoker. Tannion guessed her age at about thirty-five to forty, but would not have been surprised if she was older. She had seen them

165

166 | Wayne Elsner

all come and go, and as he was dressed in blue jeans and a T-shirt she probably couldn't tell if Tannion had any money or if he was filthy rich.

"Sure," Tannion said. "What will you have?"

"Tony, pour me a whisky sour," she called back to the bartender. Who knows what Tony poured into the glass, but it was going to cost Tannion the same no matter what. She looked at him and asked the inevitable. "You want to party."

Tannion thought to himself that now was probably as good a time as any. There may not be a need to inflict pain on anyone who was too innocent. If there was the idea that the disease started in the oldest profession, it may help the cause.

Tannion reached over and took the hooker's hand, and with a quick look he saw that she would have passed him something he didn't want if he had gone with her. It was enough for him to unleash the virus. "Thanks anyway," Tannion said. "Enjoy the drink."

Tannion dropped a few bucks on the table and headed for the door. He got about halfway before a voice stopped him.

"Why don't you want to party with the lady?" it said. "Don't you like to party? Are you a queer or something?" the voice went on.

Upon turning around Tannion found the face that belonged to the voice. A little guy sitting at one of the tables was looking up at him with an expectant smile. The reason he could smile were the two tough looking guys sitting at the table with him. Although he didn't have the typical pimp look, it was a good bet that he was mixed up in that end of the business.

Tannion walked over to the table and extended his hand to the little pimp and to Tannion's surprise the guy shook it. He didn't think the guy really had anything in mind other than to talk a little trash as he was quite social after the rocky start. It didn't matter to Tannion as the virus was released almost as soon as they touched. "Probably should touch the other two as well," Tannion thought, and he reached over and shook both their hands while talking about nothing important.

When Tannion had passed the virus on to all three of them, he stepped back and started to head to the door. He turned after a couple of steps and said to the guys at the table, "It was nice meeting you, but I would be more careful in the future who you call a queer. Not everyone is as nice as I am."

The two big guys started out of their chairs, but the pimp put out his hand and stopped them with a laugh. "Thanks for the advice," he said. "Next time maybe you'll like to party a little."

"Maybe," Tannion said as he walked out the door.

The sun had gone down in the few minutes he had been inside. The street lights had come on and the landscape had changed. "Not bad for a few minutes work. Lots more where that came from," he said as he walked off into the night.

38

Jeff Martin was up early Monday morning, but he wasn't feeling refreshed. The remainder of the last week had been lost looking for Jim Tannion. As far has he could tell Tannion was still in New York, but he hadn't been seen for a few days and there hadn't been any traffic on either his bank account or credit cards. No one falls off the end of the world. He needed to be patient.

That morning Martin had to meet a plane in from Kansas as both Mike Rallin and Bill Pansloski were coming to New York to help in the investigation. Martin considered himself lucky to not have the FBI take over the case, but the way the captain and some of the other detectives were treating him, maybe he should have the FBI in charge. Maybe that way he could get something done. At least the captain had given him some man hours to use.

The plane was on time and they had a chance to talk in the car on the way in. The FBI guys had been up early and it showed. Traveling was often stressful, and having to get up earlier than usual and sit on a crowded plane never made it fun.

Rallin and Pansloski started talking shop almost as soon as they got in the car. Rallin got in the front seat beside Martin with Pansloski in the back. If Martin hadn't pegged

Rallin for the automatic leader of this pair before, he did now. Martin filled them in on what he knew, including the conversation with the hospital security head.

Rallin started, "I understand that you haven't been able to locate Tannion yet."

"No," answered Martin. "Not yet. I have two guys watching his apartment building and four more checking the bars. With luck we should have him soon."

"Good, but when we find him, I think it may be best to not approach him. If he is the guy we're looking for we won't know it unless he confesses, and the likelihood of that is pretty slim. It may be better to tail him for a while and catch him in the act," said Rallin.

"I had thought of that, but if he is the guy can we afford to have him walking the streets?"

"If we pick him up and are unable to stick anything on him, he walks anyway and that may be as close as we ever get. This is still a free country and guys like that can disappear for a long time," Pansloski said.

The rest of the trip downtown was pretty quiet. A little discussion about the weather and the Yankees, but an unofficial decision had been made. Martin was very aware that even though he wasn't totally for the idea of letting Tannion walk around with a couple of guys following him that was the decision they had made. Now there wasn't much to do except wait until he showed up.

Rallin and Pansloski stayed with Martin for an hour talking about the case and then decided it was time to check in with the New York branch of the FBI. They took their leave but left their phone number with Martin in case Tannion showed up. They also indicated that they would take the afternoon watch at his apartment. Although Martin thought that was a bit strange, he kept his mouth shut. It had been tough getting the captain to free up a few shifts for this case, and having the FBI take one of them off his hands would probably help his cause.

Rallin and Pansloski dropped into the FBI building and reported to the commander, but were gone in a matter of minutes. A quick stop for something to eat and they were ready to take their turn at Tannion's apartment. They got there a couple of hours early. As they stopped a few houses down from Tannion's apartment they could see the detectives sitting across the street in a dark sedan that almost screamed cop. Of course Rallin and Pansloski were sitting in much the same type of vehicle, just a few more doors down.

"I doubt that Tannion would remember what I look like from that one short visit almost two years ago," said Rallin to Pansloski. "There's no sense taking any chances. I also don't think these guys are going to see Tannion today, and if they do it will be after he sees them."

"I think you're right. Now that we know what this place looks like, let's go."

Rallin and Pansloski wanted to take a look at the layout around Tannion's apartment and see what New York's finest called a stakeout, but their target for the day was a woman named Dorothy Perkins. Information gathered indicated that she had befriended Tannion at the hospital he had worked at for several months.

When the FBI arrived at the hospital they walked to the front desk and asked for security. They didn't bother to show any identification at the desk as they knew it wouldn't be necessary. Anyone who wanted to talk to security was always shown where to go. No one asked to go to security who wasn't important in some way, especially if they came in pairs and were wearing suits — looking like cops.

A quick visit to check in at security and they were shown to a room on the third floor. Perkins was on duty. Detective Martin had made the call earlier making sure Perkins would be on shift. Although they knew they were going to have to talk to her, they were both a little unsure what they were going to ask. In most cases the questions were easy, but in this one there was so little to go on, the questions were tougher. Also, they didn't want Perkins to immediately warn Tannion if she was in contact, therefore they had to be careful.

Perkins was called over the internal com system and asked to report to the room where both Pansloski and Rallin waited with one of the security staff.

As soon as she arrived, the guard informed her what the meeting was for and that the two gentlemen were from the FBI and only wanted to ask a few questions. He didn't elaborate as he didn't know any more than that. As soon as he finished, he left.

"Mrs. Perkins, my name is Agent Rallin and this is Agent Pansloski of the FBI. We would like a minute of your time, and your supervisor told us to use his office." The agents asked her to sit down in one of the chairs in front of the desk. The look on her face was one of worry mixed with surprise.

"Mrs. Perkins, we understand that a friend of yours worked at this hospital up until a couple of weeks ago," Rallin said. "I am speaking of a Mr. Jim Tannion. Is that correct?"

Perkins gave them both a puzzled look. "Yes, but what's this about?"

"We believe that Mr. Tannion may have been a witness to a crime and we need to get in touch with him. He hasn't been at his apartment for a few days and his landlady is starting to get worried."

Rallin thought if he was going to have to lie, he should at least have some of the story accurate. If Perkins decided to go and see Tannion at his apartment, the landlady would confirm that he had been missing for a while, and in fact she was probably worried about him. Probably more as it was closing in on the end of the month and she would be worried about next month's rent.

"Jim's been gone for a couple weeks and I haven't seen him since he left."

"Do you have any idea where he might be? Do you know any friends of his or places he likes to visit?"

"I don't know any of his friends. He never mentioned any and he never mentioned anyplace but his apartment."

Rallin and Pansloski asked a few more questions probing Perkins's knowledge, but in the end she knew almost nothing about Tannion's personal life. Rallin gave her a card and asked her to call them if Tannion contacted her.

Rallin made a call to the office in Wichita. There was nothing here, but maybe someone in Wichita had heard something. Rallin had asked someone to talk to Tannion's mother, relatives, and friends to see if anything would shake loose.

"Do you think that was wise?" asked Pansloski. "If he's our guy, we may be hanging out a red flag for him and he may just disappear."

"He may have already disappeared and nothing is adding up with this guy the same way nothing added up in any of the cases back home or apparently here in New York. This guy is sounding more and more like our guy."

"We still have a trace on his bank and credit cards and his account hasn't been touched for a while. He still has a good sized balance so I don't think he's run yet, but I think I have to agree. This guy is sounding pretty strange. He's lived in New York for well over a year and other than Dorothy Perkins, he doesn't appear to have any real friends at all. That just doesn't sound right." Pansloski may have hit the nail on the head.

Rallin finished with, "Unless something breaks soon, this may be a long haul, but it seems to be the only game in town, so we wait."

39

Jim Tannion was standing on the street corner outside a rather shabby looking hotel feeling pretty good about his day's work. In the past few days the virus had been set loose in many parts of town and with all sorts of rough looking characters, hookers, especially those with diseases, and anyone who looked like they needed to feel a little worse than they did.

Tannion hadn't slept for over four days, but by looking at him no one could tell except it looked like he may have slept in his clothes. Unlike the rest of the world, Tannion didn't need a lot of sleep. For the last three days Tannion had walked the streets and done his duty, and now it was time to go home. Sleep wasn't the first thing on the list, a shower was first, but a good night's sleep was going to feel good.

The bus trip was quick and after a couple blocks walk he was in front of his apartment building. It was after ten and the stars were out as he went in through the back door and up the stairs to his place. He didn't notice the two men parked in the back lane who saw his light go on.

"Bill, it's Mike. We've got him. I just got a call from Martin and they believe Tannion got home about half an hour ago. The stakeout team wasn't sure when he went by them in the dark, but when the light came on in his room they called it in."

"Okay. Now we go to the next phase."

"Right. Let's get down there."

Rallin and Pansloski took a few minutes to reach their car and get to the spot where they met with Martin. A few minutes later and they both would have been in bed, but as it was they were dressed and on their way in minutes.

"Is he still there?" Rallin asked.

"Yeah. Looks like he may be in for the night. Now what's the plan?" Martin asked.

Rallin answered, "Nobody goes near him. We need to follow him from a distance. As long as we don't lose him it doesn't matter how far back we are, but we need to keep an eye on him. We don't even have enough on him to get a search warrant let alone an arrest warrant. We need to see him in action and I think it has to be something substantial. At this point we have nothing but theories and ideas. Bill and I will take it tonight, Jeff. You might as well go home and get some sleep."

It was a long night and they took turns sleeping. "Jesus Christ," muttered Pansloski. "I'm way too old for this shit anymore." The morning sun broke out above the buildings and still nothing. Tannion had probably got a lot better night's sleep than they had. It wouldn't have taken much.

Tannion woke up just after eight and took his time getting out of bed and having a shower. He didn't notice the men looking his way when he looked out the window.

Tannion didn't move at all that day and into the night, and it was starting to look like it would be another long night when the light was suddenly gone from the window. It was too early for him to be going to bed.

"Okay," said Rallin. "I think this is it."

Tannion walked out the front door and headed down the street away from where Pansloski and Rallin were. Tannion would probably take the bus to wherever he was going and the bus stop was in the direction he was headed. Rallin had moved to a spot where they could see the front as soon as his light went out.

"Looks like his landlady was right," said Pansloski. "It looks like he's heading for the bus stop. She told us he takes the bus all the time and doesn't own a car. This may not be as bad as it could have been. It also looks like she did as we told her and didn't talk to him."

Tannion walked to the bus stop at the end of the block and sat on the seat to wait for the bus. He obviously knew the schedule as the bus was there only a couple of minutes after he sat down. The bus pulled away and Rallin and Pansloski followed a few cars behind.

If this guy was going to do anything, the hope was that he would do it quickly and that it would be something that wasn't very messy. It was never easy to write in the report that you watched your mark kill someone and you couldn't stop it.

Tannion rode the bus for over twenty minutes. When he got off he walked into an area that was not well lit or well populated. After following for several blocks, it was evident that this guy wasn't afraid to be anywhere after dark. These were places Rallin didn't think he would go without his gun.

Tannion met an older looking guy on the street and it appeared that he was probably a homeless bum. Tannion reached into his pocket and handed the guy something and then shook his hand.

"Well," said Pansloski. "The guy looks to be at least nice to the bums of the world."

Tannion walked into a bar. The poorly lit red and green neon sign over the door announced 'The Waffle'. Not what you would call a typical bar name, but in this neighborhood who knows what would be typical.

Pansloski looked at Rallin. "The guy may still recall your face, but he's never seen me. Do you want me to tail him inside?"

"No, Bill. I think we should stay together on this one. You don't know if he's meeting with a bunch of hard case friends in there, and we didn't dress for this part. You would stick out like a sore thumb."

Both Rallin and Pansloski looked like feds. They talked like feds. They walked like feds and they probably smelled like feds and they both knew it. Working undercover was not their game. Following leads, busting down doors occasionally, and bringing guys in for questioning. That was their thing. They were going to have to wait. If anything happened in the bar, they would not know anything about it until he left.

Tannion stayed in the bar for over an hour, and when he walked out he was alone. He started down the same street on foot until he came to the small park at the end. He found the nearest bench and sat down. It looked like he was waiting for someone, but whom?

A few minutes later a figure emerged from the other side of the park and walked over and sat down beside Tannion. They sat and talked for a couple of minutes before Tannion stood up. They shook hands and went in separate directions. A little over an hour later Tannion was home, obviously going to bed.

"What the hell was that all about?" was all that Pansloski could say on the way back to the apartment. "He didn't do anything."

When it looked like Tannion had settled down for the night, Rallin called in the relief team from the NYPD and he and Pansloski headed back to their hotel for some much needed rest. This was not going to be easy.

40

Tannion was feeling pretty good about the day's work. He had managed to meet and greet at least a dozen characters within a two-hour period. The guy at the park was the best though. A couple of pointed questions to some of the scum who he had already treated while in the bar, and he was told that if he went out and sat on the bench down by the park, a guy would come over and offer him sex for a few bucks or they could party all night.

"What kind of guy will come over to a bench and offer some stranger a blow job?" Tannion thought. Either he would be gay or just a guy hard up for money.

Tannion didn't really care. He thought getting rid of a few gay hookers was as good as rapists and thieves. Especially ones who thought that he was a mark. He had gone to the bench seat and then all he had to do was wait.

It only took a couple minutes and a dark figure emerged from the other side of the park and headed directly towards his bench. At first he didn't say a word, but just sat down beside Tannion. "I understand there may be something I can do for you," he finally said. Tannion looked him over and thought that the gay part had to be more accurate than just hard up for cash. "This guy probably enjoys what he does."

"What makes you think that?"

"My bench, you know. My place of business, and at this time of night that's all it's ever used for. Fifty bucks over behind some trees or for a couple hundred we can take it to a place I have. Five hundred for the night."

"Christ this guy is expensive for this area," Tannion thought, and he told the hooker exactly that. "A little steep for my blood."

"Name your price then."

"No. I think I am going to pass, but best of luck," Tannion said. Tannion stood up and stuck out his hand, and as expected, the guy took it and Tannion released the virus.

Tannion decided it was enough for the night and this time instead of continuing for a few days he decided it best to go home and recharge. There would be lots of time for more of the same the next day and for many days after that.

About an hour later he was home getting ready for a good night's sleep.

41

Nothing exciting happened over the next few days. Every night Tannion would go out to some seedy part of town and sit in a bar for an hour or so. After the second night Rallin had set up one of the New York agents with an undercover assignment to go into the bar after Tannion and keep an eye on him.

He managed to watch each of the next five nights and the report was always the same. Tannion would go up to the bar and order a drink. He would sip his drink very slowly and after a while he was often approached by a hooker, who he talked to, and then she left without him. He would put his arm around her or shake her hand, but that was as far as it appeared that Tannion was willing to go.

Pansloski figured the guy was either gay or just afraid that the diseases were not worth the risk. In the end Tannion would talk to a few guys around the bar, shake hands with a few, and then he would leave and go home. For five days in a row that was all that happened.

"If something doesn't happen in the next few days, we may have to call this lead a real bust," Rallin told Pansloski. "If Tannion is our guy, we should have seen something by now. It's been a week almost and we have nothing. We might have to admit that he may not be our guy."

"Did you see the headline this morning, Mike?" asked Pansloski trying to waste time. A stakeout was almost always boring, but this one was worse than most, and Pansloski was feeling the boredom.

"Which one, Bill?"

"The one about the mysterious deaths. It says here that there have been almost a dozen so far in the city. The first was a hooker and then her pimp and a couple of his boys — they all died on the same day. The next day there were a few more and they all came out of an area in the east end. As a matter a fact they must have been close to the place we were at last week. One of them was a bartender."

"What did they die from?" asked Rallin as he came over and took the front page from Pansloski's hands. Rallin read a few lines and then read out loud. "The medical examiner is looking into the cases and insists there is nothing to worry about. It may only be a bad case of food poisoning."

"Says here there are thirteen confirmed cases and at least that many in the hospital with similar symptoms. How the hell does this shit get into the paper? Can't these guys down there keep a lid on anything? This shit could cause a panic and it makes the front page. This wouldn't have happened back home."

"I agree," said Pansloski. "Our guys would have kept this quiet until they knew what it was. This is the kind of thing they have teams set up for. Let's head down to the bureau and see what they know. Our case is getting colder right now and the other guys have got their eyes on him for a while."

"Sure, Bill. Why not?" It sounds almost like how this case started back home. We should at least make sure they aren't connected."

A quick drive from the hotel sat them down at the New York office. Rallin and Pansloski had been given a small office off to the side with a computer link, a phone, and enough supplies to make it look like a real office. The office wasn't what they wanted today.

One of the people they had gotten to know well in the last few days was working at his desk when they walked in, and in a matter of a few minutes they had enough information out of him to think the worst. Of the dead, all of them had been in and around the same part of town where they had followed Tannion the first time he went out. They were all known to spend a fair bit of time in the bar that Tannion had gone into, and one was a well-known male prostitute.

"If Tannion doesn't have something to do with this, I'll eat shit," said Pansloski.

"Shit or no shit," said Rallin, "there's too much of a coincidence here to not come to that conclusion, but like all the other stuff going on, we can't prove a thing. On top of that, how the hell could Tannion have anything to do with something like this? As usual things just don't add up."

Rallin gave Martin a call to see if he had come to the same conclusion. He had, so they decided to get together at Martin's office in the afternoon to plot their next move.

After several hours of sitting on uncomfortable chairs in Martin's office, they didn't think they were any closer to Tannion than they had been when they first started. After some discussion they couldn't come up with a better plan than to watch him and see if he would do anything that would make the connection.

The next few days went pretty much the same as the first. Tannion would go out and come back without doing anything that would be considered suspicious. Rallin had a couple of undercover agents in the bar at all times and started keeping very detailed accounts of what he did. During the week, more deaths had shown up with the same virulent symptoms as the first few, and they all were connected to parts of town that Tannion frequented.

After the second week things had changed. More people were dying and it was becoming more evident that they were people who Tannion may have come into contact with. When Tannion left a bar on Fifth Street, the NYPD moved in and interviewed everyone in the bar. Martin and Rallin thought it was a necessary precaution and they also knew that Tannion had not been in the same bar twice in the two weeks they had been following him.

Names were taken of anyone who had come into contact with Tannion. All of them were told what the symptoms may be and to make sure they contacted the health department as soon as they felt anything. The health boys finally had the press under control and the papers were no longer carrying any doom and gloom scenarios of everyone dying.

It looked like only a certain element of society was dying and the rest of the population wasn't affected. They still hadn't been able to come up with the culprit. The symptoms all looked viral, but they couldn't find the bug.

Two days later the first patients from the bar on Fifth Street came to the nearest hospital not feeling well. A check of the list indicated they had all come into contact with Tannion, but only for a second. A couple had shaken his hand or touched him, but none of them could remember drinking from his glass or whether Tannion had sneezed or coughed, but it was starting to look like Tannion was the host.

Five days later, and more people were dead with more on their death beds. All of them had been in one of the bars when Tannion had been there. The health department hadn't found out why, but they wanted to bring Tannion in for questioning. The NYPD brass and the FBI chiefs were of the same opinion and couldn't wait any longer.

It was time for Tannion to see the inside of the FBI building. The FBI had escalated a little case from Kansas into a major case with Rallin and Pansloski at its head. As more people died, this thing got bigger every day. Problem was they didn't know whether there had been any crimes committed that the FBI should be concerned with or if it was strictly a health problem.

Mike Rallin didn't care. It was time to bring Tannion in.

42

Tannion was getting used to the routine and it was still as much fun each day as it was the first day. Walk into a bar and look around. Talk up a few people and find out what he could, and once a decision was made, release the virus. In some bars it was as many as a half dozen or more, and there was the one bar where he didn't touch anyone. It didn't take much to make the decision he needed, he knew all the marks were bad and the world would be better off without them.

Each night Tannion would get back to his place and look at himself in the mirror and know it had been a good night. He would fall asleep without a care in the world. He still had lots of cash so a job wasn't a worry and he was still enjoying himself, so there was no need to move on or to get a job. Life was good.

It was Friday night and the bar was pretty full. The crowd was lively and there were quite a few from a bike gang — they looked very promising. They were good and loud, but weren't causing any real trouble. Several of them were wrist wrestling each other and anyone else who would be willing. Tannion saw his chance.

"I've never seen a good bike gang," Tannion thought. "Maybe I can get the lot of them. They're probably a big

186

part of the hooker and drug movement in the area, and this might be a lucky night for the neighborhood."

A table near the gang came free and Tannion sat down. As soon as he sat down, one of the gang members looked him up and down and then came over and sat down in the other chair at the table.

"Hey, you look like a tough enough character," he said. "Do you think you can take the winner of the next round?" He then introduced himself to Tannion as Spider.

Tannion knew that even though he couldn't see it, there was a pecking order to the match ups and the betting was done on the side. It was time to get started.

"How about I start slow and work my way up. I haven't done this in a long time."

"Sure," Spider said. "We've got all sorts here. You can start with anyone as long as we get a chance to make some money off one of you."

The next thing Tannion knew he was sitting across from a guy with long greasy hair and a few tattoos on each arm. His hand was in the air, waiting. Tannion sat down and extended his arm and got a good grip. Tannion could hear the betting going on behind him and it sounded like the odds were on him at two to one. The guy sitting across from Tannion wasn't as big as he was, but you never know. Based on the betting it didn't sound like he was going to be very tough to beat.

The last thing they told Tannion was that the winner got a share of the winnings. As they touched, Tannion released the virus and then took it easy on him and beat him in about three seconds. The noise behind Tannion told him that it went as expected, and Spider slapped him on the back and pressed ten bucks into his hand.

"Get ready for the next guy," Spider said. "He'll be a fair bit better."

The next guy was a little bigger and a little stronger. He took a few seconds to ensure that he had the grip he wanted. When they were settled in, the judge said go, and once again it took Tannion three seconds to beat him. Tannion thought it would be best to beat them relatively easily, but not too easily.

Over the next hour there were several more matches, and that included five more with Tannion. He managed to win all of them. It became apparent that Tannion fit into exactly what they wanted, a non-biker to take on the bikers. Anything to make the betting larger. He was pretty sure that a couple of the guys had let him win, even if they hadn't stood a chance.

Big money was starting to change hands and Tannion could see that he was becoming popular and the betting on him was getting bigger. Tannion knew it was only a matter of time before they brought in the heavy artillery. There was bound to be the guy in this bunch who nobody had ever beat and was the guy who was supposed to beat Tannion and take a lot of the money out of the sucker's pockets.

At this point, Tannion didn't care. He had checked the virus into everyone he fought plus Spider and a couple gang members he managed to touch in one way or another. He also knew that he could beat the big guy when they brought him in. Bring this big asshole on.

Tannion had one more preliminary match before he was up against the big guy. He won it in the usual few seconds and this guy was pretty big. He must have been well over six feet and close to three hundred pounds. Tannion was sure he was one of the guys who appeared to let him win. The gang wanted to set everyone in the bar up. If Tannion could beat him, he could beat anyone, or at least that appeared to be what they wanted the rest of the crowd to think, and there was getting to be a pretty big crowd. People were still coming in as if they were advertising outside.

Finally they brought out the big guy. This guy wasn't very tall at probably a couple inches under six feet, but he must have been well over three hundred pounds. It wasn't just his physical size, but the size of his arms. His forearms were bigger than most people's legs, and he must have had biceps close to thirty inches. This guy was huge.

Time was given for a lot of betting and Tannion was given odds at two to one against, which made the betting on him even higher. Tannion knew if he won, the gang was going to be out a lot of money. The gang figured they couldn't be beat, but they didn't know Tannion. They were beat even before the big guy sat down.

They jostled for a few seconds with Tannion doing more of the jostling, making it look like he was making sure that he had a good hold and maybe that he was getting worried. More betting was going on and would until the judge said go. The longer Tannion fooled around getting a hold, the longer the betting went on. He was having fun with the idea that the gang members were going to lose their respective shirts.

When they finally were in position, the judge said go. Tannion decided not to use the same technique as before but to make it look like this guy had a chance. When the big guy put the first pressure on Tannion's forearm, he could tell that the guy was immensely strong, but not near strong enough. Tannion let him start to bring his arm down as if a win was coming, and then stopped him and slowly worked his way back.

They hung there in the middle for a few seconds and then Tannion slowly started him down. Finally Tannion had had enough and the big guy went down. Tannion made the final push hard enough to roll him over. As he fell to the floor the voices behind got louder. The winners were cheering very loudly, but the gang was swearing and pushing.

Tannion felt an arm go around his neck and it tried to lift him off the chair in a choke hold. He had no idea what this guy was thinking. He had just beaten their strongest guy and here he was attacking him. Tannion took hold of the arm and swung his attacker around to stand in front of him, and then he knew it was Spider.

"What the hell is this Spider?" Tannion yelled.

"Goddamn asshole, you think that was funny. No way are you getting away with this."

Somehow they thought Tannion was into the ruse and they had expected him to roll over and let them win. "Well screw them." Tannion thought. He had pretty much done that to them all. The virus was well on its way. He might have missed a few, but he had hit the majority, and he made sure that he had hit the worst of the bunch. If Spider wanted even more, well that would just be a little icing on the cake. Losing money was the least of their worries.

They, however, didn't seem to get the joke. It wasn't in Tannion's plan to have to fight his way out of the bar, but if that was what they wanted, he was very happy to oblige them. Tannion picked Spider up with his left hand and gave him a slap with his right. That was enough for Spider, but Tannion knew he wasn't alone.

Three guys came at Tannion at once from the front and they were on their asses almost immediately. Tannion reached down and grabbed one of them and hit him hard enough to do some severe damage. Quite possibly, he was dead where he fell. He hadn't meant to hurt anyone too badly, but it wasn't always possible to know how much someone's body could take.

The first two bikers had come off the ground and they were joined by a couple more who had managed to push their way through the crowd. Tannion stood there waiting for the first one to make a move, but they didn't get the chance.

There was the sound of a gun being shot off very close and then a voice called his name.

43

Mike Rallin and Bill Pansloski sat outside the bar on Thirty First Street. The van they sat in was well equipped for sound, but they wished it gave them more of an idea what was happening inside.

"Shit, I wish we had a camera in there." Pansloski finally said. "This is killing me. When are they supposed to call us in and get that guy?"

They all knew when they were supposed to go in, and Pansloski certainly knew as well. The decision was to wait until the night was obviously over, follow Tannion home, and take him outside his place. The only way they were going to go inside was if the undercover cop gave the signal.

The code signal was when he said, "Here we go again." This had been the third week of following this guy with undercover cops inside and the code had never been used. The chances of it happening now were pretty slim. The only thing that kept the possibility alive in this case was the noise coming from the speakers in the van. This was the noisiest bar that Tannion had ever been in. There was also the fact that this time Tannion was going to be picked up, but just not here.

Most of the bars were pretty quiet with some music in the back either from a jukebox or on occasion some guy playing a guitar. In this case there wasn't any music, but the crowd was loud. There were cheers and shouts and groans that made it sound like they were watching a football game. It was driving Pansloski nuts.

It was just after midnight when the noise from the bar was especially loud and then the code words came clearly over the line.

"Here we go again. Get the fuck in here before they kill this guy," the voice inside the bar said.

It was a mad scramble as the three cops in the van fought their way out while trying to pull their guns without shooting each other. It took only a few seconds to reach the front door, but by the time they opened the door, it looked like a gang fight was going on.

"Where is he?" yelled Pansloski over the noise.

Rallin could see Tannion over the top of the crowd. He was standing over a couple guys and everyone else was standing back giving him room. "Bill. Over there. The big guy over there."

Rallin moved forward to get close enough to yell at Tannion, and in the few steps it looked like Tannion was getting ready to move away, but he was surrounded by bikers. As Rallin took a couple steps closer, someone shot into the air. Rallin thought it must have been one of the gang members and it might have been directed at Tannion. He quickly moved a little closer and hollered at Tannion. "Tannion. Jim Tannion, stay where you are. FBI."

Rallin saw Tannion look up and there was a momentary look of indecision on his face, and then they locked eyes from a few feet away and Tannion made his decision. As quick as a big cat, Tannion turned away from Rallin and headed to the back door. At first there were a couple of people in his way, but he pushed them aside with ease and then there was an empty space with only one person between him and the back door to the kitchen. The problem was that the one person was agent Jason Leed the undercover FBI agent who was stationed at the back of the room.

Leed had already drawn his weapon before Rallin had said anything and before Tannion had made his move in his direction. The gun came up and he was ready to shoot as Tannion moved down on him.

"No," shouted Rallin and Pansloski at almost the same time, but the noise in the room drowned out most of the sound and it wouldn't have mattered anyway. Leed hollered something at Tannion which everyone took to be stop, FBI, or something along that line, but no one could say for sure.

Tannion was heading straight for Leed and Leed had to fire. It was obvious that Tannion had no intention of stopping. Two shots rang out and from behind, Rallin could see that both were direct hits. Tannion was thrown off stride and blood sprayed several feet in all directions. His forward momentum was only altered slightly and within a half second he had regained the step he lost. He hit Leed with a straight arm that threw him back against the wall hard enough to break his neck in several places. Tannion was out the door leaving Leed in a crumpled heap against the wall as dead as you could ask for.

Tannion had hit the door to the kitchen hard. It swung back hitting the back wall with an audible crack, and then it was swinging back to block anyone following. No one was close enough for it to hit them though, as Tannion was much too fast for that. Within seconds Rallin and Pansloski were at the door.

"Bill, check on Leed. Sharp and I will pick him up. He can't get far with two bullets in him," Rallin yelled to Pansloski. Rallin rushed through the door, looked in both directions and saw a drop of blood to his right. He moved in that direction with Detective Sharp on his tail. A few more strides and they were at the back door, which was hanging half off the hinges. Tannion had hit that door even harder than the first.

Outside, Rallin looked around, but there was no sign of Tannion. A check of the ground didn't show any blood to give them direction, and although he could see a few yards in all directions, there was no sign of Tannion. The night had swallowed him up.

"Shit. Where the hell did he go? He didn't have time to get far, and we know he doesn't own a car so he has to be on foot." Rallin gave instructions to Sharp to put out a bulletin on Tannion and to have all the hospitals put on alert for Tannion coming in with a gunshot wound. By this time Pansloski had caught up.

"How's Leed?" asked Rallin.

"Dead."

"Shit," Rallin said and then he knew he had to catch Tannion. "He can't have gone far. You go down the back alley and I'll follow the street. Sharp is calling in all cars in the area and we should have a good sweep going soon. He's probably lying in an alley bleeding to death, so let's find him."

A little more than an hour later, Rallin called the search team back. Tannion was not in the area, unless he was hiding.

"Okay, let's keep a few cars in the area and we'll continue in the daylight. If he managed to elude us then he'll need medical attention real soon and the hospitals and clinics are on alert. He'll probably show up in a corner we can't see in the dark. I saw where Leed hit him and this thing is over. It has to be," Rallin said.

The next morning failed to turn up anything. The New York Police assisted in a house-to-house search, and not only was Tannion not found, there wasn't a drop of blood anywhere. The coroner had completed his work in the bar and it was time to talk to him. He had only his preliminary assessment and he gave that to Rallin.

"The first guy with all the tattoos was killed by a blow to the head that caved in the orbital bone above the eye, and one of the bones split and penetrated the brain causing death. Agent Leed died of broken vertebrae in his neck. Death was probably instant," said the coroner.

"Agent Sharp was sitting on the other side of the room when the fight started and he saw Tannion hit the first guy and throw the next two to the ground, and then he seemed to simply stand there and wait for the rest of them to try something. There were several bikers coming at him when the shot was fired," Rallin said.

"Neither of the deceased was shot," the coroner said.

"I saw Agent Leed get off two shots. Both of them hit home and both were body shots. You're telling me that Tannion killed both of these guys with his bare hands and then takes two body shots with a thirty-eight and waltzes out and disappears without a trace. Tell me how that's possible?"

The coroner didn't have a lot to say after that. Both his charges had been wrapped and tagged and they weren't going to tell him anything else there. Now it was time for forensics. The report was a good place to start. There were two shell casings found from Leed's gun, and the only blood sprayed was AB positive, which had to be Tannion's, but other than that, there wasn't a lot of data. A second gun was found, which had fired the first shot, but it belonged to one of the gang members.

Tannion had to be somewhere — but where. Rallin knew he wasn't mistaken about having seen Tannion get hit with both shots, and the blood was real. He was not a ghost who could just disappear. He had to be somewhere.

44

It seemed as if the entire bar was fighting when Tannion heard the gunshot. Immediately afterward he heard his name hollered from a few feet away. He looked in the direction the voice came from and locked eyes with someone who looked familiar, but he couldn't tell from where. Then his name was called again and Tannion heard the words FBI, and the memory came flashing back. He almost hesitated too long, but he knew he had to get out of there. This was trouble. The guy on the floor might be dead for all he knew and it was time to leave.

Two steps and Tannion was heading for the back with only one guy in front of him. Tannion heard him yell something and then he felt the shot before he heard it or saw it. The shot hit Tannion high in the chest and knocked him a little off stride, but his momentum kept him going forward straight at the gunman.

Tannion had never felt such pain. A searing burning pain that went right through him. He was able to shut the pain off a half second after it hit, but for that half second he couldn't see anything, hear anything, or feel anything but the pain, but it was over as fast as it came.

The second shot was lower and hit beneath his ribs, but this time he was ready for it and there was no pain. Tannion could have been hit by a truck and he wouldn't have felt a thing. The second shot didn't kick him back at all, and a second later Tannion was on him. The gunman put up his arms to protect himself, but Tannion's fist went through his guard and hit him squarely in the face. The way his head snapped back, Tannion knew he was dead.

Tannion raced through the kitchen and out the back door. He knew he would be chased and possibly by some pretty fast characters. Tannion saw the nearest fence about twenty yards ahead. He hit his stride and flew over it as if a six foot fence was of the little white picket variety. Once on the other side he was out of sight, but he was not going to stop until he was a long ways away. Tannion headed for Central Park a few miles away.

The side streets were pretty deserted and he fairly flew down back alleys and sidewalks. Only a couple of times he skirted away from people so as not to be seen. Tannion was running faster than most cars went on these roads and he didn't want to attract the sort of attention a man running at forty miles an hour might attract at one in the morning in New York.

It took just over fifteen minutes to travel the five miles or so to Central Park, and once there he found what he was looking for. Deep inside the park there were places that were very dark and well hidden at night, and he found one fairly quickly. He needed to take stock.

Tannion stopped beside a thick tangle of willows and sat down. He had stopped the blood flow almost as soon as he stopped the pain so he knew he had only lost a little blood, but there was a lot of damage. The first bullet had gone in at a bit of an angle, hitting just below his heart where the rib bones had been enhanced. The bullet glanced off the bones and ripped out his left side. The bullet must have split as there was more of a large gash rather than a hole where the bullet exited.

The second bullet had hit low on the right side and had gone through. The exit route had led it through his kidney, just missing other organs. A quick repair job and a few minutes later everything was in ship shape. So here he was with a shirt covered in blood and not a mark on him. The blood had sprayed him up and down — he was a mess.

Tannion looked at his shirt and knew that it was a dead giveaway. How could a guy show up with no obvious injury, but have on a blood-soaked shirt that had two entry holes, one nice round exit hole, and a ragged tear where the split bullet had gone through it. He took the shirt off and dumped it deep into a very full garbage can on the way out of the park. They shouldn't be looking this far from the bar for things in dumpsters, and he was probably better off without a shirt than with a blood stained one. He used the shirt to wipe as much blood off him as he could before he dumped it. It was a cold night, but he didn't feel any of it.

Tannion knew that this was it. Deep shit. Not only had he possibly killed both the bikers, but he was sure that he had killed the guy at the back door. There was no way that guy could live with the shot he gave him. Not only did he hit him with everything he had, but he was moving towards him to add momentum to the punch. No, that guy was dead, but who the hell was he and why was he there with a gun and shooting at him.

And then there was the FBI agent. Tannion recognized him after he yelled FBI and he recognized him from home. Maybe he transferred to New York, but what are the odds that he would be in the same bar as Tannion.

The only answer was that they were looking for him or possibly following him. The guy with the gun was very likely an undercover cop. Yes, the shit had hit the fan. If they didn't have anything on him before, they sure as hell did now. At best it would be manslaughter, and then what? He was probably a cop killer. If they got a chance to x-ray him or test him, they might find out things that he couldn't afford for them to know.

Tannion knew he had to find his way out of town. If they had gone this far they could go further. They could have his apartment watched. They could freeze his bank account. His phone could be tapped. Tannion's mind was going a mile a minute. He knew he had to go home and take a chance on being caught. He only hoped that if the apartment was being watched, that he could sneak in or rely on his strength to get out if he was found.

Tannion was sure the cops would spend a great deal of time looking for him in the area around the bar. They had seen him get shot and would think he was seriously hurt and would be hiding close by. That was probably his ace in the hole. With them thinking they knew where he was, they might not think that he could make it home, so maybe there was no one watching his apartment.

It took a few more minutes to make his way home. He had come to Central Park to get his bearings and think, but it was also on the way back to his apartment. Tannion looked up and down all streets and back alleys to see if his apartment was being watched. His night vision gave him a real edge as he could see people long before they could see him.

The way looked clear and it took only a few seconds to make his way inside and lock the door. A light was out of the question, but once again his night vision kicked in. Sure as hell glad he worked on that part. All it took was a few minutes to take a shower, pack his suitcases and get his coat and get the hell out of there. He only had the two suitcases and they were going to have to do.

Tannion had to get out of town, and his first thought was to go as far away as he could. It was time to see California. He had always wanted to go west and this was his opportunity. There was one problem. All his money was in the bank. If they had thought to freeze his account he was in deep shit.

Tannion thought that he still had a little time as they would think he hadn't gotten very far, and this should mean that the bus depot wouldn't be watched. There was a small problem, however. He had to wait until the bank opened.

Tannion took his time walking to the bus depot, trying to look like just another guy with suitcases. By the time he got there it was after six in the morning. He carefully looked around, and seeing nothing out of the ordinary, he found a place to store his suitcases and went to find the nearest bank where he could close his account.

The closest branch of his bank was a few blocks away, so he sat in a nearby café and waited. At exactly nine the bank opened and Tannion was the first customer of the day. He tried his best to not be seen by cameras, but he knew it really didn't matter. Once they checked his bank transactions they would know that he had been there. They could probably put two and two together and see that he had been at a bank near the bus depot and know that he was gone.

Tannion walked up to the teller and smiled. "Good morning," he said to the pretty young teller. She had short blond hair made up in a stylish spike look and a very nice smile.

"Good morning. What can I do for you this morning?"

"I'm going out of town for a few weeks and need to make a sizeable withdrawal." Tannion told her. He still had over forty thousand dollars left in his account and he was going to take almost all of it. He thought that closing the account would take too long and may be even more suspicious than a forty thousand dollar withdrawal.

"Okay," she said. "May I see your card?"

Tannion gave her his bank card and held his breath. "Okay," she said again, "how much would you like to take out."

"How much is there?"

She pushed the screen around so Tannion could see that there was forty one thousand three hundred and fifty dollars and change. "I think I am going to need forty thousand," Tannion told her hoping that she wouldn't be shocked.

She didn't bat an eye, but told him that it was over her limit and she would have to get her supervisor. Her supervisor came over and asked Tannion for an additional picture ID, which he showed to her, and the next thing he knew he was walking out of the bank with forty thousand dollars in hundred dollar bills.

"That should keep me going for a while," Tannion thought. "And they can keep the rest." At least this way the bank thinks that he would be back and no undue notice should be taken. Tannion only withdrew money that was his. As far as they were concerned it was a perfectly logical and legal transaction.

"Dodged a big bullet there," He thought as he walked back to the bus depot. He still had to get on a bus though. Tannion walked into the bus depot thinking he was still probably okay, but ready for the worst. If there was anyone there waiting for him, they were undercover and he sure as hell couldn't tell them from anyone else there.

Tannion checked the out-going schedule and found a bus that was leaving in a few minutes. The fact that he was heading west and the bus north wasn't going to be a problem. He needed to get out of town, and if there were any questions as to where he was going, the only thing that would be remembered would be a ticket heading north.

The ticket was cheap and he boarded the bus without incident. A couple of hours later and he was off the bus and onto another going a little farther. It might take a few days, but it looked like he might make it to California. With any luck he might have a few days head start while they continued to look for a body in back alleys and dumpsters, or at the very least, a well shot-up guy showing up at a local hospital.

Being on the run wasn't what Tannion had in mind. His mother would be frantic, but there was no choice. He would probably not even be able to contact her. The FBI had lots of eyes and ears and a long memory. The last thing he needed was to give anyone an idea of where he was or where he was going, and unfortunately that included his mother.

Tannion had some time to think on the bus and all that he could think about was how the hell had they found him? He thought the virus was perfect, but somehow it had been his downfall. It had to be. The cops must have somehow realized that he was a common denominator and followed him. That had to be the answer. There was no way that the FBI agent from back home would have transferred to New York and then just happened to be waiting for him in a bar with backup unless they were after him.

It had to be the virus. After they thought he was a suspect they called in the FBI and thought a cop who knew him a little would be good to have on the case. Anyway, that was all in the past now, but he sure as hell wouldn't be using the virus again.

45

The call came over the radio about a few minutes after two the next day. The search had been expanded for an additional ten blocks around the already widened search area. Door-to-door had come up with nothing. There wasn't the expected body in an alley or a good blood trail leading down a darkened street. Nothing. This guy was a ghost.

The call was completely unexpected and Rallin had to question it immediately.

"What do you mean his account?" The call had come in from dispatch to his cell and it was the last thing he expected. "Tannion accessed his account, where?" he asked. "Shit that's across town. How the hell did he get there? What the hell is going on?"

Rallin called across to Pansloski. Pansloski had been working the other side of the street and was just coming out of a red brick apartment building and was looking his way.

"Bill. Come on. Get in the car. You won't believe this. Tannion took forty thousand dollars out of his account at a few minutes after nine this morning." Rallin told Pansloski what the dispatch had told him as they walked down to the car.

"Why are we hearing about this now?" asked Pansloski. "Wasn't someone supposed to be close to that end?"

"Yeah, I thought so too, but they were probably paying more attention to credit cards than the bank, and after we were on to him the main group was called off. We were probably lucky that anyone noticed anything at all."

Pansloski could only nod as he looked at the information that Rallin had jotted down. Pansloski thought for a few seconds and finally answered Rallin. "Isn't that only a few blocks from the bus station. That asshole is all shot up and he's looking for a bus out of town. Not fucking possible. I saw him get hit twice and there's no way he could make it across town let alone be looking to take a bus anywhere."

"You won't get an argument from me," Rallin replied as they both jumped into their car. It took over a half hour to get to the bank even with the lights on. As they pulled up, the discussion was still going on.

"Someone else must have been with him and saw him get hit then maybe stole his wallet and cleaned him out," Pansloski said.

"Could be. If it is, the camera will soon tell us."

Rallin had called ahead and had alerted the bank to their arrival and had asked to have that morning's video feed available. Within a few minutes of entering the bank they were in the security office in the back looking at a small screen TV.

"Holy shit, will you look at that," exclaimed Pansloski. There on the TV as big as life was Tannion. "Not only is that Tannion, but there's no sign of a gunshot wound. He isn't in any pain and he looks as healthy as a horse. The son of a bitch must have been wearing a flak jacket."

"No way," Rallin said. "Not only did I see the blood spray, but there was enough of it around the bar to know he was hit and hit hard. This has to be someone who looks like him."

The teller who had served Tannion was still working so they called her into the office. She walked in and explained that she remembered the guy as he was her first customer of the day and the fact that she had to get her supervisor to approve his withdrawal of forty thousand dollars from his account.

"We asked for two pieces of picture ID and he showed us a driver's license and some security card. It was definitely Jim Tannion," the teller said. The supervisor was called in separately and she confirmed exactly what the teller had told them.

"Shit. How's that possible?" asked Rallin. And then it hit him. "Shit, the bus terminal." Rallin was so sure that it couldn't possibly be Tannion that he had put the bus terminal out of his mind. Now it was there front and center.

Rallin and Pansloski almost ran out of the building and into their car and within a couple minutes they were at the bus terminal. A number of NYPD had been called in and had beaten them there. A quick report indicated that the exits were manned and that there was nothing yet. No sign of Tannion. Terminal security had been called and two men met Rallin and Pansloski almost as soon as they got there.

After quick introductions, Rallin filled the security officers in on the details they needed to know. "Tannion was at the bank only a half dozen blocks away at a little after nine. He may have purchased a ticket some time after that or he could have bought the ticket before the bank opened," Rallin told the security officer.

As it was only about three thirty in the afternoon, the same shift that came on at eight was still working. Rallin had a picture that the bank had printed from the video feed.

Each of the ticketing agents was approached and shown the picture. The first five said they hadn't seen the guy before, but when they got to the sixth in line, she took a quick look and said, "Sure, I saw him this morning, big guy. If I remember right I sold him a ticket and the bus left about five minutes after he bought it. That's why I remember him so well. He was cutting it pretty close and could just have easily missed his bus as caught it, and I remember that he paid in cash."

The bus had left over five hours before and it was only a two hour ride. That meant he was in Allentown, Pennsylvania, the only stop for an express bus. Or at least he was there more than a few hours ago. Now the chase was on.

It still didn't make sense that he wouldn't be badly hurt. He should have been dead or at least in a hospital, but there he was on the screen, and he was obviously running.

A quick call back to the precinct called off the search. Now the hunt was on the road.

46

The bus made its way into Allentown. As soon as Tannion got his luggage he went over to a counter and bought a map of the United States. With the FBI involved, it was very likely that every bus station would be alerted, but he thought he should still have a few hours head start. He had made up his mind to make it to Los Angeles, and although it may take a while there was no reason to take the roundabout way. He hoped the map would be good enough to keep him on course.

The next bus left almost immediately and was headed for Philadelphia. It was only a few miles south, but it's a big city. As soon as he got off the bus in Philly another bus was ready to leave and it was heading to Baltimore. At Baltimore Tannion changed plans and caught a taxi over to the airport and bought a ticket on the next available flight. It was heading for Columbus, Ohio.

He thought he should still have enough of a lead that the FBI had probably not shut off the airlines. He knew that he would need to show ID and that he would be leaving a trail a mile wide, but it was more important to get some distance even if they could trace it. If the FBI was on his tail he needed to make it as difficult as possible.

The flight took a little more than an hour. Tannion decided it was time not to press his luck any more with public transportation. There would be too many people who might have seen him. Tannion knew they could trace him at least this far, so now it was time to disappear.

Tannion caught a taxi trying not to let the driver see his face. He was dropped off at the I-70 and he immediately stuck out his thumb. Fifteen minutes later, thanks to a guy on his way to Indianapolis who wanted someone to talk to, he was on his way.

By the time he got to Indianapolis it was getting pretty late and Tannion crashed at a small motel on the outskirts of town. He slept like a log despite what was going on. His ability to knock himself out still came in handy. He paid in cash and took the time to cut up his credit cards and made sure they would never be found. He thought about getting rid of all of his identification, but couldn't go through with it. Cutting up his credit cards was tough enough.

The next morning looked like the start of a wonderful day and Tannion started out with great expectations. The motel was close to the freeway so a short walk had him sticking his thumb out looking for a ride. He found he had more time to think.

Tannion had already come to the conclusion that it must have been the virus that had been his undoing, but he had also realized that he had been in a very dark place for a long time. What had he been thinking? He had been brought up right and here he was killing people who were only doing their job. Some people even think that hookers and their pimps were doing a public service.

Tannion knew that he needed to change his thinking and his way of going about business. He still thought that what he did was justified, but only if done right. No more stupid decisions and no more viruses. Especially no more viruses.

Hitch hiking went well and a few hours later he was in St. Louis, Missouri. From St. Louis a trucker took him overnight to Oklahoma City and from there he caught a ride to Albuquerque New Mexico. It was almost easy to forget what had happened only three nights earlier and feel like he was just a guy going on a vacation.

From Albuquerque Tannion stayed on I-40 heading for Los Angeles, and then the rides became a lot sparser. It took more than two days to go the last few hundred miles, but in the end he saw the haze of the big city. Here he was in another big city which should have just as many opportunities as New York. The difference here was that the FBI was on his tail and he would have to be cautious.

Tannion checked into a rather seedy hotel on the edge of downtown in East Los Angeles. No sense going to Beverly Hills or the beach for what he had in mind. The room overlooked a dirty alley, and he wasn't sure that he would have spent a minute there if he wasn't in this situation. Tannion was well beyond the days of worrying about his health or welfare. This place would do just fine.

Tannion knew that he would have to live undercover. He paid in cash and told the old girl behind the desk that his name was Victor French. He hadn't put a lot of thought into a new identity, but when she asked him to fill out the register, he quickly picked the first name that popped into his head. The fact the last name was the same as the drunk he had the encounter with a while back was mostly accidental, but it was probably the reason the name had occurred to him.

It was already dark by the time he got to the motel, and after he had taken his luggage to the room and settled in it was time to eat and look around. The street outside that had looked a little run down when he checked in had been converted into a hooker stroll.

"Yes," Tannion thought, "this looks like my kind of place."

47

"It's been three days and not a trace." Rallin needed to talk out loud even if Pansloski was the only other person in the room and knew everything that Rallin knew. Rallin still had to say it. They were back in their office in Wichita after spending the last three days on the road.

After finding out that Tannion was the face on the video at the bank and that he had bought a bus ticket to Pennsylvania, Rallin was still having trouble believing it. A quick call to the police in Allentown and they had their people at the bus depot asking questions and showing ticket agents Tannion's picture. Meanwhile, Rallin was still skeptical.

It cost Rallin and Pansloski more than two hours, but they had to go to Tannion's apartment and have a look. The landlady let them in and told them she hadn't seen or heard Tannion come in or go out. When they entered the room it was obvious. In the bathroom sink there was a small smudge that looked like blood and there were signs of quick packing. There was nothing left to indicate that anyone was coming back. They called for a forensic team to cover the room and in particular to see if the red smudge was blood and if it was Tannion's blood.

Now Rallin was satisfied that Tannion was alive and on the run. There was no doubt and Pansloski didn't argue with him. He had to see for himself just as much as Rallin had to, but now with that behind them, it was time for a road trip. Only a few minutes out of New York they received a call. One of the ticket agents in Allenstown had recognized Tannion's picture and remembered selling him a ticket to Philadelphia.

The next several hours had Tannion leading Rallin and Pansloski on a chase across the eastern states. From Philadelphia there was another bus to Baltimore and then a flight to Columbus Ohio and there the trail seemed to have gone cold. A cabbie remembered picking Tannion up at the Baltimore bus depot and delivering him to the airport.

Tannion had used his own identification and was seen on the airport video surveillance, and the FBI in Baltimore knew exactly which ticket agent to talk to and where Tannion was headed.

"The flight landed in Columbus on schedule and the police there have no clues at this point. They've been interviewing all the cabbies and we can hope they get lucky. The dispatch knows which cabs had a fare after the plane landed and they should have the cabbies in hand very soon." Rallin told Pansloski.

It was several hours later with Rallin and Pansloski still on the road when they caught a bit of a break. The locals canvassing all the taxi drivers at the airport in Columbus got lucky when one of them remembered picking Tannion up and taking him to the outskirts of town. He especially remembered that he wanted to be dropped off on the freeway.

Rallin had been talking into his cell phone for the last few minutes and Pansloski had only heard one side of the conversation so Rallin had to fill him in. "Mike, from what I heard you say, it looks like the son of a bitch is heading home," Pansloski said.

"I think you're right. It's time for us to go home too. We can keep an eye out for him there. I don't think this guy is stupid, but you never know. We need to get in touch with his relatives and friends and get some men in there. If he calls or gets in touch with anyone in Wichita, I want to know about it."

Tannion's mother didn't take the news well at all. Tannion, in her eyes, was always a good boy who worked hard and did well at everything he did. She did admit that over the past couple of years he hadn't been himself, including quitting his job and moving to New York. He had called on a fairly regular basis at first while in New York, but he was often distant and aloof, especially when the conversation was about his work.

None of Tannion's friends had heard much of him since he left home. A couple had received phone calls, but they were almost a year earlier and they didn't have much to go on. They all said they would contact the FBI if Tannion called, but Tannion's mother was probably only paying lip service. Rallin was sure they would have to tap her phone to catch any incoming calls.

Rallin was able to get the phone tap approved very easily. Tannion had made it pretty high up on the FBI's most wanted list. If nothing else he was wanted for killing a police officer and a citizen in New York and was suspected of having killed several people both in New York and Wichita. The blood type found at the bar matched the blood type on the knife that was found on a homeless person in Wichita two years earlier. Rallin had remembered it, but when he had it checked, he found that the blood sample had been lost. There was no way to do any DNA testing. In that case it appeared the victim had died of natural causes thought to have been brought on by the exertion of struggling with someone, probably Tannion.

It had been a busy three days, and now it appeared to be a waiting game. They kept vigil for two weeks, looking for any signs of Tannion. As they worked into the third week it was looking more and more like Tannion hadn't gone home. The FBI and the police had pictures at the major places where he might enter town. The security at the airport, train station, and bus station were on alert, and the cab companies had his picture for all cabbies to see, but nothing had happened.

The more Rallin and Pansloski talked about it, the more it looked like they were waiting for a ghost. The type of ghost who could take a pair of bullets and walk away should be able to hide for a while.

At the start of the tenth week the FBI brass pulled Rallin and Pansloski off the case as another case had taken precedence. The Tannion case wasn't forgotten, but it dropped in priority. The death of the cop was given back to the NYPD, but Tannion was still an FBI fugitive. The wire taps were removed from all phones and the case was placed in the cold file. Rallin knew that it was only a matter of time until Tannion surfaced, but he was convinced that Tannion was not going home and wasn't stupid enough to do anything that would compromise his whereabouts, and he could be anywhere.

"This is bullshit," Pansloski said. "This guy will show up and we won't be ready for him. Mike, what the hell can we do?" Pansloski wasn't taking the case being cold-filed easily. It had always been Rallin who had pushed the case, but in the end Pansloski had gotten the bug. He watched Tannion hit Agent Leed, and even though he didn't know Leed very well, it had hit Pansloski hard. The last thing he wanted to do was take a break from the case at this time. In his eyes it was too soon.

"Bill, I agree with you that it's too soon, but the way it's going we could wait for a long time until we get the break this case needs. For all we know, he's living back in New York or even made his way into Canada or Mexico. He's too smart to be calling his mother now that he knows we're on to him. As much as I hate the idea of letting the case cool off, I have to agree with the captain that it's time to be patient and get on to other cases that we might have a chance of solving and wait until something happens. Tannion's face is out in too many places, so if he's still in the United States, it's only a matter of time before he makes a mistake and we catch him. It might be years, but we'll get him. Remember, there's no time limit on murder."

48

Martin was sitting at his desk at the precinct house when he got the call. Rallin had called earlier to tell him that the Tannion case was being filed for now until something came up. He said he would call back when he had more time to talk.

"Good morning, Mike. How are things in Wichita?"

"Hi, Jeff. Things are fine out here, but I can tell you I'm not happy about the Tannion case. I assume that you aren't either."

"Yeah, Mike, I've been doing some thinking since you called and told me about the case being cold filed for a while. I still can't believe it. This guy killed a cop and we're going to sit on it. That's not right."

"I know, Jeff. Not my decision and I don't like it either. The case hasn't been dropped or forgotten, but I've been told that we don't have enough people to be chasing this guy. He might be in any country in the world. He took forty thousand dollars out of the bank that morning and with that kind of money he could be anywhere. There's an active warrant out for his arrest, and if he makes one mistake we've got him."

"Okay, Mike. Do you want me to keep my files here or does the FBI want all the documentation in your files?" asked Martin

"Send me what you have and I'll put it into our files. This is not an NYPD case anymore. As soon as he crossed state lines it became an official FBI case if it wasn't already, and the files should be here. It was nice working with you, Jeff. You would make a good FBI agent if you ever decide to move on."

"Thanks Mike. I appreciate the comments, but for now there's enough crime in New York to keep me here. The only thing I ask is you keep me informed if anything does come up with Tannion. Also don't tell your bosses, but I'm not going to let it drop as easy as they are. I was able to piece this thing together before, and I'm going to keep trying."

"You do that Jeff, and give me a call when you find the son of a bitch. I want in on it as much as you do."

Martin hung up the phone feeling a little better than he had before the call. "Tannion may have gotten away for now, but he'll show up. He's still in the United States or my name isn't Jeff Martin." Martin said to himself.

The phone rang and another case appeared to be starting. Tannion will show up, but until he does, there was still work to do and Martin was off to do that job as best he knew how.

"All this work and all this paper and now it goes into a file and gets stored away until something happens," Martin said. "Not the way this was supposed to end. At least Rallin was good enough to call and tell me himself rather than me hearing it from someone in records."

Martin put the Tannion file on his desk into one large pile. He had read most of it and was starting to get a good picture of who Jim Tannion was. Everyone seemed to think very highly of Tannion. A good guy.

"Sure doesn't fit," he thought. "He just doesn't sound like the guy who would kill cops."

He took one last look at the pile of paper and then asked to have the files shipped off to the FBI. With luck he would see Tannion again. He hoped it would be soon.

49

The light that came in through the hotel window at night was usually various shades of red and green from the assortment of neon signs outside. It was never enough to read by, but it was always light enough in the room to be able to get around even if your night vision wasn't as good as Jim Tannion's.

If nothing else, it gave him plenty of light to think by. Sleep was easy once he let it happen, but as he didn't need as much as the average person, sometimes it was easier to sit and think. The topic was always the same for the first few weeks. What the hell had he done wrong and what the hell had he been thinking in New York?

The FBI was obviously on his tail or else why would that cop from Kansas be in a New York bar, and why would there be another guy with a gun waiting for him by the back door. It was an obvious set up. But how the hell did they know where he was, and why would they be following him?

There were many more questions, but few answers. How much did the FBI know? How long had they been following him? Had they bugged his apartment? What did they know and what didn't they know? Why hadn't they just arrested him?

It was finally the last question that started Tannion down the road to recovery. For weeks he had barely left the hotel room except to get food. He was extremely careful not to leave any trace anywhere and not to be seen by anyone who the FBI might have looking, but when the last question was asked he suddenly thought of the answer,

"Goddamn it. If they knew anything for real they wouldn't have been following me, they would have come up to me and arrested me, but they didn't. They obviously only suspected I was involved in the people dying. They didn't have anything solid on me at all."

"Son of a bitch," Tannion said out loud. "They sure as hell have something on me now. Shit, I know the guy by the door is dead."

Tannion knew that he had to lay low. He also knew he needed to change both his name and his identity, and he also knew that his money wouldn't last forever. He was going to have to get a job. The days on the run had gone quickly and he hadn't the time or opportunity to shave or to even keep very clean most of the time. Now he was glad that shaving hadn't been important.

A beard and longer hair could change his appearance enough to stop the casual looker from matching him to a picture the FBI might have had from the past. The one thing he didn't like, however, was not being able to contact his mother. Tannion knew that would be suicide.

As he waited in his hotel room day after day, his beard had grown quickly, but the hair was slow. After a few weeks he was feeling safe enough to go a bit farther abroad to look into other needs. First on the list was new ID. He had destroyed all his credit cards and unnecessary cards he carried, and now it was time to get rid of the rest. Driver's license, birth certificate, and social security card were all that were left.

The area for several blocks around the hotel wasn't fit for the faint of heart. It was a rough area with a mixed racial blend. There was a part that was Asian, and a black area, and a mostly blue collar low-income rental area. Together they made up a section of town that the town council liked to forget existed. For Tannion the area was ripe for all he needed.

Once Tannion made the move out of the hotel and into life on the streets, it became very apparent that the type of people he was looking for were there, but again not the big fish. He could find dealers, pimps, hookers, and tough guys, but not the real guys behind it all, but he found what he needed, people who could help him with new ID.

In a few days he had a new driver's license and birth certificate. The name he had used at the hotel was Victor French and he decided to keep it. So within a couple of weeks after coming out of hiding, Victor French came alive.

Tannion or Victor French opened a bank account and deposited some, but not all of his money into it. No way was he going to get caught the same as he had before. The money was probably safer in his pocket than in the bank and the interest rate was so low that it might just as well be under his mattress. There were times however when he would need a bank account.

Now he needed a job. His strength and youth were an advantage that the full beard and lengthening hair didn't detract from. A company a few blocks out of the area needed someone to swamp for them and haul around heavy boxes. He was given the job without any fuss. Victor French had his first job and the pay was more than enough to pay for his expenses.

Next was to get out of the hotel and find an apartment. A small apartment became available close to the hotel, and when the sign appeared in the window Tannion snapped it up. It was nothing to write home about, but it was a furnished one bedroom, one bath apartment. Not a place to bring girls home to, but he had no intention of getting to know any girls. He was back in business, but he was still on the run.

Tannion thought he knew what his mistake had been in New York and he wasn't going to make that mistake again. Tannion didn't like what he had done in New York. Somehow he had become the bad guy and that wasn't the way he thought of himself.

Tannion had a new idea. Most of the time he had been striking out against the visible few while wishing he could get at the invisible power behind the ones on the street. Maybe it was time to dig in like an undercover cop and work into a system until the big guys became apparent. Maybe it was time to sell himself as a tough guy who might do anything, and then wait. It couldn't hurt as it would also be a way of lying low.

For several months in New York he found he did his best work in the local bars. It had worked for his ID in LA, why not for something else. Tannion chose a rather large, but very seedy bar a few blocks from where his apartment was because it appeared to have the right type of characters, and enough of them. Tannion thought he would work his way into the crowd slowly meeting people, acting tough, maybe get into a few fights if need be. Any way he could to make it look like he was the kind of guy who could be recruited. The beard was a good full length and the hair was still growing.

Every night after work Tannion would take his new look to the same bar and wait. He would talk to anyone who came close. Just making small talk and trying to become known. He wanted to become a regular and see what that would do for him.

50

Tannion started to get to know a number of the regulars. The King's Head was well known in the area for being a biker bar, a rough tough bar, and he was starting to fit in. It was on a Thursday night when he was finally accepted. One of the regulars was over talking to Tannion when three tough look-ing guys came in off the street obviously looking for the guy Tannion was talking to. They marched over and in trying to get a little closer to the regular, Tannion was pushed rather unceremoniously to the side.

When the second guy pushed him, Tannion took the guy by the arm and pulled him back. It was a pretty innocent movement, but it was taken as aggression, and the focus was switched to Tannion. Tannion took a step back, and before a fight could take place, he challenged all three of them to step outside. They couldn't wait to take him up on it. The regular was forgotten for the minute.

Tannion led them out of the side door and into a small area beside the loading dock to the hotel and bar. The alley had a few cars in it, but the loading dock area was empty and large enough for a few people to file out to watch. With the onlookers was the regular Tannion had been talking to and a crowd of tough looking characters. A good fight would always draw a crowd.

Tannion had decided to draw the fight out so he wouldn't look too good. A duck here, a faint there, and maybe even take a couple shots and it would look like he was good, but not super human. The fight took almost five minutes and started with a lot of dancing around looking at each other. When the first guy jumped in the second and third came in right behind.

It looked like the three guys had never fought as a group before and Tannion was able to keep one guy in front of him blocking the other two, so he never had to fight all three at once. The first guy took a couple of punches and fell back. The second guy threw a punch at Tannion which Tannion let land and acted as if it had thrown him back

Tannion quickly gathered himself together from what looked like a hard shot to the face and hit the guy hard enough to knock him back into his buddies, and then he attacked. It looked to the onlookers as if he had seen his chance to take a couple shots when the first guy fell back into his friends, and then quickly all three of them were on the ground.

Tannion stepped back to let them get up and then did more or less the same thing. After Tannion took another hit, all three of the attackers were on the ground again. After this happened three times it looked like the fight had gone out of the attackers A minute later and two of the guys were out cold on the pavement and the third was scurrying away not looking back to see if his friends were okay.

The fight was over and Tannion had a crowd around him slapping him on the back, and one regular was looking at Tannion with more than a small amount of delight.

Tannion didn't know why the three toughs were after this guy, but he felt that he had a right to know. Maybe the door he was looking for had just opened.

Everyone went inside and sat down. The two guys in the alley were left there as if they had fought each other. The chance of them showing up inside was very small. Tannion went back to the same table he had been sitting at, and the regular followed him.

"Name's Steve Copeland, but my friends call me Six. Based on what just happened, I think you can call me Six."

Tannion had known Six for a couple of weeks. That only meant that he knew him well enough to say hello as he walked by and to know that he had been in the bar most of the times that he had been there. As a regular he had gotten to know most of the other regulars, but names were not usually part of the package.

Six was a little guy, especially when compared to Tannion. He was a few inches under six feet, which didn't help Tannion understand how he got the nickname. He looked like he was always looking for his next meal and had the shifty little eyes that reminded Tannion of a ferret.

"People call me French," Tannion said extending his hand to Six. Six took his hand for a hearty handshake and Tannion took a look. Over all, Six appeared pretty healthy. No obvious signs of anything that might be serious. Possibly a slightly elevated blood sugar level, but those types of things were always a bit of a guess.

"I really appreciate what you did back there," Six said.

"No problem. I don't appreciate being pushed around. Those guys looked like they wanted something from you. Will they be back?"

"Oh yeah," said Six. "I owe their boss some money and they were here to collect. Trust me, the big guy won't let me off that easy."

"How much you in for?"

"Shit only a few hundred dollars," Six said. "You think I owed that bastard millions the way they go about it."

"Did you have the money to give them, and did I get in the middle of something that I shouldn't have?" Tannion was hoping that Six would tell him that he was in deep shit and these guys were real trouble and was disappointed with the answer.

"Shit, no. Those punks probably get the shit pounded out of them on a weekly basis. They'll be back to get their money in a day or two, and if they see you nearby they'll do their best to ignore you and hope that everyone has forgotten their last meeting with you. You have nothing to worry about. Now if it was the Russian who works for Philips that might have been a different story."

Six went on. "And no I don't have the money today, so I'm quite happy with you stepping in."

"Will you have the money the next time?" Tannion hoped the answer would be no. He would like to buy this guy and if all it cost was a few hundred bucks that he might get back, it would be cheap.

"Shit where would I get that kind of money. I'll have to get lucky again and stay out of the way."

"Tell you what. I'm sitting on a bit of cash right now. How about I lend you what you need and get this guy off your back. You can pay me back at a more leisurely pace than he seems to be willing to get along with."

"You'd lend me eight hundred bucks? Shit we just met and you'd lend me money?"

"Sure, why not. Maybe you can do me a favor one day. The only thing is you don't get the money until the guys you owe it to are with you, and then I'll pay them. Okay."

"Sure, why not. It won't be long and they'll be back. Probably tomorrow or the next day," Six said. "I assumed I would have to lie low for a while, but that looks to be a problem solved. Thanks again."

Six was wrong. A couple hours later a fairly big guy with a full beard on a big face that had a very eastern European look to it stopped at the bar and asked for Six. The bartender pointed him over to the table where Six and Tannion were talking. As he walked over to the table, Six spotted him from a few feet away.

"Shit, French. It's the Russian." Six sat there and watched the Russian get closer, and a look of fear came over his face. His somewhat drink-flushed face lost most of its color.

The Russian moved up to the table and put both hands on it and leaned in looking directly at Six. "Six. I think you owe a little money and I am here to get it from you." The Russian said in slightly accented English. This guy might be Russian by heritage, but he had spent much of his life in the States. His English was almost perfect.

Tannion looked up at him and started to say something. "I'm not talking to you," the Russian said before Tannion could get a word out. "This is between Six and me. You stay the hell out of it unless you want to get hurt."

Tannion looked at the Russian and sat back in the chair making it look like he was taking the Russian's advice. Six looked at Tannion and stammered something about getting the money, and looked in Tannion's direction. The Russian wasn't having anything of it. Tannion listened for a few seconds and then reached into his pocket and pulled out a wad of money.

The Russian saw the money and stopped talking. "How much is it?" Tannion asked and the Russian told him it was thirteen hundred dollars.

Tannion looked at six. "I thought you said it was eight hundred, Six. Is this guy full of shit?"

The Russian obviously didn't like the way Tannion said the last piece and stepped back into a fighter's stance. "Watch what the fuck you say around here asshole or I'll squash you like a little bug."

"I don't think so asshole," was Tannion's quick reply, and it caught the Russian a little by surprise. Tannion shoved the wad of money back into his pocket and started to get up. The Russian had recovered quickly from his mild setback and grabbed Tannion by the lapels. The Russian was strong, but not nearly strong enough.

Tannion reached out, and although he knew it was probably not a good idea, he did it anyway. Tannion grabbed the Russian by his large jacket with his right hand and as he pushed the rest of the way out of his chair, Tannion lifted the Russian up with a rush. The bar ceiling was eight feet high and the Russian's head hit the top with a loud crack. He was going to have a headache. He wasn't hurt badly, but he was stunned and the fight was out of him.

Tannion sat the Russian down on his feet and told him not to move. The Russian had a funny look on his face, but did as he was told. Tannion asked the Russian how much Six owed, and when the Russian told him it was eight hundred dollars, he peeled off eight one hundred dollar bills and put them in the Russian's pocket. Then he told him to bugger off. The Russian looked at the pocket where Tannion had shoved the money and then at Tannion, and without saying a word, he went out the front door.

Only a few people in the bar had been watching when the Russian hit the ceiling. None of them seemed to believe what they had seen and none of them came forward to talk to Tannion except for Six. Six promised to pay back the money, but he had a look on his face that was beyond respect and well into fear. Strength was always something to fear in someone else, but strength like that was beyond anything Six could talk about. Who would believe him?

51

The big Russian's name was Vladimir Potenlikov, but he was known as the Russian, the big Russian, or even more commonly as Potenlikov. As he hustled out of the King's Head he pulled the money out of his pocket and quickly counted it. The boss didn't like to be shorted and Potenlikov wasn't about to start now. He stopped just outside the door and leaned against the wall and rubbed the top of his head. He was feeling sore and woozy and was having a little difficulty understanding exactly what had hit him.

He remembered grabbing the guy with Six and then his head hurt and he had the money in his pocket and was out the door. He counted the money again to make sure it was all there then he shoved it back into his pocket and got into his car and drove off. A few minutes later he parked the car at an upscale apartment close to downtown. He walked up to the doorman, who obviously knew him well as he opened the door for him without a word.

The doorman knew Potenlikov, but you could tell by the look on his face and the lack of words between them that he didn't think very much of him. Potenlikov ignored the doorman as if he was the door itself. He pushed the up elevator button on the wall. The elevator door opened and, without a backward look, Potenlikov stepped inside.

The penthouse suite was owned by Jackson T. Philips, and Potenlikov headed directly to the top where he knew Philips would be. Jackson T. Philips was big, black, and beautiful. Philips was a big man physically, but he thought of himself as being more than just that. All his help called him Mr. Philips and that included Potenlikov.

Philips was growing in the drug trade, prostitution, and illegal gambling. He was known to dabble in money laundering, fencing of stolen property, and loan sharking. Philips was the kind of guy you wanted to have on your side, and even then he was well known to have a mean streak that could flare up on his own people as well as on his enemies.

Philips had an extensive police file on him, but none of the charges had stuck. Most of the charges were drug related, and all had been dropped due to lack of evidence. Philips had close to a hundred people working for him in many capacities, and Potenlikov was his head of security. Philips didn't like having to send Potenlikov on such petty errands as collecting gambling debts, but when the three stooges couldn't get the job done, Potenlikov was called in. Luckily the stooges got the job done most of the time. This time they hadn't.

Potenlikov got off the elevator on the top floor and walked into the penthouse suite without knocking. The foyer opened into a large sunken living room that was very tastefully decorated in mostly African motif furniture and art work. A large double door was open on the right, and Potenlikov knew that was where Philips would be. As

Potenlikov walked into the room, Philips's voice greeted him. "Well did you get what you went for?"

"I sure did, boss," replied Potenlikov. Potenlikov had decided that what had happened in the bar didn't need to be told right now, even if it got back to Philips from other sources. Even Potenlikov wasn't too sure who might be working for Philips or where they may be at any time. As long as the question didn't come up, he wouldn't have to be caught in a lie. If the question did come up, then the truth would only hurt a little. If there was one thing Potenlikov knew, it was that Philips didn't like his people to lie to him.

Potenlikov reached into his pocket and counted out the hundred dollar bills that he knew were there. As he reached over to hand them to Philips, Philips saw the top of Potenlikov's head and asked, "What have you got on your head? Come closer." Potenlikov moved a step closer and held his head down for Philips to take a closer look.

"That looks like plaster dust. Where the hell were you to get plaster dust on your head?"

Potenlikov knew that he didn't have a choice now and told the entire story, ending with the guy grabbing him and thrusting his head against the ceiling of the bar and then giving him the money. The plaster dust jogged a part of the memory that was missing.

"How much do you weigh Vlad?" Philips asked Potenlikov.

'Probably about two forty maybe two fifty."

"And this guy lifted you up and smashed your head into the ceiling with one hand. Are you shitting me? Do you realize how strong that guy would have to be?" Philips reached over and took hold of Potenlikov's jacket with one hand and pulled up. As big and as strong as Philips was, he didn't lift Potenlikov up to his tip toes.

"Bullshit, Vlad. Not possible," Philips told him with a look that Potenlikov knew very well. Potenlikov knew that Philips thought he was being lied to. It took a bit of talk, but finally Potenlikov convinced Philips. Philips shook his head.

"I want to talk to that guy, Vlad. You go and bring him in. If he's as strong as you say he is, I suggest that you ask him very politely. I just want to talk to him." Philips had a small chuckle at Potenlikov's expense.

After Potenlikov had left, Philips placed a call to one of his men who he had sent to the bar to watch the three stooges. He should have been there when Potenlikov had shown up. He needed to confirm Potenlikov's story. The contact confirmed the story with even more awe than Potenlikov.

"Shit, I need this guy working for me," Philips said to himself with a wry grin on his face. "I've got to see this guy in action."

52

Tannion watched Potenlikov leave the bar and thought it probably wasn't the last time he would see the guy. Six was still all over him, thanking him and looking at him with eyes that still couldn't believe what they saw. A couple of other guys came over to say a word, but they all stopped before they got to the table and walked back in the other direction. After all, what could they say?

Tannion told Six to sit down and started asking him questions. He had fallen into debt gambling at a basement gambling joint a few blocks away. Many of these guys never seemed to wander to far from home. Everything they needed was only minutes away.

Six had lost money and, of course, the only way to get even was to keep betting until he won it back. With long-time losers like Six, that seldom happened. The house let him dig a deeper hole and in the end he owed over seven hundred bucks. With interest that made the eight hundred Potenlikov was looking for. Nobody ever bothered to calculate the percentage of the interest charged. Somehow it didn't matter. Six was lucky it was only eight hundred.

For a guy like Potenlikov's boss, this would be pretty small potatoes in the overall scheme of things, but if he looked after the nickels, the dollars would look after themselves. Or, more likely, if you let some low life asshole get away with owing a few bucks then everyone would think that he had gone soft, and then who knows what could happen. Philips never looked soft and Potenlikov was often why.

So even for a few bucks, knee caps could be broken. Six had a good idea that it was Jackson Philips behind the operation from the beginning, having worked for him in the past running errands and doing odd jobs. When the three stooges came looking for him he thought it was Philips. After he had stalled the stooges that time and they told him that Potenlikov would be coming, then he knew for sure it was Philips behind the joint.

Tannion was interested in knowing more about Philips. Six knew a little, but even if he testified under oath there wasn't enough to get the guy on jay walking. Of course Tannion had no intention of ever having anyone go through the court system. Six didn't have much else. He knew a little about Potenlikov and he told Tannion to look out for him, especially after what had happened.

Tannion went home about an hour later. If he would have stayed fifteen minutes longer he would have run into Potenlikov. As it was, only Six remained to take Potenlikov's wrath.

Six didn't know where Tannion, AKA French, lived, but he knew that he was in the bar every night and would probably be back the next day. He told Potenlikov all he could while trying not to get the beating he felt was coming. Tannion may have paid off his monetary debt, but a somewhat bigger debt had been incurred, and Potenlikov wanted a small bit of redemption. Six was at the bar early the next night waiting for Tannion.

"Shit, Six, what the hell happened to you?" Tannion asked when he saw the extent of the damage to Six's face. Both eyes were blackened with one almost swelled shut, and there was a lot of swelling over the other eye and a cut on his lip where it looked like he might have put a tooth through it.

Six didn't look like he had gone to a hospital or anything, but had only washed off the blood and let things heal themselves. The cut on the lip and another above his eye should probably have had stitches, but they weren't even bandaged.

"Fucking Russian, French. He came in after you left. He was looking for you, but when he could only find me, well this is the result."

"Looking for me? Did he come alone?"

"Yeah, but he told me he only wanted to talk to you. He sure as hell didn't want to talk to me."

"So what did you tell him, Six?"

"French, I didn't tell him anything. I don't know anything except that you come to this bar a lot and I told him that." Six's voice tailed off at the end and he shrunk back almost expecting Tannion to reach out and pound his head into the ceiling. It was all Six could do to look him in the eye,

"Don't worry about it. Anyone in the bar could have told him that and the last thing I'll do is worry about some Russian. If he wants to talk or anything else, he knows where I'll be."

About an hour later the door opened and Potenlikov walked in. It was dark out and even though the bar was not well lit, Tannion knew that it would take a minute for the Russian's eyes to adjust to the light. His eyes wandered over the bar, first looking to where Six and Tannion had been the night before. Not seeing either of them there, he swept the room.

Tannion and Six were sitting at a different table over near the bar, and when Potenlikov saw them he immediately walked their way. As he got closer Six looked up and saw him. Six went to get up, but Tannion stopped him with a word, and Potenlikov stopped beside the table facing both of them.

Potenlikov put both hands on the table the same way he had when he had first accosted Six the night before. "You," he said looking directly at Tannion as if Six didn't exist.

"The boss wants to talk to you."

"Who's the boss?" Six had filled Tannion in, but it was time to get a read of how Potenlikov and Philips were connected.

"You don't need to know that. You only need to know that he wants to talk to you, so come on."

"Not so fast. I only go where and when I want to go, so I ask again, who is this asshole you call the boss." Potenlikov stepped back obviously not used to hearing anyone talk about his boss that way. Tannion saw the look in his eyes and knew that this guy respected Philips, and that was all Tannion needed to know.

"Shit, why not. Let's go."

"Are you fucking nuts," Six cried out. "These guys mean business. You don't want to go with this guy."

Potenlikov threw a look at Six that could almost kill and Six shrunk back into his seat, immediately sorry that he had opened his mouth. After all, how well did he know French? If he got himself killed, so what.

"Don't worry about it. I'll see you later." Tannion said as he stepped towards the door placing Potenlikov at his back showing contempt for the big Russian. Potenlikov followed at a discreet distance. The late model car was double parked just outside the door as if Potenlikov knew that it wouldn't take long.

Potenlikov got in the driver's seat and motioned for Tannion to sit beside him. Tannion took his seat and waited for Potenlikov to start the car.

"Before we go, if you ever lay a hand on one of my friends again without me telling you to, I'll break both your arms. Got it?"

Potenlikov looked at Tannion and only nodded. It was one of those times when Potenlikov wished that he had brought a driver along. This guy had him worried and he didn't know why Philips wanted to see him.

53

The car ride took a little more than half an hour. The traffic was bad and the trip of only a few miles had Potenlikov in an even worse mood than when he had started the trip to the bar. Both men got out in front of a condo tower and the valet took the car. They entered the building with Potenlikov leading the way.

Jackson T. Philips met Potenlikov and Tannion at the door to the penthouse suite, and with a nod Potenlikov was dismissed. Philips reached out his hand and shook Tannion's. Tannion took the quick look that he always took almost without thinking. The difference this time was that he did think.

"I could kill him a hundred different ways," Tannion thought, but other than noticing that Philips was pretty healthy, he did nothing but shake his hand. This was the guy who was going to lead Tannion to the mother lode.

Philips introduced himself and flashed a big toothy grin that was supposed to show Tannion that nothing but good would come out of this meeting. It was the type of grin that the girls probably decided they should fall for, when in fact they fell for his physique, strength, and the size of his wallet more than anything.

Tannion had to admit that Philips was a very dynamic character with lots of charm and charisma. By the time they had talked for half an hour over a drink, Tannion had a job. It was clear to Tannion that Philips would rather have a guy like him working for him rather than having him on the other side.

The meeting ended suddenly with the phone ringing and Philips getting up and pushing a button on his desk. Almost as if he was listening, Potenlikov opened the door to the suite and walked in. "Vlad, please take our friend French back to where you picked him up. Starting tomorrow he'll be your right hand man. You can start teaching him the business first thing in the morning. French, Vlad will be ready to go to work as soon as you get here, so be here at eight sharp. Be ready."

With that Tannion was dismissed and Philips picked up the phone and started talking as if Potenlikov and Tannion no longer existed. Now that Tannion worked for him, Philips obviously saw him as property and no longer something to attain. Potenlikov ushered him out the door and back to the car then they drove back to the bar. The traffic was better and the trip took only twenty minutes. In all they had been gone for just a little under two hours.

Tannion decided not to go back into the bar and went home instead. With a lot on his mind he needed time to think. In the end, before he decided to sleep, all he had come up with was to let things come at him as they would. That and he would have to quit the job he already had.

The next morning Tannion met Potenlikov at the bottom of the condo unit at eight o'clock sharp. Tannion had decided that his other job could just do without him. They didn't know where he lived and didn't have a phone number. They were just out one worker. Tannion didn't even care about his last paycheck.

Potenlikov got into the car that was sitting there and motioned for Tannion to get in the passenger side. Tannion buckled the seat belt and Potenlikov pulled out into traffic.

There was an obvious tension in the car and Potenlikov had nothing to say. Tannion tried to make small talk, but Potenlikov ignored him entirely. It was obvious that if the boss said to work with him he would, but there was no reason to get friendly. Tannion got the impression that Potenlikov didn't get friendly with anyone.

Tannion tried to ask where they were going, but Potenlikov wouldn't say a word. Tannion sat back for the ride. It was well over an hour later when they pulled off the freeway several miles north of LA. Potenlikov got out of the car and Tannion followed.

"We're here to collect payment," was all Potenlikov would say.

It looked like Tannion's new job was going to be Potenlikov's backup. Somehow he didn't think Potenlikov needed a lot of help, but what the hell. They had parked beside a small bungalow on a street of very similar looking houses. They walked up to the door with the number 1142 marked boldly on it.

Potenlikov rang the doorbell and stepped back. The door opened and a small man with a long dark beard and long greasy hair opened the door, took one look at Potenlikov, and slammed it in his face. Potenlikov hollered for Tannion to go around back, and he immediately hit the door with his shoulder. The door crashed open and Potenlikov was in the room.

Tannion went around the right hand side and vaulted over the six foot fence like it wasn't there. As he landed, he saw the little guy coming out of the back door and Tannion maneuvered to stop him. The little guy was screaming something and running as if for his life.

Tannion took a few strides and caught the guy by the hair and pulled him back before he could get out the back gate. Potenlikov came flying out of the back door and looked very surprised when he saw Tannion there with the little guy well in hand.

"Watch out, this guy has friends," yelled Potenlikov just as three guys came rushing into the yard from next door.

"Hold it," Potenlikov yelled at the new guys on the scene. "Frank here owes us money and we're here to collect. Just go about your own business and no one will get hurt."

"Fuck you," shouted the guy closest to Tannion. "Let him go and get the hell out of here while you can."

Tannion stood still, content to let Potenlikov do the talking, but he held on to Frank without letting up. Frank was well pinned with Tannion's hand in his hair and arm around his shoulders. He was pinned as if he had been hog tied.

Potenlikov tried to explain the situation, but Tannion could tell that the guys he was talking to didn't want to listen. Tannion was a little surprised that Potenlikov was trying to explain anything at all. It didn't seem to fit his style.

These guys only saw their friend being man handled and the fact there were four of them against only two gave them strength. One of the three wasn't much bigger than Frank, but the other two were close to Potenlikov's size, which made them look bigger than Tannion.

Finally the one big guy closest to Tannion made a move towards him and Tannion was forced into action. Tannion closed his fist and gave Frank a hammer blow to the top of his head. Not enough to kill him, but hard enough to make it three against two. The closest guy came at Tannion while the other two went for Potenlikov, seeing him as the bigger threat.

Tannion side stepped the on-rushing attacker and gave him a slap to the back as he went by, which sent him into the fence hard enough to knock him down and out of the fight. Two strides later and Tannion grabbed the other big guy just as he was going to throw a punch at Potenlikov, who was being distracted by the third man. With one hand, and without either Potenlikov or his attacker seeing, Tannion threw him into the fence where he landed on top of his buddy more than ten feet away.

Potenlikov took one swing at his assailant and the fight was over. He then went over to Frank and picked him up off the ground, slapped him a few times to make him come around and then demanded what he owed him. Frank said he didn't have it and this didn't make Potenlikov happy. As it turned out, Frank owed over two thousand dollars and he was well past due.

After taking all the money Frank had on him, and what his friends had in their wallets, he was still almost two thousand short. The few bucks they had, Potenlikov considered to be payment for the hassle of having to fight them. Potenlikov herded all four of them into the living room and sat down to talk. A glass of cold water in one face made sure they were awake if only a bit sore.

Again Potenlikov did all the talking, and when they left there were a couple of broken lamps and a few people who were feeling lucky they didn't have broken bones. As Tannion was to find out later, this was the way things went with Potenlikov. Guys like Frank were known not to be able to run and they would eventually be able to come up with the money. The next visit was clearly outlined to Frank and to his friends. The next time would mean enough pain to make them miss a couple days of work and with a couple broken little fingers, they would have trouble picking quarters off the ground.

This was not the first time Potenlikov had used this method, and Tannion soon found it wasn't his last either. The only thing Potenlikov said when he dropped him off at the condo was, "Same time tomorrow."

Tannion looked at his watch. It was just past noon. "Short day," he thought. But if Potenlikov said that was all there was today, then that was all there was. Maybe Six was at the King's Head and Tannion could buy him a beer.

54

For the next two months, Tannion faithfully met Potenlikov outside the condo unit. They quickly settled into a routine and it didn't change. Each day they would either make a number of collections or act as bodyguards for Philips, and on occasion they would pick someone up at the airport or run whatever errand Philips needed run.

Tannion knew he was being tested, but what the hell, he was being well paid and time was on his side. He knew he could do whatever he wanted to Potenlikov, Philips, or anyone else who happened along, but he wanted more. These guys may be crooks and thieves, but from what Tannion could see they supplied more in the way of enterprise and employment than the negative side could destroy. These guys weren't honest, but they weren't real bad either. There had to be someone up the ladder who needed it worse than these guys did. Tannion was even starting to like Potenlikov.

The plan now was to continue to use the connections he had with Philips and see what happened. So far Tannion had been used to collect debts from illegal gambling and working with some of the hookers, but he knew there was more illicit stuff going on. He was just going to have to wait until it came along. As long as he did what he was told and earned the trust and respect of Potenlikov, it would happen eventually.

Tannion began to see the size of Philips's operation. Although at first it seemed to be quite big he realized that compared to some of the other names out there, he was really a very small player in a big pond. Tannion also knew that Philips wasn't happy being the small fish and wanted to grow.

Each night Potenlikov would report back to Philips. Potenlikov didn't exactly like Tannion, but he had a growing respect for him, and he told Philips exactly what happened each day. Tannion had never failed on an assignment, and he thought that Potenlikov and Philips were thinking that he was intelligent and that his speed and strength were incredible.

Philips must have taken all this in. After two months, he was starting to feel that Tannion might be ready to do more and maybe go out on his own. Philips had still not seen Tannion in action, but that would have to wait. The initial testing period was over, but Tannion didn't know it, and that was the way Philips wanted it. The next steps were crucial.

The drug trade was a major part of Philips's business, but in the overall supply of drugs into the greater Los Angeles area, he had only a very small part. Philips wanted more and had his eyes on a big strike.

Philips got word of a rival dealer who was expecting a large shipment of grass. The group was known as the Santos Brothers Inc., which was emblazoned on the doors of their trucks as they hauled equipment and produce back and forth from Los Angeles into the Imperial Valley just inside the Arizona border. There were two Santos brothers who ran the company along with two of their cousins.

The trucking business made the Santos brothers a good profit, but nothing like their side trade. Marijuana was routinely smuggled out of Mexicali on the Mexican side of the border into California, where the Santos brothers would happen to stop by. They would take it into town, where the more clandestine side of the operation would make the tax-free profit by packaging it and selling it on the street.

The Santos brothers were well known in the drug trade. The cops had been onto them for years, but had never been able to catch them. Word was out that they had a mole in a safe place and in deep. Somehow they always knew when a crackdown would happen and the trucks were always clean and the warehouse was spotless.

Philips had word from a very good source that a very large shipment was coming in from Mexico, and that the Santos brothers were picking it up and taking delivery in a few days. It had taken over a year for Philips to get in a position where he could make this type of strike. All he needed now was to know when the shipment was to land.

Philips was aware of the warehouse the Santos brothers used and knew it was their weak spot, and he had a plan worked out. Potenlikov and a few good men would move in on the night the goods arrived, dispose of any witnesses, and move the stuff to a safe place. Then they would lie low for a week or two and slowly move the drugs to the street.

Philips made sure that he had his own shipment in very recently and that it was well known in the right places that he was holding. Then when the Santos's shit hit the street it would look like Philips was only moving his own. Philips didn't want a fight at this stage. That would come later after he had weakened the Santos brothers enough. This was to be the first of many hits that would put the Santos Brothers Inc. out of business.

Potenlikov indicated that Philips thought Tannion would be a good addition to the team. Tannion suspected that Potenlikov thought that when Tannion got into this kind of action he would be in for good. This would be make or break for Tannion, and he knew that Philips would make sure Potenlikov had a good eye on him. Potenlikov had already assured Philips that Tannion was good. Very good.

55

Tannion knew Potenlikov had a plan, and it appeared as if Philips felt that Tannion had earned his confidence enough to be involved in the job. During the last couple of weeks Tannion had made a number of pickups and collections on his own and never once failed, but was that enough? What he needed to do was something above what was expected. Potenlikov's plan might just be the ticket.

The way he explained it, Tannion could tell that it was Potenlikov's plan and not Philips's. Philips would have made it look bigger or showy somehow, while Potenlikov made it simple. There were three guards at the front entrance to the warehouse and none inside or anywhere else. The Santos Brothers relied heavily on a little power and a large amount of looking honest and above board. How could they justify a large contingent of armed guards to guard a warehouse full of lettuce?

The plan was to have one of the boys drive up to the gate and ask for directions and then take the guards out with a silenced thirty-eight before moving in. The plan had a couple flaws. A thirty-eight isn't the biggest piece, and hitting all three without them raising an alarm or getting a shot or two off might be difficult. On top of that was the mess. A mess that might be seen from the road. Also, it was going to take a few minutes to locate and load the grass into the trucks. There was supposed to be a large shipment so it would take a while.

"Hey, Potenlikov," Tannion called out. "How about trying something a little different? If I was to drive up and get out of the car acting quite drunk and carrying a bottle, I could probably get right up to them and take them into the guard house for a drink. I could dispose of them in the guard house and the mess would be out of sight." Tannion didn't tell them how he would dispose of them, but they would be disposed of.

"I don't think so, French."

"If they don't go for it, I'll get back in the car and drive off and then you can try asking for directions." Tannion told him why he thought his plan might be better and was a bit surprised when Potenlikov changed his mind and agreed. "If I don't screw this up, I might be in for good," Tannion thought.

Two nights later and they were ready. Philips had found out when the shipment was to arrive and he had approved the plan. This confirmed Tannion's first suspicion that, although Phillips had approved the plan, in reality the plan belonged to Potenlikov. Potenlikov wasn't stupid enough to go off with his plan without the boss's okay. Or for that matter to make a change to a plan that wasn't already his own.

They parked the two trucks a couple blocks away and Tannion drove on in the sedan. As he drove up he took the full bottle of whisky out of the bag on the seat beside him and took a good long swig making sure to spill a little. As he got close to the gate he made a couple moves that made it look like he could be over correcting his bad driving, then he pulled into the parking lot.

Tannion sat behind the wheel for a few seconds until he knew the guards had seen him and were making their way towards the car. It was show time. Tannion got out of the car with the bottle in his hand and walked a little unsteadily towards the guards.

"Hi, guys," Tannion shouted at them with what he hoped was a slightly drunken slur. "Where the hell am I? I was heading for the freeway and here I am, and I don't have a clue were here is."

"This is private property, you need to move on," the closest guard said. Maybe this wasn't going to be as easy as Tannion had first thought.

"Can you at least help a guy out first? I have an almost new bottle here that should be able to pay for directions, don't you think." The first guy was about to say something when the guy behind him pushed him aside and headed Tannion's way.

"Sure," he said. "We can always find time for a lost soul with a bottle. Come over here." Tannion thought for a second that they were going to go over next to a truck in the lot and have a drink there, but Tannion wanted to get them into the shack over to the side.

"Do you have some glasses so we can share? I've got one hell of a cold and if we all go from the bottle you guys will catch it." Tannion said.

"Sure, come on up and we can help you out." He put his arm around Tannion's shoulders and started to walk over to the shack. This guy was quite a bit smaller than Tannion and had a heavy body odor surrounding him — he reeked of garlic.

His friend, however, wasn't so sure. "Forget him, Dan. We don't need to get in trouble over some drunk."

"Hey, what trouble can we get into? This will only take a few minutes and nothing's going on tonight anyway."

About then the third guy piped in. "Yeah. I want a shot at that bottle too," he said, and the resolve in the first guy weakened.

"Okay. Okay," he said as they headed for the small guard shack off to the side, leaving Tannion's car where he had parked it.

All that Tannion needed now was to make sure that all three of them came along. Tannion sure didn't have to worry about that as they all wanted to get their hands on that bottle of whisky. The night shift was probably boring as hell, and the chance to have a drink on him was too much for any of them to resist.

All four of them came up to the shack. Inside, it looked even smaller than it did from the outside. Tannion's new buddy reached over his arm and took the bottle and went to the back for something to drink from. He came back with three plastic glasses in his hand and gave one to each of his friends.

"I only found three glasses, so you'll have to drink from the bottle," he told Tannion. He went on to pour out a very generous portion of the bottle for him and his friends. When he handed the bottle back it was well under half full. As they all reached forward to touch glasses in a salute, Tannion took his chance.

There was one guy on each side of Tannion and the other was straight across from him. As they clinked the glasses against the bottle Tannion was holding, he conveniently dropped it. As it fell, all sets of eyes followed it intently — except Tannion's.

Tannion quickly pulled his arms back and grabbed the fellows on each side of him by the scruff of the neck. He then took a step back and smashed their heads together. There was a resounding smack as the two heads cracked at about the same time the bottle hit the floor. A half second later and the guy across the room looked up in time to see a fist in his face that turned the lights out. It was all over in less than two seconds.

Potenlikov wanted no witnesses and these were the kind of guys Tannion was willing to erase anyway, so a quick neck twist and Potenlikov got his wish. It was time to call in the troops. Potenlikov had picked a couple of the boys who would impersonate the guards, and the rest of them would take the trucks into the warehouse to load the stuff.

A cell phone call, and five minutes later they were set. Two hours later and the warehouse was empty of not only the shit they were after, but almost anything that was valuable and not nailed down. This was supposed to look like a hit, but not just by someone who knew about the grass, but by someone who might have been looking for whatever else there was inside. Problem was that other than a few machinery parts, the majority of the warehouse was refrigerated and full of produce. So they took a bunch of lettuce and tomatoes. For some reason Potenlikov thought stealing lettuce and tomatoes was funny.

As soon as they had the stuff put away, Tannion and Potenlikov were called up to see Philips. Potenlikov told Philips how everything went down. Philips was thinking and smiling. This was a big day for him with almost twenty million dollars worth of high quality street-ready shit. It appeared that Tannion was finally over his probation period and now he was in for real.

Not only had Tannion bumped off three guys who needed it, but he had taken a very big step in his plan. Now to the next step, and that would include playing Philips along for a while. He would be the last on Tannion's list, but for now Phillips was a tool to get him there. Tannion just needed to keep doing his job and he would wait for the next good opportunity to come along. It always would.

56

Tannion read the report in the paper of a warehouse being robbed of produce and machinery. The warehouse was indicated as being owned by a Los Angeles-based company, but there was no mention of Santos Brothers Inc. It was probably a shadow company or some subsidiary that could not be directly traced to the Santos brothers.

There was no word on anything illicit being in the place, but already the word on the street was that the Santos brothers were not in a good mood. The article went on to say that the police were at a loss to account for three dead guards. They didn't think that machinery and a few cases of lettuce warranted murder. At least they mentioned the guards. Tannion was a little surprised that the Santos brothers didn't manage to hide that part of the hit.

Tannion had hoped that his part of the Santos job would give him some credibility and open some doors. He may have gotten the credibility he was looking for from Potenlikov as the Russian had finally warmed up to him a little, and he got a hand shake and good words from Philips, but the door remained closed to their private conversations.

Tannion was starting to understand how this part of the world worked and was formulating a bit of a plan for the future. For now it would be easy, work with Potenlikov and wait for his big opportunity.

Tannion didn't have long to wait. The Santos brothers were hurting from the hit. It was only grass, so it could have been worse, but as a result, word had it that they were stepping up their operation. That meant Philips would be stepping up his operation as well.

Two weeks after the warehouse job Potenlikov, along with Tannion and six of Philips's men, were on a road outside of town waiting for the lights of a truck that would be coming down the road. In the back of the truck was supposed to be a real mixed bag. There was to be illicit drugs, with most of it being cocaine that the Santos brothers got from across the border in Mexico. There was also supposed to be some meth and probably some illegal aliens.

When the truck's headlights came into view they were ready. This was a frontal assault with a spike belt and enough fire power to make sure that it went well. The truck was being followed by two cars that were sure to be full of Santos's men. Word was that this was such an important shipment that one of the brothers might be riding along. Philips must have someone in a good spot to get that kind of inside information.

The truck went by their position at more than forty miles an hour. Potenlikov had chosen a steep uphill portion so the vehicle would slow down, but the truck had good power and hadn't slowed down as much as Potenlikov had expected. The spike belt was camouflaged under dark cloth and the driver never saw it. The front tires hit the belt and were flat before they turned over again, even at that speed. The belt caught in the tires and the ends flapped against the side of the truck making a hell of a noise. The truck came to a screeching halt only seconds after it hit.

It was all the first car could do not to hit the truck in the rear end, but the second car was not so lucky. It hit the car in front of it with a good crash. Four men poured out of each of the cars and were met with a hail of fire from both sides. It was over in seconds. All the occupants of the cars were down and out after the first burst, and the two men in the truck bailed out and ran like hell.

Potenlikov didn't want any witnesses. Tannion and three of Philips's men went after the two escapees. Within the first few running steps it was obvious that the men with Tannion weren't going to be of any use. As soon as they were off the highway, the lights disappeared and Santos's men were only vague outlines against the sky even though they were not that far ahead.

They only had a few yards head start and Tannion quickly made up the ground. Tannion didn't like guns, but he knew it would be expected of him. One shot took the lead runner in the back between the shoulder blades and it took the run out of the guy behind him. He must have heard the bullet go by him as it was only a few inches away.

He turned and put up his hands, but the second bullet stopped any words from coming out of his mouth. Tannion took both of them by the collar and dragged them back to the truck. The three guys with him caught up as he started to pull the bodies along, and they were very willing to take the load from him. The trio had looked like shit in this one, but if they came back with the bodies they would save face. They would owe Tannion for this one.

It was the first time Tannion had used a gun to do any dirty work for Philips, and he didn't like it. He made a pact with himself not to use a gun again unless it was really necessary. Then he decided it would never be necessary again.

Potenlikov put a new driver in the truck and he headed off to a secluded rendezvous with one of Philips's trucks a half mile down the road. That was as far as it could make with the tires gone. After the switch, the truck would be found over a cliff in a river nearby. The rest of the group collected the bodies, put them in the two cars, pushed them off the road, and then set them on fire. They knew that a coroner could tell that they had died of gunshot wounds, but it might fool the first guys to the scene into thinking there had been a bad accident.

A few hours later and they were at Philips's office waiting for the boss to get off the phone. Potenlikov filled Philips in and called it a night. The Santos brothers had taken a beating. The bodies were identified and none of the brothers were dead, but a couple of the big guys in Santos's organization had bought it. The few thousand that they carried in pocket change became Potenlikov's pocket change, but he shared it around so no one complained.

57

The news on the street was that the Santos brothers were very pissed off again, and this time they had a very good idea who was behind the last action. The cops didn't seem to have anything other than some gang related deaths. The Santos's knew better, but they weren't saying anything. Even the mole didn't know what the brothers were thinking, and what was worse, he didn't know what they were planning.

Philips was in a good mood. He knew that the Santos brothers were mad and hurting, and although he had heard the word on the street, he didn't think there was a chance in hell that he was suspected. He was already plotting the next attack. He thought the sooner the better. The Santos's would not be expecting an attack so quickly, and this time Philips was going for the jugular.

Philips had figured that it was time to knock off at least one of the brothers. If he could kill at least one, then the others may be in a position where they would have to deal, and Philips definitely wanted to deal. He hoped to come forward as the white knight and offer to take over the Santos brothers' area for a fee. Philips only had to make sure that the brothers didn't suspect that it was him behind the two heists.

He had a plan, but it involved a little personal risk. He was going to meet with the Santos brothers when the attack would happen. That way it would look like it couldn't possibly be him behind the killings as it could have been him getting killed.

If there was one thing that Philips had it was balls. He knew that he wasn't the smartest when it came to school learning, but he knew that he had street smarts and they had always worked him out of trouble as a kid. He was also big enough that when he had to bust a few heads on his own, it was done. His big break, however, was when he met Potenlikov. Funny thing is, Potenlikov didn't know this.

Potenlikov found Philips when Philips was a small-time pusher and some-time money lender. A small-time hood borrowed some money from him and couldn't pay. Potenlikov needed a job, and Philips told him to rough the hood up and retrieve the money. Potenlikov thought he had been hired by a pretty cool black dude with moxy and pull. Philips didn't do anything to expel that thought.

After Potenlikov came back with the money they formed a tight bond, but very clearly a boss to employee bond. From there Philips had used Potenlikov to pull a few deals, and the money from some of the drugs eventually allowed Philips to grow to where he was today. He was still pretty small time considering what was out there, but he was getting bigger, and if he could take over the Santos's operation, especially the drugs out of Mexico, he would increase in stature.

Philips and Potenlikov had been together long enough that Philips could tell what Potenlikov was thinking by the look on his face. He never would be a good poker player. Potenlikov didn't like his boss's new idea at all. It was way too risky.

"I don't like it, Mr. Philips."

"It's a good plan, Vlad."

"Anything can happen in a drive-by shooting. You could be hit."

"I'll keep back, but I need to be there."

Potenlikov knew it wouldn't do him any good to argue. Once Philips had his mind made up nothing would change it. The risk would be worth it, but only if the plan worked.

Philips knew there was a risk, but if everything went well he could step in without any consequences and agree to take over the territory. Life would be good. The remaining Santos brothers would welcome him into the family with open arms.

Philips and Potenlikov met the Santos brothers at the Metropolitan Restaurant around noon. Both Santos brothers and the two first cousins from different uncles were waiting for him. It was the four of them who made up the Santos brothers. Philips was relieved to see all four of them there, but in reality he hoped that one of them would be left alive to make the deal easier. If they all died, then the area would be a free for all.

They ordered their meal, and after the food arrived the real conversation began.

"Who the fucking hell do you think is after us?" asked the older of the two brothers and the head of the family.

"How many times have you been hit, Frank?" asked Philips not necessarily trying to avoid the question, but working up to an answer.

"Just twice, Jack, but they were both bad. Someone knew things they shouldn't have known and we haven't found the mole yet." Frank Santos had known Jackson Philips for a couple of years before Philips had found Potenlikov and started to grow. Not everyone would think to call him Jack. Philips's closest friends knew him as Jackson, but most people either called him Mr. Philips or sir. Frank was not even close to a friend, but he thought he was.

"Shit, Frank, with only two hits, why do you think they aren't just isolated occurrences and there isn't anyone after you."

One of the cousins, Dominic Santos piped in, "No fucking way those were isolated hits. They knew way too much and that means we must have a mole, and if we have a mole he has to be working for someone and that someone is dead if we catch him. That goes for the fucking mole too."

Philips knew that the guy on the inside was a potential disaster and had already had him disappear. Obviously the Santos's hadn't missed him yet. If they caught him they might not be able to trace him back to Philips, but under the type of torture that the Santos's would put him through, he would give up Philips in a minute and Philips wouldn't blame him.

"Okay," Philips said. "If they weren't isolated then it was someone who knew what you had, and wanted it for themselves. Word that I heard is you lost some heroin and cocaine in the last hit and the first was grass and, according to the papers, some machinery and lettuce."

"Shit, I wish we could get our hands on heroin these days. That supply dried up a few months ago. The last hit was mostly cocaine and some hash, but the big thing was they killed my guys. Nobody gets to kill my guys unless it's me. I lost a dozen good men in those two raids and good men are hard to find. A couple of them had been with me for years," Frank said.

The conversation went on for the entire time they were eating, only slowing down a little when the waitress was serving the food or topping up the water. Philips knew this was a business meeting when the brothers passed on anything to drink but water, and that was fine with him. A cool head was the best thing he had going for him today.

As they approached the end of the meal the check arrived and Philips attempted to pay, but the Santos brothers would have nothing of that. They may be hurting, but they still had their pride. Even if Philips had asked for the meeting, the brothers thought of it as theirs. That meant they had to pay.

They all got up from the table and headed for the door. Philips knew that one of his guys was sitting at a nearby table and as soon as they stood the message had been sent. It was too late to stop it now. As they got to the door Potenlikov hurried ahead to open it for them, and as Philips got to him he stopped to say a word, but only long enough for the brothers to get ahead of him.

As they walked out the door, which Potenlikov was still holding open, Philips called out to one of the cousins, "Hey, Tony, hold on." Philips had chosen Tony as the one cousin to live as Tony was as close to being a friend as any of them could be, the rest were acquaintances at best. Philips pointed down to his shoelace that very conveniently was undone.

"Just need to do up my lace," Philips told Tony as he bent down to tie up the lace.

That was the final signal the boys were waiting for. A car pulled out in front of the restaurant, and before anyone suspected anything, two automatic weapons were sticking out of the windows and bullets were flying. The first round of lead caught the leading Santos brothers before they knew what was happening. The second weapon was only a little slower, but to the Santos's credit, they had already moved.

It really didn't matter though as the bullets followed their movement and as there was nothing to hide behind, they all fell. It was over in a few seconds. The blood was already running into the gutter and soaking into the pavement.

Philips heard the shots as soon as he bent down. He was still close to the door and Potenlikov still had it open. Tony had stepped towards him and Philips grabbed him and together they jumped through the open door back into the restaurant.

They both lay on the floor with Philips on top of Tony to make sure he didn't get a look at anything outside, but he made it look like he was protecting him. Potenlikov had thrown himself over them both not caring about Tony, but ensured that any stray bullet would hit him and not Philips.

Before the cops got there, Philips and Tony had a chance to check to see if anyone was alive. They were all dead. Each of them had been hit with more than one bullet. Each of them was hit in a vital area, but by the amount of blood on the sidewalk and pavement, they would have bled out quickly.

The cops arrived and took Philips, Potenlikov, and Tony Santos in for questioning while the wagon picked up the dead. It had been a long time since this kind of killing had gone on in the streets, but it wasn't the first time, and the cops knew there would be more. Gangland killings were something that was thought to have only happened in the thirties, but they still happened every year in one city or another. This looked to be Los Angeles's year.

A couple of hours later the three of them were released. They gave their statements and the cops had nothing to hold them on, so they were let go. Tony was busted up pretty bad, and Philips did a good job of holding his hand as they went to the morgue to see the brothers and then made arrangements for their burial.

Philips was looking pretty good.

58

For the past few weeks, Tannion had been enjoying himself. Potenlikov had made it obvious that he trusted him. At least he appeared to trust Tannion, as long as he kept his nose clean and didn't try to go beyond his duties. He made sure to do only what was expected of him, but what Potenlikov didn't know wouldn't hurt him.

The job usually put Tannion into contact with all kinds of people, and not too many of them were of the type that earned a good honest living. There were thieves, punks, toughs, pimps, hookers, and losers. There were bums and scum of the earth and most of them thought that the world, or at least the other people on the world, owed them a living.

Tannion would do his job, which might be to get money from some loser for bad debts or outstanding loans, or to run shotgun on a drug run. The one thing these jobs had in common was they almost always included the type of people that were causing Tannion to have so much fun.

Tannion spent much of his evenings watching. He met more and more people in the business and he slowly gathered information. He was still looking for the guys at the top. The little guys would often lead to the bigger guy and Tannion watched and he learned.

Luckily the loan business and much of what they did sent them all over the greater LA area. Tannion got to know the city very well and also got to know who lived where and who was doing what.

Potenlikov didn't know that he had become a good teacher, but he filled the role very well. His knowledge of what was happening on the streets came from several years working them. Tannion couldn't have been paired with anyone better.

Tannion wasn't in on the Santos hit and, like everyone else, he wasn't even aware of how it went down until later. He was surprised when Potenlikov confided in him a couple days after it happened. This obviously proved that Tannion had gained the big Russian's confidence. Tannion felt pretty sure they had become something close to friends over the past months, but this was the final proof. At least as close to friends as anyone could be with the big Russian.

The hit did what Philips hoped it would do. Over the next few weeks he took control of all the Santos's area and bought everything that Tony could sell him at pennies on the dollar. Tony was pretty sure that someone was out to get them all, so the sooner he could sell off everything and get the hell out of town the better.

After Tony was gone, Philips found himself with a business that had more than doubled in the couple of months since the first hit, and his cost was only a fraction of what the business was worth. He was ready to make some moves, and Tannion knew that he was on the right track.

With Philips getting bigger and with Potenlikov at his side, the time was getting right. Tannion knew it was time for Philips to take on the big guys, and he was going along for the ride.

It didn't take long for Philips to prove Tannion right. A couple of weeks after Tony Santos headed out of town for points unknown, Philips called Potenlikov to get the car and drive him to a meeting with someone Tannion had never heard of. Potenlikov however quickly told Tannion that this could lead to something very interesting.

The meeting was held in an office building downtown. Potenlikov and Philips got out of the car and Tannion followed a step behind. Philips had gotten very used to this treatment as Potenlikov always had Tannion covering his back.

The elevator opened up on the thirty-first floor, and although it was not the penthouse, it opened out into a large and luxurious foyer. A quick look around revealed paintings on the walls that looked real and very expensive.

Two men greeted the Philips's party, neither of them was smiling. Philips, Potenlikov, and Tannion were quickly patted down then showed into the next room. The door opened into a large sitting room with three leather sofas angled towards the windows that looked out over the city.

There was a very noticeable lack of the types of things that an office or a relaxing sitting room would have. There was no television and no bar. They weren't going to be served drinks. The owner didn't drink and never served drinks to anyone. Something to do with his health.

There was a door to the right that appeared to open into an office, but it was only ajar, so all Tannion could see was what might have been the corner of a desk.

Three men got up off the three sofas and moved toward the door to greet the visitors or in reality the visitor and his two bodyguards. They all shook Philips's hand as if he was someone they knew or at least someone they knew of or had met before. Definitely not as friends or even acquaintances.

Ross Dennison had made his money in two of the largest trucking firms on the west coast. His two sons, Jeff and Paul, were now in their late thirties and getting set to take over the business. Dennison must have been in his early sixties, but he looked younger. His graying hair was still plentiful and cut to a fashionable length, and his suit was not off the rack.

Philips and the three Dennisons sat on the sofas and started to talk in a slightly less than normal tone. The bodyguards who had shown them in remained over by the door and Potenlikov and Tannion took up positions on the other side of the same door. The tone of conversation was low enough that although there was complete trust in the group at the door, there was still a hushed feel.

After talking for about an hour the Dennisons took Philips into the back room that Tannion assumed was an office. As they opened the door to enter, it afforded him a better look and confirmed his first impression. He saw a large desk in the middle of the room, a set of full book cases against the wall, and at least four chairs.

Once the door closed, the room seemed to sigh as some of the tension eased. The Dennison guards shifted their position and went to sit on the sofas. Without being asked, Potenlikov and Tannion did the same. It was apparent that if there was going to be any talk at all, Tannion would have to start it. Potenlikov sat very grim faced, not overly pleased that Philips had left the room alone. The three guards were not ready to pass on small talk.

"Well that was a long one," Tannion said. Getting no reaction he tried again, but it was obvious there wasn't going to be any conversation. Tannion and Potenlikov had spent the better part of another hour on the sofas without saying a word before Philips came out with the Dennisons. After a very quick hand shake, they were shown to the elevator and were soon back in the car.

The smile Philips had on his face when he came out of the room changed significantly when they got into the car. Tannion got the impression that the smile was for the Dennison's benefit and was put on. The second look in the car was real. It looked like Philips could be a bit of an actor.

59

Potenlikov handed Tannion the keys and he got in the back seat with Philips. Tannion had missed the quick nod that Philips had given Potenlikov, but Potenlikov had understood immediately. They were to sit in the back and talk strategy. Philips used Potenlikov every so often like this, and Tannion knew that Philips would do all the talking and Potenlikov would nod and grunt a lot. Philips liked to think out loud and only wanted a listener. Potenlikov was the best he had.

Tannion could hear everything and took it as a sign of trust that he was even in the car. This was the first time it had happened. Philips started with what had happened in the office and Tannion had to suppress a smile. He could see Philips in the rear view mirror and saw the occasional flash of white teeth.

The meeting had been for Philips to get to know the Dennisons. They had worked with the Santos brothers in the past, and with them gone, they had called upon Philips. The Dennisons were in charge and they saw Philips as being at best a junior partner. Definitely he was not a full partner, and he wasn't happy.

Philips was to proceed with a large shipment of office furniture and supplies that the Dennisons couldn't handle, and as Philips now had a relatively large fleet of trucks at his disposal it was time to get them back on the road. They had been sitting idle for a while since he had taken over the Santos's business, and it was time to move.

Once again Tannion had the thought that Philips wasn't really the bad guy, and now it looked like the Dennisons were probably okay as well. This next job looked like legitimate business. Tannion thought it might be a little too soon to make that decision and it didn't take long for him to be proved right. Philips went on to explain what else would be inside the furniture boxes, and although Tannion's first thought was drugs, it turned out to be illegal aliens.

The Dennisons were into a sweat shop business and regularly imported aliens from Mexico to fill the quotas and, as Philips noted, on occasion there was a good looking one who would find herself on a boat out of town bound for the Orient for sale to the highest bidder.

Tannion had heard of the sex slave trade, but didn't know that it actually existed. A tingle of excitement went up his spine as the thought of having hit the mother lode. The Dennisons were dirty and Philips was in it up to his ass. This could be interesting. This could be the big time he had been waiting and hoping for.

Tannion dropped Philips and Potenlikov off at the apartment and parked the car. He took the elevator up to the suite to get the rest of the plan, as now he knew he would be a part of it. He had come this far into the circle and there was no turning back.

The plan was simple. Potenlikov and Tannion were to fly to Houston and pick up a truck at the Dennison's yard. The Dennisons would have already packaged the goods, and all he and Potenlikov had to do was transport them across state lines. The Dennisons and Philips knew that the transport of illegal aliens across state lines was a federal offense, but it would be the price Philips would have to pay to grow into the organization. That was if Philips was willing and ready to pay the price.

Philips was eager to go up the next rung. The Santos brothers had provided the opportunity to get in with the Dennisons, and now it was up to him to take that next step. The Dennisons were deep into drugs and money laundering, the sex trade, sex slave trade, and illegal work force. All these dealings, as well as their legit businesses, had made them very rich. Philips wanted a piece. A large piece.

Potenlikov and Tannion landed at the George Bush Intercontinental Airport in Houston, Texas. The flight went smoothly and they were on time. They caught a cab into town and picked up the truck that was waiting.

The first rule was not to open the back of the truck. There was enough food and water and sanitation to last the trip. Tannion thought this may be more of a test than a real job and wasn't too worried about the consequences, except that if something happened, Philips might fall out of favor with the Dennisons. Tannion didn't want to lose access to those he wanted. The Dennisons would be a good start.

60

Why does everything have to happen at night? The trip out of Houston was easy and they headed west on Interstate 10. Potenlikov was behind the wheel while Tannion was supposed to get some sleep. It would be his turn behind the wheel later.

Tannion dozed for a few minutes then woke quickly, but he only opened his eyes a slit to see what had made him wake up. He knew it wasn't the normal truck noise or the jostle of a moving truck down a road where the truck lane was badly in need of an overhaul. It had been a sound that Tannion's overly keen ears had picked up, and it was something he had not heard on this trip before.

When it happened again Tannion was wide awake and knew where it was coming from. There was a definite noise coming from inside the box of the truck. Someone or something was moving around inside and had hit the front of the truck box. Nothing to worry about. Who knows what was going on back there, and it was none of his business.

Tannion fell back to sleep, but was awakened only a few minutes later. This time besides the noises there were voices. They were very faint and it was all his excellent hearing could do to pick them up. It sounded like screaming and it was coming from the back of the truck. Tannion looked across at Potenlikov and could tell that he hadn't heard a thing. The truck was almost soundproof, and with the road and motor noise, Potenlikov couldn't hear anything else.

Tannion knew they weren't supposed to go inside the back of the truck, but he didn't care about anyone else's rules. He thought he knew what to expect back there, but then why was the screaming going on. "Hey, Vlad, I'm wide awake, why don't I drive for a while and you get some sleep."

Potenlikov knew it was still a couple of hours before it was Tannion's turn, but driving was something the big Russian didn't really like to do, so it only took a second for him to say sure. If Tannion wanted to drive it was okay with him.

They got out of their respective sides of the truck and as they passed in front of the truck, Tannion slapped Potenlikov on the shoulder and held contact long enough to set something in motion. Only seconds after sitting in the seat beside the driver, the something paid off. Potenlikov was snoring heavily and obviously very sound asleep.

"That will keep him for a few hours," Tannion thought as he pulled the truck out onto the freeway. There was a rest stop only a few miles ahead according to a sign they had passed. Tannion pulled in, and instead of lining up where the trucks were supposed to park, he maneuvered the truck over against the trees to the side then backed up so no one else would be able to see into the back.

The slide back door was locked, but there wasn't a tell tale seal and it took Tannion only seconds to pick the lock. He hung the open lock back on the hook and, with a push, lifted the truck's sliding door up. There was no immediate indication of anything wrong, and the screaming had stopped.

There were several boxes marked with pictures of furniture in front of him and Tannion carefully pushed them aside to look behind. The first thing he saw was the bars of a cage.

Inside the cage were more people than there should have been. At first glance, there appeared to be a couple dozen people, with as many young women as there were men. The twelve women were inside the cage while the twelve men were behind the cage. At least that was where they were supposed to have been. Two of the men had broken into the cage while the others watched.

One of the men was getting off his knees and pulling his pants up, it was very obvious what he had been doing to the girl on the floor. Another guy had a knife to the throat of one of the girls and obviously had them all in fear, which had stopped the screaming.

The girl on the floor got to her feet and was trying her best to cover herself with the remnants of her top. The two guys inside the cage looked over towards Tannion and a burst of Spanish came out of the one with the knife.

"What the hell's going on here," Tannion yelled as he moved around to the open door of the cage. Tannion could see where the cage lock had been knocked off so the two could get at the girls. Behind the cage there was a crowd of men, all obviously Latino. It seemed that two of the men had had enough of looking at the girls and wanted some action.

The girls were obviously illegal, but would probably never see the light of day in the United States. The Dennisons had kidnapped them and would have them shipped to somewhere in the Orient or the Middle East as sex slaves, but the men were different. They would be put to work in one of the Dennison assembly plants or on a farm somewhere.

They knew what was in store for them as they had paid to be in the back of the truck. To them the girls were only an unexpected bonus and they felt it wasn't necessarily wrong to cut off a little piece on the way.

Tannion didn't get an answer to his first question. "I said what is going on. You," Tannion pointed at the Mexican in the women's cage, "drop the goddamn knife and get out of the cage."

By this time the two guys in the cage had looked at each other and at the crowd of guys in the back. They had exchanged enough glances to tell a few of their friends that this guy wasn't going to stop the fun. The one with the knife started towards the cage door and Tannion stepped back to let them both out. At the same time he shifted his weight to the balls of his feet waiting for what he knew was going to happen. The only thing he hoped for was that he didn't have to kill the lot of them.

The first guy came out of the cage and looked at his buddies, then attacked. Tannion had expected it and he knew how to diffuse the situation. When the knife came down, Tannion stuck out his left hand and allowed the knife to penetrate through the palm up to the hilt of the knife. Being prepared, there was no pain and no bleeding. With his right hand Tannion hit the guy hard enough to lift him out of his boots and slam him against the wall with enough force that everyone in the truck knew he was dead.

Tannion stood there with his left hand in the air with the knife very prominently sticking out and asked who was next. As he was expecting, there were no takers. He removed the knife and healed the wound. He found some wire on the floor and secured the cage door as best he could. He knew that any one of the guys could remove it, but a few words were all it would take to ensure that no one would dare.

Tannion was pretty sure that the rest of the group wouldn't say a word as he took the dead Mexican out and dropped him in the trees behind the truck. When the truck got to its destination there may be some difficulty in a final head count, but as they were never in the back of the truck, the problem wouldn't be his or Potenlikov's.

When Tannion got back to the cab, Potenlikov was still sleeping. A few hours later when Potenlikov woke up, they were several miles down the road, and he was none the wiser. By the time they dropped the load off where they had been told to, Tannion knew that the Dennisons were the type of people he was looking for, and knew that now it was time for them to feel his wrath.

61

Tannion decided that Potenlikov and Philips didn't need to know what he was going to do. At least not yet. As long as they were ready and able to move in when he did, he would be okay. The first order of business was the truck.

The trip had been long, and after driving day and night they had dropped the truck off at the warehouse around ten that night. After Potenlikov dropped Tannion off at his place, Tannion grabbed a cab and headed back to where the drop was made. Tannion got out a couple of blocks from the warehouse and went around back.

The warehouse area was relatively well lit. He hopped over the fence making sure there were no cameras on him. Tannion made his way to a side door he had seen earlier. The door was locked, but with a quick pull Tannion was inside.

The door opened into a small security office and not into the main warehouse. The man sitting at the desk had a surprised look on his face, thinking the door was locked, but then he recognized Tannion. "What the hell are you doing back here?"

"I left something in the truck."

Tannion stepped forward before the guard had time to say anything more and hit him hard enough to push him into the back wall. Tannion checked, and finding no pulse he knew he had hit him hard enough.

The room was small without any windows and only one door out the other side, and it was full of monitors. One of them showed the inside of the warehouse including the truck which was sitting where they had left it. Tannion found the switches and shut down the cameras.

Tannion moved to the door into the warehouse and walked towards the truck. As he got close he thought he heard screaming coming from inside. He threw open the back of the truck and found a scene similar to what he had found before. In the middle of the truck was the same group of Mexicans, and there was a lot of noise and sex going on.

Most of the women were screaming. Others were pleading with their captors, and it looked like none of them were enjoying what was happening. Only a couple of the girls were standing and the others were on the floor and on their backs.

Tannion hadn't expected the Dennison's to leave the truck locked for the night, but that looked to be what had happened. Obviously the wire he had tied the cage door with hadn't been enough

Tannion knew it was time to stop the party. He jumped onto the truck bed. Two of the men had moved to see who had opened the door. Tannion grabbed the one closest to him by the hair. With a good twist he broke his neck and moved to the next guy. He didn't last much longer before Tannion threw his body out the open door.

More of the Mexicans were heading towards Tannion. Tannion hit the first to reach him with a right hook. It caught him under the chin and seemed to explode on his face. Now there were half a dozen of them coming at Tannion in the enclosed space. In a matter of a few seconds there were only two guys standing, and they turned and tried to run out the back of the truck, but Tannion caught them before they had gone a couple of steps. There were no innocent men here and there would be no male witnesses.

Turning back to the women he could see they were all very frightened, and although some of them hadn't found their clothes, they were trying to hide their nudity with their hands.

"I'm not here to hurt you," Tannion called out. "Do any of you speak English?" Tannion thought it was quite possible that the girls were more afraid of him than they were of the men he had just killed. Tannion was a gringo and not one of them, but he had stopped the rapes so he hoped they would come around. They had, however, seen what he could do.

One of the girls stepped forward. She looked to be a little older than the others, but was probably not much over twenty five, and even as disheveled as she was Tannion saw she was a beauty. She had managed to find most of her clothes and had just pulled her top over her breasts before she stepped forward.

"Yes, I speak English," she said in a heavily accented voice.

"Okay. Is anyone hurt?"

She turned around and talked to a couple of the girls directly around her and was quick in returning his question. "No one is injured," she said being very careful to get the English words right. One of the girls touched her on the shoulder and said something to her. She listened then turned back to Tannion. He could tell that even if some of the other girls could speak English, this one was the den mother.

"The girls are very scared and don't know what will happen to them next, especially when they find all the dead men."

"Yes, I understand." Tannion didn't know what he was going to do either, but he knew they couldn't stay there. Even if he cleaned the mess up and dumped the bodies somewhere they would be missing and the girls would be questioned. Also there was the fact that the girls would soon be sent to some part of the world to act as concubines or whores in what would probably be a short and nasty life. He couldn't leave them to that. After all, why had he come back to the warehouse if not to set them free?

"Okay, we have to get out of here. I don't have a car so we walk." Tannion needed time to think and walking would give him the time. As they walked out the side door, he made sure that no one was watching the place and got the girls out into a side street and made a few blocks as quickly as possible.

Tannion had the den mother walk beside him and the other girls were to walk in pairs behind them with the youngest and those with the worst clothes in the middle. Tannion chose two of the older girls to bring up the rear and gave one of them his coat to cover up what was hanging out. The guy on her hadn't left much of her blouse.

As they walked out of the warehouse district they started to encounter people. At first there were a couple of guys who only looked at them walk by. There were several people out on the street and it was bound to happen.

"Hey look what we have here," said a young looking black guy from the end of an alley as they approached. He wasn't alone as three more stood behind him.

"Don't even think about it," Tannion told them without raising his voice.

"Right. Fuck you." The punk looked behind him and directed the question to each of his friends. "Have you got yours picked out yet. I get the one on the end in the jacket."

This was followed by a laugh from his friends as they stepped out onto the sidewalk.

Tannion moved closer, and without raising his voice said, "I warned you once and I won't warn you again. It will take a few more than you, and you'd have to be a hell of a lot tougher, to even get close to these girls. One more step and I'll not be responsible for what happens."

He had their attention with the conversational tone he had used and the fact that he moved to a position between the four of them and the girls. Although he may have had their attention, they still felt they had the upper hand and took the next step that he told them not to take. Tannion told the girls to keep walking.

He felt it would be best to start rather than to react. Faster than any one of them could move, he grabbed the leader by the collar of his jacket and lifted him over his head with one hand on his neck and the other on his leg with him facing away from his friends. Tannion tightened his grip on the guy's collar enough to choke any sound from coming out of his mouth.

"Okay. If you turn around and walk back into the alley and keep walking, your friend here gets to live. If you don't then I smash him down on the sidewalk with enough force to break several ribs and his back and then choose one of you. Which will it be?"

The three punks were in a real quandary. They had heard their leader say let's get the girls and now he was hanging there not saying a word, and they really wanted to get a better look at those girls. They had seen how quick Tannion had grabbed their guy and how easy it was for him to pick their leader up over his head, and now as they waited for a count of ten without moving, they could see that he wasn't weakening.

They decided they had had enough and turned around and ran back into the alley and out the other end. Tannion took his hostage and set him gently down on the ground, but while the punk was choking he had managed to reach down into his back pocket and had brought out a blade. With a snap the blade popped into position and he swung it hard at Tannion.

Tannion saw it coming even while he held him in the air and easily blocked the thrust, with his free hand he brought his fist down on the top of the guy's head. The blow brought the punk to his knees. Tannion had made sure not to kill him with the blow, but had taken a little too much off and hadn't completely dazed him.

He came up swearing and swinging. Tannion stepped back, and with a quick step forward he swung his right hand into the guy's forehead with enough force to knock him out cold. He would have one hell of a headache, but he got to live. Tannion reached down with one hand and grabbed him by the back of the pants and tossed him into a dark spot in the alley then quickly herded the girls away.

"I told you to leave, but you wouldn't listen. Now look what you made me do," he said to himself.

The rest of the walk went without incident. Tannion found a motel and rented a room. He thought of getting two rooms, but decided not to split the girls up. It would have looked a bit odd for him to have rented two rooms anyway, so one would have to do. He made the girls hide around the corner and then sneaked them into the main floor room, which had two queen size beds. Not much of a room, but they weren't in the best part of town.

Tannion could tell that the girls had been together for a while as they very quickly determined who would sleep where. The older girls got the beds and the younger girls found the extra blankets and pillows and made beds for themselves as best they could on the floor. Tannion got the chair.

Tannion moved the chair over against the door, and as soon as the girls had settled down he closed his eyes and sleep found him almost immediately. Not the deep sleep of the exhausted, but the one-eye-open sleep of the wary. Dreams came quickly and his body replenished itself almost immediately.

62

Tannion woke up as soon as it was light, but he let the girls sleep. He sat and listened for an hour before he got up and walked over to the den mother. The girls all looked so young and innocent lying asleep. Most of the girls were young, pretty Latinas, probably only fifteen or sixteen years of age. Three or four looked to be from eighteen to twenty.

The den mother looked to be closer to twenty five. She was probably not the usual age of the girls snatched off the street in some Mexican city to be sold as sex slaves. One look at her and you knew why she had been picked up. She was tall and had a strong Latin look, but what hit Tannion immediately was that she was drop dead gorgeous. The kind of looks found on the red carpet at Hollywood functions or in Europe on the fashion stages. Definitely not the looks you find in a cheap motel in East LA.

She opened her eyes just as Tannion looked down on her. He touched his finger to his lips to silence her and quickly whispered that he would be back with something to eat. He had noticed a McDonalds a couple of blocks away when they had come in last night so he headed that way.

A few minutes later and Tannion was back with an assortment of breakfasts and coffee, and by that time the girls were all up and dressed and waiting for him. A quick look at the bathroom and he could see that none of them had showered, but they had combed their hair and tried to look as comfortable as they could in the little room sitting on the two beds in what was left of their clothes.

Tannion handed the food to the den mother and watched her deal it out to the girls. After they were all settled and eating, the den mother looked at him. "Thank you. This is the first nice thing that anyone has done for us since we were piled in the back of that truck." Tannion asked what had happened, and she told the entire story.

The girls had been picked up in Monterrey, Mexico. Most of the girls had been snatched off the streets. In her case she was trying to get a ride out of Monterrey when a truck had stopped and picked her up.

Her name was Louisa Francia Fluentes. At the time she was on the road trying to get out of town to escape her husband, who had beaten her a number of times. She had gone with him to the bar, and when he was drunk and hitting on all the girls in the place, she knew the beatings were sure to follow. She had been there too many times before and knew it was time to leave.

After the story was over, the girls had finished their breakfast and cleaned up and were looking expectantly at Tannion. He looked at Louisa and asked her what the girls would want to do. Most of the girls knew a few words in English, but not enough to get by. Only Louisa and one of the older girls were fairly fluent. She told Tannion her name was Maria.

"I can see if I can get you all back home," Tannion said, but was quickly shut off by both Louisa and Maria.

"Most of us don't have anything to go back to, and I'll never go back to Monterrey as long as my husband is still alive," Louisa told him. There was a look in her eyes that told Tannion that she was telling the truth and would not be swayed from it.

"How about any of the girls going back? If I could find a way to get them home, would any of them go?"

Louisa turned and spoke quietly to the girls, and as she listened very patiently to their answers, Tannion waited. When she was finished she turned back to him.

"There is only one girl who wants to go back. Mary was taken from the street when she was walking home from school. She's only fourteen and very scared. The men in the truck raped her. She was the one you saved first and she is very thankful to you, but she would like to go home."

Tannion told the girls to stay in the room. After a few minutes talking to the guy behind the motel counter he was back in the room. He told Louisa that he had booked the room for the rest of the week. The motel clerk didn't know how many there were in the room so it would be best if the girls were quiet and kept the curtains closed.

Tannion took Louisa and walked to a used clothing store, where they bought some clothes for her and the rest of the girls. Louisa couldn't believe Tannion's generosity, but he wasn't worried about the money. They found an old suitcase at a Goodwill store and headed back. Louisa thought it would be best for Mary to have an old suitcase. New luggage would make her stand out on her trip back into Mexico by herself.

When they got back to the motel, Louisa passed out the clothes to the girls. Tannion was pleasantly surprised when they stripped down to try them on as if he wasn't in the room. Most of the girls didn't have a bra on after the affair in the warehouse, and Tannion felt his face flush.

Mary took the clothes she had been wearing and another dress that would fit her and packed them into the suitcase. Tannion took her and Louisa out and told the other girls that they would be back in a couple of hours.

The three of them caught a cab and set off for the bus station. He bought Mary a ticket to Nogales, Mexico, where she would be able to catch another bus to Monterrey. He also gave her enough money for the ticket and some food on the way. The bus was on time and they were told that it would be leaving in half an hour. There was an older Mexican woman who was going to be on the same bus. After Louisa talked to her, and Tannion had given her twenty bucks, she agreed to look after Mary until she got to Nogales.

Tannion didn't feel good about leaving Mary at the bus depot, but Louisa had talked at length with the woman and she said she would take good care of her and not to worry. The woman was going to claim the girl as her daughter when they crossed the border and would see her get on the next bus.

"Will she need a passport?" Tannion asked.

"She has her ID with her picture on it. That should be enough," Louisa told him. "There shouldn't be a problem."

"How did she manage to keep her ID?"

"She had it on her when they grabbed her and she managed to hide it in her shoes."

They picked up some pizza and headed back to the motel. It was after two in the afternoon. There were now eleven girls left for Tannion to deal with. He sat and talked to Louisa for the rest of the afternoon trying to figure out what to do. Of the ten other girls, seven of them had been hookers in Monterrey and they all saw America, and especially Los Angeles, as their big break. LA was where they would have gone if they had ever had the chance.

The remaining three girls were from poor families, and they were feeling a little home sick. All they had seen since being brought to America was the inside of a truck, a warehouse, and the Mexican men who had raped them, yet they wanted to stay. If it had been American men it may have been different, but they had been raped by Mexicans and as a result they thought they were better off in America.

Tannion had eleven young, good looking, female, illegal aliens. Seven of them were hookers, three of them had stars in their eyes, and one was fascinating. Now what the hell was he to do?

63

Tannion called from a pay phone a few blocks from the motel and talked to Potenlikov. He told him he had to take a few days off to look after some personal business, and although Potenlikov said that Philips wouldn't be happy, there wasn't much Potenlikov could do about it. Tannion wasn't worried about Potenlikov, but he knew that Philips would continue to bring people like the Dennisons into his life and he wanted that to continue.

As far as he was concerned, having sex was for fun and not for money. Tannion had already placed a few hookers in an early grave, but these were just kids who didn't know any better. The others had been spreading diseases and knew about it and didn't care.

The first order of business was to get the girls into a better place than the motel and to see about what they could do for a living.

A couple days later Tannion and Louisa found a couple of two bedroom apartments a few blocks from where Tannion lived and moved the lot of them in. The rooms were bare and Tannion had to spend a few bucks to buy some beds and other furniture.

They set up three beds in each apartment and had five girls in each. Louisa told Tannion that she was moving in with him. Tannion wasn't sure it was a good idea with what he had in mind to do over the next few weeks, but he was still mesmerized by her and couldn't say no.

Louisa introduced Tannion to each of the girls, and as he took their hand in his he checked. He found a couple of sexually transmitted diseases which he quickly healed. Tannion left them in their apartments, and taking Louisa with him, they went home. The next day he was back with Potenlikov. A week had passed since the warehouse.

The first morning, Philips had Potenlikov take Tannion up to his penthouse suite. Tannion knew he was in shit, but his only worry was how to get out of it without losing his connection. If they tried to get physical he might end up killing them both. He needed Philips alive and in his position, and Tannion had started to like Potenlikov so he hoped that wouldn't be necessary.

Philips was sitting at his desk when Potenlikov showed Tannion into the room. He was dressed in a light blue pin stripe suit that was tailored for him and must have cost him a bundle. Philips looked up when they came into the room and motioned them into the chairs across from the desk.

In a very quiet voice Philips said. "Vlad here tells me that you called last week and told him you needed a few days of personal time. Is that so?"

Tannion had been thinking of this moment for a few days and had decided that the best thing to do was to tell mostly the truth and not to lie. He just wouldn't tell all of it depending on what Philips and Potenlikov knew and what part of the story he had to tell.

"That's correct, Mr. Philips."

"Now normally I wouldn't have a lot of problem with that, French. You've been doing very good work and Vlad tells me that you've been doing as you're told and doing it well, but when you call in for time off after a job for the Dennisons, and immediately I get a call like the call I got, you can see that I might not be that happy."

Philips voice slowly rose throughout this little speech and now was at a point of getting very loud. "That call came from Ross Dennison. It seems that the truck load you dropped off should have contained twenty-four Mexican nationals. He found eleven of them dead, one missing, and one of his men dead in the warehouse. There were supposed to be twelve girls in the truck and they're missing too. Now how the fuck do you think that happened, and what was your part in it?"

By this time Philips had turned as red as his natural color would allow, and a line of spittle had formed on his bottom lip. He stopped and shook himself for a moment. He found that he was standing up with both hands on his desk, and it didn't look like he could even remember standing.

With some effort he stopped and straightened his tie and looked at Tannion. Trying to get some semblance of calm in his voice he said, "Start talking and you had better make it good."

Tannion started the story with the noise in the truck. He left out the part of putting Potenlikov to sleep and then what happened while they were driving back. He only told Philips about going back to the warehouse and finding what looked to be men raping school girls. He went on to tell of killing the men and taking the girls away and having them locked down in a safe place.

While Tannion was telling the story, Philips was watching very closely and obviously having trouble keeping quiet, but to his credit he said nothing. When Tannion finished,

Philips looked at him and then asked Potenlikov, "Did you know anything about this?"

"No, Mr. Philips. I had no idea. I was with French when we dropped the truck off and then we came back here and then I went home. I had no idea,"

Philips turned back to Tannion. "What the fuck were you thinking, French? What did you think you were doing? You stuck your nose in and Dennison is pissed. I should throw you to him and let him do what he wants with you, but he'll think I was involved. Could you have fucked this up any better?"

"I think —"

Philips only let the first two words come out before he slammed his fist on the desk. "Shut up! You have already done enough and now I have to think of a way out of this."

Tannion tried to speak again, but this time it was Potenlikov who stopped him with a hard slap to the head. Tannion saw it coming and took the slap. Then in one quick motion he took Potenlikov's arm and twisted it until he was on his face at Tannion's feet. Philips got up as if to do something about it, but one look from Tannion and he stopped cold.

"As I was trying to say, I think there is a way to make a lot of good come out of this. We tell the Dennisons that we don't know anything about this, but then we move to put them out of business just like we did the Santos brothers," Tannion said.

"You don't have any idea, French. Now let Vlad up." Philips was scrambling, but he hadn't lost his cool, and he was still trying to act as if he was in control. He had seen how easily Tannion had handled Potenlikov and had thought better of doing anything but talk.

"The Dennisons are huge compared to the Santos brothers, and they won't just hand us their operation because you asked," Philips said.

Tannion could tell that he had said the right thing and had Philips thinking. Now it was his job to get Philips to agree to go ahead with a plan that would have the Dennisons put down. All Tannion had to do was to make Philips think it was his own plan. Tannion didn't care who took credit for the idea or, for that matter, who got the prize in the end. He let Potenlikov go.

Philips listened to Tannion tell them his thoughts before he asked them to leave. Potenlikov followed Tannion out of the office and left Philips alone. Philips knew that he had to set up a meeting with Ross Dennison and find out what he knew about the botched hauling job. At the very least he had to find out if Dennison thought Philips or his men had anything to do with it.

As usual, the swagger came back to Philips very quickly. "This might just turn out to be nothing but a good thing," he thought. "As long as Vlad can keep an eye out for French. It was quite a sight seeing him in action finally, if only against Vlad. He handled him like a school boy."

Potenlikov didn't say a word to Tannion when they left Philips's office. When they were in the car, Tannion said, "Sorry about that up there." He saw a hurt look come across Potenlikov's face for a moment. Tannion knew that having bested Potenlikov again was one thing, but doing it in front of the boss was the real problem. Potenlikov had a lot of pride. Tannion thought he might have lost what friendship he had with the big Russian.

It might take Potenlikov a while to get over what happened, but it would pass. Tannion was sure of it, especially if Philips got what he wanted. Now to set out a plan that could work.

64

Tannion made his way back to his place. He had moved a month earlier and he now liked where he was living. He made sure that he wasn't followed. He wasn't worried about Philips or Potenlikov, but he didn't want there to be anyone else who knew where he lived. Having Louisa in his life and at his place had brought out a protective streak that he didn't know he had.

Louisa was waiting for Tannion when he opened the door, and the smell of cooking hit him immediately. He was going to like this arrangement, especially if she was interested in a little more. They ate supper together and talked the evening away. When they went to bed, he took the couch and she took the bedroom.

The clock had luminescent hands, but even without them Tannion could tell that it was just after midnight. Something had awakened him. His night vision was working and he lifted his head to the small sound that he had heard. He saw Louisa standing in the doorway to the bedroom.

She hadn't had time to buy any night clothes and was wearing one of Tannion's shirts. The buttons were undone. Tannion watched her come closer. He could tell that she was having difficulty seeing in the dark and he knew that she thought he would be having the same problem. He could see her almost as clearly as if the lights were on.

Tannion stood up and looked at her. There was enough light coming in from under the door and around the curtains that Louisa could see him as she got closer, and as he approached she opened her arms and welcomed him into them. She took Tannion by the hand and led him back into the bedroom.

She was very gentle as she took off the little he was wearing and removed the shirt she was wearing. It had been a long time for Tannion, and it was worth the wait.

Tannion was awake the next morning before Louisa and quietly slipped out of the room and dressed in the living room. He put on the same clothes he had worn the day before. He had a lot on his mind. After last night he knew that he had something to lose for the first time in a long while.

Tannion knew the only way to stop the Dennisons from finding Louisa and the other girls was to keep them looking in other places. An anonymous phone call to a source saying that there had been a number of young Mexican girls seen boarding a bus heading north may help, but he knew that would not be enough.

The only real way to ensure their safety was to eliminate the source of the fear, and that was his plan. Problem was, the plan had to sound like Philips had thought of it first. Tannion knew that the Dennisons were meeting with Philips again, and although Tannion was to go only as a backup to Potenlikov, he made a big deal about telling Philips that he wanted to meet Mr. Dennison

When the day arrived they took the car to the same office building where they had met previously with Ross

Dennison and his sons. Tannion reminded Philips that he wanted to meet Dennison.

"All I want to do is introduce myself, shake his hand. I like to know who it is we're dealing with. I have the girls' safety in mind, and I just want to know." Tannion tried to sound like he was almost pleading with Philips as they drove to the office, when in fact if he had to, he would just go over and grab Dennison by the hand before anyone thought to stop him.

"Sure, French. I'll introduce you. Ross already knows Vlad and he should know who you are too, but don't do anything stupid. This is just a quick trip to find out what he knows, and then I can think how to use what you have on him and how best to find his weak point."

They went through the same ritual as the first time with a quick pat down outside the door, but this time when they went in, Tannion made sure to stay close to Philips. After exchanging very brief pleasantries, Philips took Tannion by the arm and maneuvered him around in front and said to Dennison, "Ross, I want to introduce you to someone who has become very valuable to Vlad and me. French, Ross Dennison."

Dennison took Tannion's hand, but it was easy to tell that meeting one of the help's help was not something he was used to doing. At least he was civil, but it didn't matter to Tannion as he was busy. Nothing major popped up from Dennison, but there were a few minor ailments. A little arthritis and a few age-related items, but nothing that could kill him for a long time.

That was until Tannion placed an order for a slightly altered cell in his right lung. The cancer would grow very quickly and Dennison would be dead in a matter of four to six weeks. It was going to be quick and unstoppable unless, of course, Tannion stopped it.

Dennison let go of Tannion's hand and quickly took Philips by the arm and led him into the back room. He stole a quick glance at Tannion to ensure that they weren't followed. A few minutes later and they were back in the hallway to the elevator.

Once they were back in the car, the rather stern and uninviting countenance that Philips was displaying burst open. "That son of a bitch! That low down dirty son of a bitch. Who does he think he's dealing with? I would love to kick his ass." Philips was not a happy man.

Philips went on to tell Potenlikov and Tannion what went on in the back room. Dennison had told Philips about the dead Mexicans and how he knew it wasn't Philips. When Philips asked him why he knew this, he was told that Dennison knew each and every one of the men working for Philips and had his men check up on the whereabouts of them all. The only one they couldn't locate was French, and they knew that it must have been a fairly large crowd who killed a dozen men, so it couldn't be connected to him.

"That son of a bitch had the nerve to go behind my back and check out my guys, and then after he doesn't find anything, he wants me to use my men to hunt down the guys responsible. He thinks he knows who it was and wants me to get dirty and keep the muck off his head," Philips was on a bit of a rant.

Tannion was hearing just what he wanted to hear. Now was the time for him to break the news to Philips. Philips already thought that Tannion had something on Dennison and wouldn't be surprised to hear about it.

"A friend of mine has access to some medical files and he tells me some disturbing news about our friend Dennison. I understand that he has lung cancer and has only a few weeks to live."

The news took Philips by surprise and took most of the sting out of his mood. He even had a second to think. "Cancer. What does that mean? How long?"

"I was told he'll be dead in a few weeks."

"Shit, Dennison has cancer. How good is your source? Is there a possibility that this could be only a rumor?" Philips had questions. Somewhere in the past couple of days Tannion had moved into the inner circle. He might not get to stay there for long, but for now he was in.

"My source is legit and I've never seen him fail me. If he says Dennison is going to die, he's going to die. The question now is how do we make the most of it?"

Philips took a few seconds. As he held his right hand under his chin and looked up at the ceiling, you could almost see the gears grinding. The words came out of his mouth as if he was talking to himself and no one was listening.

"As long as I stay close, and as soon as there are tell tales that he can't deny, then I can move in with the idea that I'm trying as much as I can to help. With his sons not having much experience and them needing a black man in LA, it just might work. It just might work."

"Making a hit on Dennison's enemies would help to put you in his good books, and as long as they don't know who was involved, it might soften the rest of the crowd a little as well," Potenlikov said. The Russian was thinking too.

After they got back to the office they spent the better part of the night planning. When they drew to a close and had a stiff drink to ring in the morning, Tannion had a sudden realization. He was being treated almost as an equal by Philips and somehow even Potenlikov had been elevated from someone who Philips needed and trusted to someone Philips planned and confided with. Potenlikov may have even forgiven Tannion for what happened the last time they were in Philips's office.

The plan was, for the most part, pretty simple. By staying close to Dennison and knowing that Dennison thought Philips to be very clean, Philips could make a few hits that would increase his status. They would use Dennison's knowledge and Potenlikov's and Tannion's strength to cut a swath through the heads of crime in LA.

If Dennison lived long enough, they might be able to clean out a good part of the city, and Philips would take over as much as he could. By the time Dennison died, he would be in control of enough that they could take the sons out and have it all. Philips liked the plan because it gave him power, and Tannion loved it because he got to see the end of many of the scum he was sent to get rid of. It would also keep the girls safe.

The great part was that Philips thought of it as his plan, and for the most part it was, thanks to a little push. Potenlikov was along for the ride, but as long as it was a good ride he was happy. Tannion might have to touch Dennison again in case he died too soon. He needed to stay alive only long enough to pass on all his knowledge.

65

Tannion and Louisa checked in with the girls every day. Maria was very quickly tutoring them all in English and soon they would be ready to start work. The amount of English they would need to get the types of jobs they were getting was minimal. Philips had some connections, and each of them had a position waiting at one of his hotels as maids. They were not great jobs, and in a while most of them might end up out on the streets working for a living, but at least then it was their choice.

"All the girls have jobs and it's time I get one too, but I don't want to work in the hotel where they work. I was a teacher in Mexico and I would like to be one in America too," Louisa said. She had mentioned this before, but Tannion hadn't been able to give her the answer that she wanted. This time was no different.

"Louisa. I'm afraid that without being a citizen or having a green card that isn't going to happen."

"Well then I need to be a citizen," Louisa said with a matter-of-fact attitude that made Tannion smile. It was a nice thought, but it wasn't going to happen just because she wanted it to.

"I'll make a couple of phone calls tomorrow and see what I can do. The first thing for now is to keep you safe."

They made love that night with wild abandon. This was someone he couldn't afford to lose. He had to find a way to keep her safe. The next day he made those phone calls. Immigration placed him on hold for a long time, and when he finally got through he found what he needed. There were possibilities with asylum and landed immigrant status, but they were either not likely or would take forever. There was only one way that was both quick and sure. They would have to get married.

With all things that were bound to be going on in the near future, Tannion knew that marriage would have to wait. When they finally had a chance to talk about it, Louisa was not sure.

"I'm already married in Mexico."

"I don't think that U.S. law recognizes a Mexican marriage," Tannion told her, although he knew that he didn't have a clue if it was true.

"In the eyes of God we are still married."

"How about I go to Mexico and kill him for you. Would that help?" Tannion said very tongue in cheek.

"Would you? Yes, that would be the best. You kill Jose and then I am no longer married. Yes. You can go and kill him." Louisa had the straightforward, matter-of-fact way of speaking her mind that made you believe that what she said was either true, or at least very possible.

"Shit, Louisa. I was joking. I'm not going to go down to your home town, look for a guy named Jose and then kill him on the street and come home. I would end up rotting in one of your fine Mexican jails. We'll just have to wait for a while and see what happens." Tannion might have been hoping for some kind of miracle. The last thing he wanted right now was to get married, but he was definitely falling in love.

Tannion thought he could get a fake green card made up for her, but threw that idea out as too risky. He didn't want to take any chances with Louisa. Things would just have to wait. Anyway, other things were happening. Bigger things.

It took a couple of weeks for the plan to gel while they waited for Dennison to get worse. Philips had someone keep an eye on Dennison, and when he made a trip to the doctor he made sure he talked to one of the sons. It was after the Dennison's second visit to the doctor that Philips was told there was a problem and another meeting was set up.

Meanwhile Philips had been busy on the other front. There was a faction in town that was easy pickings. The King's Guard motorcycle club had been in a feud with the Dennisons for several years. There was an issue of ownership of parts of the city for both the drug and prostitution trades.

It was pretty easy for Philips to drop an anonymous phone call into the club indicating that Dennison was pretty sure that it was the Guard who had killed the Mexicans and stolen the girls — and that the Dennisons would find a way to make them pay.

Philips staged a small hit on a meth lab that belonged to the Guard. They found two men in the place and Tannion disposed of them both in quick style. After they took what they wanted they painted the words "pay back" on one of the walls. Then it was only a wait-and-see situation.

The Guard hit fast and they hit hard. It started with a drive-by shooting, and a couple of the Dennisons' men were killed very early in the battle. A couple of days later one of

Ross's sons was caught in a shootout and killed. Ross was beside himself with anger and grief. It was time for Philips to step in.

Potenlikov took Tannion and two hand picked men and waited inside the empty clubhouse the Guard were known to own and hang out in. About one in the morning the leader and fourteen men from the King's Guard walked into the club. None walked out.

One of the men Potenlikov had chosen worked for the Dennisons and the news got back to Ross Dennison very quickly. Philips had a phone call very early the next morning. He was in his office expecting the call.

Philips placed the receiver back in its cradle and looked over at Tannion and Potenlikov sitting on the other side of the desk. "I think we're in. Ross wants to talk to us this afternoon, and this time he used words that included you two. He knows what you did for him so you should expect a few good words, maybe a reward. This could be big."

66

Philips was right about a couple of things. Tannion and Potenlikov did get a few good words from Dennison, but no cash reward. Tannion knew he would eventually get the reward he was looking for, but first there was work to do. Philips had to make himself invaluable to Dennison if the plan was to succeed.

The meeting didn't take too long and there was an obvious change in the attitudes of all parties. Philips was feeling more involved and Dennison was looking at Philips through completely different eyes. Even the bodyguards smiled when they got in the elevator. Or at least what might pass for smiles.

After the meeting was over and they were back at Philips's place, Philips called Tannion and Potenlikov into his office.

"French, this is something that you started and I'm going to finish. Dennison is going to find me to be the best partner he's ever had, but there's a lot to do."

Philips handed a sheet of paper to Potenlikov. "That's a list of all the kingpins in Los Angeles freshly supplied by Dennison. As much as I hate the son of a bitch, he sure as hell knows a whole lot more of what goes on in this town than I do."

There were forty names on the list. Each of them was known to rule parts of LA, and many of them were also known to have had run-ins with the Dennisons. It had taken a lot of phone calls and talking to the right people, but Philips managed to narrow the list to thirteen names. The big thirteen he called them.

The first hit was in the north end. Julio Braggo was a small timer who over the past couple of years had pissed off the Dennisons on more than one occasion. Not enough to force them into action, but there was no love lost between them. His bunch was a good one to start on.

Braggo was left on the list because he should be an easy mark, and Dennison had made a note on him. It was always good to have Dennison happy at this point.

Tannion and Potenlikov and a few men had waited outside the house that Braggo was living in. They went in guns blazing. Braggo never saw it coming and never got a shot off. The hit went as revenge and not to gain territory, but Dennison loved it and that was all they needed.

Second on the list was a much bigger mark. Victor Viscilli was one of the biggest drug runners on the east end. Almost nothing came into LA that he didn't have a hand in. Even the Santos brothers used to ask Victor's permission to do business. Viscilli was too big for the Dennisons to do anything about, so Philips had the hit planned slightly different than with Braggo.

The plan for Viscilli was more subtle. First Tannion and Potenlikov went to an apartment where a couple of Viscilli's men were known to live and made sure they never walked out. These men were big in Viscilli's operation, but they would only be replaced. The plan was to make Viscilli think that it was Dennison making the hit, and a well-placed phone call started Viscilli's action.

A week after the Viscilli hit, Dennison took a hit of his own. It was only with a little luck that the remaining son, Paul Dennison, got out without being killed. A second hit on Viscilli took place at one of his warehouses. After taking out the guards, Philips's men loaded the trucks up with everything they could get their hands on and left it in one of Dennison's warehouses where it could be found.

An anonymous phone call and it wasn't hard for Viscilli to find the warehouse. The war was on. At that point Dennison added his men to the battle and they hit Viscilli hard at his Los Angeles home. After the smoke cleared and before the police cruisers pulled into the yard, Victor Viscilli and ten of his closest men were dead.

As luck would have it, Viscilli had called a meeting at his place to discuss what action they needed to take against the Dennisons. They were all in one room when the hit went down. Philips wasn't sure, but he thought it very possible that Dennison had someone on the inside, which made the timing of the hit easy.

The cops called it a gangland killing unlike anything they had ever seen in Los Angeles. Dennison was jumping with joy while fielding calls from the cops at the same time. The cops knew Dennison wasn't getting along with Viscilli, but the calls were easy to defend.

Ross Dennison had given enough money to charities, cops benefits, and the like to ensure that he was left alone. Unless there was irrefutable evidence, the cops would do just enough to ensure the report looked thorough, but that would be all. Dennison's name would never show up on a file.

The big thirteen were now down to eleven. Dennison had grown in area and Philips had grown in stature. Things couldn't be going better. Tannion knew they were heading in the right direction every time one of the guys went down.

Tannion still had the initial list of forty names complete with addresses and known hangouts. He kept busy on his own tracking the rest of the list and getting to see and know as much as he could. Tannion spent many late evenings watching, but only rarely doing anything. He was sure the information would come in handy after the first thirteen were dealt with. Eventually he wanted to deal with them all.

67

Philips got the call he was expecting. Dennison finally told Philips about his cancer and that he only had a short time to live. Philips called Tannion and Potenlikov into his office. He couldn't wait to tell them what else Dennison had told him.

Dennison had gone on to tell Philips that with his oldest son dead, he was worried about his youngest son taking over the operation. Dennison knew he needed someone to take care of him and lead him into his future. Philips had proven to be loyal, quick thinking, and quick to take action, and he was not afraid to take lethal action. Dennison had asked Philips to take on the role of guardian.

Philips had of course taken a few seconds to ponder the question, as if it wasn't something that he had worked toward, and then said he would be very happy to take on the job. Dennison didn't realize he had probably just signed the kid's death warrant.

That night as Tannion lay in Louisa's arms, he found sleep difficult, and instead of requesting sleep he took the time to think. Dennison was the largest crime boss in Los Angeles according to Potenlikov. Once he was gone, and the kid was looked after, that would make Philips the largest, and Tannion was one of his right hand men.

Once Philips was in control, Tannion could use the manpower of the organization to clean up the streets. Drugs, gambling, and prostitution would still be the main activities of the group. Philips had always considered theft as below him except when it met his purposes as with the Santos brothers, but the big money was in the big three.

If Tannion had his way, the prostitutes would be well-treated and clean. The drugs would be good quality and not sold to kids, and gambling would be fun and free of worry. Of course those weren't exactly the ideals that Philips would be concerned with, but it may only be a matter of time and that would take care of itself. With a smile, Tannion closed his eyes and asked sleep to come.

Over the next couple of weeks, life went on as normal while they waited for Dennison to die. Philips and Potenlikov had spent many hours with Tannion plotting direction when he did. Dennison spent several hours in the small office off the sitting area with Philips going over the business. It would only be a matter of time.

Tannion and Potenlikov made a few key hits on the list of thirteen, with Philips making sure that Dennison knew about the extent of each hit. Each hit strengthened Philips position with Dennison, but also weakened the opposition.

Tannion also took a lot of his own time to continue to watch and learn about the bigger list of forty. Almost all of his free time was spent watching and learning. At least, as much free time as he could spare from being with Louisa. Tannion didn't think there was any need to leave anyone out. There was no need to be limited to only thirteen.

Dennison died in his sleep at his home on a Monday morning. The funeral services were large and expensive and the guest list included the chief of police and the Mayor of Los Angeles. Dennison was known to be linked to the crime world, but nothing had ever been proven and he had donated millions of dollars to charity and to the city over the years. The politicians were falling over each other trying to tell the city what a great man Dennison was. Not too many people knew about the sizable personal donations that had bought some of those same politicians.

A week after the funeral, which Philips thought a reasonable mourning period, he gave Paul Dennison a call to set up their first meeting. After two similar meetings, Philips moved his office into the Dennison building and took the floor below the penthouse.

The first order of business was to take a good look at the books and get a feel for how big Dennison was. Paul Dennison was cooperating fully, which allowed him to stay alive and well. Philips had moved his men into the area and was in the process of integrating the two forces.

Tannion had moved in as well. He talked to each of Dennison's men and made sure to shake their hand to get a feel for what kind of person they were. Some he knew from experience and others he learned about through information from Potenlikov. Many of the men he had never seen before.

Dennison had a lot more men than Philips had working for him, so Tannion and Potenlikov had the job of ensuring that they were all on board. There would always be a few who thought it should be a family-run business and a few who didn't want to work for a black man.

There were a few who looked like they would make trouble and an example was made of one of them in front of the other Dennison men. After that, everything fell into place. All the heads of Dennison's house had a Philips man looking over his shoulder or the head was gone in place of a Philips man. Everything was looking good for the future.

68

Tannion's life had reached a degree of normalcy. Tannion was getting what he wanted from Philips plus spending time on his own after hours. One day it would be a meeting with one of the list of thirteen where Tannion might shake a few hands and Philips would make some sort of deal. Later he would be watching someone else from the larger list. Watching and learning.

At the end of the day Tannion would come home to Louisa. She would have a drink ready for him and supper on the stove. The only problem was that Louisa was not happy with her situation. She was not in a position to do much about it, however, and she knew it. She had a husband back in Monterrey who she hadn't heard anything from and didn't want to. She had fallen in love with the big gringo, but her first love was teaching and she felt the loss.

Tannion was well aware of his situation with Louisa and knew there was only one answer that made sense. It was a Friday night after an easy day at work where he had only some bodyguard and driving duty with Philips. Tannion had called Louisa and told her he was taking her out and that she should dress up in one of the new dresses she had bought.

He had made reservations at one of the better restaurants up town. He had already made an earlier stop and had picked out a ring. It was a little over a carat in size with two smaller diamonds set in a swirl pattern around the larger diamond. He thought Louisa would love it.

When they arrived at the restaurant they were seated at a nice table in the middle of the room. Tannion made small talk and Louisa filled him in on what the girls were doing. Two of them had disappeared and were probably back on the street.

The girls had been in town long enough and were old enough to look after themselves, and although they may be into the oldest profession again, Tannion couldn't worry about them. The mother hen in Louisa couldn't help but worry. The other girls were doing very well at their jobs and had managed to save up a few dollars, and of course there were boys.

Their small talk wound down as they ate. The restaurant was known for good food, and they weren't disappointed. The food was excellent.

Tannion waited until the dessert was brought to the table. As Louisa picked up her spoon to taste the sherbet, Tannion stood up and walked over to her side of the table. He took her hand and got down on one knee. Louisa let out an audible gasp.

"Louisa Francia Fluentes, will you marry me?" Tannion had put some thought into what he was going to say when the time came, but when it did, his mind and mouth wouldn't connect. All he could do was blurt out the one line proposal and wait.

Louisa didn't wait for a breath or a pause or hardly for Tannion to finish the question. She jumped up and crushed him with her arms around his neck. She breathed yes several time between kisses, and the people at the tables around them applauded, having seen and heard everything.

Louisa talked all the way home in the taxi. She wanted to get married right away and then work on getting her citizenship papers so she could find a job teaching. That night, with Louisa sleeping in his arms, Tannion had time to think.

Tannion didn't want to get married as Victor French. He had almost lost the Victor in the past several months as everyone knew him only as French. He realized he had been French for a year already.

He knew he was going to have to tell Louisa what his real name was. She already knew what business he was in, and it didn't matter to her, but should he tell her more?

Could Tannion tell her about being on the run? Could he be with her on the run? Questions came to Tannion that should have been there long before he proposed, but it was too late for them now. Tannion loved this woman and he had to do right by her, and that did not mean being Mrs. Victor French.

Tannion was going to marry Louisa and make her legal. He was going to tell her his real name, but as he drifted off to sleep, he knew that was all he would tell her.

69

Tannion had the day off. He was going to tell Louisa today. After a long shower and the time it took to get shaved and dressed, the morning was half over before he went into the kitchen. Louisa was there with a cup of coffee and a smile on her face that just wouldn't go away.

"You make me the happiest woman in the world," she smiled at Tannion. She handed him a cup of coffee and turned around and placed some bread in the toaster

"You make me happy too, Louisa, but there's something I need to tell you. First thing is that I love you and never want to lose you."

Louisa lost her smile for second. As it came back she told him she loved him too and that he could never lose her, but she still wanted to know what he had to tell her.

"I need to tell you more about myself and some of it you may not like."

"I don't think there's anything you can tell me that would make any difference, so why not just don't tell me."

"No, this needs to come out." Tannion took Louisa by the hand and sat her down at the kitchen table taking the seat next to her. She noted the serious look on his face and waited for him to say what he had to say.

"First, my name is not Victor French. It's Jim Tannion. I had to change my name when I came to Los Angeles so the FBI couldn't find me. I'm wanted in New York for killing a cop."

Louisa's face turned white with the news, and she got up and walked around the kitchen. She looked at Tannion and he could see that the look wasn't one of disgust but of wanting to understand. And maybe there was a little fear. Fear for what the future might have in store. She sat back down before she said anything, and this time it was Tannion's turn to wait.

"I know what kind of business you're in, and have since we met in the truck. I knew we would always have to watch out for the police, but this is different. What happened? I saw you kill the men in the truck so I know you are very capable of killing, but I have come to know and love you because you are a good, kind, and generous man."

Tannion told her what had happened in New York. He left out the parts about getting shot and racing ahead to get out of town. Even Louisa couldn't know about his hidden strengths. She had seen what he could do when he saved the girls in the truck, but she only knew he was good with his hands and that was as far as he was willing to go. Even with Louisa.

"I really didn't know that he was a cop at first and I certainly didn't want to kill him. I was just running away."

"I believe you," Louisa told him, and he could see the sincerity.

Louisa got out of the chair and went over to the counter to pour them both another cup of coffee. The smell of coffee permeated the kitchen making it smell like so many other kitchens in the city. The discussion in this kitchen however was not typical.

She still wanted to get married and become a citizen as soon as possible, and this was the man she wanted to marry. She had the thought that now she wanted to get married even sooner than before. That way if they were caught, she wouldn't be sent back to Mexico.

"I want to be Mrs. Jim Tannion and not Mrs. French," she told Tannion. She thought how strange it felt to be calling him Jim. "I want to meet your mom and the rest of your family and live a normal life. I understand that not all of that is possible, but at least I want to be Mrs. Tannion, and I want to get married as soon as possible."

Tannion knew that approaching any of his close relatives would end up with the cops starting another chase. He hadn't worried about the cops for a long time and finally felt comfortable when a cop car drove by when he was standing on the street. They were not looking for him. At least not as Jim Tannion. As Victor French, that was a different possibility.

If Louisa wanted to get married sooner rather than later, that was okay with Tannion and he was happy that she wanted to be Mrs. Jim Tannion. Tannion knew there was no time limit on murder, but he had been safe for a long time so why not for many more years.

70

Tannion was sure that it was a bad idea, but he had promised Louisa that she would become Mrs. Louisa Tannion. It seemed to have become very important to her and he wanted to make her happy.

Tannion told Philips and Potenlikov that he had asked Louisa to marry him and that he was going to go down to the local office to get a marriage license and needed some time off.

Philips was more than happy to give Tannion the day off and much to Tannion's surprise, Philips told him that he wanted to set up and pay for the wedding. Philips had grown to trust Tannion and as much as Philips would not have considered Tannion to be a friend, he was his boss. Philips wanted to use his ability to pay as his way of showing his faith in an employee. Philips also liked to show off, and what better way than a wedding.

Tannion had called the city clerk's office to find out what they needed to do to get married. He was happy to hear there wasn't a blood test requirement in California and that it didn't matter that Louisa wasn't an American. All they needed to do was to make an appointment, wait in whatever line there was, and pay their money.

They also required a picture ID and had to tell the clerk's office what their parents' names were. Tannion knew that these were problems, but thought there was an easy way around them. Tannion's Victor French ID was still the fake he had bought when he first came to town. It had worked up until this point, but now he would need a fake ID with his real name on it. The beard and hair would have to go as well.

Louisa was also a problem. She was married in Mexico, and although California may not recognize a marriage in Mexico, they may not want to marry a Mexican to an American if they knew that the Mexican was still married in Mexico.

Louisa had taken the name Fluentes from her husband in Monterrey, but her maiden name was Chavez. Louisa could use any name she wanted, and all she needed was to come up with the fake information she would need.

Tannion asked her to pick a different last name for the IDs and was surprised with the name that Louisa wanted on her fake birth certificate. She wanted to be Louisa Maria Franklin.

"I never liked the name Francia and my mother's name is Maria."

"But why Franklin?"

"I like the way it sounds. Not everyone in Mexico has Spanish or Mexican sounding names and it's close to Francia."

"Well that's different, and pretty soon we'll change it."

Louisa was very pleased and found it hard to wait the few days it took to get the new documents made. Tannion used a new connection to get documents that were more than just rough copies. They were close to the real thing and he knew they would pass the test at the clerk's office.

Tannion had to come up with different information for his birth certificate. There were several Jim Tannions in the U.S. and all he needed to do was become another who would not touch any police radar. He changed his birth date and made himself a couple of years younger, born in Los Angeles. If they checked for hospital records he hoped there would be a least one hospital where some of the birth records had been lost.

Tannion hated the idea of losing his mother in this way, and he especially didn't like the idea of not having her at his wedding, but there was no choice. At least Louisa was happy. She knew that the wedding was going to be small with only a few of Tannion's work friends attending and with a Justice of the Peace presiding. She was okay with that.

She would have liked to have had some of her family at the wedding too, but with both of them missing families it seemed easier somehow. Louisa and Tannion took a taxi to the city clerk's office. Tannion had set up an appointment, but he knew there would be a line up and they would have to wait.

A little over two hours later and they had a shiny new marriage certificate in their hands and a Justice of the Peace lined up to marry them.

Philips was making a big splash about the whole thing. He had hired a company to cater the event and had invited all the biggest heads of crime in town. Tannion thought it was a bit more than Philips would normally do for an employee, but he wasn't arguing.

Philips had gone as far as picking the date, and as long as he was paying for everything and the date wasn't too far into the future, then what the hell. Louisa wanted it to happen sooner, but she would have to wait. Only a couple of weeks and she would be married and then she could work towards what she wanted. She really wanted to be able to work in America. It was all she could talk about.

71

When the phone rang in Mike Rallin's office, Rallin was sitting back with his feet up on the desk reading a case file that had come across his desk the day before. A woman had reported a murder, but the body was nowhere to be found. The file had been passed to the FBI as it may have crossed state lines or maybe the locals hoped the FBI would take it and get it out of their hands.

The jurisdiction was suspect and Rallin didn't think there was much of a case unless a body showed up. He would have to follow the few leads and probably waste his time. It had been rather quiet so he could afford to spend some time on a case like this.

He leaned forward and picked the phone up off the desk. "Rallin here."

"Mike."

"Yes, who's this?"

"It's Jason Fredrick in Records."

Rallin knew Jason from past cases, but didn't know him well. He thought he could put a face to the name and knew him to be alright, but that was about all.

"Jason, what can I do for you?"

"No, Mike, it's what I can do for you this time. I just got a buzz from Los Angeles. One of your wanted characters may have shown up in LA. We just got a hit on the name Jim Tannion."

Rallin's ears pricked up with the name Tannion. He also knew there had been three earlier hits on the name and they all had proved to be nothing. There were, at last count, forty-seven living Jim Tannions in the United States. Each one had been checked out, including any James or J. Tannion, but all had been legit. It was only when a new name appeared that the radar went off.

"I didn't think Tannion was that common a name."

"It's not that common, but there are enough of them," Fredrick said as if the comment was directed towards him. "This time it was a marriage license. The age is different with different parents' names, and it says he was born in LA, but that could all be faked if the ID was good enough. The clerk's office is pretty good at spotting fake identification, but they're not perfect."

"Thanks, Jason. Please send me the data and I'll look into it."

"No problem, Mike, and good luck. It should be on your desk in an hour."

Rallin sat the missing person case file down on the desk, forgotten for now. Tannion was still the top case on his list even if had been cold now for almost a year and a half. He needed a break and maybe this was it. He couldn't wait to get the file in his hands.

He knew there wouldn't be a picture, but there would be an address, and although that may be a fake as well, it was a starting point. He doubted that anyone would drive to LA to get a marriage license unless they were living in the Los Angeles area, and although he knew Los Angeles was a hugely populated area, it was better than nothing.

As soon as the information was on Rallin's desk he started the search. First job was to find out where the license was issued. A couple of well placed phone calls and Rallin had the address of the clerk's office where the marriage license was obtained. There were a lot of offices in the city where someone can come in and apply for a marriage license. Luckily the license was applied for in person and not online. Now he had a place to start.

Rallin got Pansloski on the phone and filled him in on what he had so far and they agreed to meet at the airport. As soon as the call had come in from Fredrick he knew that he and Pansloski were heading for Los Angeles. After a quick check in with the boss, the flight was booked. They were ready to start again, only this time on the other side of the continent. Nothing like hitting the big cities. First New York and now Los Angeles. If this was the real Jim Tannion, he must like the bright lights.

Rallin and Pansloski checked in with the local FBI headquarters on Wilshire Boulevard. Rallin had never been to California before. Pansloski had taken his kids to Disneyland several years ago and that had been his only time in the area.

After reporting in to the bureau they were given a couple of desks in a small office off the squad room. Then they were left on their own. They didn't expect any assistance from the Los Angeles staff until they were further into the case, and that was exactly what they were told. The lead was probably like the last few and would end up as a dead end.

An hour later and Rallin and Pansloski were in front of the address given as the county clerk's office where the marriage license was issued. A quick look around and nothing looked any different than in any street in the area. Rallin wondered what he had been expecting.

The office was open until five and it was almost four thirty. The office was almost empty. They walked up to the first person they saw and flashed their badges.

"Is the manager in? We would like to talk to him," said Rallin taking the lead as he always did when it was just him and Pansloski.

The manager was in a back office and Rallin and Pansloski quickly filled him in on what they were after. He left the office for a minute, and when he came back he told them that when they closed in a few minutes, all the staff had been asked to meet in his office and they could ask their questions then.

The few minutes seemed to drag as they waited until five o'clock. Rallin was a little startled when the first of the staff came into the office. In all there were only five people who worked in the office other than the manager.

Rallin pulled a good quality picture of Tannion from the briefcase and passed it to the first in line.

"We're looking for this man," Rallin started. "We think that a man using the same name as the man in this picture applied for a marriage license here three days ago. All we need is for you to look at the picture and tell me if any of you have seen this man, and in particular was he here earlier this week."

The first man shook his head and passed the picture to the woman on his right who took a look and quickly said no and passed it to the next person. A relatively young looking, slightly overweight girl took a look, and Rallin could see recognition in her face as soon as she saw the picture.

She started talking almost immediately and Rallin had to stop her and ask her to slow down so they could understand her. She was obviously excited and nervous, and they didn't want to get anything wrong.

"Now say that again. You saw this man and did you supply him with a marriage license."

"Yes. He was here. He came up to my window and we were face to face for several minutes while we worked on his application. Is he dangerous? Am I in danger?"

Rallin had seen the nervousness and hadn't had it click that she would be worried about her own safety. "No. There won't be anything to worry about. We just want to talk to this man. He's not the type to hurt people," Rallin lied to her. He had decided it was better if they knew as little as possible. It was very unlikely that Tannion would come back to seek revenge on a clerk even if he knew that was where the information on him had come from, but there was no reason to tell her that.

Rallin thanked the rest of the staff and they took that as their dismissal. They all left with a smile as they had been the lucky ones not to have seen the guy in the picture. In their business they only saw the ones at their window, and never saw the people sitting for hours on the chairs in the middle.

Rallin was also getting excited and he could see the excitement on Pansloski's face. He jumped in with the next question. "Was this man alone or was his future bride with him?"

"California law requires both parties to be present when they're applying, so she was here. She was a very good looking Latina."

"The name on the form is Franklin. Are you sure she was Latina?"

The clerk was definite in her answer. Rallin and Pansloski continued to quiz her. She had been working at the branch for a little over a year and this was her first encounter with the police, let alone the FBI. She told them everything she could remember and after a few minutes they let her go. With a large sigh of relief she got up and left the office. Rallin assured her that they would not need her again.

Rallin and Pansloski took a taxi back to the bureau and both of them had a hard time being quiet in the cab. Tomorrow they would be getting a car from the pool, but for now they kept quiet. The cabby knew where they were going and that they were FBI agents just based on their clothes, but that was all he needed to know.

Once back in the quiet solitude of their little office, they both started talking at once. They both knew they had hit the mother lode and the next step was going to be very important. If they could find Tannion it would be removing one of the top fugitives from the most wanted list, which would greatly raise their status in the bureau, but this chase was too personal to both of them for anything else to matter.

The chase was on.

72

Tannion found it hard to go to work each day knowing that his wedding date was only two weeks away. Somehow the date had more meaning than any other day in his life and it had him jittery.

Louisa was in her element. She was working with the company that Philips had hired and she loved it. She had a big wedding the first time as both her and her ex-husband had big families and they all came as well as their neighbors and friends. It was a gala affair, but not like this.

The invitations might be costing more than her entire wedding did in Mexico. Back home she was able to keep the costs down by having everything but the ceremony at their house, and everyone brought food and drinks and had a good time. Music would almost come from nowhere as all of a sudden a band would be playing. This was going to be different.

Philips had met Louisa only a couple of times, and in this case all her instructions were given to her by Tannion. He passed her the name of the caterer and some idea of what the budget was, although it wasn't very clear. She had also been given the guest list.

She had spent the day with the caterer and after calling Tannion and knowing that he would be home at the usual time, around five, she headed for home. She was happy with the knowledge that she was going to get married in a couple of weeks and what a wedding it was going to be.

As soon as Tannion got home, Louisa started talking wedding, filling him in on some of the details of what had been planned. The biggest part was the invitations.

"Who are these people, Jim?" Louisa asked as she pointed to the guest list. She was slowly getting used to calling him Jim, but only when they were alone.

Tannion had seen the list for the first time a couple of days earlier when he had passed it to Louisa. It wasn't exceptionally long but the names on it were predominately off the list of thirteen with a couple from the larger list that Philips knew personally.

These were the guys Tannion had been watching and looking for. Philips may be thinking that the wedding was a great place to start some working relationships with the heads of large organizations, but Tannion was feeling a little more malevolent.

"Just people who Philips wants to get in the good books with."

"Are they all crooks then?"

"Business associates, Louisa. They're business associates. In this line of business it's best to keep certain words out of the conversation."

"But just between you and me, they're crooks, right?"

"Not just crooks, but the biggest crooks in town. Between them, these guys control almost all of the drug and prostitution trade in Los Angeles, in fact much of the drugs that are run up and down the west coast. These guys are big and Philips wants in. He would rather join them than fight, and I can't blame him. He's gotten pretty big himself with his merger with Dennison, but he has his sights set even higher."

Tannion hadn't said that much about work to anyone at one time in his life and it surprised him when it came out. Louisa was probably the only person he could talk to in such detail, and yet there was a nagging thought at the back of his mind. Even with the ability to tell Louisa these sorts of things, he could not tell her his deepest secret. At least not yet.

73

Rallin and Pansloski were back in the bureau chief's office early the next morning filling him in on what they had found the day before. Dealing with a new bureau chief was rarely an enjoyable experience. This one could be different.

An hour later they were in a black late-model sedan with obvious cop written all over it and heading for an area to the east of downtown. They knew the address was likely to be a fake, but they had to check it out first to get it off the list.

The address turned out to be a strip mall that was obviously not the place you would call home, but they hoped that the address given was one that may be closer to real than Tannion would have liked. If it was a last minute decision at the clerk's office, then he would lie, but he might not have been able to think of an address that would be miles away. Maybe his real address was in this same part of town.

The bureau chief had assigned him a couple of agents and the four of them split up and went in a prescribed pattern. They each had a good picture of Tannion and they were going door to door asking for people to take a look. They had decided that they would stop in stores and bars and not bother with apartments or houses. Now they needed to get lucky.

After walking for close to three hours and having his stomach tell him he was hungry, Rallin called in the other agents and they stopped at a lunch counter for something to eat and to talk strategy. Pansloski was starved and they ordered coffee and a burger and sat at a corner booth in the back to keep away from any prying ears.

They had shown the waitress the picture of Tannion and already had a no, but they never knew. Tannion could walk in and order lunch just like anyone else.

"Nothing," Pansloski said after the waitress had taken their orders. "We might be in the wrong end of town for all we know, and with just the four of us this could take forever."

The two LA agents nodded their heads in agreement, but both of them had come on board with the hope of catching a big name on the most wanted list and were not likely to complain after only a morning on the street. It was going to take more than that.

"It's all we have for now and we can't afford to go big. We give his picture to the LAPD and let them go wild, we may find someone who knows him, but more likely he'll hear about it and go to ground. He's done that once already and we know he can do it well."

They had their lunch and then went back to where they left off and started up again. What else did they have?

At three thirty on the second day Rallin's phone rang. One of the LA agents had a bite. A bartender at a bar about twenty blocks from the starting address had remembered seeing Tannion a few weeks earlier. Rallin called the other two and they all met at the bar.

The agent had taken all the information from the bartender and Rallin decided it best not to make too big a deal out of it. The four agents met outside the bar and sat in the car. Pansloski was at shotgun and without a word the LA agents took the back seat.

It appeared as if Tannion might have been in the area, but the bar had not been a regular hangout. If they were going to catch a break, it was quite likely that it would be at a bar.

A quick look at the GPS gave them a listing of bars in the area. Rallin and Pansloski split the bars with the LA agents based on the map and drove off in different directions.

The first bar Rallin and Pansloski came to was an upscale type with good lighting and little tables with a candle in the middle.

"Not the type of place Tannion used to frequent in New York," Pansloski said.

"You mean not a biker bar."

"Yeah, that and no hookers, pimps, or junkies. His pub of choice in New York always had a good assortment of the shady types if you know what I mean."

Rallin knew exactly what Pansloski meant and they might be only wasting their time, but they had decided to check them all and that was what they were going to do. After the bartender shook his head and the guy cleaning the tables agreed that they had never seen the guy in the picture, he had to agree that Pansloski was probably right.

The next three bars were much the same as they were in a more upscale area of Los Angeles and the bars were more for kids or yuppies rather than for guys like Tannion. The next bar was a couple of blocks away, and when they turned the corner into the street, they knew the area was more promising.

It was too early in the day for the hookers to be out, but it was easy to tell. The area had a slightly run down look and there were people on the streets unlike around the last few bars. This area already looked more like an area that Tannion would be in.

After striking out at the first two bars in the area, Rallin and Pansloski stood outside the third with high hopes. Tannion had been in the area, now if only they could just find his watering hole. He was bound to have a waterhole.

Rallin looked up as they approached the door and noted the name of the bar. Most of the bars in the area seemed to have an Irish or English theme with names such as The Pipe and Grill, or The Hose and Hound. This one was simply The King's Head.

Rallin spotted the bartender behind the bar. There were a number of people in the bar as it was getting late in the afternoon and already the regulars were in and a few people had come in after getting off work early. They were all quietly huddled over a beer or in the back playing pool. The bar had an eerie quiet to it as Rallin approached the bar.

Rallin pulled the picture out of his pocket and asked the bartender to take a look at it. Rallin immediately saw that there was recognition on his face. This guy knew Tannion. Now to make him talk. Some of these guys were talkative, but many didn't want to stir the regular pot by talking to cops, and this one looked to be in that lot, and there was no doubt that he thought that Rallin and Pansloski looked like cops.

"We just need to talk to this guy. He's not in any trouble, but we need to find him." He wasn't having anything to do with it, however, and Rallin could see the determined look on his face.

"No. Don't know the guy."

"I think you do and I think you had better talk to us."

"Like I said, I've never seen the guy."

Pansloski piped in at that point. "Listen, we want to talk to this guy and we think you know who he is. If you stone wall us and we find out about it, you'll be the one in trouble." At that point he pulled out his ID and both Rallin and Pansloski showed the bartender their FBI badges.

Rallin was a bit surprised when the bartender caved. He wouldn't have been surprised if the guy had a warrant against him and had decided it would be better to talk and get out than not talk and have his background checked. Probably half the guys in the place wouldn't want a background check done on them.

"Ok. I know him. He's a regular here. He goes by the name of French and he works with the Russian. That's all I know."

"You know where he lives?"

"No. I don't know where any of these guys live, but I know he's in here two or three times a week."

"Does he come in alone?"

"Not any more. He used to come alone and then sit with one of the regulars, but the last year he's either with the Russian or with some girl. I think she's his girl friend and not a hooker cause I have seen her a few times."

The information was rolling off his tongue now and he didn't need any prodding but Rallin was concerned that as soon as Tannion, or French as he was obviously known, came in the door, he would be hearing that the FBI had been looking for him.

Rallin called the LA agents and sat at the bar with Pansloski and waited while the agents came. "I need to ask you to come in and fill out a report with what you've said to ensure that we have it right. I wouldn't want to screw up anything you said," Rallin told the bartender.

The bartender put up an argument, but with a heavy sigh he knew there was no way out. He only hoped that they didn't ask him any personal questions. At this point they hadn't even asked him his name, so maybe he was safe for now.

After ensuring that the bar was covered while he was gone, the bartender left with the LA agents. Rallin had told them to hold onto him until after his shift was over then let him go. If Tannion didn't show up tonight they would have to think of something different.

Now the waiting game starts. They had been real lucky so far, and the hard part should be over. Now if only he shows up.

74

"Feels like old times in New York, doesn't it," Pansloski said. He was in the passenger seat of the car that he and Rallin were parked in just down the block and across the road from the King's Head.

"Yeah, I know what you mean." Rallin had been thinking along the same line of the times that he and Pansloski had been outside bars in New York waiting for Tannion. At that time, however, they knew where he was and they were either waiting for him to do something or to come out. This time they just hoped he would show up.

There was always plenty of time to talk while on a stakeout, but the best partner was one who could sit in complete silence for long periods of time without it being an uncomfortable silence. Pansloski and Rallin had that ability.

Rallin broke the silence. "I've been thinking about what we need to do when we see him."

"Yeah, me too."

"What have you been thinking?" asked Rallin only a bit surprised. Pansloski was a good cop, but when they were together he seldom told Rallin his thoughts until after Rallin had told his. He was good at thinking on his feet, but preferred to elaborate on a plan rather than formulate one.

"Well, I remember what he did to Agent Leed in New York. I don't think we can afford a repeat of that happening here. If it did, we may never find him again. He went into hiding so fast that we couldn't follow him."

"I agree. We need to make sure that we can take him in without getting anyone killed and without him running. Based on his ability to take a hit, I don't want to shoot him. We need to take him alive."

"It may be best to follow him and see where he lives and see if he has a weak spot or a routine that we can take advantage of. We were able to follow him for a long time in New York without him knowing. We may be able to do it again."

"I don't know if we can follow him as much now," Rallin said. "It may have been a year and a half, but he has to know there's a watch out for him and he may be a lot more careful now. Also there were enough people at the bar who saw us talking to the bartender that someone could tip him off. If we follow him it has to be just once, and then we need to take action."

"So we have a plan. It's good to have a plan," Pansloski said almost to himself.

Rallin smiled. He knew his partner almost better than he knew himself, and he was much more at ease when he knew what was in store even if the plan was as loose and limited as this one was. At least it was a plan. Hopefully it would firm up if and when they found Tannion.

At about nine o'clock, a big sedan pulled up and parked with authority outside the bar. It stopped in a loading zone, but it was apparent whoever was in the car wasn't worried about getting a ticket. Both front doors opened and two big men got out. The guy on the left was even bigger than the one on the right. Rallin instantly recognized Tannion as he got out of the car and stood in a pool of light cast by the street light they had parked under.

"Bingo!" said Pansloski having recognizing Tannion as well.

"Shit, we got lucky," thought Rallin. "Now we just have to wait until he comes out and tail him home."

It was over quicker than they had expected. They must have gone in for a quick drink as only a little more than half an hour later they both came out and got into the car with Tannion taking the passenger seat. The big guy looked even bigger as he came around to the driver's side, and Rallin and Pansloski got a better look at him.

The sedan pulled away and Rallin pulled out and stayed a few cars back making sure they weren't spotted. The big car was easy to follow and there was no need to be up close. After driving for about ten minutes the car stopped at an apartment building and Tannion got out of the car. After leaning over to say something to the driver, he closed the door and walked into the building.

"Looks like the big guy took Tannion home. This must be where he lives," said Pansloski.

Rallin knew what he was going to have to do and knew they were done for the night. He told Pansloski the remainder of the plan and pulled away from the curb. Best if they were to head back to the hotel and get a good night's sleep. Tomorrow would be the day.

75

Tannion and Potenlikov went into the bar for a quick drink after a good day. They had made a couple of collections and had driven one of the wives to the airport which wasn't why it was a good day. When they picked up the wife, Tannion had a chance to shake her husband's hand. He was high up in the big thirteen, and in a few days she would be a widow.

Potenlikov noted when they came in that Tony was not behind the bar as he usually was. They took their regular seats in the corner. The barmaid came over and Tannion asked her where Tony was, but she said she had just come on shift and he wasn't in when she got there. Maybe he was sick she thought.

They each had a beer and talked quietly. No one came near them, but that wasn't unusual. The big Russian didn't put out the vibes that said anyone was welcome to come up to the table for small talk unless they were a good friend. There weren't too many of them. The regulars knew to stay away.

They paid for their drinks and went out to the car. A few minutes later and Potenlikov dropped Tannion off at his apartment. Tannion had called Louisa earlier in the evening to say he would be a little late, and she had told him she would have dinner ready when he got home. A quick call from the bar had confirmed the timing.

Louisa was getting very excited with her work on their wedding. She could see the plans unfolding and had to tell Tannion all about them. It was all he could do to get a word in over breakfast the next morning, and when he kissed her goodbye at the door he told her to expect him home at the regular time.

It was not going to be a hard day. A little bodyguard work for Philips and then mostly sitting around in Philips's suite waiting for something to happen. Not the most fun day, but Potenlikov seemed to like that kind of day, and it was always best to keep Potenlikov in a good mood.

At five o'clock, Potenlikov deposited Tannion at the door to his apartment building. Tannion stepped out of the elevator and put the key in his apartment's door. He closed the door behind him and took his shoes off.

"Hey, honey, where are you?"

The apartment wasn't huge, but it was big enough that Louisa could be back in the bedroom or in the kitchen and may not have heard him come in. Tannion walked the length of the hallway and around the corner into the living room. Then he stopped dead.

"What the hell is this?"

Tannion took the room in at a quick glance. If Louisa hadn't been in the room, he may have turned and ran out faster than the two guys could do anything about it, but he couldn't do that.

There were three of them in the living room. Louisa was sitting on the couch in front of the window. There were two men sitting one on either side of her. They had positioned themselves about ten feet on either side and had obviously taken chairs from the kitchen to sit on. They had their guns out, but they were not pointed at Tannion. They were pointed at Louisa.

Louisa looked scared, but she must have been told not to say a word, but there were tears in her eyes.

Tannion felt the slight tug of recognition when he looked at one of the two men. He instantly knew they were cops.

"I know you, don't I?"

"Just stay where you are and we won't hurt her," said the cop Tannion thought he recognized.

Tannion's mind was working fast. What could he do? They had their guns on Louisa and he couldn't chance getting her hurt. He could probably move quickly enough to get to the first cop before he had a chance to fire, but they had positioned themselves as far apart as possible in the room. He would never be able to get to the second guy before he fired, and with their guns trained on Louisa, he couldn't risk it. He was going to have to listen to them and hope for a chance.

"Okay. Just don't hurt her." Tannion was going to play it safe and slow and see what happened.

The two cops introduced themselves as FBI Agents Rallin and Pansloski and told Tannion that he was under arrest. Slowly Rallin reached down to the floor in front of him. Tannion had glanced at what was on the ground between the cop's feet, but hadn't put any thought into what it might be. Now it became very apparent.

Rallin picked up a set of handcuffs, and without changing the direction his gun was facing, he tossed them to land at Tannion's feet. He then reached down and repeated the motion, but this time it was a set of leg irons that landed at Tannion's feet.

"Put the leg irons on first and then the handcuffs behind your back. Try anything and we won't hesitate to shoot Louisa."

"They know her name," Tannion thought as he slowly reached down and took the leg irons and clicked them in place. He could probably break the chain, but he was becoming more certain that he was caught. A slight sense of relief came over him at the idea, and it surprised him. He was tired of living under cover and not being able to contact his mother. He especially didn't like not being able to have her at his wedding. Maybe this was inevitable.

Tannion picked up the handcuffs and put them on behind his back as he was told to. "I could still get out of these and do you some serious damage, but as long as you don't harm Louisa I'll come quietly. Just leave her alone, she has nothing to do with this."

"She's coming in with us just to make sure you do as you say," Rallin said.

Tannion knew that there was nothing else he could do.

76

Louisa made more trouble than Tannion did until Rallin told her that if she was quiet they would let her go, even though they were sure she was illegal. Rallin told her that there was nothing she could do or say that would help Tannion at this time. Finally she quit screaming and settled into a few sobs.

Rallin and Pansloski gave Louisa to the two LA agents who had remained out of sight on the street until they were called in and then put Tannion in the back of their car.

"She'll be fine as long as you don't do anything she will regret," Pansloski told him as they got in the car. A few minutes later and they were sitting in an interrogation room at FBI headquarters.

"I would like a lawyer."

"I thought you would, but for now you have no need for one. We're going to do all the talking and you'll just listen. You don't need to answer any questions or say anything unless you want to," Rallin said.

Rallin wasn't sure this was how he wanted to handle this, but he didn't have any choice. The order had come directly from his superior in Wichita. His boss had been talking to the bureau chief in LA and had been convinced

that Tannion might be very useful as a pawn if he was working for Jackson Philips. The chief had been told that Tannion
was a known associate of Philips and that seemed to carry
some weight with him.

They thought that Tannion might know details about
some of the crime in LA and could be turned into a snitch
for the cops in order to keep Louisa safe and reduce any
time he did. Rallin thought it was pretty easy treatment for a
cop killer, but the boss wasn't sure they could get murder to
stick anyway. He thought that the best they might be able to
do would be manslaughter, and even then a jury might think
they had the wrong guy.

"We have reason to believe that you may be involved
in some form of criminal activity in Los Angeles." Rallin
said, not knowing if this was accurate. He needed to take
it slowly, but make it sound like they knew more than they
did. Louisa may still be the trump card in this situation.

"We have you on two murder charges in New York,
but at this time we have nothing on you in Los Angeles.
That doesn't matter to me. All I care about is getting you
the death sentence for killing an FBI agent in New York."
Rallin thought it best to give Tannion a little incentive.

Tannion held his tongue and his face showed no emotion as Rallin went on. He could have been watching television or reading a book for all the expression he showed.

"We do, however, know that you planned on marrying
Louisa and we also think that she's illegal. We won't hesitate to deport her and make sure that she never gets into the
country again."

With the mention of Louisa, a flash of emotion passed
over Tannion's face. Rallin saw it, but he couldn't be sure

if it was anger or sorrow. The flash was quick and then Tannion had complete control again.

"However," Rallin paused for a few seconds to make sure that Tannion got the idea that the however might be big for him and to see what the reaction would be. Tannion gave him nothing.

"However," he repeated. "My boss thinks that you might have information that you may want to trade. He's talking about a reduced sentence for you, and he may be able to throw in something for Louisa if the info is good enough."

At that point Tannion opened his mouth as if to speak, but he closed it again without saying a word. Rallin knew he wanted to talk and that he wanted to ensure that Louisa was okay.

Rallin turned to Pansloski. "I think we're wasting our time with this guy. Lock him up and let's get the paperwork started to get him back to New York." They hadn't been talking for ten minutes and it looked like Rallin was already throwing in the towel. He didn't want it to go this way and it showed.

"Let's see what we can get on his girl friend," suggested Pansloski, just the way that Rallin had planned. They still thought she was their best bet of getting to Tannion and they had a plan worked out ahead of time. It seemed it might work as Tannion finally spoke.

His voice came out slow and clear as if he was being very careful with what he was saying. At this time the conversation was not being taped, but it looked like he thought that it might be.

"I need to know that Louisa is okay. If I know that Louisa is okay and will be looked after, I might be able to help you. I don't care about myself, but I need to know about Louisa."

Rallin heard him say Louisa three times in a short speech and knew that she may be the only way they would get anything out of him, but Rallin didn't care. He wanted the murder charge and not some reduced bullshit because he gave evidence on a friend who sold shit on the streets or because he knew a pimp or two.

Pansloski left the room for a minute, and when he came back he told Tannion that Louisa would be brought into the room in a minute and that he was not to talk to her nor would she speak to him. He would see that she was unharmed and then what happened to her would be up to him.

A minute later there was a knock at the door and Pansloski brought Louisa in. Tannion tried to stand, but the leg irons had been set into the chair and he couldn't stand up. Pansloski had to hold Louisa from running to him, but he could not stop her from talking. She asked him if he was alright, but before Tannion could answer, Pansloski took her by the arm and pulled her back out the door.

Tannion could hear her screaming at Pansloski before the door shut behind them. A smile showed on Tannion's face briefly as he listened to Louisa yelling. The yelling was in Spanish. He knew how hot her Mexican blood could run and knew that Pansloski was getting an earful, and if Pansloski knew any Spanish, his ears were probably red by now.

"Okay, you can see that she's unharmed. Now the rest is up to you." Rallin placed a pen and paper in front of him.

"You write down anything that you can think of that will help keep Louisa in the country and maybe keep you off death row. It had better be good."

Rallin left the room and Tannion looked down at the paper. He thought he had enough in his head that would make the feds happy, but what he wasn't sure of was how fast he should reveal his strengths. He could give them Philips and Potenlikov easily enough, but he still had a list of what remained of the thirteen and that would be the bigger fish. Plus Tannion had the longer list that he was working on.

He needed a lawyer to make sure things didn't get out of hand and to make sure he didn't give them so much that they might start thinking they didn't need him. He didn't want to give them too much at the wrong time.

Tannion picked up the pen and tossed it and the paper at the door. "You get nothing until I get a lawyer."

The room was just like any other room in the building and it didn't have a one way mirror or any recording devices. Therefore no one saw him throw the paper and pen. He didn't know it, but a lawyer had already been called in.

When the door to the interrogation room opened again, Tannion didn't recognize the man who walked in ahead of the FBI agent who he had come to know as Agent Rallin. The same Agent Rallin he had first met in Kansas. The lawyer was probably in his late fifties and was dressed in a rather drab brown suit.

He introduced himself to Tannion as George Pannel, his court-appointed lawyer. Tannion knew that one call to Philips would have a high priced legal team in the room, but he knew that the case against him in New York would not go away even with a good lawyer. After all he had killed an FBI agent on duty. They didn't like that. He had decided to keep Philips out of this.

Rallin picked up the pen and paper and placed it back on the desk without a word. Pannel was telling Tannion his credentials and what he had been told by the agents. He was there to help, but he was telling Tannion that it looked like he would have to help himself by giving them what they needed.

Rallin left the room to give them the privacy they wanted with the hope that the lawyer could talk Tannion into something. Rallin didn't want this thing to drag on. Already several hours had gone by and it was almost morning, and he hadn't had any sleep since the night before. He needed to get some rest.

As he headed to his hotel room, Rallin thought Tannion looked like he might be ready to talk, but did he have anything to say? It could wait a few hours. He needed some sleep.

77

When Rallin pulled into the FBI building it was just past lunch. He was told that Tannion and his lawyer had talked for over an hour and then Pannel had left and Tannion was taken to a holding cell where he was released from his bonds and allowed to get some sleep.

Rallin asked if Tannion had a watch on him at all times and was told that an agent was outside his cell twenty-four seven and was there now. Rallin breathed a small sigh of relief and went to work on the paperwork he needed for the transfer to New York. He also wanted Tannion to get some rest. They would need to spend some time together soon enough.

Rallin placed a phone call to New York. "It's time to bring Martin in on what's happening. He deserves to know," thought Rallin.

The phone rang and after the second ring a familiar voice answered. "Martin here."

"Jeff. Good to hear your voice. This is Agent Rallin."

"Yeah Mike, I recognized your voice. It's been a long time. How are you and Bill doing?"

"Good, Jeff. We've got some good news that I knew you would want to hear about."

Rallin went on to fill Martin in on Tannion's bust and what was happening. Needless to say Martin was not overly pleased with the prospect of Tannion being a state's witness and getting lost in a witness protection program without even standing trial for what happened in New York, but he was glad to hear he was in custody.

It may not have been one of Martin's cops who Tannion had killed, but it had been a cop on his watch and somehow he felt responsible. He wanted to get some measure of revenge even if it was going to be through the court system.

Rallin told him he would keep in touch and let Martin know what went down and promised to drop in if and when they were able to transfer Tannion to New York. Rallin turned back to his paperwork feeling good having talked to Martin.

At about two o'clock the phone rang and Rallin was told that Tannion was up and was asking for him. Rallin met the agent at the first gate. After signing in and giving up his service revolver, Rallin was escorted to the cell where Tannion was being held.

The wing held six cells and Tannion was in the middle cell on the left. All the other cells were vacant. Rallin thought it was strange that they had Tannion separated from everyone else and wondered if it was because he was considered dangerous or if they were protecting him.

Tannion saw him approach and got up off the cot and walked over to the cell door. Rallin made sure to stay far enough back from the bars. He knew what this guy was capable of and didn't want to get close until they were sure he was under control.

"Thanks for coming," Tannion said in a very conversational tone, which caught Rallin a bit by surprise. He knew that Tannion was well educated and originally from a good family back home, but with all that had gone on, it was easy to think of him as just another criminal with limited education or chances as he grew up.

"I was told you wanted to talk to me."

"Yes. My lawyer and I talked it over and we decided that we only want to deal with you. Don't take it too personal as we don't necessarily trust you any more than anyone else, but you're from home and have been in it from the start, so you may be the only one who will follow through."

Rallin wasn't sure exactly how to take what Tannion said. He thought maybe he was being insulted, but at the same time being more trusted than anyone else in the bureau might turn out to be a good thing in this case. No matter what, Rallin intended to see this to the end, and having Tannion wanting him would ensure that he would be there.

Rallin didn't want Tannion to think that he was happy with the idea. He told Tannion that for now that would be fine, but eventually someone else may have to take over. No need to give him what he wanted even at this stage.

"If you can guarantee Louisa is given asylum and not sent back to Mexico and that she'll be able to become an American citizen in time, and if we can agree to a reduced sentence of some sort, I'll give you what you want."

"I won't agree to a thing if I don't see something from you first."

Tannion turned around and went over to the small table and picked up a piece of paper, which he brought back and stuck through the bars. Reluctantly Rallin reached out and took the page from his outstretched fingers.

Rallin agreed to look at what he had been handed and to come back the next day with some idea of what they might be able to offer. Tannion asked to have his lawyer present at that time and Rallin agreed.

A few minutes later and Rallin was back at his desk reading what was on the page. There were almost forty names on the list with a few dates and places, but almost no information on what he might have on the names. Not being from Los Angeles, the names didn't have any real meaning to Rallin, but he knew who might care.

With any luck the names wouldn't mean anything to anyone else and then the paperwork he had been working would get Tannion transferred to New York. He knew he would have to give the page to the chief and cross his fingers.

78

The bureau chief took one look at the page Rallin had handed him and a small whistle escaped his mouth.

"Shit. Rameriez, Jenson, Mercido, Morinelli, Spaff. Shit!" The chief was muttering to himself as his eyes scanned the names on the list.

Rallin didn't recognize any of the names except for the fact that they were off the list that Tannion had given him, but it was obvious that the chief knew the names.

"We have a huge dossier on each of these guys. Most of these guys have a rap sheet a mile long and we haven't been able to stick them with anything more than a parking ticket for years. If this asshole has anything at all on these guys, he's worth his weight in gold."

Rallin had to smile as the chief rattled off a number of old clichés.

"I understand that he'll only deal with you. Is that correct?"

"That's what he said. He wants his lawyer present and me, but he didn't make any demands about being alone or that no one else could be in on any discussions. I suspect that if he has anything, he'll spill it as long as we feed him bullshit about his girl. We may have to give him what he wants with her, but I still want him to go down for killing the agent in New York."

"I understand your feelings on the agent, but this could be big. I don't know if I've ever heard anyone use all the names on this list in one sentence. Many people may know a few names, maybe even a dozen or so, but these guys keep things among themselves and I can't think of anyone who could name them all unless he works here at the FBI, and even then he would have to be well versed. He has forty on the list including a few that have died in the last year."

The chief couldn't stop talking about the list and Rallin could see that things were starting to go Tannion's way already. It wasn't looking good for a strong case against him or for getting him to New York any time soon.

The chief made a call to someone outside, and in a few minutes a woman walked into the office. She didn't appear to be from the clerical pool, but she didn't introduce herself to Rallin. The chief introduced her as Pat. After a quick conference over the desk she walked out the door.

"I agree that we should be able to do something for the girlfriend," Rallin told the chief picking up on what the conversation had been about. He hadn't been asked to leave the room so obviously he was meant to hear what had been said.

"As soon as Pat can, she'll put together a letter for me to sign that will tell Tannion that his girlfriend will be looked after and that it will come from the governor if what he has on his list is legit and if it's good enough. When we're satisfied with what he has, then we'll get the letter for the girlfriend and start negotiations on his behalf."

"I think as long as we get his girl looked after he'll cooperate. His ability to get a reduced sentence will be a bonus for him, but his lawyer will probably push for it more."

"You might be right. As soon as things are ready I want you to present the letter. I'll have someone give you a call."

Rallin took that as a dismissal and got up and left the chief's office and went back to wait at his desk. About an hour later he got the call.

"That was quick," thought Rallin. "They obviously think this guy has some real stuff."

Rallin met an agent at the holding cell's first gate and was handed a package. Rallin pulled out the letter and checked for the signature without reading its content. He didn't really care what it said as long as it had what Tannion wanted.

A little later he was in a room with Tannion and his lawyer, who obviously had been called in ahead of time knowing what was coming. Rallin handed the letter to Tannion, but the lawyer stood up and took it first. After a quick read he nodded and then handed it to Tannion and turned to Rallin.

"Thank you, Agent Rallin. Please give us a few minutes to discuss this in private."

Rallin backed out of the room and went outside to wait. About half an hour later he was called back in.

"My client agrees in principle to what has been discussed. Please supply him with paper and pens and tell your superiors that he'll start writing what they want. My client tells me that they will want what he has and to get the governor ready."

Rallin left the room and reported back to the chief. He met Pansloski on his way out and told him what had been happening. Pansloski wasn't happy about being left out of the loop at this point, but he knew it was not his call and was quite happy to have Rallin fill him in.

Together they agreed that they wouldn't like to see Tannion get off with anything less than manslaughter, but they weren't in charge and it would be up to the court system to work out a deal.

It had been a grueling couple of days and they were both exhausted. Tannion had been taken back to his cell and he and his lawyer had parted company. A fresh looking Tannion sat at the lone table in the cell and started to write.

"This might just work," he thought. "First to make sure that Louisa is safe, and then let my lawyer worry about me."

He started writing with the knowledge that his running and hiding was done and now he could come out into the open even if it meant jail time. His mother may not be pleased with the way things had gone, but at least she would know that he was alive and she might get to meet Louisa.

A smile crept over Tannion's face as he continued writing. After all, he had made a point of knowing as much as he could about the list of thirteen for Philips and Potenlikov's sake, but his work on his own had taken him all over the city getting to know everything he could about the people on the expanded list, and Tannion knew a lot.

This was not the way Tannion expected to take them down, but it was somehow strangely exhilarating to have the government do his dirty work. He had spent a lot of his own time researching these guys, knowing where they lived, and where their areas were.

He knew hangouts, crack houses, holdings, locations of the stores, and where the money went. Tannion had spent time watching each of them and had seen people killed and bodies dumped and buried. His night vision had allowed him to see things that no one thought would be seen, and it all went down on the paper.

It took Tannion well over an hour of steady writing, and anyone other than Tannion would've had writer's cramp long before he finished. The names, dates, and places ran out of his head and onto the paper nonstop. By the time he was finished he had filled fifteen sheets of letter size paper from top to bottom.

"That should ensure Louisa is safe," Tannion hoped.

79

Tannion's lawyer made the plea bargain with a look on his face that showed that he wasn't pleased. Tannion would only let his lawyer talk about something for Louisa. Tannion had given his data to the FBI and the info was with the bureau chief who couldn't wipe the smile from his face.

A task force had been put together with extreme haste. FBI agents from all over the state and from neighboring states had been called in. This was going to be the biggest one-day strike in the history of the FBI. And it had to be done right.

It had taken a little more than a week from the time Rallin picked up Tannion to get to this point, and it had been a mad house. Rallin and Pansloski had initially not been part of the team, but as the need for more agents became apparent they were added.

Rallin found himself with Pansloski leading a team to pick up one of the thirteen. They were standing at the gate waiting to be admitted. The idea was to ask to see the man in charge, and then after the gate opened, the rest of the team would follow. With luck there wouldn't be any gun play and they could take a few of the people into custody without a fight.

Luckily the guards had been instructed to deal with the cops in a courteous manner and they opened the gate as Rallin was told they would. As soon as the gate was open Rallin swung it wide open and six FBI agents and eight LAPD rushed in behind him and Pansloski.

One of the agents held a gun on the two guards and cuffed them together around the gate. They each had a gun, which was confiscated.

"At least these guys look like they know what they're doing," Rallin thought as he saw the Los Angeles police securing the guards while the rest swept up the path on foot.

Twenty minutes later and there were ten men in hand-cuffs being led from the house and not a shot had been fired. Rallin hoped that all the other raids went as well. They had found the guy matching the name on the original list of thirteen and most of the additional names that Tannion had supplied as his closest associates. They would need to pick up a few others later, but for now it had been a good raid.

There had been a couple of women in the house, including the boss's wife. There had been a little screaming at first and then a few tears, but Rallin didn't think it necessary to take any of the women into custody so they were left behind.

If any of the other raids had been as successful, and if Tannion's stuff could hold up in a court of law, there might be some major changes in the crime situation in LA.

When Rallin got back to the FBI building there was already a crush of reporters and people outside trying to get in. Rallin and Pansloski pushed their way through the crowd and surveyed the situation. Only the few who were the heads of their organizations were being held at the FBI head quarters. All the rest were taken to the closest LAPD precinct for processing. Rallin heard that in all there were well over one hundred people taken into custody, including a handful of women.

Rallin went to the holding cell where they were holding Tannion and was let in after clearing security and leaving his weapon behind. Tannion looked up when Rallin approached the cell.

"How's it going, Agent Rallin, catch any bad guys today?" Tannion said. He had decided that even if he had asked Rallin to be his go between, Rallin was probably the only real enemy he had at the FBI. Him and maybe his buddy Pansloski.

"I don't know what your story is, but at this point I don't get it," Rallin said. "I know you were working for a guy named Philips and his friend Vladimir Potenlikov, but those names didn't show up on your list."

Tannion had supplied the FBI with a very comprehensive list. Not only were the names of the remaining thirteen on the list, but also most of their second in commands, hit men, tough guys, pimps, hookers, and front men. There were addresses, dates of crimes committed, details of murders, and even the whereabouts of a couple of bodies, but no mention of Philips or Potenlikov.

Tannion had agreed to testify in front of a grand jury if necessary or in any court room of the FBI's choosing. He had done this all with only the promise of Louisa's well being. He still hadn't made any deals for himself, but Rallin knew it was coming, and he was not happy about it.

In all there were more than a thousand charges filed in the first few days. Rallin's raid was one of the few to go quietly. Shots were fired in more than one case and people ran in almost all others. In many cases there were several charges developed based on what was found at the scene.

It had been easy to get warrants based on the initial information that Tannion had provided. These were often warrants to search homes that the cops had wanted to search for years, but could never get probable cause. The cops went in to find everything, including drugs, money, and guns.

There had been three agents and two LA police shot during the raids and one of the agents had died on the way to the hospital. On the other side there were fourteen injured and seven dead among those who decided to protect their property with force. More charges resulted.

Tannion looked out at Rallin and decided that the truth wouldn't hurt at this point.

"Okay, Agent Rallin. I'll tell you why. There will always be crime in a city this large. There will be drugs, hookers, and money, and as long as they exist there will be men to exploit them. In this case the best you can hope for is to have someone in charge who has a conscience. Mr. Philips does. He cares about his people and most of his activities are victimless. He may well be the best of the worst."

Rallin was listening.

"Most of the so-called gang style murders were the gangs killing each other off. If there was one guy in charge there wouldn't be a need for that. Mr. Philips is no saint, but I have worked with him for a while now and he's the best I've seen. If I was released I could be back with him and make sure that he stayed that way."

Rallin knew that was coming, but he was not in a position to do anything about it. "I suppose that you've instructed your lawyer to give those terms to the chief, haven't you."

"Yes," Tannion said.

"What about New York? What about what went on in New York, and what about what happened in Wichita? I need to know about them even if you don't get charged with anything."

Rallin's voice dropped to just above a whisper, but with Tannion's hearing it didn't matter. He could hear him say. "I need to know."

80

Philips heard about the busts around town almost as soon as they happened. His men had been well placed within the Dennison's and Santos's outfits and had worked their way into other households as well, as per the plan they had worked out.

What he didn't understand was why there hadn't been a knock at his door as well. Potenlikov had told him as far as he knew all his men were safe, but he hadn't seen French for a few days.

"Where the hell is French?" Philips almost yelled at Potenlikov. "Why has this happened like this? It just doesn't add up."

A knock at the door brought his attention back to the moment. A letter had been hand delivered. The courier handed Potenlikov an envelope and quickly headed back out the door. Potenlikov handed the envelope to Philips.

Philips opened the envelope and took out a single piece of paper. On it were two short sentences and a name.

"Without a little luck it could have been you. Now treat it nice and do it the Philips way. French."

Philips gave the note to Potenlikov to read.

"What the hell do you make of that? What the hell is going on, Vlad?"

"I don't know."

Potenlikov really didn't know anything more than Philips did. He hadn't seen French and hadn't heard from him until the note was delivered.

Over the next few weeks Philips found out what had happened to French and started to put the pieces together. As proceedings worked their way through the court system and the charges started to show up in the papers, it eventually became apparent what French's role was. The papers only called him a well-placed informant, but Philips knew who it was. If Philips knew, he wondered who else would know.

Louisa was held for a while by the cops, but was let go after the raids went down. Philips made a point of talking to her as soon as he knew she was back. She didn't know much, but she did know that French was in jail. With what had happened around town he knew what Tannion had been doing.

The meaning of the note became more apparent because his operation was almost forced to grow. Large holes were created as entire criminal operations were wiped out. His men found it easy to walk into areas and take over. The few remaining men who weren't picked up came out of hiding and many of them approached Philips. They would rather work for Philips than to have to strike out on their own. They may have been near the top in their respective organizations, but leaders they were not.

In a few months, as the court proceedings wound down, Philips saw his holdings grow to encompass most of the city. A few small-timers were either wiped out or added to Philips's crew. Life went on in the city as if nothing had happened. Life came back to normal, but not for some, including Philips and Potenlikov.

The cops were busy running things through the court system, but overall the streets were quiet. After a few minor operations were shut down by Philips, there was relative quiet across the city. Philips understood the threat French had made and put out the word that stopped a lot of action. This did not, however, stop any of the drug use, prostitution, or anything that could make Philips a buck. It only stopped some of the killing that had gone on in the past.

Philips and Potenlikov also knew that they needed to stay away from French. They could do him no good.

There were still drug crazed kids and old men with wine bottles. There were houses broken into and liquor store holdups to keep the dopers buying the stuff they otherwise could not afford. There were husbands killing wives for money and wives killing husbands for revenge, but much of the criminal activity had vanished. The cops had never had it so easy.

81

Rallin and Tannion spent a lot of time together over the next few weeks. Tannion slowly filled him in on what had happened in Wichita and then in New York. Tannion was very careful to make sure that what he told Rallin, or anything that he said under oath in front of a judge, only included things that a very strong man could do.

Tannion never took credit for any deaths in front of the judge, but he told Rallin, and Rallin's respect for him grew each day. Rallin would often stop and have a beer and relate some of the stories to Pansloski.

"Bill, this guy is creepy strong and he's killed more people than he has told me about, and he has told me about several, but they were all on the wrong side as he puts it. This guy's a vigilante, not a crook. He's put down guys in New York, LA, and back home,"

"That doesn't make him one of the good guys in my books."

"No, maybe not, but he thinks he is."

When it was Tannion's turn to sit in front of the judge for his trial, a deal had already been worked out and it was only a formality. He was given an outright release and then the paperwork that Rallin had been working on could kick in. The FBI in Los Angeles had nothing on him and they had no reason to hold him unless to protect him.

Everything finally wound down in Los Angeles. Tannion had been able to have visitors, and Louisa had been there on a regular basis. That was coming to an end. Rallin was going to win this one and then Tannion would be heading to New York City. The transfer finally took place and Rallin, Pansloski, and Tannion got on a flight to New York.

Tannion had refused anything to do with witness protection. He might have seen almost every syndicate or crime boss in Los Angeles put away for one offence or another, but who knew who he missed and who was sitting outside somewhere with a high powered rifle. He also had to know that some of these guys would try to run their outfit from the inside. Maybe Tannion didn't seem to care, but Rallin wanted to get him back to New York to stand trial without incident.

They arrived in New York in one piece, and just before the trial was set to begin, Rallin had a surprise visitor.

"Agent Rallin."

Rallin turned around and saw that it was Tannion's lawyer who had called out his name. Rallin hadn't seen him since Los Angeles and was a little surprised that he was still on the case.

The trial was set to start in an hour and Rallin wondered what eleventh hour deal he was looking for.

"Yes. You're Tannion's lawyer, Panel, right?"

"That's Pannel with the accent on the second syllable."

"Sorry. Mr. Pannel, what can I help you with?"

"You're the only one who Tannion will talk to and he seems to trust you," Pannel said. "I think he's making a major mistake and I would like it if you would talk to him."

"What kind of mistake."

"With the information he gave you in LA, and the success that the courts have had there, Tannion has put more people behind bars in the last few months than by almost everyone else in years. He knows that and you know that."

"I agree, but where is this going."

"The deal that Tannion made was first to be given immunity for anything that happened in Los Angeles, and that was easy. There's also a deal for him here in New York. He thinks he'll stand trial for the murder of an FBI agent." Pannel went on to explain to Rallin what the deal included in New York, or at least what Tannion thought the deal was.

Tannion wanted to take his chances with a jury trial, and if it ended up with a murder conviction, he would take the life term. He knew the chance of a death sentence in New York was pretty slim.

Rallin heard what Pannel said and couldn't believe it. With all his discussions with Tannion, not once had Tannion indicated that he would be making that kind of deal. Rallin was sure that he was going to get off without even a blot on his record. They had come all the way to New York and Rallin hadn't heard any word of what the deal might be. Now it looked like there wasn't much of a deal at all.

"But there is a deal here," Pannel said. "When he gets to trial here in New York there'll be a different deal waiting for him. The chiefs have worked it out between them and the DA. Tannion's not even aware of it, and I think he may not be happy. He seems to want to pay for everything he did here."

"That's what we all want as well," Rallin said.

"He'll stand trial for murder, but it will be reduced to manslaughter and he'll get five to twenty in a state prison.

That is if he pleads guilty. He may want to plead not guilty and take his chances. He may end up with murder after all if he doesn't take the deal."

Rallin wasn't sure how he felt about this information. He had wanted so badly to have Tannion stand trial in New York that he could taste it, but he had gotten to know Tannion and he almost liked him.

"So he gets a little jail time and with good behavior he'll be out in five years. They'll probably put him in a minimum security under a false name and he should be safe. There could be worse outcomes."

"The problem is he might not get the manslaughter charge, and even if he does, he won't accept a cushy jail term. He wants to spend his time in a maximum security prison under his real name. I've told him that would be suicide. He may be across the country, and he may have put most of the guys out there in jail, but they can reach out and if they find him, and they will, they will kill him."

Rallin knew that Tannion had his pride and he agreed to talk to him before the trial went ahead. He was able to see Tannion for a couple of minutes just before he was brought into the room.

"Not much of a deal you made for yourself."

"What do you mean? I got nothing, an outright release, nothing on my record."

"Yeah, in Los Angeles, but not here, but I know where you're heading next."

Rallin broke some rules in telling Tannion what was in store for him, and Tannion held back for a few minutes. Finally he told Rallin that if that was what they wanted to do with him, he didn't see there was much choice. He hadn't asked for a reduced sentence, but if that was what they were going to charge him with, what could he do?

He would either win the case and be free or lose and spend time in prison. Not as much time as he thought was going to be the case, but it was still time. That is unless they changed their minds when he pleaded not guilty.

"You could work out a deal to spend your time in some cozy white collar crime facility and not have to worry about anything. Take an assumed name and have Louisa come and visit every week. You could be out in your minimum time. Hell, if you wanted, you could probably not spend any time at all."

"I know all this, but I need to make amends for what I did here in New York," Tannion lied to Rallin. He hadn't meant to kill the cop in New York and he felt bad about it, but not bad enough to take the death penalty. But what better place to do what he loved to do than in prison. Not some soft paper-pusher jail, but in with the hard cases.

Even better, if they knew who he was, they would come after him and then he would have an excuse to defend himself. He would talk to the warden and let him know that he may be attacked, and if he was, he couldn't predict the outcome other than to say that he would be the one left alive in the end. What better way to conduct his business.

Tannion and his lawyer chose trial by jury and the charge was manslaughter. Tannion pleaded not guilty and both he and his lawyer were pleasantly surprised when the manslaughter charge wasn't increased to murder. It could have gone as high as murder one as it was an on-duty FBI agent, but the prosecutor left it at manslaughter. Rallin thought the reduced charge must have stemmed from what happened in Los Angeles.

Tannion's lawyer had argued that Tannion didn't know that Agent Leed was an FBI Agent and that he didn't intend to kill him. Pannel told the jury that the agent's death was an accident. The prosecutor brought in both Rallin and Pansloski as witnesses to the killing, along with another agent who was in the bar at the time. It was looking bad for Tannion.

After final argument, the jury left to decide Tannion's future. After only slightly more than an hour, the jury returned with a verdict. The jury agreed with part of what Tannion had said, and although they still found him guilty of manslaughter, they didn't recommend the maximum sentence. Instead, they reduced it to five to twenty-years, which was the minimum allowed under the state law.

Louisa had made the trip to New York and was sitting behind Tannion as the verdict came down. She was noticeably upset and tears flowed freely. Tannion wasn't given the chance to do more than say a few words to her before he was led away.

His mother didn't make the trip to New York. She had talked to Tannion by phone the night before and wished him well. She would wait for a phone call to tell her what was going to happen to her son.

Tannion said goodbye to his lawyer and was surprised to see Rallin in front of him as he was being led away after sentencing.

"I just wanted to say goodbye and to say thanks for your work in Los Angeles. I can't, however, say that I'm sad that you got some time. I wanted you to get some time."

"I understand and I don't hold it against you. Say goodbye to Pansloski for me will you."

As Tannion was led away, Jeff Martin watched the short discussion between Rallin and Tannion from his seat at the back of the courtroom. Although he would have liked to have seen Tannion get a few more years, he was happy with the outcome. Time would be served.

Tannion spent the next night in lockup waiting for the ride that would start the next five years of his life. He was able to call his mother and tell her his fate. She was hard to talk to as she couldn't stop crying. It was going to be harder on her than on him.

Tannion's final call was to the hotel room where Louisa was staying. He told her that he wouldn't be allowed to see her before being sent off, but that she could visit him in prison. They decided that she should go back to Los Angeles and get her life back in order and make the trip to see him after a few weeks. Tannion would rather it was sooner, but the distance made it difficult. Long distance relationships rarely work and he had his doubts about this one. He said goodbye.

82

The first night went as well as could be expected. Tannion had the single room without a view and all around him were the sounds of other men. Someone had a good sleep based on the volume of snoring that was coming from a few cells down. Tannion, on the other hand didn't get much sleep at all, but that was his choice.

He was excited. This was not the same as the holding cell or the county jail in LA or even anywhere in New York where he had been held before, during, and immediately after his trial. This was the big house. This could be it. This could be where the fun would begin.

He had a lot of time to think in Los Angeles. First, where would he end up and what was he going to do when he got there? In the end what it came down to was the excitement of the big house. Tannion was probably the first inmate actually excited about seeing the inside of a maximum security prison. This may be most people's hell, but it wasn't his, and he was only going to make it worse for others.

Here were all the guys he was after. Here were the rapists and the murders. The drug dealers, thieves, pimps, and anything that walked around resembling human beings, but were really scum. People you couldn't find no matter how long you worked for guys like Philips.

Tannion had seen all the movies and TV shows that tell you what goes on behind the walls of a maximum security prison. They all show the new guy getting pulled out of bed in the middle of the night. There were always a few very large and sweaty guys with tattoos who would proceed to beat on the new guy just enough so he knew who was boss, and then after a good round of sex, he was sent back to bed. The aches and pains were probably not as bad as the hurt to his pride and the humiliation.

He knew that the chance of that scenario being for real wasn't likely, but then again, how many of the guys in there had seen the same movies and television shows and thought it was their job to make it happen. There were a lot of tough guys with tattoos in the place and some of them had probably not seen a woman alone for a long time. This was not a place that was known for conjugal visits. Of course there were always the guys on the outside who knew about Tannion and wanted him dead. They were the more likely problem, and there were bound to be a few of them.

When the door was locked for the night and Tannion was alone inside, there was a feeling of loss as he knew he couldn't get past the bars, but there was a feeling of security as well because others couldn't get past them either. The feeling was only a little different than in the holding cells in county as he awaited trial. He felt secure, but he was feeling the loss of freedom much more than back then. There had always been a chance that the trial would go his way before, but from here he knew his options were limited. The excitement abated only a little.

Tannion had met the warden when he first arrived and the warden knew what had gone on in LA. He knew that there was a good chance that someone in his house would be instructed to pull the plug on him. What he didn't know was when or how to keep him safe, especially if Tannion didn't want any special treatment. In the end he agreed to just let him be and not to jump to any conclusions when someone ended up dead and it wasn't Tannion.

He knew it would happen. He had ruffled feathers of powerful men and enough of them were still alive that eventually someone would come looking for him. They knew where he was. He had made sure of that, but what they didn't know was that Tannion would be waiting.

If you enjoyed *Tannion* read on to see what happens next:

Tannion Stepping Out

Coming soon

Read on for a preview of *Tannion Stepping Out*

1

When Tannion walked into the room there were six people already there. He only knew two of them. One of them was Watson, a guard he had gotten to know a little over the years. He was standing over next to the door doing his duty.

The other five were sitting behind a long table leaving the other side with a solitary chair. It was obvious which chair was his. Tannion had never been in this room before, but he knew what he had to do. He took the seat. At least he got to sit down.

The second person in the room Tannion knew was the warden. He was sitting at the left end of the table a little away from the other four. Tannion and the warden had gotten to know each other quite well over the last five years. He had turned out to be a strict but fair man. Although Tannion respected him and almost liked him, he didn't owe him anything.

The other four were strangers, but they held his future in their hands. It was up to them to determine if Tannion would get out or not. Tannion had been there for five years, they could make it more or they could set him free. They could make him stay for as many as fifteen more years. They were his parole board. His sentence had been twenty years with possible parole after five. The charge was manslaughter.

Tannion found it hard to believe that five years had passed already. It wasn't that the days sped by, but only that when the end of a long period of time was reached, it was easy to forget the daily drudgery. He remembered the day he got there five years earlier and it seemed like only yesterday.

It had been an interesting five years, which the warden would attest to. Tannion had wanted to be there to find the men who he knew were in there and to do what needed to be done. These men were difficult to find in the outside world, but in prison they were a captive audience. It was a place where Tannion was happy to spend some time, but five years sounded like enough.

In the five years since his incarceration, more than a hundred men had been taken out of the warden's prison in body bags. That sounded like a lot, but with a prison of that size and the type of hard cases it contained, it really wasn't that large of a percentage. It may not have been that many more than the prison's average for that time period.

Some died from an act of violence, some from illness, and a few from unknown causes. Tannion had a hand in almost all of them. Or maybe that might be a little too much to say. He at least had his hand in a large number of them. More than the warden would ever know.

It had started only about a week into his sentence when the local toughs thought it best to soften him up and take what they wanted. They saw him as a potential threat and had decided to ensure that Tannion knew his place. He thought it best to become the head tough guy instead, and they gave him the opportunity. The boss's name was Gus Balkin, but he went by the name of Big Gus. From his appearance it was immediately obvious why he got the nickname

Big Gus came at Tannion with three of his men. Men who didn't get to live much longer. The warden never did find out if Tannion had anything to do with their deaths. He didn't need to know. Big Gus belonged to Tannion from that point on, as much as he didn't like it.

Because of hits put on Tannion from his time in Los Angeles there had been at least a dozen attempts on his life, and they all took place within the first year or so. Either the perpetrators gave up after the failures or all his enemies were dead. All of them failed. Tannion was still standing. The warden knew about most of them, and they had come to an understanding. Tannion was prepared to protect himself, and the warden was prepared to consider self-defense as a means of getting rid of a few he didn't like either. The warden was a very pragmatic man and could occasionally see a good thing when it hit him on the head.

The rest of them died from various illnesses or an occasional busted head, but each was based on their situation. Tannion didn't feel any remorse for ridding the place of guys the world didn't need. The world was a better place when these guys couldn't get out and repeat what had put them in prison in the first place.

The parole board was made up of three men and one woman. They all looked to be in their late forties or maybe early fifties. The oldest looking man in the middle was obviously in charge, and he started the session.

"Mr. Jim Tannion. My name is Merle Adams. I will be chairing this session. On my left is Mr. Janson and to my right are Ms. Williams and Mr. Chance, and of course you know Warden Saunders. Before we begin, do you have any questions?"

Tannion told him he didn't and Adams went on. It took only a couple of minutes to explain what the process was and it was pretty simple. They had reviewed Tannion's file and had talked to the warden. As Tannion had waived council and refused to have anyone talk on his behalf, Tannion would either get out on his own merit or spend more time inside. It would be their decision to make.

As it got closer to the date of Tannion's parole hearing he had decided that he wanted out and especially since knowing that this day was scheduled. He still felt there was a lot of work for him to do inside. It left him with mixed emotions. The decision he made was to go ahead with the parole hearing by himself, and if that wasn't good enough then he would stay. If it were good enough then they would let him out.

If Louisa had still been in the picture then maybe it would have been different. They were supposed to get married and it had been the application for the marriage license that had gotten him caught. Tannion needed to use his real name and somehow they had found them. Despite all she told him, and how much she loved him, after a year and a few months she had stopped visiting. It was almost impossible to keep that kind of long distance relationship going for long.

The parole session lasted just over an hour. There were questions from all four of the panel members and the warden was asked a few as well. He had submitted his written report and the questions were for clarification only. When it appeared that all the questions had been asked, Tannion was told that they would take a few minutes for discussion and he was taken out into the hall. Watson went with him, and even though they were still well inside the prison walls, he kept an eye on him.

When the time came, the warden stuck his head out of the door and motioned to Watson. Tannion saw the nod and stood up ready to meet whatever they had decided. His chair was still waiting across the desk from the panel. Without asking, he sat down.

The chairman was the only person who spoke. He told Tannion that they had come to a decision, and that based on his record over the five years of incarceration, and with the input from the warden, they were granting his parole. They were well aware of what Tannion had done in Los Angeles and had taken that into account along with his behavior inside. The warden must have filled them in on the attempts on his life and the results, and they obviously had decided that they were self defense and not to be held against him.

The warden had a very slight smile on his face, and Tannion wasn't sure if it was because he was happy that Tannion was going to get out, or if he was happy that he was getting rid of him.

Other than the results of the attempted hits on Tannion, he was probably what the warden would call a model prisoner. Occasionally a few hard cases would end up dead in some corner, but the prison was relatively quiet once Tannion arrived, with one notable exception.

The warden might not know that Tannion had a big hand in that exception, but Tannion would not have been surprised if he had his suspicions. The warden had his sources of information on the inside and they would have kept him informed. Tannion wondered what it might be like inside over the next few months.

Tannion was told the processing would take a couple days, and by Friday he would be a free man. They also told him that he needed to decide where he would live. They needed to set up his parole officer, and although he would be out of jail, his life was still not completely his own, but they were letting him go. He was getting out.

Wayne Elsner is the author of the *Tannion Series*, the *Talanhold Trilogy*, and *Time Tells All*. *Tannion* is the first book in the *Tannion* series and the first book Wayne has published. Watch for more of Wayne's books coming soon.

Wayne is a retired geologist who spends a large part of his time travelling the world with his wife. They are working their way up to one hundred countries visited and have no intention of slowing down.

Visit his website at **www.wayneelsner.com** for more information or follow him on Twitter @wayneelsner